DIABOLIC CONCEPTION

"Please..." she pleaded weakly. "I've changed my mind. I..."

He thrust his pelvis against hers, making her cry out.

"No...no..." she implored him, squirming under him, straining to get away.

His eyes widened and Patty found herself suddenly transfixed with horror at the sight of them. They were changing, as though a fire were burning beneath them, tinting them yellowish. Soon the color deepened, becoming dark orange. *What's happening?* Patty's mind screamed as Sam forced her to stare up at him. Is this a trick of the light? What was she looking at? What kind of creature was this?

Other *Leisure Books by Edmund Plante:*

TRANSFORMATION

GARDEN OF EVIL

TRAPPED

EDMUND PLANTE

SEED OF EVIL

Book Margins, Inc.

A BMI Edition

Published by special arrangement with Dorchester
Publishing Co., Inc.

Printed in the United States of America.

For Netta,
with love always

PROLOGUE

FROM THE RED LANTERN

Patty glanced at her reflection behind the bar, then quickly turned away her head. She hadn't liked what she'd seen, and the less she saw of herself the less she'd remember how pathetic she really looked. In that brief instant the mirror had ruthlessly reminded her that she needed more color in her cheeks, more body to her reddish brown hair and more weight on her face. Her eyes were like hollow craters, and she was as thin and pale as death. No wonder the men in this dump weren't paying any attention to her.

What the hell am I doing in here? the young woman wondered in disgust for the umpteenth time. She was the mother of two children, for Christ's sake! Shouldn't she be at home bathing her kids, tucking them in for the night, reading them bedtime stories—something like that? She certainly shouldn't be in this sleazy dive, trying to pick up men.

Patty took a sip of her vodka and tonic while watching white cigarette smoke turn red under a neon Budweiser sign above the mirror. But she deserved this little treat, she then told herself. She was 23, too young to devote herself completely to her kids. A few nights out a week were harmless, good for her, and besides, Kate, her best friend and neighbor, had insisted that she accompany her. Actually, Patty had no choice. Kate had been so stubborn, so persistent.

But now Kate had found someone—a construction worker, Patty guessed by the looks of him. So this meant Patty was alone, drinking and waiting.

"A refill, Patty?" the bartender asked, nodding at her glass, which now contained pebble-sized ice cubes swimming in a half-inch of water. How many drinks had she had so far? Patty wondered. Two? Three?

"Sure, why the hell not?" Patty said, barely able to get the words out. Things seemed to be slowing down now, and her eyelids were feeling weighty. Maybe she shouldn't have another drink, after all. But on the other hand, why should she worry about things slowing down? Especially after a hectic day with cranky kids. She needed to relax. She needed to have things slow down.

"Yeah . . . why not?" she repeated, shrugging emphatically.

The bartender gave her a small, crooked smile as he made her a fresh drink. "There you go, Patty," he said. "And drink slow." There was mild concern in his voice, which Patty caught through her alcoholic haze. She and the bartender only saw each other on Friday and Saturday nights. But it had been for almost a year now, and although they had never exchanged many words, a quiet friendship had developed between them. It was nothing strong, just something small and nice. He cared a little for her, and he was probably the only man in her life right now who did. Her father was long gone, and her ex-husband had himself a new wife to worry about.

Patty took a sip of her drink, then looked up at the mirror again. Carefully avoiding her own reflection, she studied the people around her. She spotted her friend, Kate, at one of the small round tables. A candle in a red glass globe eerily illuminated the young woman's face as she leaned over to catch something the construction worker was saying. Then she sat back, laughing, and the construction worker leaned forward to say something else. Patty could see they were hitting it off well, but then, Kate never did have any problem meeting guys. She was different from Patty, more aggressive and outgoing. She was . . . desperate.

But Patty wasn't. Not really. She wasn't as lascivious as her friend. She probably could get along without a man in her life, but right now her life seemed so hollow and empty. There must be more to it than catering to two screaming kids and an overweight mother who did nothing but watch soap operas, old sitcom reruns, and game shows all day. Patty knew that the men who frequented this lounge were only interested in booze and sometimes sex, nothing lasting. And usually she didn't care. Usually that was all she was interested in, too. But tonight, well, she was beginning to feel a little depressed. The question *What the hell am I doing in here?* was like a song that wouldn't stop playing in her mind.

Maybe it's guilt, she suddenly thought. Maybe she was feeling like one of those clichéd schoolteachers she'd read about in novels and seen in movies, the ones who roamed the streets at night looking for johns. Sweet by day, wicked by night sort of thing. Maybe she . . .

In the mirror she saw Kate and the construction worker get up from their table and leave the lounge, arms around each other's waist. Patty felt a sudden, heavy feeling in her stomach, a feeling she couldn't quite define. She experienced disgust toward her friend for being too easy, along with a twinge of jealousy and a stab of rejection. It was like the feeling she used to get when she was at a high school dance where the boys would ask all her friends to dance except her.

Then she caught someone staring at her in the mirror. Instinctively, Patty pulled her gaze away and concentrated on the glass in front of her. Already, she dimly noted, the ice cubes were melting, watering her drink. As she stared at her glass, the eyes she had seen in the mirror still lingered in her mind. The eyes had been brilliant, penetrating, like twin lanterns in a dense fog. But the color was vague. Blue? Gray?

Patty told herself that it didn't matter what color the eyes were. But for reasons she couldn't understand, her curiosity was strongly piqued. The color of those eyes, it seemed, demanded to be known. Slowly, Patty returned her gaze to the large mirror across from her. At first she fixed her attention on herself. For the second time that night she cringed at the pale, pathetic image that stared back at her, then her eyes slid reluctantly toward the right.

Their eyes met again.

Patty felt the lethargic, alcoholic haze clear. Without the fog the twin lanterns burned brightly, like the sun on a cloudless day. She felt the eyes warm her . . . or chill her. Fire or ice? Somehow she wasn't sure which, for there seemed to be a delicate line between the two. Also, Patty still couldn't decide the exact color of these eyes. If anything they seemed to be colorless. Maybe there was too much distance between them for her to tell.

Patty stared at the eyes for a long moment and experienced an attraction that she found somewhat disturbing. It actually took willpower to pull her own gaze away. When she finally succeeded in breaking the magnetic attraction, she studied the rest of the man's face.

Like the color of the eyes, his age was indeterminate. But one thing was unquestionable—this man staring at her was the most handsome man she'd ever seen in her life! His hair was thick, the color and gloss of licorice. His jaw and cheekbones were severe and prominent, hard and masculine, yet his lips seemed soft and somewhat enticing. Once again Patty felt the hot/cold sensation of fire and ice. She wanted to look away from this impeccable face but could not find the strength to do so.

The man smiled at her. Patty felt her face burn, as though she were a schoolgirl. She swallowed, then returned the smile. The man rose from the table he was sitting at, and Patty felt her heart hammer violently inside her. The man began threading his way toward the bar, toward her.

Patty took a sizeable gulp of her drink, hoping the alcohol would slow down her pulse a bit. Jesus, why was she acting like some kind of lovesick teenager?

Eyes never leaving the man in the mirror, Patty waited for him to approach her. He was tall, she noted, well over six feet. And well-proportioned. He walked with confident grace, a cross between a strut and smooth, pantherlike stride. He seemed a perfect male specimen. Only his hands seemed out of place, for they appeared too large in comparison to the rest of him. But this was minor, for this deformity was overshadowed by his otherwise breathless perfection.

The man paused directly behind her, and for a long moment the couple stared silently at each other in the silver glass. The din of laughter and conversation in the room faded in Patty's ears, as though someone had turned down the volume inside her head. Far across the lounge she could faintly hear the jukebox—a Lionel Richie number, smooth and slow.

Then the man leaned forward until his mouth was close to her ear. She could feel his breath, and for a fleeting moment thought it was icy, like an arctic wind. But of course that couldn't be possible. It was wintertime, and maybe a gust had escaped from outside and wormed its way across the room toward her.

"Where, my darling, have you been all my long life?" He fed her the corny line, but somehow, from him it didn't seem at all trite. It sounded sincere.

Patty suddenly felt shy. She smiled awkwardly, turning away from the mirror to meet him. He hovered, and once more she was reminded of how tall he was. And powerful-looking. He wore a thick black sweater, but she could still envision a hard, trimmed torso beneath the woolen fabric. Suddenly she had a strong desire to touch his body, his perfect face.

"I . . . I've been here all along," she stammered.

He chuckled. He seemed to enjoy making her uncomfortable and bashful. His colorless eyes glittered. Maybe under a different light Patty would be able to determine the color, but right now they looked like rhinestones, bright and hot—or cold. Whatever.

"You . . ." Patty paused to strengthen her voice. ". . . want to buy me a drink, big boy?"

The man laughed again. She wasn't fooling him. He could see through her, see that she wasn't as experienced and nonchalant as she pretended to be. "You've had enough to drink here," he told her bluntly, his mouth twitching in amusement. "But if you wish, I'll buy a bottle and we'll drink it together at your place."

Patty stared in surprise at his boldness. Such nerve, she thought, but yet wasn't offended. Strangely, she found herself flattered. This perfect specimen was asking her—*her*—to go to bed with him. Her body tingled at the thought of this man's body fusing with hers.

"Well, I . . . I don't know," she said, hesitatingly.

"You do know," he confidently assured her. "You are as strongly attracted to me as I am to you."

Patty continued to stare dumbly at him. His confidence and audacity were beginning to unnerve her. She knew she should tell him to go fuck off, but the domineering half of her, as he had brazenly said, was strongly attracted to him.

"You're . . . you're a fast worker, aren't you?" she replied at length.

He smiled radiantly, charming her even more. "Why waste time, eh?"

Patty cleared her throat. She took another sip, and still her mouth was dry. How could she tell this man that yes, she was tempted to have sex with him, but first she'd like to slow down a bit with small talk? This would make her feel so much better, make her feel . . . well, less easy.

"I don't even know your name," she said.

He shrugged, then blurted, "Sam." The reply was sudden, as though the name had just occurred to him.

Patty was convinced the name was fictitious, and yet, to her surprise, she didn't care. For probably the first time in her life she found herself sexually drawn to a man in a purely physical sense. She didn't care what would happen the morning after, or about developing a relationship. This would be completely sexual, nothing more. Was she finally getting to be like her friend, Kate?

"What kind of bottle do you want?" he asked, breaking her thoughts.

"Wha . . . Oh, I'm drinking vodka and tonics. But . . ."

Sam never let her finish. He signaled the bartender and asked for a fresh bottle of Smirnoff. The
bartender started to refuse, stating that it was against
the lounge's policy to sell bottles, but something in
Sam's countenance caused him to change his mind.
The bartender's eyes glazed over in mid-sentence,
then he wordlessly went into a back room and
reemerged a moment later with a paper bag. The
purchase was completed before Patty knew what
was happening.

"You have tonic water at home?" Sam asked.

"What?" She blinked, still in a daze. This was all
going too fast. "No, no I don't."

"No matter, we'll drink it straight on the rocks."
Sam then smiled broadly. "It is time for us to leave."

Patty found herself dazzled, light-headed. No
amount of drinks could ever make her feel quite like
this. "Yes," she relented finally, her voice sounding
weak and far away to her ears, "let's go."

As she climbed off the stool she almost fell, but
Sam quickly gripped her forearm with his big hand
and steadied her. He then steered her through the
crowd toward the main entrance and the coat rack,
never releasing his firm hold on her. So powerful,
she found herself thinking again as he helped her
into her coat. So masculine. So handsome.

The icy New England air slapped her face the
instant the door opened. Patty sucked in a startled
breath and instinctively recoiled from the abrupt
cold, but Sam, without the slightest pause, propelled
her onward.

"This has got to be the coldest winter," she complained, bending her head to deflect the wind.

"Car?" Sam asked succinctly. He kept his head
straight, as though enjoying the harsh air against his
face.

"I only live at the end of the street." Patty

gestured ahead at a dead end that faded into darkness. The street lamp had been broken for almost a year now (the town, it seemed, gave up, unable to repair it faster than the neighborhood kids could break it).

Patty and Sam paused before the last house, a huge rectangular structure in desperate need of repair. There were six apartments in this house, six families on welfare, including Patty's. The place, with its front storm door flapping in the wind due to a broken lock, its top glass panel smashed, proclaimed poverty and neglect. Patty covertly glanced at Sam, wondering what he thought. Sam, she could tell, was not poor. His hair was expertly styled, and his black woolen overcoat probably cost more than what the welfare department paid her for an entire week.

"Well, here we are already," she said, somewhat shamefully. "Third floor on the right."

Sam said nothing, and it was too dark to read his face as he surveyed the blocklike structure. He saw that all the apartments, except Patty's, were in darkness, the windows black mirrors. Then he looked over at the woods that began where the street abruptly ended. He stared for a while, as though in rapt fascination. "You live on the edge of darkness," he said cryptically.

"What?"

Sam didn't explain. For a moment the only sound in the night was the faint murmurs and laughter of the patrons at the bar, The Red Lantern Lounge, several hundred yards away. Patty stared at the blinking Miller sign in the distance, wondering if she was making a mistake here. She did not know this man. He could be dangerous. Could be a killer. Could be a pervert into kinky sex, into bondage or something. All she knew was that she was attracted to him, an attraction that was disturbingly powerful.

"Maybe we should forget about . . ." she began, then stopped. He was holding the broken door open for her. The naked light bulb in the foyer illuminated his face—so handsome with his eyes, still twinkling colorlessly like rhinestones. He smiled, and the magnetic attraction she felt toward him intensified. Patty shyly met his smile and stepped inside.

"We'll have to be quiet," she whispered in deference to the sleeping tenants. It was after midnight. "Maybe I should've told you this sooner, but I don't live alone."

"Oh?"

"No, I live with my mother and two kids." Patty nibbled on her lower lip, waiting for and expecting an angry reaction. Usually she told the men beforehand that she lived in the apartment with her family, but Sam had so drugged her with his charm—or whatever it was he had—that she had forgotten to inform him.

To her relief, Sam shrugged mildly. "If you don't mind, then I fail to see why I should."

Patty relaxed, her smile widening. "They're sound sleepers, though. And my room is off the kitchen, away from the others." She started up the stairs while Sam followed. For a fleeting instant she felt cheap and was disgusted with herself for what she'd just said and what she was about to do. For Christ's sake, she was behaving like a common whore. But when she glanced over her shoulder at him, she sighed as all inhibitions melted.

They reached Patty's apartment. The smell of cabbage, stale and sour, filled the dingy hallway. Patty opened the door and the stench of soiled Pampers wafted out, causing Patty to wonder if Sam had noticed the odor. But he said and showed nothing.

"Lead me to the refrigerator," he demanded instead.

Patty closed the door quietly after them, wiggled out of her coat, took Sam's, and dropped them on the couch. She then showed Sam where the kitchen was. As he began collecting ice cubes and preparing drinks, she checked on her children and mother.

A lamp from the living room dimly illuminated the shapes of the bureau and bed in her daughter's room. Vaguely, Patty could see her two-year-old daughter's sleeping form. It was just a tiny lump from the doorway. Softly, Patty moved toward the bed and kissed the child's forehead, then tucked the covers tighter around her. As she straightened and looked down at the girl, a wave of guilt and shame surged through her. What kind of mother was she to bring strange men home from a bar? What on earth was the matter with her?

Tears burned her eyes and she sniffed them back. I'm a damn good mother, she told herself. I get lonely now and then, that's all.

In the next room she checked on Frankie, her 11-month-old son. She changed his diaper, careful not to awaken him, then, as she had done with his sister, Janet, kissed his forehead and pulled the covers tighter around him. When she reached her mother's room, she opened the door a small crack and listened for a moment to assure herself that the woman was asleep. Then she gently closed the door.

"All is well?"

Patty spun around, surprised to find Sam so close behind her.

"Did I frighten you, darling?" he asked, his voice deep, almost guttural. Patty found it sexy, yet disturbing.

"No," she lied.

He grinned crookedly, obviously not believing her. Then he held out the drink he'd made for her while sipping on his own. His eyes brazenly watched her over the rim of his glass as she accepted her drink and took a small swallow.

Patty tried to feign aloofness, pretending that his scrutiny did not fluster her, but her hand holding the glass trembled. She felt uncomfortably warm, even awkward. For the umpteenth time she wondered if she was making a mistake.

"Bedroom," he said.

Patty wasn't sure if it was a statement or question. "What?"

"Lead me to it."

Patty took another sip of her drink. The tart vodka puddled on her tongue for a long moment before she remembered to swallow. This guy doesn't fool around, does he? she thought, a little stunned. This is all happening too fast—much too fast.

Sam's eyes sparkled as he waited for her response. He was so sure of himself. Had any woman ever refused him? Patty wondered. Could anyone resist such perfection?

At length Patty turned away from him and moved toward her own bedroom. He quietly followed and closed the door behind him. For a moment the room was in complete darkness. Patty groped for the lamp on the night table. Her fingers searched for the small pull chain as she glanced over her shoulder. Then she froze. Something was glowing. No, it was *two* things, and they were moving toward her. She thought of silver coins gliding forward in the air. Then her hand thawed, finding the chain. Light filled the room and the glowing coins vanished.

The only thing Patty saw coming toward her now was Sam.

And he was smiling, calmly sipping his drink as he walked. What had she seen? Patty wondered. Spots of light lingering in her eyes from the other room? She didn't believe this, but what other explanation was there?

Wordlessly, Sam put his drink down on the night table and took the glass from Patty's hand to set it down next to his. He then pulled her into his arms. Not sure why, Patty found herself holding her breath. Anticipation? Fear? Suddenly she didn't know how to respond. Put her arms around him? Tilt her face upward to meet his lips?

Or push him away?

"Relax," he urged. Again the deep timbre of his voice infused her with a mixture of excitement and trepidation.

Why am I so tense? she asked herself. She had gone to bed with strangers before. She didn't have to worry about being raped, not if she was a willing participant.

But her body remained rigid as Sam slowly and deftly undressed her.

"Maybe . . . maybe we should turn the light off," she suggested.

He ignored her, openly appraising her naked body. She shivered in shyness, fighting an urge to cover herself with her arms. Then he lifted her into his arms and gently lowered her onto the bed. She relaxed a little, for he seemed so patient and graceful. Silently she watched, like a child filled with wonder, as he removed his own clothes.

Never had she seen such a beautiful body. As she had suspected before he had taken off his sweater, his torso was trim and muscular. His skin gleamed golden from the soft light of the lamp. His legs were long, and his thighs meaty. He towered above her, and he watched her admire him. His lips curved into a thin, complacent smile as her gaze fell and rested on his penis. It was huge, out of proportion like his hands. And the most incredible part was that he wasn't yet aroused.

Excitement swiftly abandoned her, now leaving her alone with dread and fear. Patty had never seen a man this large before, and she wasn't sure if she could go through with this. But she knew she could not stop now, for she had gone too far. He would resort to force if she refused him.

"Relax," he told her again, apparently seeing the fear in her face.

Patty squeezed her eyes shut for a moment. Yes, relax, she mentally commanded. Who knows, maybe she would enjoy this. Maybe she was about to have the experience of her life.

Sam climbed on top of her, and her eyes flew open.

Sam's face loomed above her, grinning wickedly, eyes staring into hers. He wasn't heavy, but he was strong, and Patty knew that she could never push him off or roll away. Suddenly he didn't look patient and graceful to her anymore. She felt trapped, especially when his grin widened and his eyes glittered. He chuckled, a sound that came from deep inside him.

Not wanting to look up at his face, Patty turned her head. She wished she had insisted on turning off the light, but it was out of reach now. She would have to slide closer to the edge of the bed and stretch for the lamp.

Leaning on one elbow, Sam gripped her chin with his big hand and forced her to look back at him. Patty gasped in surprise and alarm. She stared wide-eyed at his face above her. She could feel and smell his breath, cold and sulfuric. He was watching panic erupt in her eyes and was enjoying it. He chuckled again, his mouth never moving. The sound was almost inaudible, something like a faint, rumbling growl.

Oh God, what have I got myself into! Patty moaned, squeezing her eyes shut. Sam's grip on her chin tightened, demanding her to reopen her eyes. She promptly obeyed the tacit command, for she could tell that if he added pressure her jaw would crumble like rotten wood.

"Please . . ." she pleaded weakly. "I've changed my mind. I . . ."

He thrust his pelvis against hers, making her cry out. She could tell his penis still wasn't hard, yet it seemed to fill her. Then she felt it grow.

"No . . . no . . ." she implored him. "I hear one of the kids crying," she lied, squirming under him, straining to get away, feeling something like a fish trying to free itself from a hook. "Please . . ."

His eyes widened and Patty found herself suddenly transfixed with horror at the sight of them. They were still gleaming, but the color was no longer indeterminate. It was silver, like the floating coins she had seen in the dark. And now they were changing, as though a fire were burning beneath them, tinting them yellowish. Soon the color deepened, becoming dark orange. *What's happening*? Patty's mind screamed as Sam forced her to stare up at him. Is this a trick of the light? What was she looking at? What kind of creature was this?

The orange eyes deepened some more, turning to the color of dark blood.

Patty began to squirm more violently. "Get off!" she shrieked. "OFF!"

He thrust harder, growing larger inside her.

"No!"

He laughed openly now, throwing his head back. Lips parted, his teeth glinted in the light. And they were not the white, healthy teeth she'd seen and admired earlier; they were yellowish with decay, some broken with jagged tips.

Patty twisted under him, raked her nails across his back, which felt smooth, hard, and cold as iron. In fact, his entire body seemed to have dropped in temperature. But he seemed unaffected by her struggle, although she could feel his flesh gather like shredded paper under her nails.

Never again, she vowed, would she bring a stranger home. Never again!

Sam continued to grow inside her, mercilessly ripping her. She could feel blood trickling out of her, feel hot pain as she continued to claw him.

"Damn you!" she screamed as loud as she could, no longer able to keep this rendezvous hidden from her family. "Get off me!"

He increased his rhythm, vicious as a savage animal. Patty kept on fighting him, now sobbing as she realized the futility of it all.

Never again! Never!

The door slammed open. Patty turned only her eyes toward it, for her head was still in Sam's firm grip. She saw her mother in the doorway, gaping in shock at the sight before her.

"What on—"

"Ma, help me! Help—"

Sam's head spun toward the fat woman in the doorway. Eyes glowing like votive candles in ruby glass, he snarled, then brayed laughter at her. The woman staggered back, hand reaching for her lips in disbelief.

"Ma, please!" Patty cried. "Call the police. Help me! Help—"

The woman hesitated, as though afraid to leave her daughter alone. Then, as fast as her rotund body would allow, she rushed off toward the phone in the kitchen.

Patty expected Sam to chase after the woman, and she began to regret having put her mother in such a perilous situation. But Sam never stopped what he was doing. Then Patty thought of her children. Little Frankie couldn't walk yet, but Janet could easily come into the room and see. . . .

Oh God, please don't let my daughter see this!

Her mother, Lydia, returned with a carving knife in her hand. Seeing this, Sam laughed at her for the second time. As Lydia brandished the weapon, ordering him in a tremulous voice to leave her daughter alone, he quickly and violently finished his horrid lovemaking, shooting what felt like ice water into Patty, then lifted himself off her and stood triumphantly on the bed, feet planted on each side of Patty. He smugly studied her body below him, stared in brief amusement at the blood that dripped from between her legs and puddled the sheet under her, then he looked over at Lydia, quietly challenging the fat woman.

She breathed laboriously, as though on the verge of a heart attack. She still held the knife aloft, but was too old and frightened to be a threat.

Sam grinned, and Patty gaped in horror at him. He looked so tall and invincible above her. What was he going to do now? Kill her? Right before her mother's eyes? Oh God, please help me, she silently cried.

I'll never bring a stranger home again. I promise. Never.

Sam grew. Before Patty's and Lydia's disbelieving eyes his extremities extended like something out of a movie with bizarre special effects. In smooth, fluid motion he expanded until his head touched the ceiling, and his hand touched her throat beneath him.

"No!" Patty screamed.

The grip tightened. The nails lengthened and became claws. Shadows writhed like elongated tentacles on the walls and ceiling, shadows cast by the monstrosity on her bed.

The knife fell and clattered on the worn, rugless floor. Lydia numbly made the sign of the cross, moaning, "Oh, my God." Then she stared at the knife she had dropped, as though seeing it for the first time. Patty gasped as the claws squeezed her throat. She thrashed and bucked in vain, her face quickly turning purplish. Then Lydia, with strength she never knew she had, picked up the knife, raised it high over her head, like a woman who had suddenly lost her sanity, and attacked the horror on the bed.

She stabbed at the leg, first the calf, then the thigh. But so thick and firm were his muscles it was like attacking leather with a butter knife. Sam released his grip on Patty and swatted at the woman, as though she were a pesty housefly.

Lydia staggered back until she fell heavily against a bureau. She cried out in pain, but never let go of the knife. Patty rolled over and tried to scramble off the bed. But Sam was too quick for her. With his hideous arm and hand he reached for her hair and yanked her back, flipping her over until she was again on her back, looking up at his grinning face.

"Why . . . why are you doing this?" she sobbed.

Sam said nothing, just simply stared, watching as though in fascination as the terror grew inside her. Then Patty heard and felt water trickling down on her breasts and stomach. Fire and ice. It took her a long moment to realize that he was actually urinating on her.

Patty screamed, and Sam laughed again. Lydia moaned, crawling toward the bed, knife in hand, and from another room little Frankie wailed.

Turning her head, Patty saw her mother struggling to her feet, and she wanted to warn her to go back, to tell her it was useless. Sam, or rather the creature who called itself Sam, would only strike her again, and this time the blow could be fatal. But Patty couldn't form any words, only shout incoherently with horror.

The hand with the elongated nails returned to her throat and squeezed, breaking into the skin and forming red crescents. Patty gasped, feeling the fight and strength leave her. The room dimmed and spinned. *It's over*, her mind whirled. *I'm 23 and one of my kids is still in diapers . . . and it's over.*

The room blurred until nothing could be seen, except for the red burning eyes. Then the crimson orbs began to fade away until darkness swallowed them. Far away she heard the sound of sirens. Her mother had called the police after all. But it is too late, she thought, feeling herself slipping.

It *is* over.

PART ONE

BOULDER AND QUICKSAND

1

Patty swam underwater as fast as she could, and yet her limbs seemed to be moving in slow motion. She looked behind her and saw the man who called himself Sam in close pursuit. She wanted to scream but could not, knowing that water would fill her, drown her. So she kept on swimming, this time changing course and pushing upward toward the surface. She took another peek behind her, and to her surprise found it wasn't Sam who was after her anymore, it was Peter the Rat, her ex-husband. And he was laughing at her, impervious to the water streaming into his gaping mouth. Patty swam faster, determined to gain distance. Above her she could see a smiling face. Faster and faster she moved her arms and kicked her legs, violently agitating the water until it was effervescent like champagne.

At last she broke surface.

"Mrs. Thompson?" She faintly heard a woman call her name. Patty blinked slowly, bemused. Sam was gone now, along with Peter the Rat. And staring at her was a young nurse. What had happened?

"You're going to be fine, Mrs. Thompson," said the nurse. Her voice was soft, soothing. She patted Patty's hand reassuringly, then stepped back to let someone else come into her vision. A doctor. Looking tall above her, he adjusted his glasses on his nose, then smiled down at her, but somehow his smile wasn't as warm and sincere as the nurse's.

"You've been through a traumatic experience, Mrs. Thompson," he told her, pronouncing each word carefully as though she were a foreigner unfamiliar with English. "You do not have to remember anything you don't want to." He paused, then, as the nurse had done, patted her hand. His smile never changed; it was frozen. "There's a gentleman in the hall who wishes to see you. A Lieutenant Wheeler from the police department. He promises not to tire you, only wants to ask a few questions."

Lieutenant? Police department? Groggily she remembered hearing police sirens. Then she remembered.

Sam. On her bed. His head brushing the ceiling. His hand—no, claws—clutching her. She reached for her throat and felt the tender skin.

"But, of course, Mrs. Thompson," the doctor quickly added, "you do not have to see him now, if that's your wish."

Now. He had said "now." That meant if she didn't see him now she'd see him later, didn't it? So why put it off?

Patty struggled to find her voice; it seemed the last to awaken. "It . . . it's okay. Bring him in."

"You sure you feel strong enough, Mrs. Thompson?"

Patty nodded. The doctor in turn nodded at the nurse behind him, a signal to summon the detective in the corridor. Patty closed her eyes a moment as she waited. An unbidden image of Sam filled her mind, his mouth a sneer, his eyes burning cinders. She quickly reopened her eyes, her heart thundering from the horrible memory. Maybe she shouldn't talk to the detective, after all. He would make her relive everything that had happened and . . .

"Mrs. Thompson?"

Another voice betraying concern. Another sympathetic smile. Patty nodded weakly in acknowledgement.

"I'm Detective Lieutenant Allan Wheeler, police," he introduced himself, speaking in a low whisper, as though afraid that Patty and anyone else in the delicate hospital would shatter if he spoke louder. He was a small man, about five feet five, sporting a heavy moustache. He wore, of course, the obligatory trench coat, but unlike the baggy, limp kind Patty had seen detectives wear on TV and in movies, this one looked relatively new and fitted him snugly. There were no wrinkles, Patty found herself thinking. He was orderly and immaculate, the kind who would iron and fold his underwear before placing them in a drawer. "If you've no objection," he said, as though expecting that there would be, "I'd like to ask you a few questions."

Patty braced herself, then nodded at him to proceed.

Wheeler glanced at the doctor and nurse, silently commanding them to leave the room. The interrogation, his look told them, was to be private and confidential. The doctor gave Patty a final look, then wordlessly left with the nurse.

"Mrs. Thompson, please describe as accurately as you can what happened at your apartment last night," Wheeler said, pulling out a pad and pen from his shirt pocket.

This was a question? Patty sighed, feeling for the first time a throbbing soreness in her pelvic region. "A man tried to kill me. He . . ." He what? Tried to rape her? No, she couldn't say that, could she? She had every intention of having sex with him. It was only at the last minute that she . . .

"He what, Mrs. Thompson?" Wheeler prompted gently.

Patty's eyes widened as she stared at the detective. How much should she tell him? How much would he believe of her story? Sam wasn't even a man, for God's sake. He was . . .

Her eyes began to fill with tears. Her vision blurred, but not enough to miss the frustration in the detective's countenance. "I'm sorry," she said, "but it was so horrible."

Wheeler nodded briefly, indicating that he understood. "Can you tell me the name of this man? Can you describe him?"

He's not a man, Patty wanted to say, but couldn't. Wheeler would think she'd been hallucinating. He would tell the doctor, and the doctor would have her transferred to another floor, to the floor where the doors were locked and people wandered aimlessly, mumbling and plucking invisible things out of the air.

"He called himself Sam," Patty said after a long silence, "but I don't think that's his real name. He's very tall, and his hands, they're big, they don't go with the rest of him. Out of proportion."

Wheeler wrote everything down rapidly and neatly. "You remember the color of his hair, his eyes?"

"Black. Blacker than any hair I've ever seen. His eyes . . ." her voice faltered. How could she tell him the color of his eyes? They had glowed like silver coins in the dark. They had gone from colorless to silver to yellow to orange and finally to crimson. "I don't remember," she said.

Wheeler looked disappointed. "Anything else?"

Patty shook her head, suddenly very tired. She didn't want to talk about it anymore, didn't want to remember more than she had to.

The disappointment grew more evident on Wheeler's face. He quickly masked it with a smile when he saw that Patty was watching him. "Not much to go on," he said, stuffing the pad into his pocket, "but we'll get this guy. Mark my word."

Patty didn't believe him but said nothing. She knew nobody would ever get Sam. Nobody. She knew this the moment she'd seen him grow to the ceiling. He was invincible.

Nobody, but nobody would get him—or rather, *it*.

Patty closed her eyes and began to swim under-water again.

When she surfaced, her vagina felt raw, burning with pain. Without opening her eyes she rocked her head back and forth on the pillow, moaning. At first she thought she had delivered a baby and was suffer-ing from the tear he or she had made and the doctor had stitched. And then she remembered.

Sam. The monster.

She opened her eyes and was surprised to find someone else in the room with her, sitting in a chair. She blinked repeatedly until her vision cleared.

"Ma," she whispered, suddenly feeling like a little girl again who had been away from her mother for too long. She wanted to leap into her plump arms, bury her face in the woman's ample bosom and lose herself in the no-nonsense smell of Ivory soap. But Patty was too weak to do this and, of course, too old.

"Ma," she said again, "I'm so glad to see you."

Lydia, she noted, didn't seem to share the same sentiment. Her pale face was tight, and her eyes were angry sparks. She laboriously pulled herself up off the chair and stood at the bedside. "You feeling okay?" she asked, her voice as tight and controlled as her face.

"Yes, Ma."

There was silence as each woman surveyed the other. Then Lydia exploded. "What's the matter with you, for God's sake?"

"Oh Ma, please don't," Patty pleaded wearily.

"You almost got y'self killed." She ignored her. "And you could've gotten me and the kids killed as well."

"Ma, take it easy," Patty urged. But Lydia's face was already flushed, and she was starting to pant. It was from all that fat around her heart, no doubt. And from all the smoking she did. (She'd be smoking right now if the hospital let her.) "I know it was stupid of me, and I'm sorry."

"Sorry? You've no idea how scared I was. Could've had myself a stroke or heart attack, y'know."

"Ma, I said I was sorry."

There was another long silence as the women continued to stare at each other.

"But I suppose this ain't gonna stop you none," Lydia said, disgust evident in her voice.

"About meeting men?"

"About going to that hell hole you go to and bringing home God knows what. When are you going to smarten up and stop?"

"I'm all done, Ma."

"Sure." She did not believe her.

"I mean it. I got the scare of my life, too."

Lydia, realizing her daughter was serious, sighed with relief. "Why do you do it, Patricia? It's not the way I brought you up."

Patty looked up at the ceiling and thought about it, but there was no definite answer, nothing black and white. "I don't know, Ma. I know I'm not going to get anywhere just staying at home, and Kate kept insisting I go with her to—"

"That Kate is no good for you," Lydia spat out. "She's a bad influence."

"Ma, I'm twenty-three, too old for you to worry about anybody influencing me."

Lydia sniffed, then pushed the chair closer to the bed and sat heavily into it. "My back," she grunted. "Can't stand up long like I used to, y'know."

Yes, Patty did know. That, along with her recurring migraines, dizzy spells, allergies, touch of arthritis, hot flashes, chills, ingrown nails—the list of ailments was endless. Yes, Patty knew all right, having heard complaints from her mother almost every single day since Dad died.

Patty waited until her mother was comfortably seated, then said, "Where are the kids?"

"In the hallway. A nurse is with them. Kids are not allowed on this floor, y'know."

Patty didn't know, but she nodded anyway. She wished she could see her children now. Maybe it would help her forget what had happened. Maybe seeing something good and wonderful would erase what was bad and horrible.

"Do they have any idea what happened?" she asked, hoping the answer would be no. But as soon as the question left her lips she remembered hearing Frankie screaming from his room.

"Little Frankie don't remember nothing, of course," her mother replied. "All the screaming and commotion woke him up, but he don't remember nothing. But Janet . . ."

Alarm surged through Patty. "What about Janet? You think she saw him?"

"No. She was in the corner of her room, shivering and clutching that rag of hers. Never said nothing. But let me tell you, she was petrified. No," she said again, shaking her head thoughtfully, "but she must of thought you were being attacked by a bogeyman or something. I had to tell her you were all right. Too bad the hospital has dumb rules, otherwise I'd bring her in here and show her that you're . . . well, still alive."

"Poor baby." Tears welled up in Patty's eyes.

"Should've thought of that before you brought that monster home," Lydia snapped.

Patty was silent. She reached for a box of tissues on the bed tray and wiped her eyes.

"Weren't you aware of the dangers?"

"I . . . I just didn't think about them."

"Humph! Any idiot would know that only bums hang out in that hell hole."

"There are some nice people who go there," Patty said lamely. "And it's not a hell hole, Ma. It's a lounge. A respectable—"

"A bar is no place to look for men, Patricia."

Patty groaned inwardly. Her mother would never understand. She came from a time when divorce was a shocking rarity. She was one of the lucky ones who had a lasting marriage, a marriage that only death could terminate. So how could she understand Patty's conduct, understand her frustrating search for companionship, sexual or otherwise?

"Where do you want me to look, at church bazaars?" Patty retorted.

"Not a bad idea, actually."

"Oh Ma," Patty sighed impatiently, "who from a church would want a divorcee with two children? I don't even go to church, for God's sake."

"Maybe it's time you started again."

"Ma, let's change the subject. Okay?"

Lydia's lips promptly tightened. Patty had

affronted her, and now she felt a rush of guilt.

She reached out, held her mother's hand, and said earnestly, "I'm not going back to that lounge again. It's a promise."

Lydia's mouth visibly softened. "A promise, Patricia?"

"Yes, a promise." Seeing relief in her mother's eyes, Patty smiled. The promise would never be broken, she silently vowed. From here on she was going to change her life, improve it somehow. No more bars. No more picking up strangers. The man who called himself Sam had frightened her enough to keep the vow forever. Never, never would she want to meet someone like him again.

"How did he get away?" she wondered out loud. "I remember hearing sirens, but nothing after that."

Something clouded Lydia's eyes, a protective sheen of some kind. She looked at Patty, then averted her head and gazed past her, out the window where thick gray clouds could be seen, promising snow. "His hand was on your throat when we heard the sirens," she said. She seemed to be detaching herself, pretending she was recounting something she had seen on TV or read in a novel, something fictitious. "As the sirens grew closer his hand became smaller. It was awfully big at first, then it became normal in size. His legs became shorter. I guess they shrank, but I didn't see them shrink. I just noticed that his head wasn't touching the ceiling anymore. And the space between the ceiling and his head got wider and wider. Then his eyes—they were bright red and glowed—stopped being so bright. They grew dimmer and dimmer until there was no more light in them. That was when I thought maybe he was rolling his eyes up into his head or something, but then the whites started to fade, too. They turned grayish, then black. And before I knew it, there were no eyes at all, only empty sockets.

"The sirens finally reached the house and I heard footsteps running up the stairs and down the hall towards the apartment. But I knew then that the police would be too late, they would not see this man. He was disappearing too fast. His arms and legs shrank into his body, then his body shrank until only his head was sitting on top of you, grinning at me. And by the time the police made it to the bedroom the head was gone. It faded, Patricia. Faded until you could see it no more."

Lydia's eyes were still glazed over, but she finally pulled them away from the window and focused them on her daughter. There was a long silence. Outside in the corridor nurses rushed about. A patient coughed in another room.

Gradually Lydia's eyes cleared, mirroring a vicious struggle to remain sane. "My God, Patricia," she whispered. "What kind of monster did you bring home?"

"I don't know, Ma," Patty said, also in a low voice. "I don't know."

Three days later Patty found herself home again, spooning oatmeal into little Frankie's mouth. The baby swallowed half of the mushy cereal and ejected the other half onto Patty's T-shirt. Sighing, Patty got up from the kitchen table to get a towel. She moved painfully, feeling her stitches pull. Detective Wheeler, upon learning of her violent injury, had demanded details of the cause, but she had lied and told him the assailant had ripped her with his bare hands. Wheeler had winced and sworn at that, but she knew if she had told him the truth he would have arranged an appointment with a psychiatrist.

Frankie pounded on the highchair tray, demanding more oatmeal. Face scrunched up and red like raw meat, he wailed, drowning out the sound of the TV in the other room.

"In a minute, sweetheart, in a minute," Patty said mechanically as she wiped the oatmeal off her shirt. She contemplated changing it when she saw the wet brown stain, then decided against it. Who, besides her family, would see her anyhow?

She returned to the table, taking the towel with her. The baby continued to wail until Patty plugged his mouth with a spoonful of food. This time Frankie swallowed it all. Patty sighed again, in a mixture of relief and exhaustion.

Lydia, sitting in her favorite recliner in front of the TV, glanced over at Patty through the open doorway that separated the two rooms, briefly sized up the situation, then lit a cigarette and resumed watching *Three's Company*. Not too far away Janet played silently in a playpen. Janet's the quiet one, Patty found herself musing, while her brother is loud and demanding. Such opposites. Janet, who was now two, had been mild-mannered even when she was Frankie's age. Patty wondered if this meant her son would always be hotheaded and impatient. God, she hoped not!

Janet, as though sensing her mother's attention, looked up from a toy in her hand and over at the kitchen. Patty smiled at her, and the girl's blue eyes brightened. She grinned broadly and waited a moment, as if to see if Patty would come to her, then returned her attention to the object in her hand. She seemed happier, now that her mother had noticed her.

Such a beautiful child, Patty thought, feeling her insides swell with pride. The girl had her mother's red hair but had her father's big blue eyes—beautiful, sparkling pools. It was because of these eyes that Patty had fallen so hard for her ex-husband, Peter the

Rat, the name she had later christened him with. And it was these same eyes, she knew now, that charmed other women and took Peter away from her.

Eyes were dangerous things, she suddenly realized. Sam's eyes had enchanted her, also. They had charmed her, tricked her, deceived her.

Frankie screamed, demanding in his language, "More food! More food!"

"In a minute, sweetheart." Patty dipped the spoon into the cereal, then into the baby's mouth. "There you go." She watched her son swallow, then fed him another mouthful, catching with the small spoon the remains that oozed out the corner of his mouth.

Why did I let myself be charmed so easily? she asked herself. Why did I go to the lounge every weekend? Was it because I wanted to get back at Peter for what he'd done to me? Because I wanted to show him that I didn't need him, that I could easily find myself another man? Was that it?

Patty tried to put her mind on something else. She didn't like to think about Peter. She didn't love him anymore, but nevertheless the way he had cheated on her still hurt. She was carrying his baby while he was seeing someone else. He had stayed with Patty until Frankie was born—out of pity and out of guilt. Not because he loved her. No, definitely not that.

"Waa-wahhh!" Frankie wailed.

Patty mechanically added another spoonful, then gave him some milk.

And then there was Sam.

Patty tried to dislodge the thought from her mind, but it was no use. She knew she would never forget that . . . that creature. Even now she could feel a chill whenever she remembered his hand—claws—closing around her throat. She had almost died that night. She had come close.

Patty shivered at the horrible realization. Lydia, who had happened to glance over from her chair, caught her. "What'sa matter, Patricia?"

Patty mentally calmed herself. She took a deep breath, then forced herself to shake her head. "Nothing, Ma. Felt a draft, that's all."

From the expression on her mother's face, she could see that she didn't believe her. But Lydia said nothing and returned her attention to the TV screen.

"Waa-wahhh!"

"In a minute, sweetheart, in a minute."

Would she ever forget Sam? Forget that horrible night?

Only Frankie's crying answered her. Patty momentarily silenced it with oatmeal.

After both kids were tucked away for their afternoon naps, Patty visited her friend, Kate, in the apartment below. Unlike Patty's place, which was nondescript, Kate's apartment was flamboyant with bubblegum-pink walls and cheap prints adorning them. The windows were framed with fake satin drapes, and the floors were covered with pseudo-fur throw rugs (bunny white in the living room, leopard in the bedroom). Patty always wondered what Kate would do if she won the lottery. Go berserk and put Joan Collins to shame?

And another thing that was unlike Patty was Kate's figure. Although skinny, like Patty, she was incongruously bosomy. Also, her hair was not natural in color; she was a bottle blonde with a brown wavy path bisecting the top of her head. What on earth do we have in common? Patty found herself asking. Then she remembered. They both had kids and had been dumped by their husbands.

"Hey, kid, great to see you." Kate beamed sincerely when she opened the door and saw Patty. "Come in, come in. Beer with me, or the usual?"

"The usual," Patty said, following her friend into a pink kitchen, complete with a fuzzy heart-shaped rug beneath the sink. In silence she sat at the table and waited as Kate prepared instant coffee for her and took out a bottle of Miller from the refrigerator for herself.

"Heard what happened to ya, kid," Kate said when she finally sat down. "I've been meaning to see ya at the hospital, but . . ." Her voice trailed off and she shrugged, as though to say: You know how it is, not much time for anything.

"It was a close call, Kate."

"Yeah?" Kate pushed an errant strand of hair back behind an ear, then took a sip from her bottle. "But you're okay, aren't ya?"

Patty nodded, then shook her head. "But never again."

"Now what kind of talk is that?"

"You're gonna have to start going to the Red Lantern without me, Kate."

Kate stared hard at Patty, apparently not believing her ears. "Hey, I thought you had more guts than this. Exactly what did this guy do to ya?"

How much did she know? Patty wondered. What did she hear through the grapevine, which certainly must have spread firelike throughout the building? "What do you think he did, Kate?" she asked hedging.

She shrugged. "Slapped you around, I figured. Gave you a few bruises. Am I right?"

How much should I tell her? She would believe me, wouldn't she?

Maybe. But she would also tell everybody else in the building. She is a friend, but not one you could confide in and trust.

Patty decided to reveal only half of what had happened. "He tried to kill me, Kate. He was awfully strong and . . . he had his hand on my throat and tried to strangle me."

"Oh, my God." Kate's brown eyes grew round and huge. She seemed genuinely sympathetic. "I had no idea it was this serious. I just thought you had picked up a bondage freak or something, not a psycho."

"Well, my mother saved me. She called the police."

Kate took a hearty swig of her beer, as though endeavoring to mitigate the shock. "Is he . . . is he still loose?"

"I don't know. He . . ." Patty stopped, almost blurting "disappeared into thin air." She took a deep breath, then repeated, "I don't know."

"Gee, kid, I'm sorry. Now I wish I had made the time to see you at the hospital."

"Oh, don't be silly. I know how busy you are with your kid and all."

"But it's still no excuse, especially when your best friend almost died, for Christ's sake!"

"Now don't start getting goofy on me, Kate."

Before Kate could make a reply, her two-year-old son, Jason, began to cry in another room. Kate promptly rose from the table. "Nap time's over," she groaned as she left the kitchen. When she returned, it was with her son balanced on her hip. His legs were long, Patty noted as she watched them dangle in the air. He was growing up fast. She could remember when Kate had brought him home from the hospital, so tiny in a blue blanket. It was about the same time Patty had brought Janet home. Time was passing swiftly.

Life was precious.

And she had almost lost it.

"Patty?"

It was a moment before she realized Kate was speaking to her. "Oh. What?"

"You were in faraway land."

"I was just thinking . . . about life in general."

Kate was silent for a moment, too busy mashing what looked like cold carrots in a bowl. When she was ready to spoon-feed her son while he sat on her lap, she replied, "You know that what happened to you was a once-in-a-blue-moon sort of thing, don't you?"

Patty didn't answer, only waited for her to elaborate.

"Hey, kid, you can't let one bad apple turn you off on all the other juicy apples in the bunch. Now, can you?"

"Kate, I almost died."

There was silence. The child on Kate's lap looked curiously at Patty, then at his mother.

"But you can't stay cooped up in this godforsaken place and not go out," Kate said finally.

"I've been doing a lot of thinking. I'm going to start doing something with my life. I'm going to take some night courses, in accounting, I think. Going to get myself a job when Frankie's a little older and not too much trouble for Ma. And, you know what, Kate? I'm going to get off welfare. And I'm going to get me and my family into a real nice apartment. Maybe even a house with a stupid old picket fence. How's that?"

Kate shrugged, as though to say "No big deal," then said, "I want the same things, kid. I don't like being on welfare any more than you do. They act as if you owe them your life. They're worse than the jerks who want a piece of ass just because they bought you a drink or something. But I still think the best way to get out of here is by keeping a lookout for some nice guy with a decent living."

"But you're not going to find anyone nice at the Lantern."

"That's where you're wrong. I found myself a decent fella just last Friday when you . . ." Her voice trailed off, unable to finish.

"But it's dangerous," Patty insisted.

"I know that, but so are a lot of things. Even eating can be dangerous. You could choke. But are you gonna stop eating?"

'It's not the same."

Kate shrugged for the umpteenth time. "Hey, it's your prerogative to do whatever you damn please."

Her voice was light, but Patty could tell her friend was disappointed and annoyed with her. And in a way she couldn't blame her, for no woman wanted to walk into the Red Lantern alone. There was a sense of security and confidence in numbers.

"I'm sorry," Patty said quietly. She finished her coffee and left the apartment.

The following Friday evening Patty watched from her bedroom window as Kate walked toward the lounge. Her heart seemed to skip a beat as her friend grew closer to her destination. She felt as though she were Kate. What if Sam were waiting inside the lounge? Would he charm Kate? Would she bring him back to this building? Would the same thing happen all over again, but this time without the police arriving in time?

Patty read a Janet Dailey novel for a while, then returned to the window. She saw two men outside the bar, smoking and inhaling the cold night air, then she returned to her bed and her novel. Her kids were sleeping, and her mother had retired early with indigestion. Patty read a chapter, then fell asleep. She dreamt of two silver coins floating toward her. When they were close enough to touch, she reached out. And as soon as her fingers made contact with the coins they exploded into two fiery balls of red flame. Then she saw something open, like a horizontal door in the air. Like the balls of flame, it was fiery and red. In rapt fascination Patty watched as the entrance expanded wider and wider. Then she heard laughter—Sam's unmistakable laughter. Then, in sudden, shocking awareness, she realized what the growing entrance was. It was a mouth—and it was coming rapidly toward her!

Patty bolted upright on the bed, dropping the paperback that had been resting on her chest. It took her a full minute to realize she'd been dreaming, that Sam was not in the room with her. She waited until her heart ceased to thunder, then she returned to the window. She stayed there until she finally saw Kate emerging from the bar—alone. She watched until she was certain her friend was safe inside the building, then she went back to bed, and this time slept peacefully.

Every weekend night, for a month and a half, Patty stood at her window and watched her friend come and go from the lounge. Twice Kate emerged with someone else, but it wasn't with Sam. Both times it was that construction worker Patty had seen her with on that horrible night. Patty continued watching, worrying about her friend's welfare, until she found something else to worry about. Herself.

She tried to ignore the possibility—told herself repeatedly that it was nerves that had made her skip her period for the last two months—but intuitively she knew she was only fooling herself.

She was pregnant.

2

The doctor confirmed her dreaded fear. No mistake about it, he had told her, you are with child.

Patty kept her pregnancy a secret for another month, trying to decide what to do. How could she keep a baby whose father was . . .

What *was* he?

Over and over she contemplated having an abortion, although before this she had adamantly disapproved of such a thing. It's taking a life, no matter how formless it is, she had told everyone whenever the subject was discussed.

It's your body and you should be able to do what you want with it, was the usual reply.

And she had always countered with the fact that there are two bodies now, not one, and you have no right to wipe out the new one.

Sometimes the argument would become heated, especially with Kate, who was for abortion rights. But Patty never changed her belief. Life began at the moment of conception, she believed, and to remove life was an act of murder. As far as she was concerned, there was no argument.

But this time it was different, wasn't it?

For one thing, she shouldn't have been pregnant in the first place. She had been on the pill. So what had happened? Had there been something wrong with the pill? Or wasn't it the pill at all, but something else? Sam.

She didn't understand, but then again she didn't understand anything about Sam either.

Patty found herself unable to sleep at night, and she found herself barely able to take care of Janet and Frankie. She felt drained, as though her lifeblood were leaving her, pint by pint. At first she thought that maybe it was the baby inside her drinking her blood, like a vampire. It was possible. Anything was possible after having sex with . . .

No, she finally decided, it wasn't a vampire. It was her mind that was debilitating her. She needed to talk to someone, to express her feelings and fears. Kate was the first person she considered seeing, then she quickly changed her mind. If she told Kate she was pregnant, everyone in the building would soon know about it, especially if an abortion was decided. And she wasn't ready for that yet.

Then she thought of her mother. She could already see the look of disgust on Lydia's face, but the woman was going to learn about the pregnancy eventually, anyway. So why not tell her now? And at the same time Patty could discuss everything that had been preying on her mind.

She waited until the children were asleep, then she simply clicked off the TV set that her mother was watching and sat in a nearby chair next to the woman's recliner.

"Wha—" Lydia stared at her in a mixture of confusion and annoyance.

"Ma, I need to talk."

"Fine, but can we talk with the set on? That was one of my favorite episodes of the Jeffersons, y'know."

"This is important."

Lydia sighed, resigning. She reached into the pocket of her frayed, floral housecoat and pulled out a package of Salem and a Bic. Patty watched her in silence as she lit a cigarette. The woman looked as though she hadn't seen daylight in years, so pale and oily was her skin. And her hair—when was the last time it had been washed? Last week? All this woman did, it seemed, was eat, watch TV, and chain-smoke. Not much of a life. But then, Patty's life wasn't all that much better either.

"Well?" Lydia demanded impatiently. She had already slipped the cigarette package and the Bic back into her pocket and was now waiting for Patty, who was staring at her with a faraway look in her eyes, to say something.

Patty's eyes cleared as her reverie broke. "Ma, I don't know what to do," she began slowly. "I'm pregnant."

The last word lingered in the air like an echo.

Lydia inhaled deeply, then slowly let out smoke. "I'm not surprised," she said after a long silence.

"Ma!" Patty wailed in a mixture of frustration and anger. "I didn't come to you so you could start that 'I-told-you-so' bit. I came to you because I'm so damn confused."

"About what?"

"About . . . about whether or not to keep the baby."

The disgust Patty had foreseen on her mother's face was now openly staring back at her. "I thought you were on the pill," Lydia said.

"I was, but . . ." She lifted her shoulders and eyebrows, showing that she was just as surprised and flabbergasted as her mother that the pill hadn't worked. "Maybe some practical joker at the drugstore slipped another kind of pill into the vial. An aspirin, maybe."

Lydia thought about this as she inhaled on her Salem. Then she shook her head, vaguely at first, then firmly. "No. A little pill wouldn't stop that—whatever it was—from getting you pregnant. It must of been his intention all along."

"To get me pregnant?" This hadn't occurred to her until now. Had she been used? Had she fell into some kind of trap? "Oh God." She closed her eyes, feeling something cold course through her veins and chill her heart.

"Patricia!" Her mother snapped at her to reopen her eyes and get a hold of herself.

"Oh, Ma, what have I done?"

"You've fornicated with the devil, that's what you've done."

Patty recoiled as though her mother had physically slapped her. "You don't know for sure it was . . . the devil."

"Humph! Who else could've changed the way he did?" Lydia's pallid face had momentarily filled with blood. Aware of this, she became silent and waited for her heart to reduce its beating. She took several drags of her cigarette, letting the smoke calm her, then said in a quiet voice, "I prayed for you every night, Patricia. I prayed for God to keep that horrible creature away from this place. But now I see that this creature is coming back—through you."

"What do you think I should do?"

"Do?" Lydia echoed, as though Patty had asked an absurd question. "You can't possibly be considering keeping the baby, can you?"

"Well . . . yes," Patty replied in a small voice.

"Oh God, I don't believe this."

"I'm against abortion, you know that. And so are you," Patty reminded her.

"But this is different, totally different."

"It's a life. I'm not sure I've the right to kill it."

"Patricia, have you forgotten that the father of this child tried to kill *you*?"

"What has that to do with the child itself?"

"Everything. The father is a killer and only God knows what else. The child will be the same."

"Not necessarily."

"Don't be stupid, Patricia."

"But I'm not, Ma. The child is also half mine, and I'm not a killer."

Lydia gave this some thought as she crushed her cigarette out in a plastic ashtray and promptly lit another. "You have to get an abortion," she said at length. "You can't take a chance."

Patty sat back in her chair, experiencing an overwhelming urge to cry. But she fought back the tears, knowing that this would not solve anything. She was a grown woman with a difficult decision to make, so she'd have to act like a grown woman, not like a child resorting to tears whenever the situation seemed impossible.

"I'll have to think about it some more," she mused out loud.

Lydia shook her head repeatedly, disgust more evident in her face. "You're gonna be the death of me yet, Patricia. No wonder I have these sharp pains in my heart all the time. It's cuz you worry me so." She took in a deep breath, then let out a woeful, theatrical sigh. "Patricia, you have nothing to think about. And the longer you wait, the harder it'll be. You must get an abortion!"

It was an order, not a suggestion, and Patty resented this. Maybe she had made a mistake talking with her mother. She had wanted her to help make a decision, not force her into one. She had wanted to discuss all the pros and cons. She had wanted to make a decision she would never regret.

"I still have to think about it," she said firmly.

"You *are* going to send me to my grave. My God, Patricia, aren't you afraid? Repulsed? How can you stand it knowing that *thing* is inside you?"

"Ma," she protested angrily, "don't call it that! It could be a normal baby. A beautiful, innocent baby. You've no way of knowing for sure."

"Please, don't yell at me like that." Lydia's voice suddenly turned to a whine. "You know I can't take it when you yell at your mother like that."

Patty compressed her lips in frustration and (now it was her turn) disgust. Her mother had now switched to the self-pitying role. She did this whenever she knew she was losing control of a situation or argument.

"Sorry I bothered you," Patty muttered as she realized there was nothing more to discuss. She rose from the chair and switched the TV set back on.

"Now look at that," Lydia said angrily as she saw the credits roll up the TV screen. "You've made me miss my favorite episode of the Jeffersons."

"G'night, Ma," Patty said tiredly. She kissed the top of her mother's head and, without another word, retired to her bedroom.

Several times Patty actually had her hand on the phone to call Sheila Seligmann, who lived in the apartment house across the street and who had had two abortions. It would only take one phone call to learn of her doctor's name and number and another to schedule an appointment. It would be simple. And according to Sheila, she would only have to pay the doctor a little at a time until the debt was paid.

Yes, it would be simple. And yet Patty found herself pulling her hand away from the phone each time.

The decision would be so final, and this was something that needed a lot of thought. She even sat at the table and jotted down all the pros and cons on a piece of paper. She had ended up with more reasons why she should have an abortion than not, and still she crumpled the paper and threw it away. She seemed no closer to a decision than when she had begun the list.

Weeks went by, and her mind, like water that had been constantly churned, became progressively cloudy. When the wintry weather took a sudden turn and became unseasonably warm, Patty took advantage of the pleasant change by taking her two children for a stroll to the playground at the other end of the street. Maybe the fresh air and change of scenery would help clear her mind, finally help her come to a decision.

The sky was a cloudless, pale blue. The temperature was in the high 50's, not beach weather but still warm in comparison to the frigid weather that had preceded it. The dirty, crusty snow that had been pushed against the apartment house by the street plows was melting rapidly, softening to lumpy mush. A thin stream ran along the gutter, sparkling in the sunlight. For the first time in months Patty felt good, felt as though she were awakening from a lethargic trance. It was as if she had been living in a shadow and was now stepping out into a patch of sunlight. The light, she knew, would disappear shortly, so it was important that she enjoy as much as she could of it now.

Slowly, leisurely, she strolled toward the playground, little Frankie in the stroller and Janet holding onto the lower end of the handle while taking tentative steps. Frankie wailed in protest, not liking the unfamiliarity of his surroundings. But the wind muted his cries and Patty ignored them until he finally relented and fell asleep. Janet, unlike her brother, reveled in the change of scenery, the crisp air, and the warmth of the winter sun. Her eyes were huge and she was actually glowing.

We should do this more often, Patty thought.

When they passed the Red Lantern Lounge, Patty instinctively turned her head away from it, as though afraid direct eye contact with it would somehow harm her and close the distance that she had worked so hard to create. After the lounge was behind her, she found she had been holding her breath as well. She slowly exhaled, forced herself to relax, and concentrated on her destination.

To Patty's surprise the playground was not alive with screaming children and gossiping mothers, but she didn't mind. If anything she was relieved. It wasn't only change she was seeking; it was peace, too. And here, in the snow-clad playground, it was peaceful. The rusty swing set was still. The wooden benches were vacant.

Yes, she'd be able to think clearly here. Maybe if she sat here on a bench for a while, an answer would come. While Frankie slept and Janet played in the diminishing snow in her waterproof suit, Patty tilted her face to the sun and let the heat burn away the doubts and troubled thoughts that plagued her. After today, she resolved, I will make up my mind once and for all.

But Patty was on the bench for only a few minutes when voices shattered the warm peace. Turning her face away from the sun she saw two mothers entering the playground, four children running ahead of them. Patty groaned with disappointment. Now the silence was broken as the children jumped onto the swings and squealed with delight. The swings creaked as the cold, rusty chains scraped the equally rusty overhead bar that supported them.

But the disappointment was ephemeral as Patty reminded herself that she hadn't expected to see the playground empty in the first place. She shouldn't expect to be the only one taking advantage of the mild weather. She was just early, that's all. There would be more. After all, the playground was the only place around here that resembled a park. The rest of the neighborhood consisted only of apartment houses without yards, a barroom, and dense woods. The Red Lantern Lounge and the playground were the only places that people in the area could congregate.

The two mothers smiled in greeting at Patty, and Patty returned the smile. Then she turned her face toward the sun again. She closed her eyes, the darkness behind her lids turning reddish as the sun tried to penetrate them. She let her thoughts surface slowly in her mind.

Why should I have an abortion? Let me count the reasons.

But before she could think any further, Frankie woke up and began screaming in distress. Feeding time. Sighing, Patty took out a bottle of milk that she'd brought along and plugged the baby's mouth with it, letting him hold the plastic container himself with his tiny hands.

Will I ever make up my mind? Patty wondered. Was she subconsciously procrastinating until it would be too late to get an abortion? Was that what she was doing? Maybe she should take up jogging or something equally exertive. Maybe she could jar the baby loose inside her, make her miscarry. That way it would be an accident.

It wouldn't be an accident if you make it an accident, dummy!

Oh God, what to do? What to do?

She saw someone else enter the playground, someone she'd only met once, someone who lived two houses away from hers. It was a young mother pushing not a stroller but a wheelchair across the shoveled ground. The woman chose a bench directly across from Patty.

Patty surreptitiously studied the child in the chair—a boy about five years old. He was leaning to one side of the chair, and his arms and hands, she noted, were unnaturally contorted, bent severely at the wrists and elbows. Even his features seemed contorted—his mouth twisted, one eye closed, the other hooded. Cerebral palsy? Muscular dystrophy? Patty felt her heart reach out in sympathy to him.

Not wanting the woman to catch her looking at her handicapped child in obvious pity, Patty closed her eyes and returned her face to the sun.

Why should I have an abortion? Again let me try to count the reasons.

Would that woman across from her have had an abortion if she'd known her son would be in a wheelchair like this? If she could, would she have prevented him from coming into this world? Would it have been the humane thing to do?

As though to find an answer, she stole a glance at the woman and the child. The woman was saying something to the boy, and both seemed to be smiling. Patty wasn't sure why, but she found this surprising. They shouldn't be happy, she thought. They should be miserable. They should be bitter.

The woman caught Patty looking and she smiled. Patty felt her face color, like someone who had been spotted doing something illegal. Patty forced herself to smile back, then in embarrassment quickly averted her head and feigned sudden concern with Frankie's bottle. It had slipped a little, so she positioned it more snugly between Frankie's hands.

If the woman had known, would she have had an abortion?

Why was that question so damned important? Maybe she should change the question a little. If she, herself, knew she was going to have a handicapped child like that boy in the wheelchair, would she prevent it with an abortion? To be truthful, she had to say yes.

But when she stole yet another glance, she could see that the mother truly loved her son, and the son actually seemed happy.

Did she love her son when she had first learned of his handicap? Had she panicked and immediately thought she had a burden on her hands? Somehow Patty was certain that this was exactly how the woman had felt at first, but she could see now that the woman had gradually accepted her hardship and made the best of it. And because she had come to terms with this, she began to love her son. And her son, in return, was given a ray of light; her love made him love back. And now this woman was probably relieved that she had never done anything foolish and final like having an abortion.

This woman had no way of knowing, before birth, what kind of baby she would have. No woman, for that matter, had that guarantee. It was a gamble that all pregnant women had to take—including Patty. She'd just have to take a chance. Who knows, maybe she'd be one of the lucky ones and give birth to a healthy, beautiful baby. Or maybe she'd be the unfortunate one and bring into the world a . . .

Whatever kind of baby she delivered she knew she'd have to be like the woman sitting on the bench across from her; she'd have to accept the child, no matter what, and try to love it. Otherwise, if she had an abortion she'd never know what kind of baby she had killed. And the guilt, she knew, would eventually kill her.

She could see now that she had no choice.

Back at the apartment she found her mother

sitting, as usual, in front of the TV. As Patty crossed the room to enter the kitchen, Lydia asked, "Make up your mind yet, Patricia?"

Patty stopped in mid-stride. Her mother's eyes were still fixed on the TV screen, where Dick Clark was hosting a game show.

"Yes," Patty said quietly. "I've decided to keep the baby."

Lydia said nothing. Her face was stony and her eyes never moved from the screen, as though she were more interested in the TV show than in her daughter's decision. But Patty wasn't fooled. She could sense a flickering of many emotions behind the dispassionate visage. And the emotions, she knew, were dread, fear, and a touch of panic.

3

It was a boy—six pounds and twelve ounces—and it had the strongest pair of lungs that the nurses on the maternity floor had ever heard.

On the first day Patty declined to feed or hold the baby, affecting dizziness and exhaustion, so a young nurse fed him. Over and over Patty told herself that it was the truth, that she was exhausted. Labor had been long and difficult. When they had told her the baby was only a little over six pounds, she had been surprised, certain a monstrous ten pounder, at least, had been pushing its way out of her. Hearing her son's first cry, she had turned her head to look, still expecting to see a monster complete with cloven hoofs and horns. But instead, she had seen the doctor holding a normal-looking infant upside down by its feet. Patty had wept, flooded with relief, then closed her eyes and fell asleep. The delivery and trepidation had drained her.

When she had awakened in the maternity ward she found herself wondering if she had dreamt everything. Then a nurse entered and asked if she wanted to feed her "darling baby boy." After she had told her she wasn't strong enough, she felt a rush of guilt. Why had she lied? She was alert and rested, even a little restless now. Her mother had always been amazed with her resiliency, her ability to spring back no matter how hard the blow. So why had she declined to hold and feed her baby?

Was she afraid of it?

On the second day she steeled herself and took the baby in her arms. The guilt she felt mushroomed inside her and spread throughout her body, almost to the point of tears. What kind of mother was she to refuse to hold and feed her baby, especially when it was so tiny and helpless? The small, round face looking at her seemed angelic, hardly anything to fear. She could almost feel love emanating from the infant, seeping into her body like heat.

There's nothing to be afraid of, she told herself. Nothing.

He's a normal, healthy baby. Normal. Harmless.

She gently twisted the nipple of the bottle back and forth in his mouth until he caught on and began to suck. He drank the cream-colored formula in spurts, all the while keeping his huge, blueberry eyes fixed on her. Again Patty could feel the flood of warm love emanating from him and saturating her. This baby openly adored her. Unlike her other two children when they were newborns, this one seemed more aware of who she was—the mother, the one whose body had nurtured and sheltered him for nine months, the one who had let him grow and live.

There was unmistakable intelligence in the infant's eyes. Patty's other children never seemed this alert, their eyes never as penetrating. And for a fleeting moment Patty was tempted to ring for a nurse to take the baby away. She felt as though she were under examination, uneasy and transparent.

And she felt certain that the baby knew she had, at one time, almost aborted him.

But the temptation ebbed as she experienced another flood of warmth. *I forgive you*, the baby seemed to be saying as his eyes adoringly watched her.

After the baby's feeding was done, Patty unwrapped the blue blanket to examine the rest of him. She gasped loudly the instant she saw his hands. Actually there was nothing wrong with them, no sixth finger or anything like that, but they seemed too large for the small arms. They were out of proportion.

Like his father's.

Hastily, Patty wrapped the baby back up, and this time she gave in to temptation and pressed the button at her bedside to signal the nurse. While she waited, she carefully avoided eye contact with her newborn son. But still, without seeing, she could sense a change in him.

A young nurse, barely out of her teens, entered the room. "Yes, Mrs. Thompson?" She kept a warm smile. Naive, Patty found herself thinking. She probably thinks babies are literally bundles of joy and wants a dozen of them someday.

"Please take the baby," Patty said. "I'm very tired all of a sudden."

As Patty expected, the nurse was surprised and confused. How could anyone not want to cuddle a baby forever? "Oh, sure, Mrs. Thompson." She gingerly took the baby from Patty, as though he were a delicate glass figurine, and cooed, "Oh, you're such a cutsie, cutsie little one."

As the nurse left the room, Patty caught a glimpse of the baby's eyes. She'd been right when she had sensed a change in him. There was no longer love and adoration in those eyes. What she'd seen when the nurse had carried him out of the room was silent, smoldering rage.

But a baby does not know what rage is, Patty told herself as she lay alone in the hospital bed. She was letting her imagination instill fear in her. She had not seen anything in the baby's eyes. Maybe disappointment or distress, but nothing else. He was a normal, healthy baby.

"Harmless," she said, then bit her lip as she realized she had spoken out loud.

I love my baby, she thought. I love him. I love him.

He is adorable.

Maybe his hands were a little too big for his arms, but in time the arms will grow and the hands will look smaller. Right?

I love my baby.

The eyes hadn't mirrored rage. Just my imagination.

I love my baby. I love my baby.

Patty turned on her side and tried to fall asleep, but her stomach was filled with something heavy and cold.

I love my baby.

Tears began to seep through the corners of her closed eyes, dampening the pillow under her. Far away she could hear the crying of infants, the talking and laughing of nurses.

I love my baby. I love . . .

After what seemed like a long, long time, she finally fell asleep.

"Feeding time, Mrs. Thompson," the sunny young nurse announced.

Patty opened her eyes and saw her son in the nurse's arms. The cold, heavy sensation returned to her stomach. "I . . . I don't feel too good. Maybe you should feed him."

That surprised, confused look again.

"You don't mind, do you?" Patty added.

"No, no, of course not," the nurse said. "Is there something I can get you?"

Patty shook her head. As the nurse carried the baby away, Patty made sure her eyes never met the baby's. Soon she could hear the nurses in the hall discussing something in love voices. "Baby" and "post-natal blues" were the only words she could catch, but it was enough. They were talking about her.

Postnatal blues. Was that why she didn't have the strength or desire to feed her baby? Of course, that was it.

I love my baby. I have the classic postnatal blues, that's all. But I definitely do love my baby.

Oh, yes, I love my baby. I love my . . .

She closed her eyes and drifted off to sleep. This, it seemed, was something she was doing a lot of lately.

Patty was miserable with guilt when she woke up the next time. She was not suffering from post-natal blues; she had only been deceiving herself. She was afraid of her baby, pure and simple, and that was why she had been reluctant to feed or hold it. Because of its father, she was certain the baby, too, was a monster.

She wasn't giving it a chance. And not only that, she was still calling the baby "it." She hadn't even thought of a name for the baby. All the while she had been carrying it—*him*—she had deliberately kept her mind on other things, on anything except the baby. Therefore, no name was even considered.

Well, the baby was here now and could no longer be ignored. She was his mother and had made the decision to keep the baby, so she would have to start behaving like a mother.

Remember the woman with the child in the wheelchair? Remember the vow that was made, the one about accepting whatever should happen?

Patty took in a deep breath, as though to gather inner strength, then slipped into her robe and slippers. She started toward the nursery at the end of the hallway, moving slowly, for each step was pain-ful. At the wall of glass, behind which the babies could be seen in a row, Patty stopped and searched for her son. It was easy, for there were only four infants, and only one was covered with a blue blanket while the others were covered with pink. All four babies were sleeping.

As Patty stared at her son she felt a blend of love and regret surge through her. Her son looked so peaceful and . . . the word "angelic" came to her mind once more. How could she not love this baby? She wished she had never refused to hold him. Would the baby, in his subconscious, always remember that she had rejected him in the first days of his life? Had she psychologically marked him? God, she hoped not.

What will I name him? She leaned her forehead against the glass, and a small list of names passed through her mind until she thought of one that seemed to fit. Richard. Richard Thompson. Yes, that had a nice sound to it.

"Hello, Richard," she said softly at her sleeping son. "Mommy loves you. And Mommy will feed you and hold you from now on." Confident and proud of the vow she had just made, she then returned to her room.

The next morning the young, pretty nurse gave Patty her son and a warm bottle of formula. Patty eagerly took Richard into her arms and fed him. When she was done and Richard was back in the nursery, she realized she'd been tense all the while she was holding him. And what's more, not once had she looked directly at Richard's face.

Again a wave of guilt flooded her. Although she had had Richard in her arms and fed him, she still ignored him.

Well, the next time would be different, she promised herself. If not, then the time after that. Eventually she'd relax, accept and enjoy her son. She would just have to be patient, that's all.

Patty and her mother, Lydia, stood at the glass window, silently watching the infants in the hospital nursery. Patty's children, Janet and Frankie, had been left at home with Kate.

"Isn't he beautiful, Ma?" Patty said of Richard.

Lydia was poker-faced. "You've made a mistake, Patricia."

"What are you talking about?"

"You know very well what I'm talking about." Her voice was a tight, yet loud whisper.

Patty uneasily glanced around her to see if anyone could be listening. A nurse and a cleaning woman in a white, polyester pants suit were nearby, but they were in deep conversation.

Back to her mother, Patty spoke in a soft whisper, "Give Richard a chance, for God's sake."

Lydia ignored her. "You should've had that abortion, I'm telling you."

"Why are you saying this? Richard hasn't done anything. Look at him. He's just a baby. So innocent, so little. Look at that face, Ma, just look at it."

It was true, the baby did look as though it had descended directly from heaven. The face, unlike the others, was smooth and untroubled. It was not grimacing in distress but was the countenance of contentment and peace. But still, Lydia wasn't convinced.

"A mistake, Patricia. A mistake."

"Oh stop it, Ma. You're being unreasonable, and you know it."

"Unreasonable? His father is a demon!" Lydia spat out the last word.

Again Patty looked around her. No one was in the room anymore. There was only a nurse on the other side of the glass, out of earshot.

"Ma, please. I don't want to discuss his father. I want us to forget about him."

Lydia said nothing, but her face was still stony and cold as she stared at her grandson. It had been so different when Janet and Frankie were born. She practically glowed with pride and love the moment she had seen them, actually begging nurses to let her hold each baby. But now, the glass window didn't seem to be enough of a barrier to separate the two.

"I don't want his father ever mentioned," Patty went on, keeping her whisper but adding a firm tone. "You understand, Ma? I especially don't want the kids to know who the father is—"

"*What* he is, you mean."

Patty nodded impatiently. "I don't want any of them to know. That goes for Richard, too. I want us all to love each other, be a happy family."

Lydia snorted. "You always were a dreamer, Patricia, you were. Must of been from all those romantic comic books you used to read when you was little." She shook her head ruefully. "Should've stopped you and set you straight right then. Should've drilled it in your brain that the real world is different, that there is no prince charming and—"

"What on earth has this got to do with us being a happy family?" Patty cut her off.

"You're expecting too much if you think we can all be a family."

"We can at least try."

Lydia's ample chest rose, then fell in a dramatic sigh. "It's warm in here. Or is it me? I must be coming down with something."

"I said, at least we can try," Patty repeated, determined not to let the subject go unfinished.

"It will be difficult," Lydia said, after a long pause.

"But will you try?"

Before the plump woman could answer, a lilting voice said, "Hello, Mrs. Thompson." It was the young nurse who adored babies. "Admiring your son, aren't you? Can't blame you. He's soooo cute."

Patty managed a smile, but Lydia remained grim. The nurse never noticed, her eyes glittering as they feasted on the sleeping infants on the other side of the glass.

"Strange baby, though," she thought aloud, a comment that was almost inaudible.

Patty responded swiftly, as though the nurse had shouted the remark through a bull horn. "What?"

"Oh, it's nothing, really," the nurse quickly added, a little flustered. Then she smiled radiantly, as though attempting to erase everything. "He's soooo cute," she said again.

Patty fought an urge to grip the nurse's arm and squeeze information out of her. "How is he . . . strange?" she demanded.

The nurse's smile diminished slightly in brilliance. "Oh, I shouldn't have said strange, Mrs. Thompson. You see, I'm relatively new here, so I haven't really seen all that many babies. I'm sure your son is really norm—I mean, he's not at all unus—I mean . . ." Her face was rapidly turning to a raspberry color.

"Please, just tell me why you think he's strange," Patty said, fighting to keep impatience and alarm out of her voice.

Both Lydia and Patty gave the nurse their full attention. The nurse groaned, seeming to be chastising herself for getting into this mess. Slowly, carefully, she said, "Again I say it's nothing. I was just impressed at how strong he was. And how . . . well, moody. One minute he's so peaceful, like right now, and in the next . . . well . . ."

"What?" Patty urged.

The nurse hesitated. "Well, he seems to have quite a temper. That's all. No big deal, I'm sure." Now that she said what she had wanted to say, she brightened her smile again.

Like a dimmer switch to a light fixture, Patty thought remotely. There was more, she knew. The nurse was holding back something. "And?" Patty pressed.

"And nothing. He has a temper. I sure hope I didn't offend you, Mrs. Thompson."

"No, of course not. But I still don't understand why you'd find a baby's temper tantrum odd."

Once more her smile dimmed. Patty could see that the nurse had finally found it useless to evade the situation. "Well, usually babies—remember now, I've not been around them that long—they cry because they're hungry, they need to be changed, or they have colic. But your son, he cries so much harder, so—oh, I don't know—fiercely is the word, I guess. He seems, not distressed like other babies, but . . ." she groped for the right adjective ". . . furious. As I've said before, I'm new at this, so you shouldn't worry about anything I've . . ."

Patty stopped listening to her. She was reminded of the rage she had seen in her son's eyes when the nurse had taken him away. That had unnerved her, for she, too, had thought that rage or fury in a baby was strange.

"Well, I better be going." The nurse glanced at her watch, then turned her smile on full force. "I'll see you later, Mrs. Thompson."

Patty watched her hurry down the corridor. Her mind was numb from what the nurse had told her. *He seems, not distressed like other babies, but furious. I was just impressed at how strong he was.* Strong? What did Richard do to make her say that?

Lydia muttered something.

"What?" Patty asked, turning back and finding her mother still staring at Richard.

"A mistake," she muttered again, then moved away from the window.

Three days later Patty was ready to go home. She packed her clothes and the few toiletries that the hospital had generously given her into a canvas tote bag, then waited for Kate and a taxi. Patty found herself tense while her mind raced with disturbing "what-ifs."

What if Janet and Frankie don't like Richard?

What if her mother openly expresses hostility toward the baby?

What if the baby proves to be dangerous like his father?

What if . . . what if . . . what if . . .

Kate arrived 20 minutes later, made a fuss over Richard, saying he was "simply gorgeous," then helped her into a cab. Kate babbled incessantly as they rode home, but Patty was too preoccupied to catch anything that was said. Yet she managed to nod and shake her head at all the right times.

When the cab halted in front of their apartment house, Patty hesitated to move.

"What's the matter, kid?" Kate asked solicitously as she paid the driver.

Patty waited for the cab to drive away. "I'm afraid they're not going to accept Richard," she confessed, clutching the baby close to her while subconsciously avoiding eye contact with him.

"Now why would you be afraid of that?"

"I don't know," Patty lied. She thought of telling her that Lydia hadn't accepted Richard, but changed her mind.

"C'mon," Kate encouraged, hurrying toward the main entrance. "Show 'em their new brother. They'll love him. Trust me."

Inside Patty's apartment only Janet, who was now three, greeted them. Her pretty face glowed at the sight of the baby in her mother's arm. "Ooooh Mommy," she squealed with approval. "He's bootiful!"

Little Frankie had other things on his mind. He was walking on wobbly legs from chair to table, pulling down cushions, magazines, and unbreakable knickknacks. All the breakables had been put away or raised out of reach.

And Lydia cast a brief glance in Patty's direction, lit a fresh cigarette, then returned her attention to the TV screen.

Patty felt a heavy sinking feeling, but she quickly willed it away. This is only the first day, she reminded herself. Janet already loves and accepts the baby. In time, Frankie and even her mother will do the same. In time they will all see what a lovely baby Richard is. They will accept him as a member of the family, and the family will be happy and close—in time.

Repeatedly, she told herself this. But somewhere deep inside she wasn't convinced. There was an uneasy feeling she couldn't ignore, a feeling that kept telling her that all would not be well in the family.

4

Five years had passed, but not swiftly.

Something hovered perpetually in the air, something invisible that everyone seemed to know would fall someday. And when it did fall it would be disastrous. How everyone in the family knew this wasn't certain, but it was in the air, waiting for one wrong move, waiting for something to trigger its dreaded plunge.

It was like a boulder precariously sitting on the peak of a steep mountain, Patty thought many times. Patty and her mother remained on edge, since the day Richard was brought home from the hospital, and Janet and Frankie sensed the unease in their mother and grandmother, together becoming aware of the unrelenting tension in the apartment. As to the cause, the two children had no idea.

For five years Patty kept waiting for Richard to change, as his father had done on that horrible night. She kept expecting him to extend toward the ceiling, to sprout claws, to curl back his lips and growl. But other than an occasional burst of anger and an amazing display of strength whenever he gripped someone's finger or wrist with his tiny hands, Richard had shown no abnormal traits.

Five years was an awfully long time to wait for something to happen, to wait for that imaginary boulder to crash down on them.

Janet and Frankie were now in school most of the day, leaving Richard alone with his mother and grandmother. Frankie had never spent much time with his brother, claiming the boy was too babyish, but Patty could tell there was more to this than what he claimed. Frankie had never even tried to get close to Richard, but Janet was different, the complete antithesis of Frankie. She was quiet, thoughtful, and gave her baby brother a lot of attention. She was patient with him, played with him, taught him things. She, it seemed, was the only one in the family who truly loved him.

Patty kept telling herself that she too loved Richard. It was just that she had been too busy over the past five years. Whenever Richard called for her there always seemed to be something burning on the stove, or the other children's needs were more urgent, or she was in the middle of cleaning the oven, floor or bathtub. She would always ask Janet to take care of whatever it was that Richard wanted.

Now that Janet and Frankie were in school, Patty found herself alone with Richard most of the time, her mother lost to the countless shows on TV. She began to feel vulnerable, like a lone soldier who had lost his comrades and was the sole army. She could feel his eyes watch her every move. Whenever she went into another room he would follow her, not saying anything, just wanting to be close to her.

Patty used to sneak over to Kate's apartment whenever the boy took a nap. This was the only way she could momentarily escape that horrible "boulder." But lately the visits to the flamboyant apartment were becoming less and less frequent. Although Kate, like her, no longer went to the Red Lantern on weekends, the two women found themselves with hardly anything to talk about. Kate now had a boyfriend, a police officer named Howie who was four years younger than she. And he was the only topic that seemed to be of importance.

Soon Patty found herself spending a good deal of her time soaking in the tub, since the bathroom was about the only place Richard wasn't allowed to be with her. But every time she left the room she'd find him waiting for her on the other side of the door. The boy, apparently, was lost and lonely without Janet.

Five years, and Patty still didn't know her son very well. Like her mother who had lost herself to television programs, Patty had lost herself to the household chores and her other two children. It wasn't until now that she realized she had never really looked directly into Richard's eyes, had never hugged him, and—she couldn't believe this was true, but it was—had never even kissed him.

What had ever happened to the vow she had made, when she had come home from the hospital? If that mother could love that boy in the wheelchair, why couldn't Patty love her son that way? Why?

Sam.

Would she ever forget who Richard's father was?

Now Patty busied herself peeling potatoes and carrots for a beef stew. She could feel, rather than see, Richard's eyes on her back. As usual he was silent, a boy of few words. He sat at the table for long minutes, staring and staring. He literally gave everybody goose bumps with his quiet scrutiny, everybody except Janet, of course.

He was an odd one, but then what would you expect, considering his father was . . .

Patty shook her head, as though to toss the unbidden thought out of her mind. When would she ever stop thinking about that horrible man/creature? Peeling vigorously, she contemplated asking Richard to leave the room and amuse himself elsewhere, then she quickly changed her mind. Richard was her son, for God's sake! How long was she going to ignore him? Now was a good time to pull him close to her, to prove that she really did love him but had been too busy to show it.

And it was the truth, in a way. She did love her son. It was just that he made her feel so uneasy. She was afraid that he'd unexpectedly show a side of him that she wouldn't like—his father's side—but he hadn't done anything horrible yet. He had been a good boy. Quiet. His eyes made everyone ill at ease, but he was still a good boy—so far.

Managing a smile, Patty turned around to face her son at the table. As she had suspected, his eyes were fixed on her. It took him a few seconds to realize that he was now looking at her breasts and not her back. He lifted his gaze until it reached her smiling face. He didn't smile back; he rarely ever did.

"Something on your mind, Richard?" Patty asked, in what she hoped was a motherly voice.

Richard stared blankly at her, as though unable to comprehend what she was doing, or trying to do. This was something out of the ordinary. His mother had never looked at him straight in the eye nor spoke to him like this before.

Patty struggled to keep her own eyes from shifting away. Although Richard's eyes were blue, not colorless like his father's, they were pale and brilliant. Almost luminous, she thought, suppressing a shudder. Would they glow in the dark? One thing was certain—she wasn't going to try and find out.

Richard had been a beautiful baby, Patty reflected as she studied his face, but he wasn't even cute now. Only his eyes were outstanding. Every part of him seemed to be growing separately, rather than together as they should. His head was much too big for his body, as were his hands and feet. His neck was long and too thin. His shoulders and chest were frail protruding bones, the flesh barely concealing them. He looked like an undernourished child, but ate almost incessantly. In fact, he ate more than his brother, Frankie, did, and Frankie was on the heavy, solid side—the class bully. And Richard's hair, although black and striking in color, was limp and always oily, no matter how often it was washed. His nose dominated too much of his face, and his mouth too little.

No, he was no longer beautiful or cute. Patty hated to admit it, but her son was very close to being ugly.

Patty felt a rush of pity for him. She wanted to pull the boy into her arms. His father had been handsome, the handsomest man she had ever seen. So, since his father's good looks obviously hadn't been passed down to his son, maybe nothing else had either.

But Patty still found herself unable to hug the boy.

"Mommy, what are you thinking about?" Richard asked, his eyes huge, probing Patty's face.

Patty fought to keep her motherly smile. "I asked you first. What's . . . what's on *your* mind?"

The boy's eyes remained on her face. Why couldn't he look elsewhere? Why did he have to stare like that?

"I miss Janet," he said.

"I know you do. She'll be home in another hour."

There was a long pause and the unrelenting stare.

"How come you never talk to me?"

"But we're talking right now."

The boy shook his head, a flash of impatience appearing in his eyes. "I mean before, Mommy." Then the eyes softened and mirrored what looked like sadness. "How come you never talked to me before?"

Patty glanced at her mother in the other room, as though hoping the woman would pull her eyes away from the TV and interrupt this conversation. But no such luck.

She cleared her throat. "Well, I guess it's because you were too busy with Janet before."

Again that horrible, implacable gaze. Could he actually see through her? Did he know that she had just lied to him?

"And I've been awfully busy when the three of you were here," she added, grasping at anything that would sound convincing. "I never meant to neglect you, if that's how you feel."

"Neg . . . huh?"

"Neglect. It means not pay attention to. I never meant to not pay attention to you," Patty explained, at the same time praying that he'd believe her. She knew the truth was that she had been ignoring him, but she couldn't help it. And now she was sorry, for she could see how sensitive Richard was.

"I'm really sorry," she said, this time truthfully.

His eyes brightened at once. Apparently he was uncertain about everything she had told him, but he knew the apology was sincere. He smiled, the only quality he had that was beautiful. Too bad his smiles were infrequent. But then, Patty reflected, maybe it was the rarity that made the smile a gem.

"We'll talk a lot from now on, okay?" she promised.

The boy nodded and, like a shooting star, his smile quickly disappeared. "Mommy?"

"Yes?"

"Where's Daddy?"

Patty's mouth fell open while her hands mechanically peeled a potato. She remained speechless for several long seconds, then caught herself and closed her mouth. "Daddy?" she echoed while her mind raced.

Richard nodded, eyes big with curiosity.

"Frankie said we don't have the same daddy. Is that so, Mommy?"

"Well, uh . . ." Patty wiped her forehead with her forearm, for it seemed to have suddenly grown too warm in the kitchen. How had Frankie found out that he and Richard had different fathers? Who told him? Kate? Lydia? She couldn't think of anyone else. Damn! She had wanted to keep this buried in the past. She was tempted to lie and tell Richard that he had the same father as Frankie and Janet did. That way he would not feel at all different from the rest of the family. But she feared the truth would come out eventually and he would resent her for lying to him, probably never forgiving her. Maybe it would be best to face it head on.

"Yes, I'm afraid it's true," she finally conceded, quickly adding, "but that doesn't make you less mine than Frankie or Janet."

Richard said nothing to that, only studied her, as though measuring her every word. Patty found herself relieved that she had told the truth about his father; he certainly would have detected the lie immediately.

"Where's Daddy now, Mommy?" Richard repeated.

Patty finished a potato and reached for another while he waited. She didn't want to answer the question, but there seemed to be no way out. She searched her mind for the gentlest word possible, but couldn't find any that would soften the hard fact that the boy's father had deserted him. With Janet and Frankie it was a little different. There were snapshots of Peter the Rat for them to see, and they knew their mother had been married to him at one time. But Richard's father had been a one (terrible) night thing. How could she tell her son about him?

Of course she could never, never tell him what

his father was—not that she was certain, herself.

"Mommy?" Impatience flashed in his eyes again. Its intensity startled Patty for a moment, and Richard, seeing this, quickly controlled himself. He always had these strange, quick flare-ups. They reminded Patty of bolts of lightning in a clear sky. Would they someday get out of hand and become violent? Would the sky become dark and stormy?

"Mommy?" Richard said again, this time patiently. His hands were folded on top of the table, like a well-behaved pupil in a classroom.

"I don't know where your father is," Patty admitted at last. "I'm sorry."

"Why are you sorry, Mommy?"

"Because . . . because I know how much it must mean to you to know where your father is, to know what he looks like and everything."

"I know what he looks like."

Patty lifted a brow in surprise. "You do?"

"Yup."

Patty waited for him to continue, expecting him to elaborate, but he didn't. He just sat at the table and watched her. He seemed to be studying her reaction. She was sure of it.

"How do you know what he looks like?" she finally had to ask.

Richard shrugged. "I do," he said simply. "I see Daddy all the time."

"Where?"

"In my head."

Patty frowned. Taking a potato, the peeler, and a bowl with her, she sat down across from Richard. She tried to appear nonchalant by continuing to peel the vegetable in her hand, but her fingers were hesitant and stiff. "What do you mean in your head?"

"I see his face."

Patty gawked at him. She wished he would stop giving her short answers and explain on his own, without having her coax him. He was doing this deliberately, she suspected. This was his way of getting her attention, which, of course, was something long overdue.

"You dream about him?" she asked.

"Yeah. I see him when I'm awake, too."

Patty's hand working the peeler loosened a bit, smoothly and deftly skinning the potato, but the rest of her body remained tense. "What does he look like?" she asked, although not sure she wanted to hear his reply.

Richard was silent and thoughtful for a long moment, rolling his eyes upward. Then he returned his gaze to his mother's face. "He's got black hair and funny eyes."

"Fun . . ." She swallowed and started over. "Funny eyes?" Her hand kept working, no longer peeling off the skin but stripping the potato itself.

"Yup. But I can't see 'em all the time. Sometimes it looks like he ain't got no eyes at all. Just whites."

"I don't understand."

"Understand what, Mommy?"

Patty found it difficult to move her mouth, to find her voice. "Understand how . . . how you can see him."

"He's got black hair and funny eyes, don't he?" Richard asked, his own voice suddenly high with excitement and pride, like a child who had just guessed a right answer to a quiz question.

Patty nodded numbly. "Yes, but—"

"I told ya, I just see him in my head. Sometimes I see him, and sometimes I don't." He shrugged as though to say: Simple as that.

Patty looked down at the potato in her hand, now half its original size. She couldn't believe what she was hearing. Her son had described his father perfectly. How could he have known what he looked like? Had Lydia told him? Or was it true that he could see his father in his head?

"Mommy, why are you white?"

Patty blinked, trying to focus her eyes and swimming mind on the boy sitting across from her. "What?"

"You sick, Mommy?"

I'm going to be, she thought. "What else do you know about your father?"

"I know a lot 'bout him, but I don't know where he is. I wish you did."

"I don't have any idea at all where he is." Her voice was faint, didn't even sound like her own. "And I think it would be best if you try to forget about him. You have me, Richard. You have Janet, Frankie, Grandma—"

"But Daddy keeps calling me."

"What?"

"Well, I don't hear him or nothin'," he admitted, briefly lifting his shoulders and dropping his head in a sheepish gesture. "But I see him smile at me. So I figure he wants to see me, but I don't know where he is."

This is only a child's wild imagination, Patty told herself, now gripping the potato tightly. Only a child's imagination.

Then how come he could describe his father so perfectly? A lucky guess? Funny eyes—could that possibly be a lucky guess?

Lydia had told him, Patty decided. Yes, that's what it was. Lydia had told him what his father looked like, and the boy took it from there.

Simple. All so simple. She'd have to have a talk with Lydia and demand to know why she had done this.

"I can 'member stuff, Mommy," Richard said, scrunching his face as he tried to explain. "Funny stuff. I 'member you in bed with him. But you ain't sleeping, 'cause your eyes are open. And you're scared. Maybe you just had a bad dream, I dunno, but Daddy's looking down at you and—"

Patty gasped, her hand flying to her mouth.

Richard stopped in mid-sentence. "What, Mommy?"

Oh, my God, did he really remember what he was saying? But it was impossible! He hadn't even been born then. This was all her mother's doing. Had to be!

She glared through the open door into the living room and saw her mother in the recliner, but Lydia was oblivious to the conversation in the kitchen. Patty began to seethe inwardly. Yes, this definitely was all her mother's doing.

"Mommy, now you're mad." Richard sounded upset. "I didn't mean to make you mad."

"No, no, it's okay. Mommy's not mad. Look, why don't you go to your room and play. It's almost time for your nap."

That lightning in a clear sky flashed again. Anger? It was gone as quickly as it had come.

"I want to talk to Grandma," she explained.

Disappointment was evident in the boy's face. He blew out an exaggerated sigh, pouted, then reminded her, "You said we're gonna talk a lot from now on."

"Yes, and we will," she promised.

That seemed to cheer him up a little. He jumped off the chair, then to Patty's surprise ran over and hugged her. Patty dropped the potato that was in her hand, too stunned to catch it as it rolled off the table. It landed with a soft thud on the floor.

"Love ya, Mommy."

Patty instinctively tensed. "I . . . I love you too," she said. She commanded herself to loosen up and hug her son back. But by the time her body listened, Richard was off and running toward the bedroom he shared with Frankie.

For a full minute Patty sat immobile in her chair. In a short space of time she had experienced a violent whirlwind of emotions—confusion, disbelief, horror, anger, shame. Now she felt dizzy and numb from it all. Woodenly, she turned her head toward the living room, the direction in which Richard had run off. But it wasn't the boy she now saw. It was her mother. And seeing her made the anger rush back.

"Ma, how could you!" she cried when she reached her mother in the recliner. Her voice was sharp but low so that Richard would not hear her.

Lydia looked up, startled to see her daughter glaring down at her. Then she dramatically clutched her chest. "My God, Patricia, don't scare me like that."

But Patty was beside herself, feeling hot blood rush to her face. "I told you not to tell anyone about Sam."

"Sam?"

"Richard's father!"

"But I—"

"And you told Frankie that Richard didn't have the same father, didn't you?"

"Well, yes, but—"

"Why?"

"Pul-leese, Patricia, get a hold of yourself."

Patty drew in a deep breath, held it in her lungs for a long moment, then exhaled slowly. "Why?" she said again, this time in a controlled voice.

"I told Frankie because he was curious about the facts of life and about his father. It slipped out that Peter had left shortly before Frankie was born. And

Frankie—you know how bright that kid is—simply put two and two together. He wanted to know how you got pregnant with Richard if Peter never came back."

"And you told him it wasn't Peter, but someone else," Patty finished acidly.

"That's right. But," Lydia quickly added, "I emphasized how lonely you were, and that what you did was a terrible mistake you regretted very much. Had to say something, y'know, or the kid'll lose all respect for ya."

"Thanks, Ma," Patty said sarcastically.

"Now, if you're calmed down, think you could get me a cup of tea? My knee is acting up again."

The request fell on deaf ears. "But why did you tell Richard about Sam?" Patty demanded.

"I didn't tell him nothing about—"

"Don't lie, Ma. Richard just gave me a good description of him—"

"But I didn't—"

"—right down to the eyes. And what's more, he started to describe how I looked when his father was in bed with me."

"Patricia, pul-leese!" Lydia's voice was surprisingly sharp, jolting Patty into silence. "I never told Richard anything about his father." Lydia now spoke quietly, in a tone that was unmistakably sincere.

"Then you must have told Frankie, and he must have told Richard."

"No." The woman shook her head positively. "I told him you had a brief affair with a man, but I didn't go into no details."

"Maybe you told Janet."

"No."

"But . . ." Patty grasped for an answer ". . . how does he know what his father looked like? How does he know that I was petrified when . . ."

She stopped and stared at her mother. There was naked fear in the woman's eyes, then something hazy covered them.

"Lucy's coming on now. It's gonna be the one about the candy factory," she said flatly, turning her head toward the TV set. "It's one of my favorite episodes."

5

Lydia lit up a cigarette then sat back in her recliner and watched the Brady kids plead with Alice, the housekeeper, to come back to the family. Although Lydia had seen this episode at least a dozen times, she still found herself moved. She felt a brief sting behind her eyes, especially when the housekeeper dabbed her tear-filled eyes with a hankie. Lydia then took a deep drag of her cigarette, and the tender moment passed.

She had been very touchy and sensitive lately. A symptom of old age? Maybe she had suffered a mild stroke and didn't even know it. She remembered reading somewhere that one side of your brain, the thinking side, controlled the other side of your brain, the emotional side. If the thinking part of your brain was weaker, then the emotional side would dominate. So maybe this was why she'd been on the verge of crying a lot lately. This had been happening ever since Patty had yelled at her.

Yes, it must have been a stroke, and it must've weakened the thinking side of her brain. She was damn lucky to still have some control over her body, to still be alive. She crushed out her cigarette (it was unhealthy to smoke more than half), waved aside the smoke that surrounded her face, then lit another.

Glancing toward the kitchen, she listened for her

daughter. She couldn't hear anything. Must be in the bathroom, taking one of her long, foolish baths again. Lydia was thirsty and wanted a nice cold glass of decaffeinated Diet Pepsi. (She'd prefer caffeinated, but her heart didn't need any unnecessary stimulants. God knew that having someone—no, make that some*thing*—like Richard living under the same roof was enough to keep the old heart banging like a jogger's.) But Lydia was having these dizzy spells lately, probably brought on by that stroke of hers, and she was afraid to get the drink herself.

"Patricia?" she called, then listened, inclining her head toward the kitchen. Nothing. "Patricia!" she shouted louder.

"What, Ma?" Patty finally answered in annoyance. The voice was far away, from the bathroom.

"Patricia, when you're finished get me a glass of Pepsi, that horrible decaffeinated kind. All right?"

"Yes, Ma."

Lydia waited, half-expecting her daughter to say "In a few minutes," or something like that, but there was only silence coming from the kitchen and bathroom area—no noise of movement or water splashing in the tub. Lydia sighed, frustrated. She'd have to wait until Patty was damn good and ready to finish her bath. Lydia would have to wait patiently for her drink.

Where is Richard? she suddenly wondered.

Don't give a damn where the brat is! she, as abruptly, told herself.

And yet her eyes searched the room for the boy. She didn't like having him in the same room with her. There had been an argument about this once.

"But this is the only room with the TV," Patty had said.

"I've been here longer. And don't forget, it was *my* social security checks that bought the TV in the first place," she reminded her.

Patty then had mumbled, "When I go to night school and then get myself a job, I'll buy a set for him."

But Lydia knew that before Patty could get a job she'd need someone to take care of Richard, and Lydia sure as hell wasn't going to sit for him and be alone with him. And since there was no Day Care Center in this town, the nearest being something like 20 miles, Patty would just have to wait for at least another year, until Richard was old enough to be in school.

Lydia knew she wasn't being fair, but also, she knew she wasn't being unreasonable either. Richard was, by no means, your ordinary five-year-old kid. His father, she was certain, came straight from Hell.

After the woman was certain the boy was not in the room with her, she relaxed and concentrated on *The Brady Bunch*. The show was over, the credits were rolling and the cast in little boxes were glancing and smirking at one another. Then *Barney Miller* came on. She didn't like this show, but it was either this, *The Match Game*, or cartoons. And besides, she was afraid she'd get one of her dizzy spells if she got up from the chair to change the channel. Maybe, when she got her next social security check, she'd buy one of those remote control gadgets. It would no longer be a luxury but a necessity, since she was getting old and her health wasn't what it used to be.

She watched *Barney Miller* for a few minutes, then remembered that her throat was still dry. She listened again for sounds in the bathroom or, hopefully, the kitchen. When she heard nothing, she yelled, "Patricia, for heaven's sake, what's taking you so long?"

"Just give me a few more minutes," Patty replied peevishly.

"Patricia, if you make me get up and if I fall . . ."

she began, then stopped. Richard had appeared in the open doorway between the living room and kitchen.

Apparently, he too was waiting for Patty to come out of the bathroom. Now he stood between the two rooms, silently staring at his grandmother. Lydia, as though she had seen a ghost, quickly looked away and focused her attention on the TV screen and Hal Linden.

She blocked it out of her mind that Richard was still in the doorway watching her. She studied Hal Linden's prominent moustache. Was it really that thick and dark? The hair on his head was incongruously gray and light. Or did he use mascara or something like that to get it that way?

Through the corner of her eye she saw Richard come closer. *Go away,* she mentally ordered. *Go to your room and play. Go back in the kitchen and wait for your mother.*

Just go away.

Richard quietly sat on the couch. He folded his hands on his lap while his feet dangled an inch from the floor. As Lydia watched TV, he watched her, his face frowning as he concentrated.

Go away!

She seemed to be fascinating and puzzling him at the same time.

Lydia felt as though her heart and lungs had suddenly forgotten how to function. She snuffed her cigarette out and, with trembling fingers, lit another. This time she didn't bother to push aside the smoke that hung around her. Let the haze obscure her face; that way the brat wouldn't be able to study it as clearly.

Goddammit, get lost!

Richard sat like a statue, an ugly statue, she thought—big head, big hands and feet, scrawny body, something like that alien E.T. He didn't move, except for his feet; they dangled as though they were weightless and in a soft breeze. His eyes were still riveted on her.

Lydia told herself to ignore him. He'll go away. Just don't show him that you're nervous or even afraid, and he'll get bored and go away.

Could he smell fear, like some animal could? she suddenly wondered. It wasn't really all that far-fetched or impossible. Anything could be possible with this kid.

She drew in a deep drag of her cigarette and, for the first time since she was a teenager, coughed from the smoke. She instinctively reached for her throat, then dropped her hand as her breathing returned to normal. With eyes watery from the strain, she glanced at Richard. He was still staring at her, as though nothing had happened.

Go away go away go away go away . . .

She took another drag, and this time managed to inhale and exhale smoothly. She turned her attention to the screen. Why was he staring at her like that? Why couldn't she ignore his presence? Pretend he wasn't even in the room with her? He certainly was silent enough.

But she couldn't; his presence was as conspicuous as a blinking neon sign, and his silence as loud as a rock concert. He simply was impossible to ignore.

The uneasy feeling gave way to annoyance, then finally to petulance. "What are you staring at, kid?" she snapped.

The boy didn't even flinch. "You, Grandma," he replied frankly.

"Didn't your mother ever tell you it's impolite to stare?"

"No."

Never was much of a talker, Lydia noted. But his eyes . . . oh, his eyes . . .

"I'm watching TV," she told him brusquely.

"I know."

So you're bothering me with your horrible eyes. With your horrible presence.

So please go away.

"Haven't you something better to do?" she asked, then forced herself to add, "sweetheart."

The bogus endearment surprised the boy, then something crossed his face and his eyes hardened. Lydia had not meant what she had said. He could tell she had tried to fool him.

"Sweet . . . heart," he echoed, his voice strangely distant, as though turning the word over and over in a remote corner of his brain.

Lydia felt a chill. *Go away. Please get up and go see your mother. She should be about done with her goddamn bath.*

"Grandma?"

"What is it now?" she snapped, her tone harsh with impatience. It was either this or speak in a quavering voice.

"How come you don't like me?"

Lydia found herself speechless, staring at the boy while he stared evenly back. After what seemed like a full minute, she said, "I never said I didn't like you, kid."

"I can tell, Grandma."

The TV droned on, but it sounded faint and far away. Only Lydia's breathing was loud.

"Look," she said, "Grandma's not feeling too good t'day. Just let me relax and watch some TV, all right?"

The boy said nothing, but he didn't move away either. His feet continued to dangle loosely while his body sat straight and rigid. And his eyes watched her.

Go away. For God's sake, just go away.

Again Lydia tried to ignore his presence and again found it impossible. She shifted uneasily in her chair, but could not get comfortable anymore.

"Am I bothering you, Grandma?" he asked flatly.

"Yes," she hissed before she could stop herself. Then in a calmer tone, she said, "I really want to see this show."

"You hate *Barney Miller*, Grandma."

Now how did he know that? She didn't remember ever telling him, or anyone else in the family.

"Why don't you like me?" he asked for the second time.

Lydia's mouth was really dry now. She needed that Diet Pepsi desperately. "Patricia!" she shouted, much louder than she intended. "Patricia, I need that drink!"

No sounds came from the kitchen or bathroom.

"Why don't you like me, Grandma?"

Lydia could feel her heart thumping wildly in her chest. Certainly she was about to have a heart attack. "Please," she moaned, reaching for her chest, "just leave me be."

"Why don't you like—"

"Patricia! Patricia!" She twisted her head and body in the chair, in the direction of the kitchen and bathroom. "For God's sake, answer me!"

In an instant Patty appeared in the doorway, a towel around her torso, water puddling the floor beneath her. "What's the matter, Ma?" Alarm and puzzlement were in her face and voice.

"I'm trying to watch TV, Patricia, and your kid is bothering me."

Patty glanced at Richard, who was quietly sitting on the couch, hands folded on his lap. His eyes never looked over at her; they were fixed on his grandmother, watching the woman overreact to his implacable scrutiny.

"Come on," Patty said to him, extending her hand for the boy. "It's almost time for your nap."

"You always say it's time for a nap," Richard said without looking at her. Something about Lydia was fascinating him.

"That's because you're a growing boy, and growing boys need all the sleep they can get."

Richard hesitated, then finally pulled his attention away from his grandmother. "Aw, all right," he surrendered. He got up from the couch and held his mother's hand. Patty visibly stiffened the moment he touched her, while Lydia relaxed, still holding her chest to still her racing heart.

As Richard left the room, he said, "Grandma doesn't like me." It was a statement, cold and confident.

Lydia shivered, took the afghan that was folded over the back of the chair and wrapped it around her shoulders.

Janet glumly watched the rain pelt against the window of her bedroom. It was a Saturday morning with nothing to do. Grandma was watching an old black and white rerun of *Father Knows Best*, something that didn't interest her or her brothers. And her mother was downstairs visiting her friend, Kate.

"Let's play hide-and-seek," Frankie suddenly suggested.

Janet brightened at the thought. She turned away from the window to face her brother, who was sitting on her bed. Her other brother, Richard, was sitting cross-legged on the floor, quietly paging through her science textbook. The chapter dealing with the stars and the solar system seemed to be fascinating him.

"You wanna play, Rich?" she asked.

He looked up from the book at her. It took a moment for the question to sink in. "Yeah," he finally said.

Frankie rolled his eyes upward in disgust at the slowness of his brother's reply. Janet shot him a warning glance. She wished Frankie would be nicer to Rich. So what if he seemed stupid at times. She suspected he wasn't as dumb as he looked. Rich stared a lot, and she had to agree that it was creepy sometimes, but they weren't dumb stares. Rich, she was sure, was thinking all the time. No, he wasn't dumb at all, and Frankie was the dumb one for thinking his brother was.

"Who's gonna be it?" Frankie asked.

"Me," Janet said.

But Frankie was looking at Richard, waiting for him to volunteer instead.

Richard studied his brother's face for a moment, then replied, "Okay."

Frankie laughed, obviously thinking, "Dumb bunny!"

As usual, Janet glared at him. Frankie ignored her, keeping his attention on Richard. "You know how to count, don't ya?"

"One, two, three, four . . . four . . ."

Frankie rolled his eyes upward again.

"Nobody taught him," Janet said, defending her little brother.

"He coulda learned from *Sesame Street* or somethin'," Frankie said.

"How could he? Grandma watches TV all day, and she doesn't watch *Sesame Street*."

Frankie sighed irritably and dramatically. Janet knew he did this on purpose to make Rich feel inferior. Why did he pick on him like this? she wondered. What had Rich ever done to him? It didn't seem fair. She felt bad for Rich. Nobody, it seemed, liked him too much. Well, she wasn't like the others. *She* liked him.

"I said I'll be it," she repeated.

Frankie waved her off, dismissing her. Turning to Richard, he asked, "You know any nursery rhymes?"

Again a blank (or thoughtful?) stare. Then Richard intoned, "Hickory dickory dock, the mouse went up the . . . clock. Hickory dickory dock . . ."

Frankie nodded, expecting him to go on. But that was all Richard knew. "Dummy," Frankie muttered under his breath, then flashed an exaggerated smile. "Good. Can you say it over again? Two times? Real slow?"

Richard nodded. "Hickory dickory—"

"Not now. Inna minute. First I want you to close your eyes, an' when I say go, say the rhyme two times, real slow. We're gonna run and hide, and you're gonna have to find us. Got that?"

Richard absorbed everything his brother had said, then nodded.

"Good." Frankie turned to Janet, who was scowling at him for treating Richard like a two-year-old instead of the five-year-old that he was. "Ready?"

Janet stiffly nodded.

"Okay, close your eyes," Frankie told Richard. "On your mark, get set . . . GO!"

"Hickory . . . dickory . . . dock . . ." Richard began, pausing between each word, pressing his palms against his closed lids.

Janet and Frankie fled from the room. The moment they reached the living room they separated. Frankie ran in the direction of the kitchen while Janet squeezed herself into the narrow space between the back of the couch and the wall. Before she hid completely from sight she heard a startling crash, a sound of something shattering on the linoleum floor in the kitchen. Janet glanced at her grandmother in the recliner, but she was asleep, oblivious to everything.

". . . clock . . . hickory dickory . . . dock . . ." came the small voice from Janet's bedroom.

Janet thought of investigating the sound of the crash, but Richard was now starting on his second round of the nursery rhyme. She'd find out later, she decided, then slipped deeper behind the couch.

"The . . . mouse . . . went . . . up . . . the . . . clock . . . Hickory . . . dickory . . . dock . . ."

Except for the drone of the TV, there was silence. Janet listened intently and soon could hear her little brother's running footsteps. Then she heard her grandmother groan and shift her large body in the vinyl chair, waking up and making squeaky rubbery sounds as she pushed herself upright. Janet heard Richard run toward the kitchen, then she heard her grandmother emit a loud gasp. Unable to restrain her curiosity, Janet peeked around the couch.

Lydia was gawking at something in the kitchen, pointing while her plump face was flushed with anger. "My mug! My favorite mug!" she was saying.

Janet crawled out from her hiding place to see what was going on. She found her grandmother's ceramic mug, something that was probably older than Janet herself, in several jagged pieces on the floor. Standing near it, looking over at Lydia, was Richard. As usual his face was blank, his eyes round and cloudy.

"You . . . you . . ." Lydia stabbed her index finger at him from across the two rooms ". . . you broke my favorite mug!" Her voice was almost a shriek, so furious was she.

Richard slowly began to shake his head in denial.

"I've had that mug for years!" She nearly screamed the last word. "My husband, God bless his precious soul, gave it to me. That mug meant a lot to me, you . . . you . . ." No adjective seemed strong enough to fit the boy.

"I didn't do it, Grandma," Richard said defensively in a small voice.

"Didn't do it?" Lydia sneered, not believing him. "How can you dare stand there and say you didn't do it?"

"But I didn't, Grandma."

His big eyes looked shiny, and Janet suddenly realized it was tears that were making them that way.

"If my husband was here right now," Lydia went on, her voice rising and rising, completely out of control, as though she had been waiting a long time for this moment to vent her fear and dislike toward him, "he would whip you good. He'd take that belt of his and he'd . . . he'd . . ."

"Don't yell, Grandma." Richard pressed his palms against his ears.

"Yell? You should be thankful I'm yelling and not skinning your hide, you brat!"

The last word slammed into Richard like a bullet. His shiny eyes brimmed over with tears and spilled down his cheeks. This sudden display of emotion surprised Janet and Lydia, and for a brief instant nothing was heard except Lydia's heavy breathing and the incessant droning from the tube. Then Richard ran past everyone toward his bedroom.

Janet thought of running after him, to soothe her little brother, but her other brother appeared in the kitchen.

"Hey, what happened?" he asked.

Lydia, nostrils flaring, lighted a cigarette, saying nothing.

Janet suddenly remembered that she had heard the crash in the kitchen while Rich was reciting the nursery rhyme in the bedroom. So this meant it was Frankie who had broken the mug.

She said, "Rich got blamed for breaking Grandma's mug."

Frankie looked down at the broken remains on the floor. "I told ya he was a dummy." He shrugged.

Janet couldn't believe her ears. Certainly he knew he had broken it; he must have heard the crash and known he knocked something off the kitchen counter as he had fled past it.

Picking up the broken pieces and sweeping the rest into a dustpan, she hissed at her brother, out of Grandma's hearing range, "You broke it and you know it, Frankie."

"I did not," he denied, his voice, too, a whisper.

"You did too. Rich was still in my room when you knocked it down. I heard it."

Aware that he was caught in a lie, Frankie then shrugged, his countenance now betraying indifference. "So what?"

"So go tell Grandma."

"You crazy?"

"But Grandma thinks Rich did it."

"So let 'er."

"Frankie!" Janet wailed, her clenched fists tiny balls at her sides. "That's not fair."

Frankie shrugged.

"How come you don't like him, Frankie?"

He thought about this, then shrugged again. He went to a cupboard and pulled out a box of Count Chocula.

"Ooooooh, yoooooou!" she exploded, then spun on her heel and stormed back toward the living room. "*I'm* gonna tell Grandma then."

"Go 'head, see if I care," she heard him say as he poured the cereal into a bowl.

Lydia was already engrossed in something on the

TV screen. Janet had to nudge her twice to get her attention.

"Yes, dear?" Her grandmother glanced briefly at her, smiled, then turned her eyes to the TV set. Her face was white, like those albino bugs Janet had seen in her science textbook, like the ones who lived under rocks or the ground.

"Rich didn't break your mug, Grandma."

"Ummmm?"

"It was Frankie." Janet quickly glared at her brother in the other room. He watched as he sat at the kitchen table, eating his cereal. He didn't seem uneasy at all, but then, that was because he knew Grandma favored him over Richard. He knew she'd be on his side, and this realization infuriated Janet even more. "Frankie broke your mug, Grandma," she emphasized, her voice urging the woman to do something, to rectify what had been done.

But Lydia stared raptly at the TV screen. Although her face never changed expression, Janet could tell that something was going on inside her grandmother's head. She could almost hear the thoughts racing in her mind.

"Rich didn't do it." Janet tried to drill it into her grandmother's head. "Frankie did it."

"It was only a mug," Lydia said after a long pause. "It's over and done with."

"But Rich got the blame for it."

"I made a mistake," Lydia said simply, her eyes still avoiding Janet. "When you get to be my age, you make a lot of mistakes. Your eyes and ears ain't what they used to be."

"Grandma, you gotta tell Rich you're sorry."

"I will, dear, I will." But the promise didn't sound sincere.

Janet said, "I'll go get him now, Grandma."

"No, not now. Later. Okay?"

"But why not?"

"Because . . ." Lydia reached for her forehead and began rubbing it. "Because your poor grandmother has an awful headache."

Janet didn't believe her. "Are you gonna tell Rich you're sorry you yelled at him, Grandma?"

"Of course." Lydia smiled to assure her. "I already said I would, didn't I?"

But Janet still didn't believe her. She clenched her fists and kept them at her sides again. It was all so unfair. She didn't know why, but she was sure that her grandmother didn't like Rich at all, and this was probably why Frankie was so mean to him. He knew Grandma didn't like Rich, and he figured she would like him more if he sided with her. And Mom, Janet suspected, didn't like Rich all that much either. Janet had seen the way she had managed to avoid him, had seen the way her mother stiffened whenever she was near him.

Disgusting, Janet thought. I'm never, never gonna be mean to Rich. Never!

Indignantly, she spun around and stalked toward her room. As she plopped herself down on her bed, she wondered what it was that made her grandmother and mother dislike Rich so. What on earth had he done?

Richard wiped away the tears with his forearm, then sniffed back the rest. The tears, for reasons he could not understand, enraged him. When Grandma had yelled at him he felt everything inside him collapse. His chin and lips quivered, his knees buckled, and his heart, heavy like cement, fell to the pit of his stomach. He had seen immense loathing in his grandmother's face. It was unmistakable. It didn't matter if he wasn't at fault; the loathing was there. And he knew, somehow he knew, that his grandmother would not have yelled at Janet or Frankie if she thought they had broken that stupid mug. He was the one she didn't like, and the mug was only an excuse.

And this awareness triggered something inside him. It seemed to make his blood churn and bubble. It made his muscles tighten and made his internal organs—and not just his heart—throb. And it made his vision change. He didn't see red, but he saw darkness. The shadows in the corners of his and Frankie's room, where the dreary light from the rain-splattered window couldn't reach, deepened and became a true black. The air dimmed, as though a curtain had been drawn. The bed and bureau darkened, becoming black forms without features.

Everyone around him became darker as the rage inside him grew. Soon it was like the interior of a theater, for although everything was black, he could still see his way around. He had had moments like this before, whenever his temper had flared, but this was different—more intense, and lasting too long.

And it frightened him.

New tears flooded his cheeks. "Mommy!" he screamed, then ran out of the room and out of the apartment. "Mommy! Mommieee!"

He ran to where he knew his mother was, at Kate's apartment. His small fists banged violently at the door. "Mommieee! Mom—"

The door swung open. It was Kate. "Hey, it's your kid," she shouted over her shoulder, then stepped aside to let Patty through.

"Richard, what on earth is wrong?" Patty said, hesitating a moment, then lifting him into her arms.

"Mom-my," he hiccuped, relieved to be close to her and smell her comforting soapy aroma. The darkness began to recede. Color returned. He leaned his head against her shoulder and felt her stiffen.

Was he leaning on a boo-boo she had? He quickly pulled his head away from her.

"Black," he tried to explain. "Everything black."

His mother said nothing, so he knew she didn't understand. Then, sniffing back his tears, he said, "Grandma doesn't like me, Mommy. And . . . she's gonna make you not like me, too. Mommy, don't let her do that."

Again his mother said nothing. Richard then leaned his head on her other shoulder.

She had a boo-boo there, too.

6

Later that night, when the three children were asleep and Lydia was in the kitchen drinking tea, eating buttered raisin toast, and complaining about insomnia, Patty decided to bring up the subject that had been bothering her since Richard had run to her in tears. She made herself hot chocolate and joined her mother at the table.

The apartment was unusually quiet, for once the TV shut off and silent. April rain still splashed against the darkened windows.

"Richard thinks you don't like him, Ma." Patty decided to be blunt.

"Patricia, pul-leese, I've enough trouble sleeping without you giving me more bad thoughts to keep me awake. Maybe I should see a doctor about this. I haven't been able to sleep nights for almost a week now."

This wasn't true, and Patty knew it. Her mother was trying to steer the conversation into another direction. "Ma," Patty spoke slowly, as though to keep her patience from flying out of control, "Richard came to me in tears today. He knows you don't like him."

"Oh, you know how kids are," Lydia said lightly. "They always think they're getting picked on. They think all grownups dislike them."

"But you don't like him," Patty reminded her.
"And he obviously knows it."

Lydia's eyes blinked nervously, her lips
twitching. She took a sip of her tea. "I was never one
to hide my feelings. You know that, Patricia."

"You could hide them if you try."

Lydia thought about this for a moment, then
shook her head. "No," she said, "not when it comes
to Richard. No."

"He's a sensitive boy. Can't you see that?"

Anger flashed in her gray eyes, shining like
polished metal. "I don't exactly see you smothering
him with affection," she countered.

"But at least I'm trying."

As the anger slowly faded, she sighed in defeat,
then shook her head repeatedly. "I can't help it, but
he makes me so nervous. I freeze every time he
comes near me. I keep remembering that horrible
monster—his father. I can't forget it, Patricia. I'm
sorry, but I just can't."

"Maybe if you really try," Patty insisted.

Lydia was still shaking her head, like a machine
that had been left in motion. "Can't. Can't. Keep
thinking of his father. Can't."

"He thinks you're trying to make me not like
him, too."

This seemed to surprise her. "He's blaming me?
I've no control over you. Never could control you. If I
could, you'd never have gone to that hell hole in the
first place and picked up that . . ." Her voice trailed
off. "You made a mistake," she said after a long
pause.

"I wish you'd stop saying that."

"And I wish you had listened to me. He's like
having a stick of dynamite around. Y'don't know
when he's going to blow up—like his father."

"Maybe he won't be like his father," Patty said.
"Maybe we're worrying for nothing. Maybe he's just

a normal, innocent boy."

"His temper," Lydia reminded her.

"A lot of children—and adults—throw temper tantrums. It's nothing unusual."

"But he's . . . he's . . ." Lydia struggled to search for the words she wanted. "He's calm, almost like he's in a trance one minute, nice and peaceful, then in the next he's furious, like something had snapped inside him. And his eyes, they give me the creeps." She shuddered, then promptly took a sip of the hot tea as though to warm herself.

Patty felt an overwhelming urge to cry. She understood her mother's reluctance to love Richard, but she was also saddened that her son wasn't receiving any affection from her. And another thing that was burning her eyes with imminent tears was the awareness that she, herself, found it difficult to love Richard. He made her uneasy, made her freeze with fear, too, but at least she was trying her damndest to hide it.

Was she succeeding? she wondered. Did Richard suspect the truth, that his mother was struggling to love him?

A noise caught the two women's attention. They both turned toward the living room, then glanced quizzically at each other. The floor had creaked. Had someone been listening from the other room?

Patty quickly rose from the table and reached the living room in time to see the door to Frankie and Richard's room close. Which boy had it been? Except for the creak in the floor, there had been no sound. So this meant that someone not wanting to be heard had moved stealthily, had eavesdropped.

Patty opened the door to the boys' room. Both seemed to be asleep, but one, of course, was only pretending. Frankie? Richard?

Intuitively, she knew it was the latter.

As she closed the door quietly, she remembered

the conversation she had had with her mother, the conversation that Richard must have clearly overheard. A cold, heavy lump began to grow in her stomach.

Lydia smiled as she dreamt of her late husband. He was young, about 30, and she was a slim, youthful 27. She had been so pretty then, so alive. In her white sundress and a wide-brimmed hat, she ran through a field of dandelions on her pappa's farm, and behind her was her handsome husband-to-be. They were both so much in love then. She kept running as he kept chasing her, until she found herself inside a white steepled church. Suddenly the dandelions were in white porcelain vases, coloring the altar. And her sundress was now a wedding gown, her hat a veil. Her fiancé finally caught up to her and pulled her into his strong arms, kissing her. She heard bells, sweet melodic bongs, then she was running again, this time with her new husband. Through the field they ran blissfully. Then she found a black, rectangular hole in the ground. She managed to skirt it, but not her husband. Oh no, he fell into it!

Lydia stopped, horrified, and looked down and found her husband gone. The cavity in the earth was black and deep. Then she looked down at herself and saw that her dress was no longer white. It was like the hole—black.

Then Lydia grew old, fat and sickly.

Then Lydia began to cry. And the cold tears on her cheeks woke her up.

Through blurry eyes she saw that the TV was still on. A meteorologist was talking about flood warnings in low areas, about the amount of rainfall breaking records for this time of year. She wiped away her tears. She often dreamt of her husband, who had died of a cerebral hemorrhage several years ago, and the dreams usually left her miserable and depressed. She missed him. God, how she missed him! Since his death she had lost something, that indefinable something that used to make her feel alive.

Sighing, she started to heave her heavy body up off the recliner, to shut the TV off and head for her bedroom. But something stopped her, startled her. She fell back into the chair.

Richard was staring at her.

Had he been staring at her all this time? Had he been sitting quietly on the couch, watching her sleep, watching her dream, watching her cry?

Lydia's first reaction was that of indignation. She felt as though he had spied on her and invaded her privacy, for nothing was more private than her dreams of her late husband. But the hot anger was quickly replaced by a chill. The boy's gaze was different this time. Although the rest of his face was stony and devoid of discernible emotions, the eyes were burning with obvious contempt.

"What . . ." Lydia swallowed, waiting until she had more control of her voice. "What do you think you're doing?"

The boy said nothing, his eyes glowering implacably at her.

Lydia found herself breathing heavily and rapidly. She mentally warned herself to slow down; she was hyperventilating, panicking needlessly. This was only a little boy, she told herself. Only a little boy.

"It's late. Go back to bed," she ordered. She tried to sound authoritative and firm, but her voice shook.

Still the boy glared at her.

The heat of his gaze made her sweat beneath her housecoat—cold sweat, chilling her even more.

"Go to bed," she hissed vehemently, anger and desperation born of fear.

The boy stepped closer.

Lydia gripped the arms of the chair, puncturing the vinyl with her nails. *He's only a little boy, only a little boy* . . .

An image of Richard's father filled her mind. She could see that handsome face turn ugly, see the fingers turn to claws, see the mouth open and reveal yellow, jagged teeth, hear the growl from deep within.

Lydia fought with all her mental powers to erase the hideous man/creature from her mind. "What do you want?" she demanded.

He paused inches away from the chair.

She pressed against the vinyl back, wishing she could push the entire recliner and herself away from him, but nothing would budge. Richard stood before her, eyes leveling with hers.

"Stop staring at me like that," she cried. She thought of shoving him away from her, but wasn't sure if it'd be a wise thing to do. She was, she had to admit, afraid.

Finally, he spoke. His voice was deeper than usual, probably because it was thick with loathing. "I hate you," he said, simply and unequivocally.

The blunt admission stunned her. She had heard those three words from her other grandchildren before, but they had been uttered out of frustration or fleeting anger. But this was different. Richard had said the words calmly and profoundly. He hated her. It wasn't only obvious in his voice; it was in his face, in his eyes. Even his stance and silence emanated the intense hatred he felt toward her.

Lydia pressed harder against the back of the recliner. "Go . . . to . . . bed." She was pleading now, barely able to get the words out.

"You don't like me," he said, scarcely moving his lips, which were pulled back in something like a fixed snarl, " 'cuz you don't like my daddy."

"You don't understand."

"But I don't care, Grandma," he went on as though she had never spoken. "But you're trying to make Mommy not like me."

"That's not true—"

"You told her I was creepy. You told her Daddy was a monster," he said. Quite apparently he had been the one eavesdropping earlier this evening. "You told her I was a mistake."

Lydia closed her eyes. She couldn't believe this was happening. Maybe she was still dreaming. Yes, that was it. But when she reopened her eyes, Richard was still there, glaring at her with those penetrating eyes of his.

"Just . . . just please go to bed," she said. "Grandma isn't feeling very well."

"Why am I a mistake?"

"You don't understand," Lydia repeated, her breathing and heartbeat accelerating. She was beginning to feel faint. "When you're older, you'll understand."

But Richard could not be placated. His face steadily reddened, and his eyes burned. Never had Lydia seen so much hate in a face.

"Please," she moaned. "Leave me alone. I'm ill, I'm cold, I'm—"

"You said Daddy was a monster. How come?" Richard demanded.

Not knowing what to answer, she said nothing. Once, when she was a little girl she had played with a small poodle and had thought it harmless. But it had a wound near its hind leg that she hadn't known about, concealed beneath its fur. When she accidentally touched it the dog bit her. She still had the tiny scar on her arm from it. And right now Richard reminded her of that dog. He had been harmless, but he could snap at her in a flash. She would have to be careful not to touch a sore spot.

"Why was Daddy a monster?" He was close to

shouting now. Certainly someone would hear him and come running.

"I didn't mean what I said," she lied, stalling for time and raising her voice so that the others would wake up and interrupt this horrible conversation.

"Liar! Liar!" Richard half-sang, half-hissed. His face was twisted in contempt. In all the temper tantrums that Lydia had seen him throw, he had never looked this furious. It was almost beastly.

Like his father when he had disappeared.

There was a resemblance. She could see it clearly now. It was not in the features, but in something that was pouring out from within—something animalistic emblazing the eyes, twisting the mouth, flaring the nostrils. Something savage. Something evil.

Lydia groaned. She couldn't endure being cornered in the chair any longer. Taking a deep breath to brace herself, she plunged forward, one hand out to keep the boy away from her, to shove him aside if necessary. But to her surprise Richard violently pushed her back down, with strength that a boy twice his age would possess.

"Richard, I'm your grandmother," she scolded instinctively, then regretted her outburst. She was definitely in no position to reprimand this boy at the moment.

"Let me go," she pleaded, her voice soft, almost a sob. "I'm tired. Very tired. All right . . . dear?"

The last word triggered something explosive inside Richard. His face swiftly darkened, from red to an ugly purple. He lifted both hands to his head and clutched fistfuls of hair. Then he tilted his head back toward the ceiling and emitted a long, wrathful wail.

Lydia stared at him, petrified. She was certain her heart would come to an abrupt, final halt. Remotely, she thought of covering her ears with her hands to muffle the ululation, but she was paralyzed.

She found herself watching the veins in his neck bulge like TV cables.

Oh my God, she moaned inwardly. *I was right, He is a monster like his father. He is going to change. And he is going to* . . .

"I hate you, Grandma!" he shrieked, spittle flying in her face. "I HATE YOU!"

Then he kicked her in the shin. Pain tore through Lydia, pain so sharp and agonizing that she thought she'd pass out then and there. Her eyes bulged in panic when she saw the boy swing his leg back in readiness to strike again.

"No!" she pleaded, her voice reduced to a whimper.

"You're gonna make Mommy hate me," he said. "I know you are. I just know it."

He slammed his foot into her leg again. There was only a soft corduroy slipper on his foot, yet it felt as though he were wearing a steel-toe boot, so much strength was behind the kick.

Now Lydia was reaching for her bruised leg, sobbing and breathing spasmodically. Certainly she'd not live through this. "Go away . . . go away . . ."

"I hate you," he reiterated through clenched teeth.

"*Richard!*" a voice screamed from the doorway.

The boy spun around; Lydia looked up with relief. Patty was looking at them, her face white with shock. Peeking from behind her were Janet and Frankie, eyes wide with disbelief and alarm.

Richard took two steps back, away from his grandmother, then calmly met his mother's stunned gaze. As he stared at her, the rage drained slowly from his face and returned to where it had come, from somewhere deep inside him. "I did what I had to do," his eyes seemed to say. Then he looked back at his grandmother with a final, lingering glance.

There was no regret or guilt in his expression, only quiet contempt. Then, without a word, he disappeared into his bedroom.

Lydia clutched her leg, weeping uncontrollably. "I'm going to die, Patricia. I'm old. I can't take this kind of abuse. I'm going to die!"

At the same time her mind screamed *Monster!* as Richard's savage visage filled it. *Monster! Monster!* But she didn't say the word out loud.

She didn't dare.

7

The next morning Richard could not remember everything that had happened the night before. There had been too many shadows. He remembered being mad at Grandma, and he remembered that everything around him, including his grandmother, had darkened, as if a heavy cloud had passed over the sun. But there had been no sun, or moon for that matter. It had happened indoors.

Also, he remembered a funny hot feeling inside himself; it had started somewhere in his belly and had spread throughout him, even to his head. As the fire inside him got hotter and hotter, he got madder and madder. He remembered that clearly, and he remembered Grandma whimpering in pain, but he hadn't seen her face too well. It had been too dark, especially around her eyes and mouth, which had looked like two black holes and a deep wormy gash. The rest of her face had been gray and blurry.

But he remembered going to sleep and then Frankie trying to wake him up. Frankie was really mad at him, but Richard kept pushing him away, more asleep than awake. Then their mother had come into the room and told Frankie to leave him alone and go to sleep.

Now Frankie was glaring at him, and there were

no shadows. The morning sun, slanting through the window, brightly lit the small room, which was crowded with a single dresser and a bunk bed. Richard, on the top bunk, rubbed his eyes to free them of the gritty remnants of sleep and the image of his angry brother. But when he looked down again, he found Frankie still glaring up at him.

Frankie was mad at him because of last night, Richard intuitively knew. But he smiled anyway, hoping that maybe he was wrong, that maybe his brother was mad at something else and not him.

But Frankie, pulling on his jeans, hissed, "Shithead!"

The smile faded like smoke from Richard's face. "What'd I do?"

Frankie yanked a T-shirt down over his head and twisted himself into it, his movements jerky and angry. "Turd!" he sneered when he was done dressing. He then began shoving books into his backpack. Today was Tuesday, a school day.

"Huh?" Richard frowned, climbing down the ladder attached to the bunk beds. He was in Frankie's old pajamas, which were too baggy and too long, causing him to step on the ends and move awkwardly.

"You heard me, squirt," Frankie said, now looking down at him. Richard was two heads shorter.

"I didn't do nuthin'."

"You hurt Grandma."

Richard strained to remember details of everything that had happened last night, but the shadows and burning heat had made everything fuzzy. Only Grandma's whimpering penetrated the haze.

"You kicked her, jerk," Frankie snarled.

"Stop calling me names."

"Shithead!"

"I don't 'member nuthin'."

"I'll bet."

"But I don't. Honest."

"I oughtta kick *you*," Frankie said, then shoved his little brother, making him stumble backwards.

Richard felt that burning sensation in his belly again, but he fought it. He also noticed the room had dimmed a little, but after he blinked it brightened again. Maybe this time it really had been a passing cloud shrouding the sun.

"I didn't mean to kick Grandma," he said.

Frankie's mouth curled in a sneer and his eyes narrowed to a slit. He was big for his age, known to his classmates as a bully. He was proud of his reputation and right now enjoyed challenging his brother. Richard knew he should be afraid of him, but somehow he wasn't. Somehow, for reasons he could not understand, he felt superior to him.

"I oughtta kick ya real good," Frankie threatened once more.

"Leave me alone." Richard's voice was surprisingly calm, devoid of fear.

Frankie shoved him again, but this time Richard kept his bare heels firm against the floor and didn't move.

"Grandma ain't done nuthin' to you, so why'd ya kick her?" Frankie demanded.

"I didn't mean it. She got me mad."

"I thought y'didn't remember."

"I 'member she got me mad," Richard said.

"Creep," Frankie spat. "You made Grandma cry last night. And n'body makes Grandma cry and gets away with it. Got it, squirt?"

Before Richard could answer, Frankie gave him another shove, this one more violent than the others. Richard stumbled backwards until his body slammed against the wooden ladder to the bunk bed.

Again the room dimmed and his belly burned.

And again he fought the change that was taking place.

"Grandma got me mad," he muttered. "She shouldn't of got me mad."

"If ya make her cry again I'm gonna knock your brains out. Got that?"

Richard said nothing, too busy trying to keep the room bright, his belly cool.

"Got that?" his brother demanded. Once more he shoved him.

"Stop it."

"Stop what? This?" Frankie shoved, then grinned defiantly.

Sunlight faded.

"Stop . . . it."

Frankie laughed, then with both hands pushed his brother with all his might, sending him sprawling onto the bed behind him.

Fire erupted in Richard's belly, then it warmed the blood in his veins, making it boil and spread like lava through his arms and legs. Calmly, while seething inwardly, he rose from the bed and turned to his brother. He stood inches before him, looked up at his face and openly defied him.

There was a flash of uncertainty and self-doubt in the older boy's eyes, then he spread his legs and hooked his thumbs on the pockets of his jeans, a stance which seemed to help restore his confidence. For a long moment no words were exchanged, then a triumphant smile began to melt across Frankie's face. He seemed certain that he had succeeded in intimidating Richard, for the younger brother hadn't pushed him back or even cursed him.

Then Richard surprised him with a powerful shove.

"Hey," he cried, but Richard did not wait for him to catch his balance. He threw his entire body on him, knocking them both onto the floor. "Hey!"

Frankie shouted again, his voice shrill with disbelief. Apparently he was thinking this was all wrong; it should be the other way around. *He* should be the one on top.

But Richard had lost control. His brother and the surrounding room were shades of gray and black, and inside him a fire raged, boiling and seething. Like a volcano, he had exploded in heat and violence. He pinned Frankie to the floor with a powerful strength that not only surprised the older boy but terrified him.

"Get off me, ya jerk!" He thrashed, shoving his body upward to throw Richard off, but Richard clung to him like some kind of parasitic monster. Frankie tried to roll away from under him, but found he could not budge, for his younger brother's limbs seemed to be everywhere around him, like iron posts.

"I . . . I'm warning ya! If ya don't—" Frankie stopped abruptly as he saw the look on his brother's face. More than anything in the world, Richard wanted to hurt him—not kill him, just hurt him in the most painful way possible—and this was evident in his face.

He bared his teeth, which were only baby incisors, but they could have been crocodile's teeth to Frankie. The boy was staring up at his brother in frozen horror.

Richard laughed, loving the control he now had over his brother, the school bully. And to think he was two years younger. The feeling of power was delicious, probably the best feeling ever.

Gradually, Frankie thawed from his frozen state. He began to squirm, and Richard laughed again. It was like watching a bug trying to get away, and it was Richard who would decide whether or not it would.

"You little shit!" Frankie spat in a sudden burst of

energy and fury. "Get off, get off, get off!" He bucked wildly, heaving and thrashing until his face was livid.

Nasty little bug, Richard thought.

"If you don't get off, I'm gonna make you ... sorry," he panted, still pushing upward to throw Richard off.

Maybe I'll squash you, little bug.

"I'm warning ya," Frankie threatened.

Y'don't scare me, little bug. Richard widened his smile, showing more baby teeth.

"Awright, you asked for it!" Frankie, with all the strength he could muster, lifted his head and bit his brother's forearm.

The pain was sharp and excruciating, and yet there was something pleasurable about it. It was almost as though Richard couldn't decide whether or not he liked it.

The bug bit me, he thought in amazement as he looked down at Frankie, who was now also as black as a bug to him. He could barely make out the features, but he knew his brother was stunned that there had been no outcry of pain.

Gotta bite the bug back. Gotta let it know that it's not nice to bite.

Richard then opened his jaw, dropped his head, and clamped his teeth on his brother's shoulder, tearing through the shirt and piercing the skin.

Frankie screamed.

Richard gnawed at the flesh and the cotton shirt, reddening them with blood. He twisted his head savagely and sank his teeth deeper into his brother's shoulder. He felt and tasted sweet, sticky liquid in his mouth and fleetingly thought of cherry juice.

Frankie screamed again, this time not in protest but in pure terror. "Mom! Mom!"

The door to the room flung open.

"Frankie! Richard!"

Hands struggled to pull Richard off his brother. "Richard! RICHARD!"

It was his mother's voice, and hearing it made him lose some of his strength. Suddenly his jaw wasn't so powerful anymore. It began to ache, and the pain ceased to be borderline pleasure.

Patty had tried to yank him off by pulling at his pajama top. Now her fingers were in his hair, forcing his head back. Richard finally relented and sat upright, straddling his brother. His mouth dripped blood and his teeth were smeared with pinkish froth. On Frankie's shirt at the shoulder there was a deep, blackish-red stain, a wet oval that was rapidly growing.

"Oh my God," Patty moaned.

Panting, Richard jumped off his brother. The darkness began to fade. He could now see that his mother's face was moon-white and her green eyes were filled with worry and apprehension. And he saw that it was Frankie, and only Frankie, that she was concerned about. There was love in her face—strong, motherly love—something that he had never seen when she looked at him.

Patty dropped to her knees before Frankie, who was sobbing hysterically and clutching his wound. The blood seeped through his fingers, staining them. "You're okay, baby. You'll be okay," she assured him. Then she jumped up and ran to a phone in another room, almost knocking Richard aside in her haste.

Richard felt that burning sensation in his belly again. He didn't like the way his mother had looked at Frankie. He wished she would worry about him like that sometimes, but he managed to extinguish the fire inside him.

He climbed up the ladder to the top bunk and sat there, where he could separate himself from everything and let the violence—or whatever it was—leave his body completely. This was when he spotted Janet by the side of the door, half in the room and half out.

Their eyes met, and he saw confusion in hers, but also compassion. Unlike their mother, she was concerned about him, and this awareness helped make his violent feelings evaporate more quickly.

Patty returned. "An ambulance is coming right away," she said to Frankie, a white cloth in her hand. Kneeling before him, she clumsily and hastily unbuttoned his shirt, carefully unsticking the saturated fabric that was clinging to the wound. She winced as she did this, then emitted a gasp as she fully saw what Richard had done. The flesh was shredded meat. The blood pooled on the ragged surface, then streamed in different directions, like thin streams, down toward his neck, across his chest, and down his arm.

Richard, from his top bunk, looked down with regret. Why had he done this? It had all happened so fast. And like the incident with Grandma last night, it was hard to remember the details. Everything was black and fuzzy.

"I . . . I didn't mean it, Mommy," he said. But his voice was too small for her to hear him. Janet, however, had heard, and their eyes met and held for the second time.

Then the ambulance arrived and Patty helped Frankie to his feet, pressing the white cloth against his shoulder. Together they left the room, left the apartment and rode off in the ambulance to the nearest hospital, 20 miles away. The sirens weren't blaring, so Richard knew it was not a life and death situation. But still, he didn't feel any better.

Why had he done it?

He had acted like a dog he'd seen once on TV, a dog attacking a rabbit.

"Don't feel bad, Rich," he heard Janet say. Her voice was soft, soothing.

Richard said nothing, only stared at her. Janet climbed up the ladder and sat next to him on the bed. Then she wiped something off his face. A tear. Richard was surprised, for he didn't know he had been crying.

"He's an awful bully," Janet said. "Nobody in school can stand him."

"I bit him like a dog," Richard replied slowly, as though in a daze. "I didn't mean it, Janet."

His sister commiseratingly wrapped an arm around his thin shoulder. "I know that. And you know what? I'm glad. Frankie deserves to be pushed around. Everybody else is afraid of him, but you're not. I bet'cha he'll never push you around again."

"He kept shoving me," Richard said, remembering. It had happened just before everything started to dim. "He made me mad, then . . . then . . ." Suddenly his mind went back to the night before. Grandma had made him mad, too. "I didn't mean to hurt Grandma, either."

"Well, you shouldn't have done that, but I think I understand why you did it."

"You do?"

"Sure. I bet you think she's not as nice to you as she is to Frankie or me. Am I right?"

Richard mulled this over, then said uncertainly, "I guess so."

"Sure I'm right." She nodded positively, keeping her arm around him. "But you shouldn't let Grandma bother ya. I think she's not as nice to you 'cause of your temper. You've got a bad temper, Rich. I hear Mom and Grandma say so all the time."

"I can't help it when I get mad," he said.

"Sure ya can. Just count to ten."

"Can't count."

"Oh, yeah. Well, say that Hickory Dickory Dock rhyme real slow. Bet'cha that'll make your temper go away."

"Think so?"

"Sure." She smiled, then hugged him. She felt so warm against him. She cared for him and made him feel good.

Now if only his mother would do the same.

But remembering the apprehension on her face when she had seen Frankie, Richard knew she would not be nice to him when she came back from the hospital. She was going to be mad at him. Mad as hell.

Only stitches were required, since Frankie already had had his tetanus shot. But Patty needed sedatives. The incident had left her weeping uncontrollably. She had lied and told the emergency room doctor at the hospital that a kid she'd never seen before had fought with Frankie and bitten him. She just couldn't bring herself to tell him the truth, that it was her own son that had behaved like an animal. Primal, motherly instincts? She didn't know, but she just couldn't do it.

An image of blood kept flashing into her mind—not the blood from Frankie's wound, but the blood that trickled from Richard's mouth. This made her shudder violently, hug herself and weep.

Ma was right, she thought. I made a horrible mistake.

A nurse sat with her for a while, trying to assure her that everything was going to be fine, but the nurse knew nothing about Richard. She just presumed it was Frankie that Patty was upset about, and Patty didn't correct her.

I have an animal at home. What to do with it, now that it's wild? Drop it off at the nearby animal shelter?

By the time Frankie was ready to leave the hospital, Patty was a little calmer. At least the tears had stopped. Patty and Frankie took a bus home. When they reached the apartment house, Patty ordered her son to stay in the living room and watch TV with his grandmother, for she wanted a few minutes alone with Richard. Janet, she already knew, was in school.

She found Richard sitting cross-legged on the floor of his bedroom, engrossed in a jigsaw puzzle of Big Bird. Keeping his head down, his eyes looked up at her when she entered the room—and they weren't eyes belonging to an animal. They were sad eyes, timid eyes.

Patty felt some of the anger leave her.

"Why?" was all she could manage. Her voice was quiet, very heavy with grief.

"I'm sorry, Mommy."

"You behaved like . . . like a wild animal, Richard. Not like a good boy at all."

"I didn't mean it."

"Why did you do it?"

Richard lifted his shoulders then dropped them in a shameful "I dunno" gesture.

"You fought so viciously!" The anger and hysteria rushed back. Patty tried to will herself to be calm, but it was useless. She needed to get it all out, to lash out at him. "You were violent with Grandma, too. Richard, I'm not going to tolerate that kind of behavior."

Richard quietly stared at her with remorseful eyes. She knew he was sorry for what he had done, but still . . .

"Don't you have any control over your behavior?" she demanded.

"No, Mommy," he replied frankly.

"Can't you try to have some control?"

"Something funny happens to me."

"Oh?"

"Yeah. I get all hot inside, like I'm on fire. And everything gets dark, like it's nighttime."

"Nighttime?" Patty echoed, her stomach tightening.

"Yeah, Mommy," she heard him say, his voice now sounding far away. "Do you get like that when you're mad?"

"What?"

"Hot inside and—"

"No," she said, louder than she intended. She immediately saw she had startled and hurt him, and knew she should apologize for snapping at him but couldn't. "I . . . I'm getting a wicked headache."

"Mommy?"

"What?" Again her voice was too loud, too harsh. "What?" she repeated, this time softly.

"You think somethin's wrong with me?"

"No. Yes. I . . ." Her hand rushed to her forehead and rubbed it. "I've got to take some aspirin," she murmured, then turned on her heels. She was almost out of the room when he called her again.

"What is it now?"

"Please don't be mad at me."

"You have to learn to control your temper, Richard. You have to promise you'll try as hard as you can."

Richard mulled this over, as Patty once more started to leave the room.

"Mommy?"

She stopped, saying nothing and waiting.

"I don't know if I can do it." There was a distinct tear in his voice. One half of Patty wanted to comfort him, but the other half remembered the blood dripping from his mouth.

"Mommy, please don't stay mad at me," he said.

"I'm not mad," she replied flatly.

"A kissie, Mommy?"

The request stunned her. "What?"

"You kiss Frankie and Janet all the time."

She stared blankly at him. "My head . . . it's really killing me," she blurted out, then hurried out of the room.

8

Richard stood immobile like a stone and stared out of his bedroom window. Behind him Frankie was sleeping in the lower bunk, tossing and turning, throwing the covers aside, then moments later retrieving them. It seemed to bother him, even in his sleep, to be in the same room with Richard.

But Richard didn't care. He just stared out into the darkness and let himself slip away. He focused on the crescent moon, letting its platinum brilliance penetrate him until he could feel its cold light seep into his brain and glow inside his head.

He continued to slip . . . slip . . .

And Frankie continued to stir restlessly in his sleep.

It was late, for nothing could be heard in the apartment, not even the droning of the TV in the living room. Silence seemed to permeate the street below, as well. The Red Lantern Lounge was closed, and without its Miller sign blinking on and off, it was a silent, black block, out of reach even from the feeble moonlight.

Far away, on another street, a car motor started up then faded away. On the other side of the apartment house, where the woods stretched on and on and the darkness progressively thickened, an owl hooted.

But Richard paid no attention to the faint sounds; he concentrated only on the silence and the pallid light of the moon. He let himself slip some more until he was completely detached from his surroundings, until he could feel a strong presence germinate inside his mind, growing and then filling it. It seemed to have developed from somewhere deep inside him, from a place where his memories were stored, memories that encompassed other lifetimes as well as his own.

His father's memories as well as his.

"Daddy," the boy whispered into the silence. He had done this many times before and never knew what to expect. Presently one of his father's many images floated like an apparition inside his head. "Daddy."

Sometimes his father was handsome, the handsomest man the boy had ever seen. And sometimes, like right now, he was very frightening. The eyes were orange-red, like twin orifices of bubbling volcanoes, and the skin was crusty, flaking off in dry pieces whenever he touched or moved his head. The nose and lipless mouth were crude, deep holes, where things sometimes came out—things like worms, beetles, and greenish mucus.

Whenever Daddy looked like this, Richard found himself afraid, but there was no place he could run to and escape, for his father was inside his head and would simply run along with him. So he remained at the window and absorbed the moon's pale light.

"Daddy, change," he pleaded softly.

The head of a small snake peeked out from his father's mouth, gazed vacantly at its surroundings, then retreated inside. A moment later lips began to form on the mouth, then the mouth began to smile, a wonderful, captivating smile. Soon the rest of the face transformed into the one that Richard liked and wanted so much to see—thick black brows, pale sparkling eyes, full lips, flawless skin.

Richard clapped his hands together, delighted. "Hi, Daddy." He held his breath, excited as usual, wondering what he'd say or do today. Sometimes his father would tell him strange stories about the land where he lived. Often they were spooky stories, but he liked them just the same.

But now, to his disappointment, his father's image was changing again. His skin had dried up and was falling off in strips, taking with them the lips and nose. Once more he was a horrible creature, like in the stories he sometimes told, and Richard was scared again.

"Change back. Change!" he cried. Behind him Frankie turned over in his bed but didn't awaken.

Richard pulled his eyes away from the moon, hoping the sudden movement would shatter the image of his father. But as he expected, the image stayed with him. This time it was more vivid than usual, and his father was uglier than usual. Because of the incidents with Grandma and Frankie? he wondered. He didn't know why, but he was certain he had guessed right.

"Daddy, change back, change back!"

His father laughed, a deep, raspy sound.

Richard wished he could run to his mother. He wanted her to comfort him, as she had comforted Frankie earlier this morning, but he knew his mother would not want him, would probably be furious at him for bothering her.

A sadness enveloped him. His father, aware of this, threw his head back and laughed louder. Mouth wide open, something could be seen deep inside, wiggling. The tail of the snake Richard had seen earlier?

Change . . . Change . . . Change . . .

Sometimes Richard hated his father, hated the way he teased him, hated him more than Grandma and Frankie. But unlike Grandma and Frankie, the dislike he felt toward his father seemed to make his father happy. It seemed the more he feared and loathed his daddy, the more delighted his daddy would become.

Go away! Richard mentally commanded.

Most of the time he liked to summon up the image of his father. It was usually fun and exciting. He had discovered how to do this when he was about three, when he had stared at a lamp and fell into a trance. All he had to do now was concentrate on an object and let his mind go blank. But getting his father out of his mind was much harder than getting him into it.

He tried to think of something else. He thought of his mother but quickly pushed her out of his mind; she only seemed to make him sad. He thought of Grandma, and she instantly angered him.

Because of her, Mommy doesn't like me. She called me a mistake.

Why was it so important that his mother love him? He wasn't sure of the reason, but something deep inside him just simply knew this. His instincts or genes—whatever it was—knew that he needed his mother's love, or else he would . . .

Would what?

His father threw his head back again and brayed as Richard tried to think of the answer.

Stop it, Daddy! I . . . I hate you, Daddy!

This seemed to only delight his father further. The laughter rose to a grating crescendo, causing Richard to cover his ears. But, of course, this did no good.

I hate you and I hate Grandma!

And don't forget Frankie. Don't forget the way he shoved you around, as if you were a lump of shit.

And I hate Frankie, too!

His father's raucous laughter now sounded as if it

came not from one throat but from a thousand, and Richard's head was much too small to accommodate all this. Soon it was going to explode. He was sure of it, could feel the blood pounding, feel the noise push against the interior walls of his skull, cracking it.

Then through the laughter he heard his father say, "Let your feelings grow, my son. Don't let them die. Let them grow—grow—grow!"

"Too loud, Daddy," he complained, still futilely covering his ears.

You hate me. You hate your grandmother and your brother, his father shouted in Richard's mind. *Now tell me, son, how much do you hate us?*

The boy said nothing but thought, *A lot! A whole lot!*

Keep hating us. Fill your insides with this feeling. Let it make you strong. Let it make you powerful. Hate, son. Hate. It is power. It is a force. Hate me. Hate me.

Richard bit his lip, as though struggling to control the hot, thick emotion that was worming its way through him.

No, don't hold it back. Let it grow.

Now the heavy, burning feeling was filling every inch of him.

Hate your grandmother.

He was going to explode with the feeling. He could feel it.

Hate your brother. He already hates you.

Richard grabbed fistfuls of hair. The moon disappeared and the fire inside him broke loose. "I hate all of 'em!" he cried, then in an eruption of rage lifted a lamp from the bureau and flung it against a wall. Its ceramic base smashed loudly on impact, and Frankie bolted upright on his bed.

Turning around, Richard caught his brother fleeing the room. Another molten bolt seared through Richard as he remembered the concern and

love his mother had shown toward Frankie. Yes, he
hated his brother, all right. There was no doubt
about it now. He hated him because he was jealous of
him. It isn't fair, he thought. Why does Mommy like
him and not me?

He picked up his brother's backpack, which was
heavy with books, and flung that against the wall. It
hit with a loud thud, then fell to the floor making
another, but softer, thud. Tears filled his eyes, but he
was unaware of them. He spun around looking for
something else to fling.

*Hate me, hate your grandmother, hate your
brother.*

The room was now too dark for him to find anything, so his hands groped wildly and blindly for an
object. They probed a wall and found the bottom
edge of a calendar, almost out of reach. He yanked it
down and tried to hurl it across the room, but it only
sailed through the air for a few feet, then fluttered to
the floor, scarcely making a sound. This seemed to
intensify his fury. He wanted to hear loud, violent
sounds, sounds that would match his rage. He
searched some more. His foot soon touched one of his
brother's sneakers, which had been left in the
middle of the room. He kicked it as hard as he could,
but to his frustration it only made a soft, rubbery
smack as it struck the wooden bed.

*Hate me and your grandmother and your brother.
Hate me and . . .*

His mother suddenly appeared in the doorway,
and light flooded the room. Everything was visible
now but still dim through his wrathful eyes.
Shadows seemed to be everywhere, more darkness
than light, and his mother's face was ugly. There was
nothing bright or shiny about it, just a grayish,
bleary moon with deep craters for eyes and a ragged
ridge for a mouth. Suddenly, for the first time, he felt
a strong wave of contempt toward her. For one long

instant he experienced an overwhelming urge to hurt his mother—even kill her.

He frantically glanced around him, found Frankie's other sneaker and hurled that at her. The shoe sailed past, missing her by several inches.

"Richard!" she shouted, her voice sharp and shrill.

"I-I-h-ha-hate . . ." the boy sobbed, frantically in search of another weapon in the room.

He was still looking when Patty seized him by the shoulders and shook him. "Stop it!"

Richard's head rocked back and forth while his mother's hot breath fanned his face. The sharp odor of vodka permeated his nostrils and surprised him. This smell was something new.

"What's the matter with you?" She was close to shouting. In the doorway Janet and Frankie nervously watched.

"Maybe he's having a 'leptic fit, Mom," Janet said. "I got a boy in my class who had one once."

Patty ignored her, now gripping Richard by the upper arms, clutching until her nails were piercing his skin, fingers pressing into the thin bones. She was furious, an emotion released by long repressed fear and frustration and magnified by the alcohol. "I said I will not tolerate this, Richard!" she screamed.

"Ud-ud-ha-hate y-you!" he stammered, tears streaking down his face.

"Fine, hate me. But I still will not tolerate your temper tantrums anymore. Now get a hold of yourself!"

Through the tears he searched her face. It still reminded him of a scarred moon, but there was something glinting in the craters now. Concern? Love? It could have been any number of things, he knew—like fear or rage—but he chose to believe it was love and concern, for this was what he wanted to see.

Gradually his body began to relax. His mother's face lightened. The craters became green eyes, like sparkling gems, and the ridge transformed into a pink mouth. So pretty. She was so pretty.

"Ud-ud-i-love you, M-Mommy," he said.

The abrupt change startled her. "Well, that's better," she said hesitantly, releasing her grip on him.

He wrapped an arm around her neck and snuggled close to her. The hot feeling inside him retreated to his belly and cooled, and now there was a lingering warmth. He smiled, reveling in the new calm feeling.

"You're not going to throw any more fits?" he heard her say.

He shook his head against her breasts. Her body was stiff and her arms were not around him, but it didn't matter. He had seen something in her eyes. She cared about him.

Don't be an idiot, son. She hates you. Just like the rest.

Richard buried his face deeper into his mother's warm chest. She loves me, he insisted, determined to block out his father's voice, which was now faint, going away like the last tendril of smoke.

She loves me, she loves me, she loves me. I saw it in her eyes. There was something there. She loves me.

His father said nothing.

Richard fell asleep, at last content.

After Patty had carried Richard's limp body to his bed she returned to the kitchen, where she had started drinking vodka and tonic. She had thought drinking would help numb her, keep her nerves steady, for lately she'd been more tense than usual. She felt as though she was on the verge of shattering like a piece of delicate glass. Until now Richard had been . . . tolerable. Previously he had thrown plenty of temper tantrums, but now they seemed to be much, much worse, even dangerous. In the last two days he had attacked Grandma and Frankie. What was next? Would he hurt someone seriously?

She finished the glass she had left on the table, refilled it, then took the drink with her to her bedroom. How dangerous was he? Was she worrying needlessly? Maybe she should have punished him, spanked him and forced him to sit for an hour facing a wall. Why hadn't she done that right away at the very beginning, when he had thrown his first fit?

She took a long swallow of her drink, wincing as the burning liquid went down. She knew damn well why she had never punished her kid. The answer was ridiculously simple. She was afraid.

And she would always be afraid.

She took another mouthful of her drink: one part tonic water, two parts vodka.

Eventually she fell into a troubled sleep.

Patty was reluctant to take Richard with her when she went marketing, for he was coming down with a cold, but Lydia adamantly refused to be alone with the boy. And since there was hardly any food in the apartment and Lydia presumably wasn't healthy enough to do the shopping for her, Patty had no choice but to take the sneezing, coughing, sniffling child with her.

A bus dropped them off at the market. While Patty pushed a metal cart down the aisles, dropping food into it, Richard wandered off, promising not to stray too far. As Patty reached for the same items she had been buying over and over again since she'd first gotten married, she found herself sinking into a depression. She picked up a box of cereal, checked the price, then disgustedly tossed it into her basket. Why was it that some things changed all the time, while other things didn't at all? Every week she'd buy the same things, it seemed, but the prices certainly changed, almost every week. Her life, she reflected dismally, was somewhat similar—no change. Since her husband, Peter the Rat, had left her, nothing had changed. Except, of course, for Richard. But she was still in the same apartment, still on welfare, still single.

She was in a rut. Or maybe quicksand was a better word. She was stuck, sinking deeper and deeper toward her death.

Patty abruptly shook her head, as though to dislodge the dispiriting thoughts from her mind. She reached for a jar of instant coffee, the cheapest on the shelf, the brand she'd been buying automatically for over six years. Her hand held the jar for a moment, then pushed it back and took a jar of Taster's Choice instead. It was more expensive, but it was a change. And right now that seemed very important.

How was Peter the Rat doing these days? she wondered as she pushed the grocery cart toward another aisle. Someone had told her not too long ago that he had left his second wife and was now working toward his third, an 18-year-old waitress at a Chinese restaurant. Each woman he picked was younger than the previous one. Was he afraid to accept the fact that he, himself, was getting older? Well, his life was certainly changing all the time.

Where is Richard? she suddenly wondered. Usually he would rush back with a box of candy or something ridiculously overpriced to drop into the basket. And usually she would order him to return it. Maybe his cold was making him listless today.

She pulled down a family-size can of Franco-American spaghetti, the kids' favorite Saturday lunch for almost five years now. Patty sighed, placing the can into the basket. Someday things *will* change, she resolved, and that someday would be in the near future. Next year, in fact. Richard will be in school, and that will give her the chance to take some courses, develop a skill of some kind, and get a job. She would have done this much sooner if Lydia hadn't refused to cooperate and take care of Richard.

Yes, next year would be good. Things would definitely change. She would no longer be on welfare, and she would no longer have to pay the grocery clerk with food stamps and pretend not to notice the scornful faces of the people waiting behind her.

Her spirits began to lift.

And then she'll meet a lot of nice men on her new job, whatever that may be. Maybe she'll be a legal secretary and meet lawyers. Or maybe a medical secretary and meet doctors. Yes, her life will change. She'll make damn sure of it!

Now where had Richard disappeared to?

She quickened her pace toward the next aisle. When she saw he wasn't there, she proceeded to the following aisle. Still she couldn't find him. Damn him, she thought. She had told him not to stray too far ahead.

She tried to concentrate on her shopping, but something that she couldn't quite define nagged at her. A mother's sixth sense, or was she simply an alarmist? She told herself the latter was true; she was getting nervous for no reason. What could possibly happen to her kid in a grocery store?

Nothing, she told herself. All those horrible things you read in newspapers about children disappearing only happen to other people. The chances of it happening to your own kid must be about one in a million, or two million, or three.

But still the uneasy feeling wouldn't go away.

Finally she abandoned her cart and went in search of Richard. She checked the frozen food department, the delicatessen, the bakery department, the magazines and paperback section.

She couldn't see him anywhere. Was he hiding behind one of the many food displays, ready to jump out at her? No, he never played games like that with her before. Usually he was well-behaved in the market, staying within two aisles of her.

So where was he?

Her throat constricted.

Maybe he had gone to the employees' bathroom. Yes, that must be it. But when she asked a worker if there was a little boy in the rest room she was told there wasn't. Maybe he was looking for her, she decided, and she went back to where she had left her food cart. No sign of Richard.

Now her stomach was twisting into a knot, tight like her throat. Damn him, damn him! she cursed inwardly. Maybe it was time she started spanking him. He was getting to be incorrigible.

She left her basket again and hurried outside to the parking lot. Her eyes swept the area, but there were too many vehicles for him to hide behind. She then walked between the rows of cars. When she had covered the entire lot and looked down the street on both sides, she went back inside the store, once more going up and down the aisles.

Where on earth are you, Richard?

When I get my hands on you I'm going to spank you good and hard. I'm all through letting you get away with everything.

But, deep down, she knew she would not get her hands on him.

She went to the courtesy booth and had the young woman there page the child. When that failed, the security officer began to search for him.

Patty's head began to pound, and by the time an hour had passed, the headache was so intense it almost blinded one eye.

"Oh, my God, I don't believe this is happening," she moaned.

The store manager let her into his office and gave her some aspirin and a cold soda, for she had become unbearably warm. The officer and several employees continued to search the premises, even checking the spacious storage area where cartons of food were stacked to the ceiling. They searched until there was no possible place he could be. Then they returned and regretfully told her that the police would have to be notified.

Richard Thompson was missing.

9

Patty wasn't sure if it was the sedatives the doctor had administered or a natural defense mechanism, but she found herself numb and detached for several days. She was participating in a drama but not living it. She found herself answering endless questions. People seemed to come from everywhere, so many of them she'd never seen before—police officers, a detective, three reporters, several mothers with baked goods. Even young children came to her, claiming they had searched everywhere, even the woods next to the apartment house, for Little Richie, the name that the media had given her son to wrench the public's heart. WHERE IS LITTLE RICHIE? the headline of the local weekly paper had asked. LITTLE RICHIE LAST SEEN SHOPPING WITH MOM, another paper printed. HAVE YOU SEEN LITTLE RICHIE? queried photographed flyers that one sympathetic librarian had Xeroxed and distributed throughout the town, fixing them on car windshields and store windows.

"Please find my boy," Patty had said on a local television station, staring vacantly into a camera. Her eyes and voice pleaded with the people who were watching, but her heart had been only a hollow organ, pumping mechanically and feeling nothing.

For several days afterward the phones at the police station, the television station and Patty's apartment rang incessantly with people insisting they had spotted Little Richie. Several witnesses said they had seen a boy walk into the woods. A search party was promptly organized, volunteers coming from as far as 20 miles. But after the third day optimism and fervor faded, and the party drastically thinned. Little Richie was still missing and the towns-folk's tongue began to wag viciously.

I just knew Patty Thompson was an unfit mother.

Did ya know this kid has a different father than his brother's and sister's?

I just knew Patty Thompson was a whore.

Did ya know Little Richie sometimes went to bed without food 'cuz his mother took the grocery money to go to the Red Lantern?

I just knew Patty Thompson was a drunk and a slut. Why on earth do they let people like her have children?

Well, I do feel terribly bad for the poor kid, but this was bound to happen.

Patty was aware of the scorn spreading around her but was too numb to care. She kept to herself most of the time, staying in her apartment as though waiting for the nightmare to blow over like a bad storm.

While the people condemned her for staying isolated and not caring, she called Detective Lieutenant Wheeler daily, hoping to hear new developments on her son's case. But every day, in his low, whispering voice, he'd disappoint her. "Sorry. No lead yet. But I assure you we're still working on it, Mrs. Thompson."

Several times Patty wanted to cry and allow her tears to fill the emptiness inside her. She hated this hollow feeling; it made her feel more dead than alive. Why couldn't she be like her daughter, who was bursting into tears about three or four times a day? Her son, she noticed, cried a little the first night, but after that seemed indifferent. And her mother didn't seem to care at all. In fact, she even seemed glad that Richard was gone.

One evening Patty sat alone with her mother in the living room while the children were asleep in their rooms. She watched her mother for a long moment as the woman stared, engrossed at something on TV. Patty needed to talk openly, honestly. She waited until a commercial was on, then quietly asked, "Ma, what do you think happened?"

Lydia glanced sharply at her, obviously annoyed that the subject was brought up. She lit up a cigarette. "Probably wandered out of the store and somebody picked him up," she said bluntly.

"Why?"

"How should I know? There are a lot of weirdos—and creatures—out there in the world. You, of all people, should know that."

"Do you think he's all right?"

Lydia frowned at her, as though wondering if her daughter had lost a part of her mind. "Only somebody who's not all there upstairs would kidnap a kid, so I'd rightaway presume he'd do crazy things to him."

"Ma!" Patty cried, protesting her mother's bluntness. She felt a rush of fear for her son, but still there were no tears.

"You asked." Lydia shrugged, puffing on her cigarette.

"You don't care about him at all, do you?"

"Y'want me to be honest or nice?"

Patty stared disbelievingly at her. How could her mother be so callous? "Never mind," she finally murmured.

"You know damn well what the answer is, Patricia." She went on, anyway.

"But he's only a little boy."

"He's an imp—literally."

"Oh Ma, you're being horrible."

"No, honest. And that's something you're not being."

"That's not—"

"It *is* the truth," Lydia snapped, now looking fully at her and defying her. "I'm relieved, Patricia. And so are you!"

Patty recoiled, blinking repeatedly. Her mouth fell open, working soundlessly, about to protest, then closed in weary surrender.

Was it the truth? Was she devoid of anguish because she had not wanted to accept her true feelings? Was she really relieved that Richard was now gone from her life?

No, a voice inside her declared. But the voice was weak, not at all convincing.

Feeling sick, she went into the kitchen, made herself a vodka and tonic and carried it to her bedroom. She lay on top of her bed, not bothering to turn down the blankets, and sipped her drink in the dark. She thought of Richard, thought of the monster that was his father. After a long while tears at last began to film her eyes. But were the tears for Richard, or tears of shame? Not wanting to know, she tried to think of something else. She thought of the imaginary boulder that had been sitting precariously on the summit of the mountain. The big rock had finally fallen, and luckily it had rolled down the other side of the mountain, leaving her and her family unscathed.

Yes, she was lucky.

Maybe it was for the best. Maybe she could now go on with her life and climb out of that quicksand she was in.

"I *am* relieved," she admitted out loud in the dark room. There now, I've said it. I am relieved, but not happy.

She drained her glass, put it on the floor by her bed, and fell asleep.

PART TWO

A STRANGER RETURNS

10

It was a warm day in April, and it would have been pleasant if the trees weren't still naked and the ground wasn't muddy and the sky dull with the threat of rain. The playground at the end of the street was alive with children and mothers, the first time in a long while, for it had been an endless, frigid winter. Rumors had it that a strange teenage boy had been seen sitting on a swing several weeks ago when it was sheathed in ice. Also, it was said that he had been spotted on a cold night in February, swinging slowly under a half moon. And it was said he was dressed in tattered clothing, hardly warm enough for the biting temperature.

It was rumored that the boy was Richard Thompson.

Patty ignored the rumor; supposed ghost stories were always popular among people when someone had died untimely or disappeared mysteriously. She hadn't seen Richard for almost eight years now, and she had succeeded in keeping him in the past. Whenever his name was mentioned or his unbidden face flashed into her mind, she would force herself to think about something else. At first it had been a struggle, but as time passed, it became easier and easier. Now it was something her mind did automatically and easily. Her brain was programmed to wipe out any mention of Richard, almost as if he'd never existed.

It was better this way. There was no pain this way.

Her life had changed quite a bit since he had disappeared. She was still living in the same apartment with her mother, who not only had grown fatter but was now half-blind with cataracts (a condition that Patty suspected was more imaginary than real). But Patty was now working as a receptionist for a small insurance company. The pay was not much, but at least she was now independent, no longer on welfare. She had managed to buy a new living room set for the apartment and stylish clothes for her two teenage children. Peter the Rat's checks for child support had grown more and more infrequent, along with his jobs. But the best change of all was Myles.

Myles Forbes was a mechanic who owned his own garage at the other end of town. He was 37, nine months older than she, and was tall with dark longish hair and brown pensive eyes. He seemed sullen most of the time, but when he smiled or laughed it was as if he'd plugged himself into an electrical outlet, for his face would brighten like a lamp. He was a quiet man, always deep in thought, and he was a gentle, sensitive man with hands that were incongruously rough with calluses and stained at the nails with black grease. He was a man she adored, a man she loved immensely.

Someday they were going to be married—he had already given her a diamond ring in good faith—and they were going to build their own house, somewhere in a respectable neighborhood. It would be nothing fancy, but it would be pretty with a big yard, flower gardens, a bay window, and cats. She had always loved cats, but her landlord prohibited pets.

Yes, more change was in store for her.

Now she sat on a bench in the playground, basking in the warm, spring sun. It was a Saturday afternoon and her day off from work. Later tonight she'd prepare dinner for her family and Myles. Then with Myles she'd go to a movie, or maybe just spend an evening at his apartment. There would be no interruptions there, for he lived alone. His first wife died from leukemia shortly after they were married. He had no children and had devoted most of his time to his garage, but he never brooded over his wife's death, just as Patty never fumed about her ex-husband or lamented over her son's disappearance. Whenever she and Myles were together, only the present and the future existed. As far as they were both concerned, there was no past; they both were born on the day they met, less than a year ago.

Patty smiled in remembrance. It was a clichéd collision of carts at the food market. She had been in a hurry, since Saturdays and Sundays were her only days off to get things done around the apartment, and Myles had been his usual, pensive self. He told her later that his mind had been on a car that needed fixing at his garage and not at all on his shopping. When their carts crashed there was a moment of surprise and annoyance, then embarrassment. A bag of potato chips had fallen from Patty's cart and they both reached for it simultaneously. Then their eyes met and they both laughed, probably because they didn't know how else to react. A few minutes later, in another aisle, they met again. And to Patty's surprise he asked her out to a restaurant and the theater. Patty promptly declined, but when they met again in yet another aisle, she told him she'd changed her mind and would love to go out that night with him.

And that night had been the beginning of a beautiful, beautiful relationship.

"Hey kid, what're you smiling about?"

The voice broke in on her reverie. She turned and

saw her friend, Kate, joining her on the bench.

"Oh, I was just thinking about Myles," she said.

"Ah." Kate nodded knowingly. "Men, they hog your mind, don't they?"

Smiling, Patty nodded in agreement. Kate, she noted, had changed a lot, too. Gone was the bottled blonde. Now her hair was a natural sandy color, and she wore scarcely any makeup. She was no longer colorful, but that was because she found no need to fuss with her appearance anymore; she had already caught her man and, like Patty, was engaged to be married. Her fiancé, Howie, was a police officer, a boisterous man in his early 40's with a beer paunch. On several occasions, when Kate wasn't looking, he lewdly cupped and squeezed Patty's rear. She would have slapped him or, at least, said something, but she hadn't wanted to hurt her friend, who was always within hearing distance.

Kate did not live in the same apartment house with Patty anymore. She and her son, now 16, lived with Howie in a six-room clapboard house several streets away. A step up, but not much. Patty suspected that Howie would never marry Kate, that the relationship would never grow beyond the live-in stage.

Now and then, especially when the weather was pleasant, the two women would get together. "Couldn't find ya at the apartment," Kate was saying, "so I thought I'd look here."

The playground was the only nearby place where one could enjoy the half-decent air and warm sun. It was either this or the woods; none of the apartment houses on the street had yards, only small muddy strips separating the buildings and the sidewalks.

"Thought I'd take advantage of the weather and get away from Ma and the kids for a while," Patty said.

"Remember when we used to bring the kids here? Now we use this place to get away from 'em." Kate shook her head at the irony of it.

In silence the women watched children laugh and scream with delight on the swings and jungle gym. It felt wonderful to listen to them at play without worrying about your own children falling and injuring themselves.

After a long while, Kate said, "Have you heard the rumor?"

Patty looked at her. Kate kept looking straight ahead. It was apparent she had to muster up courage to ask the question.

"Yes, I've heard."

Now Kate turned to look at her friend. "What do you make of it?"

Patty shrugged. "Just a ghost story."

Kate stared intently, looked away, then turned back in renewed determination. "N'body's saying anything about a ghost. They're saying Richard is back."

"Sitting on a swing in the middle of the night in February?" She gave a short laugh.

"Well, uh . . . maybe that part is a lie. But—"

"But how would anyone recognize Richard?" Patty quickly pointed out. "He would be thirteen now. And a thirteen-year-old kid would not look the same as he did when he was five."

"He would have the same hair color, same features, same—"

"No." Patty shook her head adamantly. "Hair darkens with age. Features change as you grow. Everything changes. No," she said again, "nobody who'd seen him before could possibly recognize him now."

Kate shrugged, suddenly not wanting to argue anymore about it. She changed the subject to Myles and Howie, and together the two women talked about their future, their plans, their dreams. They were laughing and talking breathlessly, like teenage girls discussing an upcoming prom, when the sun began to sink behind the trees, taking with it the unseasonable warmth.

"Oh, my God, it's late," Patty said. It was chilly now and the playground was silent. She had been too engrossed in conversation to notice anyone leave. "I want to cook supper for Myles tonight." She jumped up from the bench.

"Yeah, me too. But not that I *want* to."

The two women hugged each other, resolved to visit more often in the future, then departed, each hurrying toward her own private world.

In the next half hour Patty rushed about preparing a meat loaf supper, Myles' favorite. He had told her he liked her meat loaf even better than filet mignon. Of course she didn't believe him, but she was flattered just the same. And so whenever she invited him for supper, it was for a meat loaf. Frankie hated it, but then there wasn't much that Frankie liked besides McDonald's burgers and fries, and greasy pizzas from a Greek pizza restaurant. While Patty cooked, Janet set the table. Frankie stayed in his room, pumping iron, and Lydia, in spite of her semi-blindness, watched TV.

An hour later Myles was at the door. Patty sighed with relief, for the timing was perfect. Everything was done; if she had started 15 minutes later she'd have been caught rushing frantically about the kitchen, her face flushed, her body perspiring profusely. But, thank God, she had had time to change and catch her breath.

Myles kissed her, then handed her a bottle of wine. Patty laughed, for it seemed silly to have wine with meat loaf.

"I told you, your version is better than any filet mignon," he said, reading her thoughts. "And with that you would want wine, right?"

"I suppose." She smiled, taking the bottle. Already she felt her insides grow warm and sluggish, and she hadn't even taken a drop of the wine yet. Myles' mere presence affected her this way. "Sit down at the table. Everything's ready," she told him and Janet. Then she called out to her mother and Frankie.

When everyone was at the table, the food served and the wine poured (Frankie and Janet were allowed one glass each, although drinking was nothing new to Frankie, who had been caught drunk several times from keg parties thrown by his friends), Myles proposed a toast. "To a wonderful family that I will soon be proud to be a part of." It was a corny line, but it still managed to touch everyone. Lydia liked Myles because he sympathized with her countless ailments, and Frankie admired him because of his knowledge of cars, and Janet was delighted that her mother had finally found true love with a storybook prince.

Yes, Patty thought as she raised the goblet that held the gleaming, red wine, we are going to be a wonderful, wonderful family.

Everyone simultaneously took a sip, except Frankie, who gulped more than half the contents of his glass. Patty shook her head ruefully at him; he was growing up too fast, throwing away his childhood in a foolish haste to reach manhood.

"Delicious, Mom," Janet said, complimenting her cooking.

Lydia nodded in agreement, but then complained. "Too much salt for my blood pressure, Patricia. You know I can't have too much salt."

"A little won't hurt you, Ma."

"Well, if I get a stroke it'll be on your conscience."

Patty glanced at Myles, who winked affectionately

at her. Deep spiderweb lines framed his warm, brown eyes. There was so much kindness and warmth oozing out of him that she was tempted to lean forward and smother him with kisses. But instead, she forced herself to take another sip of her wine and concentrate on her food. She was chewing on a forkful of green beans when she heard something from the living room.

Myles heard it too, for he looked up from his plate along with Patty. It had been a soft sound, like a click. It had been the front door, Patty realized, now recognizing the sound. The door had clicked shut. But who had opened and closed it? Everyone was here in the kitchen.

Patty listened, expecting to hear more, but only silence came from the other room. Maybe a draft had pushed open then shut the door. She looked over at Myles and saw that he had other ideas.

"Someone's in the living room," he said, staring at Patty in puzzlement, as though expecting her to know who it could be.

But Patty raised her brows to show that she was equally baffled.

Frowning, Janet and Lydia looked up from their plates, having not heard anything. Frankie was too busy wolfing his food down.

There was a pause as most of the family listened for another sound. When none came, Myles said, "I'll check." He wiped his mouth with a paper napkin, then rose from the table, tossing the napkin down. He stopped at the open doorway between the two rooms, looked around for a brief moment, then stepped inside. He searched, even peering behind the couch, but there was no one. He opened the bedroom doors that led off the room but still found no one. He returned to the kitchen and shrugged.

That was when Patty saw something behind him. At first she thought it was a shadow behind his arm, then she realized it was actually another arm.

"Behind you." She pointed, barely able to utter the words. Now she could see a glimpse of a head behind Myles.

Myles spun around, then staggered back in surprise at the person standing behind him. "What the hell . . ." His voice broke in mid-sentence as his right hand instinctively clenched into a fist at his side.

The person looked at him evenly, then regarded everyone around the table. Myles glanced quickly at Patty, not knowing what to do, for the person was not making any threatening move.

"Who are you?" he demanded.

The person said nothing, his calm gaze fixed on Patty. There was a heavy hush in the room as recognition slowly surfaced within Patty. Her hand rose to her mouth and her eyes bulged as she studied the boy behind Myles. He was tall, almost as tall as the man next to him, and he was skeletal, his pale skin stretched to the limit over his frame. Every bone in his body seemed to protrude sharply; his cheek-bones were twin shelves on his face, his brow a prominent ridge, his jaw a severe bow. His hair was long, thin and straggly, almost reaching his bony shoulders. He wore old, faded jeans and a denim jacket over an equally faded black T-shirt. On his feet were battered, blue Converse sneakers, a ragged hole near one outside toe. He seemed to be somewhere in his early teens.

It was Richard.

Patty felt the blood drain from her face. She had thought no one, including herself, would ever recognize her son, for too many years had passed. But there was no mistake about whom she was seeing now.

"Who are you? What do you want?" she heard Myles demand of the boy.

But Richard's eyes were still focused on her. As though in a slow-motion dream, she rose from the table, then stood, frozen, staring back at him. The rest of the family glanced in confusion at the boy in the doorway and at Patty. They did not recognize him, not until they were aware that Patty knew this boy. Then they studied him, examining every feature.

"Rich!" Janet blurted in sudden recognition. She leaped from the table and rushed past her mother toward him.

Eyes still riveted on his mother, Richard took a step back and held his hand up against his sister. "Don't," he said, his voice flat.

Janet halted, as though she had been slapped. "What?"

"You may catch something."

"Oh, Rich," she wailed, tears filling her eyes. Her arms were out, but he took another step back, now pulling his eyes away from his mother and turning toward her.

"Hello, Sis," he said. There was a small smile on his lips, as if he were too weak to produce anything bigger. His eyes glittered for a moment, but they were like deep wells, glinting intermittingly whenever light was in the right position to reflect on the waters far below. And the color was that of clear liquid—colorless. "I missed you."

Janet broke into a huge smile while tears freely streamed down her face. "Oh, God, you're still alive. Thank God!" Again she made an attempt to hug him, and again he stepped back.

"No." His voice, although weary, was firm.

Janet's smile faded, the sting of rejection evident in her countenance. Her hands dropped to her sides.

"Not now," he added, as though to alleviate the hurt he had caused her. "I'm not well and do not wish to spread anything."

"What's the matter, Rich?"

Richard didn't answer. Instead, he returned his gaze to his mother, snatching her eyes with his, like one would swipe a moth with a hand. "Hello, Mother."

Patty found it difficult to speak. She knew she should be overwhelmed with joy that her son had finally returned, that he was still alive. She should be blubbering hysterically, spilling tears as her daughter was doing, but she couldn't seem to respond at all. She was numb, staring disbelievingly at the teenage boy in front of her.

"Is this Richard, your missing boy?" Myles asked her incredulously, his fist no longer ready to strike.

"Yes," she managed to reply.

Another hush fell around the room.

"Hello, Mother," Richard repeated, quietly demanding a response.

He talks so differently, she thought. So formal. So distant. She swallowed, then said, "Thank God, you're still alive."

"Don't thank Him."

Patty frowned, not comprehending.

"He did not keep me alive."

The frown deepened, then disappeared as Patty decided to question the cryptic remark at another time. "Oh, Richard, I can't believe what I'm seeing. It's been so long." She pushed her wooden legs forward and opened her arms to embrace him.

"No!" he warned sharply.

She stopped short. And, as her daughter had done, dropped her arms uselessly to her sides. "What is it you're afraid we'll catch?"

"I've been sick, Mother. I've been sick for a long time."

"I'll call a doctor for you."

"Not now. Maybe later."

Patty glanced at Myles, then at her family,

wondering what she should do next. This was not at all as it should be, she thought again. This should be a rejoiceful moment with tears, whoops of joy, hugs and kisses—not this awful awkwardness, not this heavy silence between words.

"I'm so glad you're back, Richard," she said, putting as much feeling as she could into her voice.

"Me, too," Janet said.

Frankie and Lydia silently watched.

Richard briefly glanced at them, and for an instant his eyes glittered like hard ice. He said nothing.

Patty cleared her throat, suddenly yearning for the wine she had left on the table. But it would mean taking too many clumsy steps to get it. "This is Myles Forbes, Richard."

Richard looked disinterestedly at him, then back at her. He seemed filled with hostility, she reflected, cold and resentful. "Myles is my fiancé," she explained.

Now the eyes seemed to flash in a burst of . . . of what? Fire? Anger? What?

"Is something wrong?" she asked.

The detachment quickly returned. Richard stiffly shook his head. "I'm tired, Mother. I wish to lie down."

"Of course. Later we'll talk." She smiled encouragingly, but his lips never curved upward.

"Same room?" he asked.

"Yes. We still have the bunk beds."

Frankie's head shot upward as though a bolt of electricity had struck him. He opened his mouth to protest, then thought better of it and snapped it shut.

Richard surveyed everyone in the room again, each in turn, then without another word or change of expression, left. Patty stared dumbly after him, her hand to her throat.

"My God," she whispered. It was still too in-

credible to believe. Eight years, and he was still alive!
Eight long years!

Myles' arm went around her; his face, betraying
confusion, watched her. "You sure it's Richard?"

Patty nodded. Everything had changed in the
boy, and still she could tell it was her son. It was in
his mannerisms, especially in the eyes, although
they, too, had changed considerably.

The room was suddenly cold.

"Not much of a homecoming," Myles com-
mented, a hint of disapproval and surprise in his
voice.

"It was so unexpected," Patty explained. Dimly
she saw her mother and children at the table looking
up at her. Except for Janet, no one seemed elated that
Richard was back. The air was pulsating with
tension. How awful we must look to Myles, she
thought.

The room grew even colder.

Lydia shivered. "Meat loaf's cold already," she
complained under her breath, dropping a napkin
over her plate and rejecting it.

Patty turned up the thermostat in the living
room. Until now it had been a comfortable day.
When she heard the clanking of the heat in the pipes,
she went back into the kitchen. "Maybe we should
give him a party tomorrow," she contemplated out
loud.

"Wonderful idea, Mom," Janet said enthusiastic-
ally.

"We'll have a cake. Buy some presents." Patty
looked at Frankie and her mother, who both nodded,
going along with her, but she could tell they were
forcing themselves. She knew they were wishing
Richard had never returned. She looked at Myles,
hoping he wouldn't notice. But she could see that he
had, for his face was now dark, his brows meeting in
a deep frown.

"I don't believe you people. You all should be ecstatic. For Christ's sake, a boy who has been missing—for what, seven, eight years?—is home again. You should be jumping up and down. You should be—"

"Myles, please," Patty interrupted softly, "you don't understand."

He looked at her incredulously. "You're right, I *don't* understand."

"*I'm* excited," Janet protested, affronted.

"Yes, you are," Myles admitted, "but the rest of you—"

"Myles, we'll talk about this later," Patty said. There was pain in her voice, and he caught it. He moved away from her, filled his glass with wine, and leaned against the refrigerator. While he drank he watched everybody from this slight distance.

Lydia was as white as the appliance behind Myles. Patty was also pale, looking as though she'd faint at any moment. Frankie seemed lost in thought, brooding as he toyed with his food. He looked uneasy, dread evident in his face. And Janet was like Myles, puzzled over everyone else's reaction.

"I'm going to have to call Lieutenant Wheeler," Patty verbally reminded herself. "And Doctor Siddons."

"What do you think is wrong with him?" Janet asked.

"I don't know, sweetheart. There's so much we don't know about him."

"Amen," Lydia said.

Patty glared at her, mutely warning her not to say much else.

Lydia struggled to push her ample body away from the table. "Something's wrong with the heat, Patricia? It's damn near freezing in here."

"It was all right until . . ." Patty's voice trailed off, unwilling to complete her thoughts.

"Until *he* came," Lydia finished for her. Then, on heavy unsteady legs, she wobbled toward the new recliner in the living room.

"He's like a stranger," Janet said to no one in particular.

"He always was," Lydia murmured in reply from the other room. And before anyone could respond, she was already engrossed in the fantasy world of television, the only place to find escape.

11

Detective Wheeler extended his hand, but Richard pretended not to have noticed. It was the following morning and the family, including Myles, was in the living room, all attention focused on the 13-year-old boy who was still clad in the same dirty clothes he had arrived in. Patty and Myles hadn't had any sleep the night before, spending most of the night talking and thinking about the boy. Patty had explained that Richard, as a child, had made most of the family uneasy with his violent temper. She told him that his father had been a one night fling at a weak moment, and Myles had been sympathetic and wonderful. She then told him that the father had been like an animal—but that was where she had drawn the line. She couldn't bring herself to say that the man had hideously transformed himself and then disappeared like a creature from a horror film.

"He's a boy who needs a lot of love," Myles had told her, when the apartment was silent and they were alone. He kissed her, made love to her, and for a beautiful moment she truly believed that love, indeed, could cure anything.

"In the mood to talk?" Detective Wheeler was now saying, taking a chair from the kitchen and pulling it close to Richard on the couch.

The boy said nothing, only sizing up the short,

162

mustachioed man for a long moment, then his eyes swept over the others in the room. He seemed to be weighing how much he should reveal. Finally he returned his gaze to the detective and gave him an indifferent shrug.

Wheeler cleared his throat, then leaned forward, elbows on his knees, hands clasped together in midair between his legs. He was like a father trying to descend to the level of his small child, and Richard seemed aware of this, for he abruptly sat back against the couch, his eyes glazing over as if determined to be distant.

"Do you remember your family here?" Wheeler said, ignoring the silent rebuff.

"I came back here, did I not?"

"Right. Stupid of me. Why did you come back, Richard? Did you escape?"

"No, I came back because I wanted to," the boy said flatly.

"Mind telling me where you've been the last eight years?"

"With my father."

Patty let out a stunned gasp, causing everyone in the room to glance at her. In the past she had prayed that it was not Sam who had taken the boy. Now she felt a chill. Was the temperature in the room dropping again?

"Who is your father?" Wheeler asked Richard, digging into a shirt pocket for a pad and pencil.

"He calls himself many names," the boy said.

Wheeler stared blankly at him.

"To mother he called himself Sam."

"Yes, that's the name on file," Wheeler nodded in remembrance. "But what's his last name, Richard?"

"I was never told. It did not matter."

"Then what last name did you use in school, Richard? You did go to school, didn't you?" When the boy didn't answer, he added, "You talk good for a kid your age."

"Well."

"What?"

"I talk *well* for a kid my age."

Wheeler blinked, then lifted a brow in faint amusement. "Yeah, right. Anyway, what name did you use when—"

"I never went to school."

This time Wheeler's brow arched in surprise, remaining this way for a long second before dropping and meeting the other brow in a wary frown. "Never?"

"My father taught me everything I needed to know."

"Is that right?" Wheeler couldn't seem to decide whether or not to believe him. "Like what kind of things?"

"Important things. Things that they don't teach you in any schools."

"Care to give me an example, Richard?"

The boy gave him a small, arrogant smile, a smile that was devoid of warmth. "I know that light and darkness are the two forces of the cosmos. I know that these forces compete with each other. I know that they should coexist in a harmonious balance, but they frequently do not. One often rules. And I know that it is the stronger half that—"

"Whoa." Wheeler held up a hand. "Sorry to interrupt, son, but you've lost me."

"I am not your son," Richard said coldly.

"Just trying to be friendly . . . Richard."

Richard stared at him with hard, glinting eyes.

The detective waited until the boy's countenance softened a little, then said, "Do you know how to read and write?"

"Father taught me."

"I see. Do you read and write good?"

"Well."

"Uh? Oh, yeah. Well." Wheeler gave a short, awkward laugh. "Guess you can read and write, then. Tell me, do you know where your father is right now?"

The boy didn't answer.

"Does your father know you're here now?"

Still he said nothing.

"Did you tell your father?"

No answer.

Wheeler glanced over at Patty in frustration, as though wishing she could somehow help him elicit more information from the boy. Richard followed his gaze and saw Myles pull his mother closer to him. This upset him, for something flashed in his eyes, something reddish. Then he looked away and fixed his attention on the detective.

He doesn't like Myles touching me, Patty thought. She contemplated moving away from her fiancé but didn't know how she'd explain the sudden withdrawal. Maybe she was just letting her imagination run away with her. After all, Richard seemed to be glaring at everybody; he had returned as a bitter, hostile boy.

"My father disappeared," the boy finally said.

"Disappeared how?" Wheeler asked.

"He has his ways."

"And you're not about to reveal them to me, right?"

Again silence was the reply.

Wheeler blew out a small gust of air, looked down at what he'd written so far, then asked, "Richard, do you remember the day you disappeared from the grocery market eight years ago?"

"I remember."

Wheeler waited expectantly for him to say more, but the boy instead looked over at his mother and Myles again. He stared openly until Patty uneasily moved a few inches away from her fiancé, so that her body was no longer touching his. Satisfied, Richard then turned back to the detective.

"I would like to hear whatever you're willing to say about that day," Wheeler said, encouragingly. "And if you don't want to talk about it, then that's all right too, Richard."

"Don't do that."

"Do what?"

"Talk down to me."

"I'm sorry, Richard. I wasn't aware—"

"But I will tell you anyway—because I want to," Richard interrupted, lifting his angular face in a smug, confident manner, as though declaring he had nothing to hide or be ashamed of. "Father was waiting for me in one of the aisles, and when I saw him I ran to him. There was no force. The minute I saw him I wanted to leave with him."

"You knew immediately it was your father?"

"Yes."

"You had seen him before this?" Wheeler asked. Patty had told him at the beginning of the case that this boy had never met nor seen his father.

"I'd seen him many times in my mind."

"Care to explain that?"

"It is not necessary for you to know." The boy airily dismissed the question. "I simply knew it was he, and I followed him out of the store. He took me to his place."

"And where was that?"

"I don't know."

"Did you leave in a car?"

"A bus."

"Oh." Wheeler sounded disappointed. Apparently he had been hoping a description of a car or possibly the number of a license plate would lead him to somewhere. "How long were you in this bus before you reached your father's home?"

"I don't know."

"Hours? More than a day?"

"I don't know."

"Would you say your father's home is very far away?"

"I slept on the bus. I think my father made certain of that."

"What do you mean?"

"He made me sleep whenever he wanted me to."

"Did he give you drugs of any kind?"

"No."

"Maybe he slipped things into your drinks or food," Wheeler surmised out loud.

"It is not necessary for you to know," Richard said for the second time, his tone flat yet determined.

Wheeler stared at him, then with resignation, continued in another direction. "Can you describe your father's home, Richard?"

"It was an apartment, but not like this one. There was no furniture in it. And it was dark in there most of the time."

"No windows?"

"There were boards over them."

"I see." Wheeler kept his voice emotionless as he quickly jotted the information down on his pad.

Had he been living in a condemned building? Patty wondered. My God, no wonder he looks so sickly. She looked up at Myles, who was a head taller than she, and found his face grim and filled with compassion for her son.

Suddenly Lydia began to pull herself up and out of her recliner. "Tired," she murmured, a lie that fooled no one. "Gonna go lie down for a spell."

"No," Richard said, his voice a quiet command.

Lydia looked quizzically at him. "What do you mean, no?"

Richard gave her a mirthless grin. "I want you to hear what I have to say," he said, then added with false endearment, "Grandma."

Lydia hesitated, then fell back into the recliner.
The boy's cold smirk widened. "Don't blame me if I
fall asleep here," she said under her breath. "I need
my sleep, y'know."

"Can you tell me more about this place?"
Wheeler asked, turning his attention back to the boy.

"It was full of bugs and rats," Richard said easily,
as though he were describing the carpeting and wall-
paper. "I remember I didn't like the smell of the
place and that it was cold, but I got used to it."

Wheeler's face was stony, but his eyes mirrored a
blend of sympathy and disbelief. "Anything else?"

"A rat bit my toe once when I was sleeping. I
thought it was just a bug at first. They don't bite, not
all of them, anyway. But rats, they know how to
bite."

"Did your father take you to a doctor or a hospital
for treatment?"

"No. I never told him about it."

"Why not?"

"He wouldn't care about something like that."

The detective fell silent for a brief moment, as
though waiting for a sudden wave of emotion to pass.
"How long ago was this?"

"I was six."

"How long did you stay at this place?"

"Long enough."

"What does that mean?"

"It is not necessary for you to know."

"Right. Uh, do you have any idea why your
father took you to this place?"

"I told you, I followed him."

"But why?"

"I don't know. Sometimes it is he whom I want,
and sometimes it is . . ." The boy glanced over at
Patty, a strange sadness and longing in his eyes. Then
he abruptly looked away, as if the sight of Myles so
close to her was too agonizing. He didn't finish the

sentence.

"Could you tell me something about the kind of life you and your father shared?" Wheeler asked.

"We did everything together. He taught me a good deal, so much more than any school could teach me."

"Do you know what your father did for a living?"

"He existed."

"I mean his job," Wheeler patiently clarified. "What kind of work did he do?"

"I knew what you meant. He did not need a job. There were enough rats and bugs to live on, and the cold did not bother us. There was no reason for a job."

"Are you saying . . ." Wheeler stopped to swallow. Another wave of emotion seemed to be sweeping through him.

"Tired, tired," Lydia suddenly and firmly blurted out. This time she succeeded in lifting herself up off the chair. Before Richard could demand that she sit back down, she was in her bedroom, closing the door on the sickening interrogation.

"You ate rats and bugs?" Wheeler asked.

"Yes."

Patty's hands bunched and unbunched the fabric of her blouse at her stomach. She was going to be sick. Myles pulled her closer to him, and she was tempted to tell him to leave her alone in front of Richard. Couldn't he see the boy did not want him near her? But she was too weak to say anything. Yes, she definitely was going to be sick.

"Your father made you eat those things?" The detective was now having difficulty maintaining a placid facade.

"He did not force me. He never forced me. He ate them and I saw how much he enjoyed it. So . . ." Richard shrugged mildly ". . . I did the same."

"Are you talking about one incident, or was this something done regularly?"

"Often."

It was a long moment before Wheeler could speak again. "What did you eat besides . . . those things?"

"Whatever was around. My father said he didn't need to eat, only did it because it was something he liked to do. He taught me that most of the fun was in the catching of food, not in the actual eating of it."

"I see." Wheeler's voice was deep and faint. "Since your father didn't work and you didn't go to school, what did the two of you do with all this free time?"

"I slept. The cold and dark and my father made me sleepy."

"What did you do when you were awake . . . besides eating?"

"Father taught me how to read, and he brought me books from the library and bookstores."

"What kind of books?"

"A lot of kinds. Father seemed most fond of biographies written about Hitler, and the works of the Marquis de Sade. We did some of the things he wrote about."

"The Marquis de Sade?" Wheeler's voice grew even fainter, barely audible. Patty, forgetting her son's obvious disapproval, pressed closer to Myles, as if in desperation to escape into the comforting warmth of his body. She couldn't believe what she was hearing. She had never read any of de Sade's work, but she knew enough about them, knew that the French writer had written about sexual perversions in the foulest and sickest way imaginable. She knew the word sadism derived from this man from the 18th century. What did Richard mean that he'd done some of the things that this writer had written about? Richard was only 13, only a child.

Patty didn't want to hear this, and most of all, didn't want Frankie and Janet to hear it, either.

"Maybe we should continue another time," she suggested.

The detective quickly understood her wish to stop the interrogation. "Very well," he said, leaning back, "we'll call it a day. Why don't we pick up again at the station, let's say tomorrow morning? That way we can talk in a private room and—"

"You mean in a room with a one-way mirror where policemen and doctors could observe me from the other side?"

Wheeler looked surprised. "No, I didn't mean that at all, Richard."

Richard's mouth curved in a lopsided, snarl-like grin betraying distrust. "I want to talk *now*," he said emphasizing the last word. "I may not wish to talk tomorrow."

Not knowing what to do, Wheeler looked questionably at Patty.

"Frankie, Janet," Patty said, "go find something to do."

"Aw, come on, Mom," Frankie protested. "We're not little kids anymore."

Janet remained silent. She seemed indecisive, curious to stay in the room, yet not certain if she wanted to hear anything more about her younger brother.

"Frankie, Janet, please," Patty said imploringly.

"How can we be close as a family if there are to be secrets between us?" Richard pointed out, going against Patty.

That settled it for Frankie, who promptly sat back against the couch, folding his arms across his chest like one waiting for a good movie to begin. It was an attitude that Patty found annoying and insensitive. Next to him Janet still seemed indecisive.

Richard's hard eyes glittered as he looked over at

Patty. He seemed strangely pleased that he had momentarily won over her. He smiled smugly, then turned to the detective, deliberately taking his time.

"Father has taught me so many pleasures," he said, finally continuing. "That's what he called them—pleasures. I was scared at first. I remember wanting to go back to my mother. I remember crying for her, but there was no one around to hear me. Only father and I lived in that place; I never heard or saw anyone else in the other apartments. Only me, Father, and the rats and bugs. And I remember my father laughing when I was crying. His laugh is different all the time. Sometimes it's deep, like a rumble you could feel under your feet, and sometimes it's high, like the wind. His laugh used to scare me, but I got used to it. But then, it's not his laugh you want to know about, is it?"

Only silence answered him. He could see he had everyone's rapt attention. He dropped his smile.

"It is the pleasures you want me to talk about," he said, his voice hardening. "I cried the first time, but as I said before, he only laughed. Then he told me there was nothing to be afraid of. He told me to stop fighting him. He told me that I would never enjoy him if I didn't stop being afraid and stop fighting him. Try it, he said. You will like it, he said. Try it. Try it. Do you know what he wanted me to do?" Richard asked, his eyes widening, shining like ice under light. There was resentment in those eyes, but Patty couldn't determine whether the bitterness she was seeing was directed at his father or at her.

After a lengthy pause, he fixed his gaze on Patty. When he had her eyes locked with his, he said in a slow, distinct voice, "He wanted me to suck his cock, Mother—and I did!"

Something invisible and sharp kicked Patty in the stomach. She winced. Then Janet let out a sob and ran out of the room. Richard watched her leave, as though in mild fascination. For a moment the cold hardness left his eyes and in their place was sadness. The door to the girl's room banged shut, and the ice promptly returned to the boy's eyes. He looked back at his mother. Yes, he definitely was blaming her for everything that had happened to him.

"Like his laugh," he said evenly, "I got used to it. He has quite a big cock, doesn't he, Mother?"

Patty's hand shot to her mouth. Her eyes squeezed shut. Oh my God, she moaned inwardly. It *is* all my fault. If only I hadn't brought that monster home from the bar. If only . . .

Tears seeped through her closed lids and coursed down her cheeks.

"Mother, answer me when I talk to you," he demanded without raising his quiet, cold voice.

Myles turned to the detective. "Why don't we finish this another time, eh?" he pleaded, embarrassed.

Wheeler blinked, as though in a daze, then nodded. "Uh, right. Look, Richard, we're going to call it quits for—"

"Did I shock you?" Richard mocked astonishment. "I thought nothing shocked your kind."

Wheeler ignored him, rising from the chair and slipping his pad and pen back into his pocket. His face was grim, his dark eyes smoldering. When he was out of the boy's hearing range and alone with Patty and Myles, he could no longer restrain the fury he felt. "We don't have much to go on," he said, "but we'll get that . . . that son of a bitch!"

Patty could have told him not to bother, that it'd be useless. You would literally have to go to Hell and back to find the boy's father, but she said nothing, for she was struggling to fight a fresh wave of tears. With Myles she walked Wheeler to the door, nodded appreciatively when he said he'd keep in touch, and nodded again when he urged her to take the boy to a psychoanalyst as well as a physician for a thorough examination.

"I'll get that son of a bitch," he vowed again, then was gone.

Patty closed the door, then buried her face in Myles' comforting chest. This seemed to be the only way she could escape for a moment, to smother the guilt that was mushrooming inside her. If only she could go back in time and start over. If only she hadn't gone to the Red Lantern that night. Richard would have never been born and would never have been subjected to . . .

"Oh God, Myles," she sobbed, pressing harder against him.

It was all her fault.

At length she pulled herself away from Myles and looked over at Richard, who was still sitting on the couch. Frankie had left, and the boy was alone, glaring. At first she thought his quiet contempt was focused on her, but she soon realized she was wrong. It was solely on Myles. And the look was unmistakable.

For reasons she could not understand, her son hated her fiancé.

12

Richard stood at his bedroom window and watched the slow onset of daylight. He watched the darkness of early morning gradually pale, turning from black to gray to white to cobalt. He watched the thin, shredded clouds brighten, the edges turning pink as the sun's first burst of rays appeared. And he watched Myles Forbes get into his car that was parked on the street below and drive off.

Richard's nostrils flared. He didn't like Myles, didn't like him from the first moment he'd seen him. He knew he had no reason for this strong feeling against the man who had done nothing harmful to him. He had even gone out of his way to be pleasant. But still Richard disliked him. Jealousy? He wasn't sure. The only thing he knew was that he cringed whenever Myles' grease-stained hands touched his mother. It was almost as though Myles had touched him as well.

Richard looked over his shoulder at his brother sleeping on the lower bunk. "Frankie," he called loudly.

His brother stirred but didn't awaken.

"Frankie, I'm talking to you." Richard's voice rose sharply.

Grunting, Frankie finally opened his eyes. "What'd ya want?" He scowled at him.

"What does Mother see in that turd?"

"Huh?"

"You heard me."

Frankie yawned. "Leave me 'lone." He turned over and tried to go back to sleep.

Richard moved close to the bed and looked down at him. His shadow shrouded the bottom bunk. "How long has Mother been with him?"

"Go 'way."

"Does she love him?"

No answer.

"Frankie, answer when I talk to you."

"I'm not a dog."

"You look like one."

"Beat it."

A corner of Richard's mouth twitched. Frankie didn't like him—it was as obvious as a full moon on a clear night—and Richard found this amusing. He wanted to laugh. He wasn't sure why. But then, there were so many strong emotions inside him that he didn't understand.

"Does . . . Mother . . . love . . . Myles?" he repeated slowly, as though speaking to someone with a hearing impairment.

Frankie groaned in resignation. He opened his eyes again and balefully looked up at his brother. "Why don't ya ask her, huh?"

"I'm asking you."

Frankie looked as though he wanted to spit at Richard, but something restrained him. Fear? Richard's mouth twitched again at the realization of this.

"I guess she loves him," Frankie finally admitted. "Now will ya leave me alone?"

"Where does he live?"

"Near his garage someplace."

"What garage?"

Frankie disgruntledly told him. It was called,

fittingly, Myles' Auto Repairs, and it was at the end of South Main, which was about six miles from here.

"What does she see in that piece of turd?" Richard asked again.

Frankie didn't bother to reply.

"Answer me, shitface."

"What did ya call me?" Frankie slid up to a sitting position, the bully in him overcoming the trepidation he had felt moments earlier.

"Shitface."

"You better watch your—"

"Shitface, shitface, shitface."

Frankie threw back the covers in a quick, confident manner. His face was dark as he made a threatening move to get up and advance on Richard. He was muscular from daily workouts and was undoubtedly the biggest kid in his class. Everybody was afraid of him—but not Richard. Richard wasn't afraid of anything.

Frankie stood inches away from his brother, lifted his hand for him to see clearly, then clenched it into a large, solid fist. "Take it back, squirt," he demanded.

"Shit . . . face!" Richard shouted, spittle spraying.

A frothy drop hit Frankie's cheek, near the eye, but he made no move to wipe it off. Instead, a look of uncertainty crossed his face. The bully in him, Richard saw, was shrinking back to hide somewhere deep inside.

Richard laughed, a quiet, low rumble like one of his father's many laughs. What was it that Frankie had seen to make him lose courage? Had he seen something in Richard's face that he didn't like? A feral glint in the eyes? Richard laughed again, this time in a strident giggle.

"Creep," Frankie muttered, backing away. "Just leave me alone." He turned, reached for his terry robe on the hook behind the door, and left the room.

"Shitface!" Richard shouted one last time after him. Then he broke into another peal of laughter.

He walked to Myles' garage. An overweight, middle-aged gas attendant asked him if he wanted anything, but Richard ignored him, walking into the concrete, gasoline-smelling structure until he found Myles in a chicken-wired enclosure, sitting at a big metal desk and frowning over the heap of paper-work in front of him.

Myles didn't see him right away, so Richard stepped closer until his shadow darkened the papers, manuals and catalogues that cluttered the desk. Myles looked up in annoyance, then in surprise.

"Well hi, Richard, what brings you here?" He smiled uncertainly.

Richard said nothing as he let his eyes roam about the small enclosure that was Myles' transparent office. On the wire partitions, greasy tools hung from hooks. A centerfold of a bosomy blonde salaciously looked back at him, her lips parted with a tip of tongue protruding. A Playboy calendar told him it was April. A rusty Coca-Cola thermometer told him it was 64 degrees. He watched the red mercury drop a degree, then turned his attention to Myles who had been waiting, a tentative smile still on his lips.

"How long have you been seeing my mother?" he asked.

The question surprised Myles, for one dark brow lifted in a perfect arch. "You don't beat around the bush, do you?"

"I do not see any reason why I should."

Myles nodded, as though saying, "Can't argue with you there." He reached for his pack of Pall Malls on the desk. As he lit a cigarette his eyes never left Richard. "Why do you want to know?" His voice was light, yet guarded.

"Because she's my mother."

Myles nodded again. In agreement? Understanding? Richard found himself getting annoyed. Like that Detective Wheeler, Myles was looking down at him, going along with him because he thought he was just a dumb kid. But Richard was not a dumb kid; he was a hell of a lot smarter than most of these assholes who were more than twice his age.

"You plan on marrying her?" he asked Myles outright.

Myles blew smoke into the already smoky room. "I love your mother, if that's what you're asking."

"What I am asking is if you plan on marrying her?" How plain can a question be? Richard thought. Yes, like Wheeler, this was another asshole.

"I really don't think it's any of your concern, Richard." The tone was calm, even friendly, yet firm.

But Richard didn't care how firm it was. "She is my mother, and it is my concern," he replied, equally calm, friendly and firm.

Myles stared at him for a long moment. Richard could almost hear the mechanic's thoughts. Be careful, the man seemed to be thinking. We do not have your usual problem brat here. This kid has been missing for eight years, eating rats and bugs and sucking cocks. No siree, it's a delicate situation. Tread carefully, or something might snap, or worse, explode.

"How do you like my garage?" Myles' smiled widened. It even managed to reach and warm his eyes.

Richard glared at him in response.

"Do you like cars, Richard?"

Damn him! Damn them all! Who did they think they were to feel superior to him, to be so condescending? "I hate cars," he spat. "All I like here is the smell of gasoline. And do you know why? Because it tells me that this place could turn into a fireball. Just like—" he snapped his fingers "—this!"

"What are you insinuating?" The voice was no longer calm and friendly.

"I do not insinuate. I, as you've already noticed, do not beat around the bush."

Careful, careful, Myles seemed to be thinking again. He took a long, pensive drag of his cigarette. "If you try to blow this place up, you'll be the first suspect. Now, I'm sure you know that already, Richard."

"Let them suspect me. If I want to turn your garage into a fireball, I will. You can lock me up, but it will be after I have the satisfaction of knowing that this place is gone."

"Why are you doing this?"

"Doing what?" Richard grinned, affecting ignorance.

"Threatening me."

Richard shrugged. "Maybe because you do not agree that your business with my mother is also my business."

"Look, I love your mother very much and, yes, I do plan to marry her someday. But right now I've a lot of financial problems. The garage is not fully established yet. The bank owns more of it than I do. But when I get on my feet—"

"Are you fucking her?"

"What did you say?" The mechanic leaned forward, his voice a harsh whisper, betraying a mixture of incredulity and controlled anger.

Richard didn't repeat it; he didn't have to.

"Get out of here," Myles hissed.

The boy didn't even flinch, but moved closer to the desk. "Stay away from my mother."

"I said get out of here."

"Not until you promise."

"Promise, hell! Look, kid, if you don't leave now I'm going to get nasty. And you're not going to like me when I'm nasty."

"I do not like you now."

A nerve in Myles' jaw jumped, as though the wrath in him were trying to pound its way out. He was silent for a long moment, struggling to keep his composure. Then, pointing a threatening finger, he warned, "Don't make me use force on you, kid."

"Stay away from my mother. Stop fucking her."

The nerve throbbed violently. Myles' face turned the color of an ugly sunburn. The warning finger joined his other fingers and the hand curled into a fist.

Quick with the fist, Richard reflected as he glanced at it, one end of his mouth twitching with amusement. Myles, he could see, had violent instincts, but Richard wasn't afraid.

Myles, as though suddenly aware that he, a full-grown man, was threatening an undernourished and possibly mentally unbalanced 13-year-old, un-clenched his fist. "Just please go away," he said as quietly as he could.

"That is precisely what I am asking you to do."

Myles took a long drag of his cigarette, then as he let out the smoke his eyes darted around the wired enclosure. He seemed frustrated, contemplating what to do. Physical violence was out of the question, and the boy didn't seem to know the meaning of "get out."

"And if I don't do as you ask?" he said.

Richard smiled. "I'll do something I'd very much enjoy."

"Goddamn you!" he exploded. "Get out!"

A mechanic, whose head had been under the hood of a Pinto, curiously looked over at the office.

Richard laughed, and this time obeyed.

Richard watched from a corner of his mother's bedroom in the dark. Pale moonlight feebly illu-

minated the sleeping form on the bed. It breathed
slowly and rhythmically in deep slumber. It was a
peaceful night, and it affected him close to the point
of tears.

There seemed to be no sense of moderation with
him. Everything seemed to be one extreme or the
other. There were no grays—only black and white,
ice and fire, violence and peace, love and hate.

Nothing in between.

And right now he was overwhelmed with the
love he had for his mother. Like the hate he felt
toward so many others around him, the feeling was
uncontrollable. He couldn't hide in the corner for
very long; he had to move closer to the bed, closer to
his mother.

Half of her face was visible in the ghostly light.
The tension that was usually evident in the visage
was gone. Eyes were closed, the mouth soft and
relaxed, and the skin was smooth and pale, free of
cosmetics. Like a virgin from a Victorian period, he
thought. She appeared so serene, so beautiful.

With a gentle finger, he touched her lips. She
jerked away in her sleep, as if he had given her an
electric shock. He let a minute pass, then touched her
again. This time she stirred but didn't pull away.
Richard smiled. Her lips were soft. He liked soft
things. And hard things. And cold things.

He traced the outline of her lips with a finger.
There was a strong temptation to kiss those lips, but
he was afraid she'd wake up. He knew she wouldn't
understand. She'd think the kiss was something
sexual, so he forced himself to be content with his
fingers.

After he completed the outline of her mouth he
moved on to her cheek and explored the softness of
her skin. Yes, it felt exactly as it looked—warm and
smooth. Then she shuddered and pulled the blanket
closer to her face. Richard quickly withdrew his

finger.

Did his touch repulse her, even in her deep sleep? Didn't his mother have any love for him at all? Oh, he knew she sometimes tried very hard to be nice to him, but he also knew it was something that did not come to her naturally. She just did not love him the way she loved her other children and the way she loved Myles.

But why? He loved his mother more than anything, for she was half of him. Why couldn't she love him back?

He caressed her hair, smoothing it. Like her skin it was soft to the touch. He leaned forward until he caught the fragrance of apple shampoo. He buried his face in her hair to absorb more of the clean, fruity smell.

Cleanliness and filth. Light and darkness. Good and evil.

Gently, he pulled the covers back and climbed in bed with her. He waited until all movements caused by his sudden weight on the mattress ceased, then he slid closer until his body was touching hers. Her warmth was wonderful, and he couldn't seem to get enough of her.

She shivered for the second time.

He withdrew for the second time.

Then he went back to caressing her hair, tracing her features with a finger. So beautiful, he thought over and over. His mother was so, so beautiful. If only he could kiss her. If only she would love him back.

She made a grunting sound, and at first he thought she would turn her back to him. But instead, her eyes opened and saw him in the platinum patch of moonlight. There was a moment of vacuous staring, then confusion. Her forehead wrinkled, as though she were wondering if she were dreaming.

Richard smiled warmly, hoping this would keep

her subdued. It was like being close to a bird; one
abrupt movement and it would flutter away.

"What . . . what are you doing here?" she asked
in a small voice.

"Admiring you," he replied softly.

"Admire . . . what?"

Richard, saying nothing, gently stroked her hair.
She quickly pulled her head back, alarm now mixed
with confusion on her face. "How long have you
been here?" she demanded.

Richard still didn't answer, too preoccupied with
studying every feature on her face—so delicate, so
unlike his father.

Then to his disappointment, she began to move
away from him. Soon she was off the bed, reaching
for a robe, although she was already decently
covered in a long, flannel shirt. "Richard . . . why?"
was all she could utter.

"Mother, you're upset. I didn't mean to make
you—"

"Of course I'm upset." She snapped on the overhead light, then squinted at the harsh brightness,
covering her eyes with a hand to shield some of the
glare. "This is my room. You have no business here."

Richard was tempted to remind her that he knew
Myles had been here and shared the bed with her,
but he could see that she was upset enough already.
In fact, she was trembling now, as though
frightened. Was he scaring her? That was the last
thing he wanted. He wanted her to be at ease with
him.

"Mother, please, don't be afraid," he pleaded.

But the trembling grew worse. "What do you
want?" she asked, as if he were a killer who had
cornered her, as if it would be money he was after
and not her life.

"I just wanted to look at you, to touch you.
Nothing else."

She gawked at him, as if he had said something obscene.

"Mother, please come back to bed."

She took another step backward, clutching the folds of her robe tighter around her. "I . . . I'm your mother, Richard. Mothers don't . . . don't . . ." She couldn't finish.

Don't what? he wondered. "I just wanted to feel how soft you are. You're so beautiful. I just wish I could hold you."

"Richard, stop!" Patty squeezed her eyes shut, apparently wanting to wipe out everything in front of her. The trembling grew worse, now shaking even her voice. "I-I'm your m-mother," she said again, as though this should explain everything.

"You don't understand." Richard could now tell she thought it was sex he was seeking, but she was wrong. "I just want you to love me," he said.

"Richard, please leave," she pleaded, her eyes still shut. When he didn't answer, she opened them. He was still in her bed without any sign of moving from it. "Didn't you hear me?"

Richard sighed dolefully. He had alarmed her, and there seemed to be no way of reversing this, of making her understand. "Why won't you love me back?" he asked desperately.

"I . . . I do love you."

She didn't sincerely mean this; he could tell. It was in her voice, in her eyes, even in the small way she lifted her chin. He said, "Then why won't you let me touch you?"

"Because I'm your *mother*!"

"Stop saying that."

"Because it's sick, Richard," she blurted. "It's . . . it's incest!"

"No." Richard firmly shook his head. "It is not sex I want. Please come back to bed. Let me be close to you. Let me touch you. Let me admire—" He stopped abruptly as he saw the repulsion in his mother's face. Oh, why didn't she understand? What could he say or do to make her realize that it was nothing sexual he wanted? He experienced a sinking feeling. It seemed so useless. Then he felt a rush of anger.

Fire and ice. Black and white. Good and evil.

The placid glow he had felt toward his mother was now rapidly turning to frigid ice. Hate surged through him. His father had been right about her, after all. She was nothing more than a common whore. She wasn't beautiful. She was an ugly cow, a smelly heap of shit.

He glared contemptuously at her, and she recoiled until her back was pressing against a bureau. "Please leave, Richard," she pleaded, almost sobbing with fright.

He hesitated, then finally complied. It was either this or do something he'd regret.

13

Frankie was awake when Richard came into the room, but he pretended he was asleep. Through slitted eyes he watched his brother move in and out of a patch of moonlight in the center of the room. Creep! he thought. Why did he have to come back? Why didn't he just stay where he was and continue sucking his pop's popsicle, the faggot?

Frankie knew he should be feeling sorry for his kid brother and sometimes he did, but most of the time he found himself not liking the kid. There were too many things about him that made his skin crawl. Jesus, the creep used to eat rats and bugs. How could anyone do that? Frankie doubted he'd ever do that, no matter how hungry he was. And what's more, the creep had weird eyes. Before Richard had disappeared his eyes were spooky, the way he kept staring and staring. But now, they could scare the shit out of you. They were a funny pale color, sorta light gray, just a shade darker than the whites of the eye. And sometimes, especially when he was mad, which seemed to be practically all the time, the color would change. Sometimes it would be reddish, sometimes yellowish. And another thing, Richard's skin was a wimpy color. Was he afraid of the sun or something? He was too white, and the dark patches under the eyes made his face look even whiter.

Yeah, he was a creep all right.

So why should he have to share a room with him?

Shouldn't judge somebody by his looks, he reminded himself. There were a lot of funny looking kids who weren't so bad once you got to know them, but this was different. Richard wasn't funny looking or ugly; he was creepy looking, like something in a horror movie. And besides, he wasn't the only one that wasn't glad the kid had come back home. He wasn't stupid; he could tell that Grandma was disappointed. And Mom wasn't thrilled either. It was obvious by the way she was always nervous whenever Richard was around her. Only Janet seemed happy, but then she was stupid like that. She was too soft, too goofy. He could remember a time when a dumb hamster had disappeared for a week. When it came back she'd cried for two days because she was so happy.

Why didn't Mom and Grandma like Richard? Was it because they didn't like his looks? No, that couldn't be it. There had to be something else. Maybe it was because of his temper. He could remember, as if it had happened yesterday instead of eight years ago, when Richard had him down on the floor, biting at his shoulder. It had felt as if he had a wild wolf on top of him. Maybe it was because of that incident that Frankie could find no compassion for his brother. The kid was an animal. It was as simple as that. And also, he didn't like the fact that a young, smaller kid could best him in a fight. Nobody else his age, let alone younger, could do that.

Now Richard was pacing back and forth, in and out of the spectral light. He was furious, for it was evident in the rapidity and restlessness of his gait. Once he shot a look at Frankie, and Frankie closed the narrow slits he had been peeking through. Had the creep seen him? Did he know he was being watched? Frankie lay as still as possible, waiting for a few minutes to pass, then he dared another peek, opening his eyes to a thin squint.

Richard was now at the window, looking out into the night. White moonbeams speared him, making him look somewhat like a stage performer in a spotlight. He stood very still and Frankie found himself thinking that Richard was actually absorbing the moonlight, feeding on it, like a plant assimilating nourishment from the sun. Why wasn't he moving? Until a minute ago he was pacing like a caged animal. What was he doing? Was he really drinking in the moonlight?

Jesus, maybe he was a werewolf or something. Maybe he was going to change. Anything was possible with Richard; he certainly was creepy enough.

Frankie suddenly felt very cold. He slid deeper under the covers until only the top half of his head was exposed. Richard then pivoted, shooting another glance at him, and this time there was a wide, mirthless grin on his face.

Frankie instinctively closed his eyes. He knows, he thought, he knows I'm watching him. There was a low laugh, then silence and stillness. Frankie's heart thundered in his chest, and he willed it to be still. There's nothing to be excited about, he told himself. Big deal if the creep knows I'm watching. Big fucking deal!

Convinced that he had no reason to be ashamed or afraid, Frankie reopened his eyes. This time it was no more than a hairline slit. He half-expected to see Richard glaring back at him, but the boy was back to staring out the window, basking in the eerie, ghostly moonlight.

Once more there was a stillness and silence that was disquieting. Only Frankie's heart seemed to move, make noise. Frankie dimly wondered if his brother could hear the hammering heart, for it seemed incredibly loud and vibrant in the strange hush. He tried to calm it, will it into silence and placidity, but only succeeded in making it race more furiously. He half-expected his brother to suddenly turn around in annoyance, but he didn't. He seemed to be in a deep trance. Had to be.

For a long time nothing moved, then something stirred. Or was this only Frankie's eyes, suddenly weary from the strain of peering through fractional slits? Frankie closed his eyes to rest them, then opened them again. Everything was as before, immobile like a picture. Yes, he decided, it had been his eyes playing tricks, after all.

Then he saw something stir again. It was slight and quick, causing him to doubt if he had seen any movement at all. Maybe it was a rat, he thought. Maybe his brother was some kind of a weird Pied Piper attracting rodents, attracting them so he could eat them.

Jesus! Frankie would have to stop thinking like this; he was scaring himself with his own vivid imagination. Nothing moved, he told himself—tired eyes, active imagination, that's all.

There, he saw something move again!

It wasn't his imagination or eyes. He *did* see something. It wasn't moving now, but it was something on the floor behind his brother. He was certain of it. Something had crawled, writhing in a single wavy motion, then stopped.

But what?

All Frankie could see on the floor was a small braided rug, clothes he had flung in a heap, and Richard's . . . shadow?

It moved again, smoothly and slightly, like something undulating under water.

Frankie rubbed his eyes with the heel of his hand and looked again at the black form on the floor. It

seemed blacker than anything he'd ever seen—
blacker than black. Maybe it was the contrast of the
silver-white moon that made it so dark.

It stopped, then moved again.

What the hell was this? Maybe he was dreaming.
Yeah, that was it.

No, it wasn't. He was awake, and his eyes were
really seeing a wavering shadow.

He looked up at his brother, hoping to catch him
moving also. But Richard was still motionless at the
window, his back to him. Only his shadow moved.

Peter Pan, Frankie thought crazily. His brother
was Peter Pan, the boy who had lost his shadow.

But Peter Pan was a character from a fairy tale.
This thing before him was real.

The shadow grew long, like the kind you see late
in the afternoon, and as it grew, like a crawling
liquid, it became thinner. The extremities thinned
like stretched worms, and they squirmed like
worms, too.

Maybe that's what they were—worms or eels or
snakes or . . .

Frankie squeezed his eyes shut for the
umpteenth time. Start over, he seemed to be commanding his mind. When you open your eyes again,
you will see nothing weird, only an ordinary
shadow. Got that? All right, one . . . two . . .
three . . .

The shadow was still there, but it no longer
resembled a human form. There were more than
four elongated appendages now; there were about a
dozen, all wavering, writhing like tree branches in a
wind storm.

Frankie stared, mesmerized. This *is* a dream, he
decided positively, and he would wake up later.

The appendages continued to expand, thinner
and longer like black spaghetti. The shadow spread
across the room, reaching the walls and his bed.

Dream. Dream. Dream.

"Dream," he finally said out loud, not caring if his brother heard him. In fact, he was hoping Richard would hear. Maybe it would jolt the creep out of his trance and stop the shadow from approaching. "Dream," he said again, louder. Maybe his own voice would wake him up. But nothing changed.

The appendages kept creeping toward him. Were they something solid, like snakes? Would they coil themselves around him, squeeze the shit and life out of him? Not wanting to find out, Frankie backed his way across the bed until he felt the hard wall behind him.

The extremities slid up the walls, up the bureau in the corner, and up the bed. They followed the contours of the furniture like thick lava, up the wooden legs and onto the top of the mattress, then flowing across it toward Frankie, who was crouching against the wall.

He looked desperately at Richard, who was still basking in the moonlight. "Rich," he cried. It didn't matter how cowardly he sounded. It was only a dream anyway, wasn't it?

His brother didn't turn around. The shadow was only inches away.

"Rich!" This time he screamed the name.

And this time Richard did turn around. His head and body moved fluidly, as though he were on a slowly revolving turntable. Frankie stared, transfixed, waiting for the complete turn, for the face to reveal itself. And when it finally did, Frankie felt a scream rise and freeze in his throat.

A face without skin was staring back at him.

It grinned coldly at him, the white glow from the moon making it appear bluish.

Frankie scrambled along the wall, not daring to cross the bed where the shadow still writhed. He climbed over the footboard, then dashed toward the door, all the while keeping his eyes fixed on the gleaming skull. He saw in numb horror that the eye sockets were empty—deep black sockets—and somewhere inside something glinted, something red.

Frankie yanked the door open—a dream a dream a dream—but it was a dream he would finish in the living room on the couch.

He kicked the door shut, feeling some relief and a sense of security in having something solid between him and his brother and the shadow. Then, in the dark, he groped his way toward the couch, no moonbeams lighting his way. Soon he found the sofa, as well as the folded afghan at one end of it. He lay down, covered himself, and tried to fall asleep—or wake up, since he was dreaming.

But instead of closing his eyes, he found himself staring into the darkness. When he had come into this room he couldn't see anything, but now shapes of the furniture and objects around him were beginning to appear out of the gloom, like things emerging from a thick, black fog. The stillness and silence, save for his thundering heart, were back. The sense of security he had felt a moment earlier was gone, especially since he now could see the outline of his bedroom door. He had a lousy, gut feeling that it would soon open.

And he was right.

Richard lingered in the doorway, then stepped into the living room, his form a shade darker than his surroundings. He moved as though he could see clearly in the dark and didn't pause until he was standing above Frankie.

Won't this dream ever end?

Frankie, curled up in a fetal ball to keep most of his body under the small afghan, said nothing, didn't even move, and Richard did the same. For a long moment, which seemed like an eternity, the boys

were stationary, like trees in stagnant air. Then
Frankie heard Richard laugh.

Bastard! Faggot!

"Why are you frightened?" Richard asked, after
the laughter had subsided.

Frankie feigned sleep.

Laughter again, but different this time. It was
deeper, a man's laugh, not a boy's. When this, too,
subsided, Richard said, "You cannot fool me, Frankie.
No one can fool me anymore. So don't try."

Frankie hesitantly opened his eyes. Stop being a
coward! he mentally commanded, but still couldn't
bring himself to speak.

"Did I scare you?" his brother asked mockingly.
Even in the darkness his teeth could be seen, faint
and white. And there was that reddish light again,
where the eyes should be.

Frankie swallowed, although his mouth was dry.
"You don't scare me," he forced himself to say.

"Then why do you smell the way you do?"

"Huh?"

"You smell like the rats I've cornered. It's the
same smell, Frankie."

"Beat it, will ya."

"It's called the smell of fear, Frankie. And right
now you stink with it."

Go away, go away, go away!

"What did I do that almost scared the shit out of
you?" Richard demanded.

"You didn't scare me, jerk," Frankie insisted.

"You're not very smart. You know that, don't
you, Frankie?"

No answer.

"You remind me of a dumb animal," Richard
said, after a long pause. "You'd keep howling,
hissing, squeaking right up to the end. Instead of
trying to think of a way to get out of a bad situation,
you'd just keep shooting your mouth off. Yes, you

really are a dumb animal, Frankie."

"Look, if you don't leave me alone, I'm gonna knock your frigging . . ."

Light flooded the room, startling him into silence. He squinted, not sure what had caused the standing lamp beside the couch to go on. Then he saw Richard's hand letting go of the pull chain. Richard, whose skin and eyes were back, laughed stridently and brusquely the moment he saw his brother's stunned, fearful expression.

Then Frankie saw the shadow on the wall behind his brother. It was bigger than Richard, reaching the ceiling—too big, too black.

A dream.

Outside, a gust of wind hit a window, gently rattling it, then was gone.

"Your smell is getting stronger," Richard told him, keeping his grin. His eyes were shiny and cold, like balls of ice.

"Why don'tcha just go away?"

"Tsk, tsk. Everybody's been telling me that lately. Why is that, Frankie? Haven't I been away long enough?"

But Frankie's attention was too riveted on the shadow for him to answer. His mouth fell open as he gawked at the shadow changing shape. The long arms stretched, then twisted themselves into something like a pair of licorice sticks. Then they straightened and shrank into the thick torso, which ballooned, then deflated, as though voluminous air were being pumped into it, then abruptly released. Then the torso thinned until it was no thicker than the extremities.

"You didn't like me before, so why should you like me now, right?" he heard his brother say, amusement rather than resentment evident in his voice.

"You're . . . different," Frankie replied, barely

able to utter the words. The shadow was charming him and, at the same time, scaring him. It seemed to be pulsing with a life of its own. And for one quick instant something round, like a head, appeared, and inside this head a mouth opened. It was a fiery red, irregular stain, which vanished as fast as it had appeared.

Frankie inched his way off the couch, gaining distance from his brother. "Go away." This time it was a plea.

"What is it that frightens you so much, big brother?"

Frankie, moving backwards, tripped over a magazine rack that was stuffed with K-Mart flyers and his mother's old true confession magazines. He almost fell on his rear, but awkwardly caught himself. He quickly stood taller, squaring his big shoulders to regain composure.

The shadow twisted and untwisted itself.

"Behind you," he finally blurted.

"You see something, Frankie?" his brother mocked.

"Your shadow, it's . . . it's . . ."

"It's what, Frankie?"

The boy swallowed, looked at his brother for a moment, then turned his wide-eyed gaze to the shadow. "This ain't real," he said, mostly to himself. "No way."

Richard gave him a crooked grin, then said, "Watch, Frankie."

There was a moment of silence as Frankie's eyes remained on the shadow, and Richard's on Frankie. The temperature in the room was markedly lower than it was a moment ago, yet Frankie's face was spotted with sweat.

The shadow continued to writhe and sway as its owner stood motionless. This time the inky shade seemed to move with purpose. It grew rapidly until it extended not only to the ceiling but halfway across it. The shape was once more of Richard, only many times magnified. Then something sprouted from the head. Horns? They curved, ramlike. The arms began to grow again, until they were longer than the body itself. At the end of the arms were hands with lengthy, clawlike fingers. Behind these arms something flapped. It took Frankie a moment to realize he was seeing wings—not feathery angelic wings, but something batlike. As these wings fluttered, hot wind seemed to fan his face.

But of course this was only in his mind, in his dream.

He saw the shadow tilt its head back and lift clenched fists to the heavens. Then he heard a guttural howl.

Shadows don't make noises, he told himself. He glanced over at Richard who still was watching him and smiling.

He heard another beastly outcry. It did not come from his brother. It was from the shadow.

And the shadow, he recognized for the first time, was in the shape of . . . a devil.

"Aw, Christ," he moaned, once more backing away from Richard. "This ain't fuckin' real. Can't be."

A dream.

But when he felt warm urine run down his leg he knew, with chilling certainty, that he was awake.

14

The morning did not bring sunshine as Patty had hoped. Since she had pleaded with Richard to leave her bedroom she had stayed awake waiting for daybreak. She desperately needed something bright and warm to help melt the cold knot in her stomach. *Incest*, a voice kept shouting in her mind, as though it were the ugliest and filthiest word in existence.

Incest. Incest. Incest.

Nothing happened, she reminded herself, but maybe next time something *will* happen!

No. She would always have control.

Nobody has control over Richard now, idiot.

With trembling hands she made herself a cup of coffee, then sat down at the table and tried to drink the coffee leisurely. But her mind was a whirlwind.

What to do?

Incest. Incest. Incest.

Nobody has control over . . .

The coffee spilled over and splashed onto her shaking hand. With a muffled sob she lowered the cup onto the table and buried her face in her hands. Please God, help me, she silently prayed. How should I handle this? Should I send him away to some special place? Should I give him another chance?

He desperately needed help. Hadn't Lieutenant Wheeler already urged her to send the boy to a psychoanalyst as well as a physician? She would make an appointment right away. But in the meantime were she and her family in any danger?

Don't be silly, part of her scoffed. The boy did not use force of any kind. You're overreacting, Patty Thompson. Richard is not a psychotic killer or anything like that. He's a confused and lonely boy, that's all. What she had seen last night was someone starved for love and affection. Period.

Yes, she was overreacting. Her son had had a terrible and damaging childhood. Imagine living with that horrible father of his and the things that monster had made him do. The thought of it alone brought tears to her eyes. The poor boy had been raised like an animal. It would have been no different if a wolf had adopted him into the pack.

Compassion and a lot of attention were what the boy needed right now. The last thing in the world she should do was send him away. She had behaved poorly last night.

Well, it would be different from now on. She'd no longer cringe at the sight of him, and next time she'd not mistake his need for affection as something sexual. These were vows she was determined to keep, but when Richard entered the kitchen a few minutes later, the cold knot in her stomach grew colder and tighter.

Merely the sight of her son made her uneasy.

"Hello, Mother," he said in a flat, bitter voice.

Patty managed a smile and a nod, afraid that if she spoke her voice would be as shaky as her hands. She suddenly wished the other members of the family were up and in the room with her.

Compassion, she reminded herself, then got up to make breakfast for the boy. She would pretend nothing had happened last night.

"Eggs and toast?" she asked, opening the refrigerator.

The boy shook his head, declining.

"Cereal, then?"

"Nothing."

"You need to eat something . . ." Her mouth formed to add "sweetheart" but the word wouldn't come out. "You look like you could gain a few pounds, you know." She closed the refrigerator.

Richard said nothing. His face betrayed no emotions, but there was a hint of turbulence in his eyes. Patty was reminded of distant, summer storms, the ones you could see brewing and gaining momentum in the far horizon and flashing vague heat lightning. Not directly threatening, but not exactly calm either.

He sat at the table and watched her. She needlessly wiped her hands on a towel by the sink and smiled again at him. He did not return the smile but only stared and stared. Just like before, she thought. When he was five he used to stare openly and silently at her and everyone else in the family. Only this time it seemed much worse. The eyes weren't filled with curiosity or confusion; now they were stormy. Resentment? Contempt? Hate?

God, she wished someone else would come into the kitchen now. She sat down at the table where her cup of coffee was cooling, not knowing what else to do. He still watched her in silence. Was he doing this deliberately? Was he making her uncomfortable just to amuse himself?

To her relief, Janet came into the room, yawning. "G'morning, Mom. Rich." She smiled sunnily. Richard brightened momentarily, then the dark visage returned. Janet had sparked something in him. For an instant there the sun had poked through.

A few minutes later Lydia entered, glancing only once at Richard. She gave him a stiff "Good morning," then asked Patty if she'd make her some tea and toast. "Stomach's too queasy for much else," she murmured as she sat at the table, chair slightly but obviously angled away from Richard. "I think I'm coming down with the flu or something."

Patty, filling the aluminum teakettle with water from the faucet, said nothing. Silence thickened in the air like pudding. Lydia cleared her throat, then lit a cigarette. She inhaled deeply, exhaled, and cleared her throat again. Janet began humming softly, as though endeavoring to cut through the silence, but it only seemed to emphasize it, if anything.

This is not a family anymore, Patty found herself thinking as she placed the kettle on the stove. Everyone is uncomfortable. It wasn't like this at all when Myles had tried to include himself into the family. Sure, there had been some awkward silences and moments, but never quite like this. This was not the result of shyness over someone new joining—or rather, rejoining—the family. This was something altogether different. Everyone, except maybe Janet, seemed to be on guard.

Yes, that's what it was, she decided—wariness, not awkwardness. She and Lydia did not trust Richard. They were afraid of him. But this, of course, would have to stop.

She waited for the kettle to let out a strident whistle, then dropped a tea bag into her mother's cup and poured the steaming water into it. She then went on to make toast. When that was ready and buttered, her mother muttered a mechanical "Thank you" and carried the small breakfast into the living room to eat as she watched TV.

Patty felt a twinge of resentment. Why couldn't her mother at least try to be nice to Richard? Why did she always have to "escape" like this?

Richard, as usual, was watching her. Patty gave him a fresh smile, hoping it would mask her feelings. "Have any plans today?" she asked.

His head shook, almost imperceptibly.

"Would you mind seeing Lieutenant Wheeler again? I'm sure he has more questions he'd like to ask you."

Richard shrugged indifferently.

The thick silence came back. Janet switched on the radio over the refrigerator, turning the dial in search of a station she liked. She took her time, for it was something to do. Tinny songs and voices waxed and waned repeatedly until she finally found some rock music that was free of static.

Then she sat down near Richard and continued eating the cereal she had started. Now, with the radio going, Janet seemed more at ease. Patty wished it were that easy for her.

Frankie entered the room, then stopped short at the sight of Richard. He appeared indecisive as to whether to continue forward or quietly recede. His eyes darted uneasily about the kitchen, pausing briefly on Patty, then on his sister, but carefully avoiding contact with his brother.

"Good morning, Frankie," Patty said, adding a lilt to her voice to encourage him into entering further.

But Frankie, she saw with disappointment, had changed his mind and was starting to retreat. His face was unusually pale, almost as pale as Richard's, and his eyes were shifting restlessly, something she'd never seen in him before.

"Can I talk to you later, Mom?" he said, and before she could answer he was gone.

Frowning, Patty glanced at her daughter, wondering what she thought of Frankie's skittish behavior. Janet promptly betrayed intense disapproval. It's unfair, she seemed to be saying. Nobody was giving Richard a chance. Well, she wasn't going to be like the rest of them.

"Want to go see a movie with me, Rich? After I

get out of school?"

The unexpected invitation surprised him. "Movie?"

"Sure. Or maybe we can go to the mall and get you some new clothes. You're gonna need some for when you go back to school, you know."

Richard thought about this, then slowly shook his head. There was regret in his voice as he said, "I am not going to school."

"Of course you are. It's the law. Right, Mom?" she asked, turning to Patty.

It took a moment for Patty to answer. She had been holding her breath, somehow expecting Richard to lose his temper over his sister's insistence that he go to school, but to her surprise Richard seemed moved instead of rankled. He was smiling now, a smile that was soft and actually warm. His sister's concern had obviously touched him.

"Yes, it is the law," Patty finally said, "but the situation is different here, Janet. We're going to have to look into this and find out what to do."

"It's too late," Richard said, his tone flat but confident.

"Well, you still need new clothes," Janet said, refusing to give up. "And I bet you'll be simply gorgeous."

Richard laughed, a mirthful, infectious laugh. She had flattered him and he was enjoying it. Even Patty found herself smiling at the sudden, warm change in him. "I don't know," he was saying modestly.

"Well, *I* do," Janet insisted. "With a little weight and nice clothes, you could look like Rob Lowe."

"Who?"

"Lowe. He's the sexiest and most gorgeous movie star ever."

"And you think I could look like him?" he asked skeptically.

"That's right. You kinda have his hair coloring. And your eyes are light and . . ."

Patty ceased to listen as she caught a glimpse of movement in the living room. It was Frankie, urgently signaling her to come to him. "I'll be back," she said to her other children in the kitchen, then left to see what Frankie wanted.

"Mom, I'm not going to share the same room anymore with that . . . that thing in the kitchen," he hissed, so only she could hear him.

"Why? What happened?" She'd never seen her son like this. He looked like a drug addict in desperate need of a fix. He seemed to be losing all control, one second on the verge of weeping, then in the next twitching with terror in his eyes. "Frankie, are you on something?" she demanded.

"No," Frankie replied furiously. "It's him. Him!" He stabbed a finger in the direction of the kitchen.

"Calm down, for God's sake." She grabbed his hands and firmly pressed them together to still them, to steady him. "Now what are you talking about?"

Frankie took in a deep breath. This relaxed him a little, but still his eyes were wide and fearful, wildly darting back and forth from her to the kitchen. "I'll take the back porch. It's big enough to make into a bedroom for me."

The porch he was referring to was four-by-six in size and boarded up to conserve heat in the winter. No one ever sat out in it, and over the years junk had accumulated, turning it more into a storage area than a porch.

"Only a bed would fit in there," she told him. "Frankie, I don't understand. You already have a nice room. What did Richard do?"

"He . . ." The boy shook his head in frustration. He didn't want to explain. Couldn't explain. "I'm not going to be in the same room with him anymore." He was almost shouting.

Patty shushed him with a finger over her lips. "Was it something he said? Something he did?"

"He . . . he . . . Just keep him away from me!"

"Frankie, he's your brother," she reminded him.

"I don't care."

The outburst, although a whisper, was loud and vehement. From the recliner Lydia looked over at them. When she saw they would not include her in the conversation, she turned her attention to the TV screen. Lucille Ball was bawling about a plan that had gone awry.

"You have to give Richard more of a chance," Patty gently urged her son. "I know he's . . . well, strange, but you have to remember he's part of this family. He's still your brother. He's my son."

"No, Mom. You don't understand."

"You're right," Patty admitted. "I don't. So why don't you tell me exactly why you don't want him in the same room with you?"

This time he made an effort to explain, but it seemed like trying to swallow something too repugnant that he had put in his mouth, something that would make his stomach heave. "Last night he . . . he . . ." Frankie paused and tried again. "Maybe it was a dream, but he . . ."

"I'll take the porch," a voice said quietly.

Heads swung toward the doorway to the kitchen. Richard was watching them. Patty felt a rush of shame. How long had he been there? Her mind quickly tried to recall everything that had been said between her and Frankie. Was there anything irrevocably damaging?

"You don't have to take the porch," she said, after the shock of surprise faded.

"I don't need a big room, Mother. I don't have very many things anyways."

"G-Good!" Frankie's voice cracked stridently,

something that hadn't happened since he first reached puberty. "It's settled."

"No, it isn't," Patty objected, but Frankie had already turned and was hurrying out of the room. Like a frightened animal, she reflected, so uncharacteristic of him. The boy was usually cocky, strutting out of a room, not skittering. What had happened? What had Richard done to him?

Puzzled, she turned to question her other son, but he was gone. He had slipped back into the kitchen to enjoy (by the sound of his laughter) his sister's company.

"He desperately needs help," Myles told her later that evening. They were at his apartment, for she needed time away from Richard, to see things more clearly at a distance. Sitting on the sofa while Willie Nelson twanged softly on the stereo, Patty rested her head against Myles' solid neck. They had just finished making love, but it hadn't been as good as usual. Richard had been on Patty's mind while her body responded, somewhat perfunctorily, to Myles' touch.

"He doesn't want us seeing each other, sweetheart." Myles kissed the top of her head, as though to confirm that this was something that would never happen. "Your son doesn't like me. No, that's putting it too mildly—he hates me." He then told her about the threat Richard had made. "He insinuated that he'd blow up my garage if I didn't stay away from you. Was he like this before?"

Patty wearily shook her head against him. "He had a terrible temper, but he wasn't this . . . this . . ."

"Bold?" Myles supplied.

Patty said nothing, but "evil" was the word that had come to mind. She thought of her son's father and for a brief moment relived the horror of that hideous night. She shuddered.

Myles wrapped his arms around her. "You cold?"

"I'm okay," she assured him, snuggling closer, seeking warmth from his body. Should she tell him about Richard's father? Tell him that Richard's father was actually something out of a nightmare? How would Myles react? With skepticism? With repulsion?

God, she hoped it wouldn't be the latter. She wouldn't know what she'd do if she lost Myles. Just the mere thought of losing him made her aware of how much she actually loved him. "Oh, Myles, don't ever, ever leave me," she said.

"Have no intention, but I might lose a garage in the meantime." He said it lightly, but Patty knew the garage was his whole world. He had worked hard to establish his own business, and it wasn't until recently he began making any profit from it. To lose it would erase at least five years he had put into it; it would crush him. "Think he'd carry out his threat?"

She caught the dread and uncertainty in his voice and wanted to assure him that Richard had only been bluffing. Frankie did this all the time when he couldn't have his way, but then, Frankie wasn't Richard.

"I don't know, Myles," she told him honestly.

Myles fell silent. Willie Nelson sang about being on the road again, and Myles seemed to be listening. But his mind, she knew, was churning with questions. At length he said, "Why do you think he wants to keep me away from you?"

Patty didn't have the answer to that, either. The only reason she could think of was that her son was jealous of Myles. But then, that seemed absurd. Her love for a man should have nothing to do with her love for her children.

"Maybe I better hire a night watchman," Myles said, worrying again about his garage. "Just to be on the safe side."

"Maybe we should not see each other anymore, like Richard wants."

"No, never," Myles said, tightening his arms around her.

"But, darling, you love that garage, and I don't want you to lose it because of me."

"I love you more, sweetheart." He buried his lips in the softness of her hair. "So much more."

"We have to do something about Richard. Something. I caught him in bed with me last night."

Myles stiffened, then silently waited for her to continue.

"He didn't try anything," she added, "but he scared me. He said he wanted to touch me. He wished he could hold me. But he's not a baby anymore. I couldn't keep him in bed with me, so I made him leave."

"You did the right thing."

'He got so angry. I guess I hurt him and made him feel rejected. Oh, Myles." She emitted a cry that was a cross between a sigh and a sob. "It has always been so difficult with him. I want to be a good mother to him, but I don't think I am."

"There you go again, blaming yourself for losing him. Sweetheart, you heard the kid. He left with his father voluntarily."

Voluntarily? No, Patty decided. Charmed was more like it. His father had charmed him, in probably the same way he had charmed her at the Red Lantern.

Again she was tempted to tell Myles everything about Richard's father and again decided against it. "That's not what I meant," she said. "I'm talking about my feelings toward Richard. He's my son, Myles, and I should love him. And sometimes I think I actually do. But most of the time I don't think I love him. I just pretend I do."

"That's because he's been gone a long time. He's a

stranger to you now."

"No, that's not the reason," Patty said, feeling her eyes burn and her throat swell. "It was even before he had disappeared. I was pretending I loved him on the day he was born. Isn't that horrible of me, Myles? His own mother *pretending*."

"You've been under a lot of stress," Myles said gently, kissing a sensitive spot behind her ear.

"I *want* to love him," Patty said, as though he hadn't even spoken. "And he wants me to love him. But I can't. I just can't, Myles."

"It's okay, sweetheart. It's okay."

"No, it's not. Oh Myles, I feel so guilty all the time."

"You've no reason to feel that way. You do love your kid, and do you know why I know that? Because you wouldn't be feeling guilty if you didn't. And know how else I know? Because you have so much love in you."

Patty desperately wanted to believe him, but she didn't. She did not love her son. It was a painful admission, but it was the truth. *She did not love her own son.* But whether or not she did, he was still her child, and she, as a mother, was obliged to take care of him. The guilt was something she would have to learn to live with.

"What do you think I should do?" she asked Myles, tilting her head to look up at him. She had held back her tears, but her eyes were still shiny in the dim light from a small lamp on the other side of the room.

"We'll help him," he replied. "We'll get him professional help."

"What if he refuses?"

"Then we'll have to force him."

"I don't think that'll be easy."

"Then we'll have to trick him."

Patty was ready to tell him that this wouldn't be

easy either, but his lips were suddenly on hers, causing her to swallow her words.

"I love you," he said, his voice deep and muffled.

"I love you, too, darling," she responded, pressing closer to him. So very, very much, she thought.

"Nobody will keep us apart," she heard him mutter, his tone strong with resolve.

And she wanted to believe him. But there was a heavy intuitive feeling inside her that was filled with doubt—and dread.

If Richard wanted to separate them, he would.

And there wouldn't be a damn thing that she, or Myles, could do about it.

15

Shortly after midnight Myles drove her home in his Ford pickup, a faded, blue rusty junk heap that he'd bought several years ago from a Christmas tree farmer and transformed into a gleaming, cherry-red masterpiece. Myles had wanted Patty to spend the night at his apartment, but this was something she could never bring herself to do. She wanted to be home when her kids got up in the morning, not be returning from a night out. Maybe this was unreasonable of her, even hypocritical, since her family already knew she was sleeping with Myles, but she still refused to have it any other way.

When Myles dropped her off at her apartment, she saw Richard in the window, glowering at her. Even from the sidewalk, three floors below, she could feel the heat in his eyes. Doesn't he ever sleep? Why is he furious with me? Then she realized he had seen Myles kiss her before driving off.

Maybe he was jealous after all, she mused as she hurried into the building to escape his burning gaze. Maybe he had the classic Oedipus complex or something like that. Definitely something must be done.

But when she reached her apartment she decided to wait until morning to talk to Richard. He'd be calmer then, and she'd be able to reason with him better.

When morning came, she still found herself hesitant to approach him. Already she found that he had moved to the porch, even had separated the bunk beds and moved his half out. Now Richard was alone, and Patty noticed that his bed was untouched. Didn't he *ever* sleep?

"Richard, we have to talk," she finally said.

The boy quietly waited. The incurious expression suggested that he had been expecting this. As usual, he was at the window. Had he been standing there since she had last seen him?

"Why do you look out the window so much?" she asked.

"This is not what you wanted to talk to me about," he replied.

"No, it's not," she conceded. "But why are you at the window all the time?"

"Life's energy abounds us," he said cryptically.

"What?"

"I like to bask in the rays of the sun and the moon."

She frowned, puzzled. "Oh."

"But you already admitted that this is not why you are here, Mother."

"No. No, it's not."

"It is about Myles."

Patty looked at him in surprise. He had made the statement so flatly and confidently, as though he had read her mind.

"Yes, that's right," she said with some difficulty. Was it really possible that he was a mind reader? Had ESP? Suddenly she felt stripped of all her protective clothing, naked and cold. "How did you know that?"

He shrugged calmly. "I know."

"Did you read my mind, Richard?" she demanded.

"It is not necessary for you to know."

Patty stared at him, feeling the chill and her

nakedness intensify. Yes, he can read minds. She was suddenly certain. How much had she revealed? Had he seen her inability to love him completely? Oh God, he knew exactly how she felt toward him. She had been—was—transparent to him.

"Tell me about Myles," he said, as though directing her wandering mind back on the original course.

"Myles, Myles," she murmured, straining to clear her head and start over. "He told me about the threat you made."

"So?"

"But that was cruel. His garage means a lot to him. And besides, you could get into a lot of trouble. What if something did happen to the garage? You would be blamed."

"I never said I would *not* do anything to his stupid garage."

"Oh, Richard, you couldn't possibly mean what you're saying."

"You know I could mean it, Mother."

Patty found herself momentarily speechless. Richard was cold and indifferent. Yes, she did know that he was deadly serious about what he had said. There wasn't the slightest doubt that he was capable of destroying Myles' garage.

"But why?" she asked, pleading for an explanation.

"I don't like it when his dirty hands are on you."

"But, Richard, Myles and I love each other."

His face hardened. "I know that."

"Don't you want Myles and me to be happy?"

"You can be happy without him."

"Richard, I don't understand. What has Myles done to you to make you dislike him so?"

"I told you why. I don't like his dirty hands on you."

"That's not a reason."

"Stay away from him, Mother." It was a command.

"You can't tell me who or who not to stay away from."

"Whom."

"What?"

"From whom not to stay away," he corrected.

Once more Patty was stunned into silence. How dare he make a command! How dare he correct her! Then she reminded herself she was dealing with a boy who needed psychiatric aid, which was the purpose of this conversation to begin with.

After drawing in a deep breath to calm herself, she said, "I want you to see a doctor, Richard."

"A psychiatrist," he said, knowingly. Reading her mind again?

"That's right. I think you'll find it helpful."

"I do not need to see a psychiatrist, and I am not going to see one."

"But Richard."

"No."

"Why not?"

He turned away from her and peered out the window, terminating the discussion. Patty stood behind him, indecisive and frustrated. How could she convince him that he needed help? Should force be used?

"No," he said.

No to what? she wondered. No, he could not be convinced that he needed help? No, that force could not be used?

Patty hugged herself, although the chill was deep inside her. Then she quietly left the room before he could pick up any more of her thoughts.

"He refuses to see a psychiatrist," she told Myles on a pay phone outside the Red Lantern, not wanting Richard to overhear the conversation. "I don't know what to do, but he really needs one."

And I need one, too, she thought. Her hand was shaking, hardly able to hold the phone receiver steady. *My son used to spook me with his eyes. He had made threats. He climbed into bed with me. And now I know he can read my mind.*

I am going to crack. Soon. I can feel it.

"Pat? Are you still there?" Myles said.

"He reads minds," she blurted out.

"Huh?"

"He has ESP, Myles."

"Honey, what are you talking about?"

Patty rubbed her forehead. She could almost hear faint cracking sounds behind it. Her mind was like a ball of ice, now splitting into hundreds of cracks.

God, she needed a big glass of vodka and tonic. Make that one part tonic water and two parts vodka. No, make it vodka and a splash of tonic water.

"Honey? Honey?"

"Still here," she said weakly.

"You all right?"

"Just a little scared, that's all."

"About Richard?"

"Yes. Somehow we've got to get him to a psychiatrist."

"What did you mean about ESP, sweetheart?"

"Never mind," she said dismissingly. He wouldn't believe her, so there was no sense explaining it. Maybe a psychiatrist might make the discovery, perhaps through hypnosis or something. He or she would find other things and probably have Richard institutionalized. It would be best for everyone. She would have peace of mind. Of course she'd visit him daily and . . .

"Is there a bad connection here?" Myles said, petulance now edging his voice. "I keep losing you."

"I'm sorry, Myles. I've so much on my mind. Do you think we can force Richard to see a psychiatrist?"

"Force?" he said, weighing the thought. "To tell you the truth I don't think there's a psychiatrist who will see a patient on an involuntarily basis, let alone one at a clinic. I think I remember hearing they can only help those who want to be helped."

"But we've got to do something, Myles," Patty insisted.

Silence ensued on the other end of the line for a few seconds, then Myles said, "We could take a chance and get him to a psychiatrist. Once he's there maybe the doctor will take a look at him. Maybe I'm wrong and he'll help the kid, no matter whether it's voluntary or not."

"But first we have to get him there," Patty said.

"Right."

"And how are we going to do that? I'm sure I don't have to tell you how stubborn he can be—and maybe even violent."

Myles paused and then said, "I'll trick him."

The appointment was to be at 2:00 o'clock Wednesday afternoon. "Be careful, Myles," Patty said after she had told him on the phone. You would think she was talking about carrying a wild lion to a vet the way she was fretting. She really had nothing to worry about; Myles had it all planned, and he was confident nothing would go wrong. When he was a kid, 16 or somewhere around there, he had been picked up for breaking and entering a TV and radio shop. He had landed in a juvenile detention home. Since then he'd been pretty straight, but he was sure he knew how rebellious boys thought and felt. They were a paranoiac bunch and usually liked to be treated like men, not kids. Or they liked to *think* they were being treated like men.

So that was what Myles planned to do—make the kid think he was Big Man.

But, of course, he'd make sure not to talk down to the kid, remembering this was something he resented and had a knack for detecting readily. It'd be easy, Myles thought confidently. He'd talk to him as if he were one of the guys at the garage. No fucking sweat.

At 1:00, an hour before the appointment, Myles was in Patty's kitchen. The clinic was little less than a half hour away, but Myles wanted some extra time to work on the boy.

"Tell him I'd like to see him," he told Patty, "and then disappear. This is going to be man to man stuff." He winked.

Patty's face was drawn, and her hands were absently rubbing the sides of her jeans, up and down.

"Relax, honey." Myles pulled her into his arms and kissed her. Her body slackened slightly, but her eyes were sparking anxiety. Like a frightened old woman or little girl, he thought. Somehow the two were alike. Myles held her tighter, wanting so much to protect her. "You're worrying needlessly," he told her softly. "What could the kid do, except maybe throw a bratty tantrum when he sees a shrink, eh? I'm bigger than him. I'll keep him under control."

"Myles," she said, then stopped. There was something she wanted to tell him but was hesitant.

Myles stroked her hair. It was the color of a polished penny, the texture of corn silk. "What is it, honey?" he prompted.

"Be careful of your thoughts."

Frowning, Myles pulled his head back to look at her face. "Thoughts?"

She nodded, looking embarrassed. "I told you I think he has ESP."

"Oh, you mean that crazy stuff you see in the movies, like in *Carrie* and *The Fury*? The sixth sense or something?" he said, laughter creeping into his voice.

Patty's face reddened, and he quickly willed
himself to be serious. She cleared her throat and
continued, "I'm not sure, Myles, but I think he can
read minds."

"You really believe this?"

"I don't know. I believe anything is possible with
him. I'm just telling you to be careful, that's all. Just
to be safe, don't think of anything you wouldn't
want him to know about. All right?"

Myles shrugged, his lips twitching. "Sure."

"I'm serious, Myles."

"I know that, honey."

She studied his face. There seemed to be something else she wanted to tell him, then decided
against it at the last minute. "I'll go get him now,"
she said.

As she turned to leave, Myles gave her an
affectionate slap on the rear, but she showed no
acknowledgement of his touch. Myles watched her
leave, mentally shaking his head with sympathy.
That boy was doing a number on her, aging her. The
kid had only been back for five days and already
there were shadowy patches under her eyes and
nerves twitching on her face. And what was with
this ESP shit? Sure, the kid was spooky-looking, but
what gave her the idea that he had some weird
powers? Something he had said or done?

Myles helped himself to a can of beer from the
refrigerator. Then, leaning against a counter, he
drank the beer and listened to the droning of the TV
in the other room. He was almost finished with the
can when Patty returned, Richard preceding her.

It took all the will power he had not to wince at
the sight of him. Christ, the kid was a real spook. No
wonder Patty was thinking crazy thoughts about
him. Never had Myles seen anyone so pale; even a
corpse couldn't be worse than this. And the dark
hair, which was too long and stringy, hiding some of

his forehead made him look even paler. Black and white, he thought.

Then he quickly reminded himself not to gawk. His job was to make the kid feel at ease. Lifting the beer can in a friendly salute, he said, "How're ya doing, Rich?"

Richard didn't answer but only watched him from across the room. Myles glanced at Patty, who caught the silent reminder and quietly retreated. Then he looked back at the boy, who was still staring at him. Reading his thoughts? No way. The kid was deliberately defying him, that's all. He could tell; he used to do it himself to grownups when he was that age. It was a way to make yourself feel bigger and better.

"Think your mom will get mad if you have a beer with me?" he asked.

"What do you want?" Richard ignored the question.

"Hey, take it easy. Don't have to be hostile," he said, now holding the beer can aloft like a white flag signaling truce. "I just thought you and I could have ourselves a little chat. You know, man to man."

The boy's face was noncommittal.

Myles downed the rest of the beer, watching him over the aluminum rim. After wiping his mouth with his forearm, he said, "Sure your mom wouldn't let you share a beer with me? Sure could use another."

"I don't drink," Richard said flatly. He was still standing near the doorway, as if impatient to leave the room. His body was rigid, hands at his sides.

Stiff as a goddamn mannequin, Myles thought, and just as creepy. "Lighten up, will ya," he urged. "I'm not gonna bite."

"I am not afraid of you," he replied in that flat voice again.

"Good, good. Now we can have our talk." Myles

crushed the beer can, then belatedly remembered that Patty saved returnable bottles and cans for petty cash. Ah well, it was only a nickel. He threw the can into a waste basket under the sink, then smiled indulgently at Richard. "Aren't ya curious to know what I want us to talk about?"

No answer.

"Care to go for a little ride, Richard?" he suggested. "We'll be able to talk better. No walls with ears in my truck. Know what I mean?"

Richard took his time to think about it, eyes never leaving Myles' face. There were moments that Myles was tempted to avert his head and escape the unwavering scrutiny, but determination prevailed. The boy, he believed, was looking for signs of guilt and deception. But he mustn't have found any, for at length he said, "All right."

"Great." Myles broadened his smile. It was easier than he had thought it'd be. "Go get your jacket."

"I do not need . . . never mind." The boy left the kitchen, then returned a moment later wearing his faded denim jacket.

"All set?" Myles said. When the boy didn't reply and just waited for him to make the first move, Myles muttered flippantly to himself, "All set."

In silence they walked down three flights of stairs, then headed toward the red pickup that was parked in front of the apartment house. Myles started to open the passenger door for the boy, then caught himself in time. The kid would think he was being patronized if Myles tried to be courteous. Kids had a thing about good manners. It was a sure sign of a phony. Truly nice people didn't have to act nice. He should know; he used to think the same way once.

Myles started the motor, then glanced at his watch. Getting the boy into the truck took less time than he'd figured. Now he'd have an extra 15 minutes or so to kill. If he reached the clinic too soon the boy would have to wait for the appointment, something he most likely wouldn't do. Myles would probably have to fight with him.

"Where are we going?" Richard asked, his voice breaking into Myles' thoughts.

"Huh? Oh, riding 'round." There was a faint odor in the confines of the truck, a cloying, rotting smell, like apples gone bad. He rolled down the window an inch or two on the driver's side, then lit a cigarette. "Want one?" He shook his pack of Pall Malls until one cigarette peeked out.

"No."

"Don't smoke either, huh?"

"No."

But you eat bugs and rodents, and shit, too, I bet. But no, pardon me, you don't smoke or drink. He slid the pack back into his shirt pocket and kept his smile.

The truck pulled away from the curb and headed north, a scenic route, bouncing and lurching like an ancient railroad car.

"Needs shocks," Myles said. There was no comment, not that he expected any. "Wanted to talk about that threat you sorta made about the garage, and about your mother and me," he said after a short silence. He was hoping for a strong reaction—a heated dispute would eat up the time—but he was disappointed. Richard seemed to have lost interest in him and was gazing out the window.

It was a cold, gray day. Only the scarlet buds in the otherwise denuded trees were a reminder that it was spring. It was hard to believe that only last week the temperature had been summerlike, somewhere in the 70's.

They passed the high school, a modern concrete and glass structure visible through a stretch of nursery-grown hemlocks.

"That's where you'll be going, I guess," Myles

said, inclining his head in the direction of the school.

"No." The reply was firm and positive.

"No?"

"I am smarter than anyone else in there. And that includes the teachers."

Is that so? Cocky bastard, this one. Myles decided not to push it. Let the shrink deal with this and force the kid down a rung or two.

"Well, school ain't the reason for this ride," he said. The boy slowly turned away from the window to look at him. Through the corner of his eye Myles thought he saw an amusing smirk, but it was gone when he glanced fully at him.

"Man to man talk," the boy said, the mockery now in his voice.

Myles felt something cold grip his belly. Angrily, he ignored the sensation. He'd be damned if he'd let a wimpy 13-year-old get the best of him. "That's right, Richard. Man to man," he said, taking a long drag of his cigarette. "And real men don't beat around no bush. They beat 'em, sure, but not around 'em, if you know what I mean."

"I know what you mean." The small laughter was still in his voice, but Myles noted the laughter was at him, not with him.

"Probably shouldn't be cracking dirty jokes with ya," he mumbled, "but I just wanted ya to feel comfortable, treat ya like I'd treat the other guys."

Richard said nothing. His attention had turned to an approaching fork in the road. The left fork would lead to thick woods and a steep incline, and the right to a moderately populated area. Myles started to turn the wheel to take the latter road, when Richard quietly commanded, "The other."

Myles obeyed—not because he wanted to, but because something from a remote region in his brain seemed to have awakened and taken control of his hands. Also, it clouded and changed his thoughts. He was suddenly reminded that there was plenty of time to kill. He'd drive along this road for a while; there was no harm in it. And besides, he hadn't been this way for over two years. It'd be a pleasant change. Later he'd turn around and get back on that other road and . . .

"Are you afraid that I might blow away your precious garage, Myles?" Richard asked bluntly, interrupting his slow, dreamlike thoughts.

"I wouldn't like it," Myles said, feeling as though he'd been drifting on a gentle pond and was now trudging on shore. "That's for damn sure."

"That does not answer my question. Do you think I'll do it? Do you think I'm bluffing?"

"I don't know," Myles said truthfully, "but I'm hoping you're bluffing, Richard."

"It would be so easy. Your smelly business is a grease box. One match and it would be gone. So, so easy."

Myles could feel sweat pooling under his armpits, dampening his shirt. He also felt a little woozy, as if he had a beer or two after a day without eating. It must be the truck. Too small inside here. Not enough air. He cranked down the window some more.

His head still felt funny, full of sticky spiderwebs.

"I've never done anything to you," he told Richard, using, he hoped, what was his most placating voice. "You've no reason to destroy my garage."

"You love that garage, don't you?"

"You bet your—" He stopped and got a hold of himself. "Yes, Richard, very much."

"Do you love it more than my mother?"

"Yes. I mean, no. I love them both equally."

"I warned you to stay away from my mother."

"But you've no right to do that."

"I warned you to stop fucking her."

"I love your mother, Richard. I love her very

much."

Richard was silent for a minute. He stared intensely at the road in front of him, his bony face grim. There was no trace of a smirk, and when he looked back at Myles, there was a reddish glint in his eyes, a glint that was ephemeral, but long and bright enough to penetrate Myles' foggy daze and almost make him lose control of the truck.

"I don't care," Richard replied in a sepulchral voice. "I don't like you, and I don't want you with her."

"But why don't you like me?"

Again Richard fell silent. This time he didn't speak until he saw a wooden sign nailed to a large pine tree. LOVERS' POINT. Beyond this a narrow, gravelly road veered right. "Take it," he ordered.

"But what for? It only leads to the top of a hill, a dead end." It was a steep incline, terminating abruptly at a waist-high stone wall. It was where teenagers parked to drink and make out in the late hours. It was the town's highest point where, on separate occasions, a lovesick girl and a male homosexual had leaped to their deaths.

"Take it," Richard repeated in a slow whisper, sounding like a hypnotist. "Take . . . the . . . road."

Once more that vague something woke up in his brain, like a sleeping Nessie stirring in a stagnant lagoon, and controlled his thoughts.

Why not? I've all the time in the world, don't I? It'll be good to enjoy the view for a while.

The truck dipped in and out of holes in the bumpy road, which was scarcely wide enough for two compact cars to pass. Tree branches along the passenger's side scraped the door and slapped the windshield, sounding much louder and more menacing inside the vehicle. Yet Richard never flinched. He sat, as though rooted in fascination, while Myles steered the truck onward, like an automaton.

They rode in silence for several miles. Up. Up.

Richard looked away from the window and watched Myles. He seemed amused at what he was seeing, as though Myles' face was entertaining him like a television screen.

Reading my thoughts? Myles wondered, but felt no rush of alarm. In fact, he felt nothing except a strange, floating detachment. He was driving the truck up to Lovers' Point, and he knew he was doing this, yet it didn't matter. It was all right. It wasn't what he wanted to do orginally, but it was all right.

They reached the summit, stopping inches before the crumbling wall of stones. So many of the rocks had worked themselves loose since Myles had last been there, so many years ago. Now the wall was uneven, gaping wide and almost to the ground in some spots. It would not take much force to push through the barrier, Myles found himself thinking dully, now feeling a faint stab of uneasiness. How deep was the drop? 800 feet? An even 1000?

"You wanted to talk," he heard Richard remind him.

"Yeah." His tongue felt swollen and dry. What was happening to him? Why was he feeling sluggish like this?

Richard grinned at him, but it was like seeing a face that was underwater, blurry and undulating.

"Let's . . . let's talk," Myles said, the last word too loud and hollow to his ears. The cloying smell of rotten apples returned, more potent this time. It's Richard, he suddenly realized. But why—how did he smell like that? Was he carrying something that had gone bad? Was he, himself, rotting?

The odor grew stronger, and Myles rolled the window down all the way, cupping his nostrils with his other hand.

"Guess what, Myles, I'm not going to do anything to your garage," Richard said, maintaining his grin. "Does that make you happy?"

"Yes. Very much." He could barely get the words out. Christ, the smell—it was literally making him sick. He wanted to get the hell out of the truck but wasn't sure if he had the strength.

"I knew you would be happy, Myles," said the boy, "but there are other ways I can keep you away from Mother."

Myles experienced a fresh stab of alarm, and this time it wasn't faint; it was knifelike, cold and numbing. "What are you talking about?"

Richard purposely widened his eyes, like one trying to frighten a listener while telling a horror tale. But in this case there was nothing to tell, only something to show. In disbelief, Myles saw the pale irises in the boy's eyes turn red, as though filling with blood, and saw the color spread until the black pupils were gone. Then he saw the whites of the eyes become pink, reminding him of strawberry milk. He watched the color darken until it was the same deep shade as the rest.

What in fucking hell is this?

Richard tilted his head back and brayed.

Myles grabbed for the door handle, panic shooting adrenaline into his veins. But at that moment Richard's head swung toward him, eyes still wide and bloody, grin still fixed, and paralyzed him with his stare. Myles helplessly looked back, his hand still on the handle but unable to move it. He felt as if his blood had turned to ice, felt as if hands were inside his head, fingers squeezing his brain and playing with it as if it were putty.

ESP, Patty had said. Y'mean like in *Carrie* and *The Fury?* he had said. The two movies were about kids who had mental powers that could kill.

Richard watched, still laughing, a sound which was now confined to the throat, muffled and vibrating. The eyes had taken on a shine, glowing like twin red lanterns. He was enjoying this immensely.

"Do you like this place I picked, Myles?" he asked.

Myles said nothing, couldn't even if he wanted to.

"You wanted to take me elsewhere, to a psychiatrist, didn't you? But I wanted to come here." Knowing he wouldn't get an answer, he looked away from Myles and feasted on the view beyond the ragged wall. Treetops and rooftops spread before them. There was a network of streets with vehicles that looked like tiny Matchbox cars moving along them. And far to the right a white church steeple pointed at the cloudy sky. Richard, intrigued, studied this for a long moment, then looked away in sudden rejection. "I know all about Lovers' Point," he said, somewhat boastfully. "There is so much I know, Myles. So much more than you do."

Myles barely heard him. He felt trapped inside his own body. Was this how a person suffering from a massive stroke felt? Unable to move no matter how much one tried? The brain was still alive but the body was dead. And was this what he was actually having—a stroke?

Why are you doing this? he demanded. *What have I done to you to deserve this?*

"I know that two people killed themselves by jumping off this cliff," Richard went on, calmly sitting back against the seat. "There are a lot of boulders down there at the bottom, and big pointy spruces and pines. One girl, Marietta was her name, about fifteen, leaped off here because she caught her boyfriend fucking her mother. Marietta was a pretty girl. Do you remember her, Myles?"

Who the hell are you? What are you?

"Speechless, are you?" Richard said. "Well, you don't have to talk, just listen. Marietta was prettier in life than in death; there's no argument there. And know why that is? She didn't have a face anymore after she jumped. She fell into a big spruce down there and slid the rest of the way to the ground. The bark of the tree peeled her skin off, some of her scalp, too. Nobody knew who she was when they found her, except for the family dentist. She couldn't have done worse if she had rubbed her face off with an electric sander."

Why are you telling me this?

"Am I holding you too tight, Myles?" the boy suddenly asked. "Is this better?"

Myles felt the pressure ease. Now he could move his head in small, jerky motions, along with his hands, although the fingers were bent and clumsy. He tried to say something, working the muscles in his throat, but only a gurgle and spittle escaped from his mouth. *Please,* he pleaded with his eyes, *I was only trying to help you, get a doctor to help you.*

Myles squeezed his eyes shut, as though frantically trying to block out the boy next to him. He couldn't believe this was happening. He felt as if he were on a bad LSD trip or something, not that he had ever taken any acid or drugs before. Narcotics were for sissies. Booze was the stuff that real men used.

"And then there was Ben," Richard continued. "He was twenty-two when he jumped. He was gay, but didn't want to be. But girls just didn't turn him on like the boys did, so he dove off the cliff. He never made it to the ground, though. A broken tree caught him in midair, in the stomach. They said he looked like a piece of beef on a skewer. Nasty trees down there." Richard paused, then turned to Myles. "Still too tight?"

Myles, sweat now worming down his face from his scalp, managed a nod. Almost instantly he felt all the pressure leave. To his relief he had full use of his body again and his voice was back. "How did you do that?" he demanded in a low, stunned whisper.

Richard shrugged his frail shoulders but did not answer.

Myles then stared at the steering wheel in front of him. Could he leave now? Would he be stopped?

He looked over at Richard, as though waiting for permission.

God, what was this kid planning? Why did he tell him about those two suicides?

Myles' skin began to crawl. The kid was indirectly telling him that they, too, would be leaping to their deaths. Wasn't he?

But he couldn't force him to jump. Could he?

He made you paralyzed for a moment there, idiot!

"I-It's time we leave, wouldn't you say?" he said, struggling to keep the fear out of his voice. He expected Richard to object, but the boy just shrugged again, not agreeing or disagreeing.

Myles hesitated, not sure of what he should do next. A stream of sweat ran into his eyes, but he didn't wipe it away, determined not to let the boy see him weak and discomposed. Fighting to keep his hand steady, he turned the ignition. He was surprised to hear it spurt to life, half-expecting Richard to freeze the motor as he had frozen him. Then he shoved the truck into reverse and gripped the steering wheel. The truck shot backward and relief flooded Myles as he gained distance from the wall. Then he turned the vehicle around and began the long descent.

Too easy, a voice nagged at him, Much too easy. He forced himself to ignore it, thinking instead that he was back in control.

Gotta get the kid to a shrink, and gotta get him there fast. Lord knows what the doctor will find.

Then he heard Richard laughing, his head

leaning back against the top of the seat, looking upward.

The sweat on his face turned cold, chilling him.

Shut up, he wanted to yell at the kid. SHUT THE FUCK UP! But instead he asked, "What are you laughing at?"

"You think . . ." he spat between laughter ". . . you have it . . . all under . . . control."

Myles floored the gas, desperate to gain more space between him and that fucking wall.

The laughter continued, rising to a maddening crescendo, then Richard said, "Watch . . . this . . . Myles."

The truck gained speed, but to Myles' horror it was going the wrong way. It was going backwards. Back toward the wall.

"No, no . . ." Myles slammed on the brakes. Nothing. He pulled at the gears. Nothing.

"No, no!"

He yanked at the wheel to pull the truck off the road. He shot a glance at the rearview mirror and saw the wall, saw it come closer and closer.

"No!" he screamed. He heard the wall explode and Richard's shrill peal of laughter. It seemed to go on and on, rising and rising. He screamed again and heard his own voice drown out Richard's.

Then he heard nothing.

16

Patty watched *One Life to Live* with her mother, but with the exception of two heartrending, hysterical scenes, she couldn't lose herself to the soap opera. Her eyes perversely slid to the digital clock on top of the TV. What were Myles and Richard doing now? she asked herself each time. At length she left the couch and looked out the window in Richard's small room. She stood for almost an hour, again asking herself, over and over, what Myles and Richard were doing now.

She contemplated taking a hot bath. That usually relaxed not only her body but her mind as well. And besides, watching and waiting for someone's return was like waiting for a telephone call, and everyone knew that a watched phone would never ring. So she drew the tub in the bathroom and sprinkled rose-scented oil into the water. When she sank into the warm water and enveloped herself in the perfumed steam, she was reminded of the many times when Richard was a small boy waiting outside the bathroom door whenever she took a bath. She remembered how annoyed she'd been because of this. He had made her so uneasy, so nervous—just like he was making her now.

Maybe she had made an awful mistake letting Myles go off alone with him. Myles had been too assured, not serious enough, but then, that was because she hadn't told him what the boy's father was. Now she realized, with a sickening feeling, that if she had explained everything, he would have treated the situation differently, would have been careful.

What were they doing now?

Were they at the clinic? Was Richard being analyzed? Was everything under control? Oh God, she dearly hoped so.

When Patty finally stepped out of the tub, her skin shriveled and the water chilly, an hour had passed. It was now a little after 4:00. Certainly they weren't at the clinic anymore. Maybe Myles and the boy had actually hit it off and were now having a snack somewhere—McDonald's or Kentucky Fried. They could be anywhere. Or they could be at Myles' apartment for some reason.

She called Myles' number. The phone on the end of the line rang and rang.

Maybe they were at the garage. She hung up and called there. A mechanic answered and told her that he hadn't seen Myles at all today.

She dully hung up, her stomach queasy, as though she had eaten something too heavy. What now? Read the romance novel she had started last week, *Love's Wildest Promise*? No, the words would only blur and not penetrate her mind.

Absently rubbing her hands on her thighs and hips, Patty began pacing the kitchen. She knew she was worrying prematurely, but her stomach was still uneasy. It seemed to know something that she didn't. It seemed to be telling her that something horrible had happened.

Suddenly Patty wished her other kids were home to talk with her and help pass the time, but Janet had gone to the library after school to do research on a term paper, and Frankie was over at his buddy's house to lift weights together. And her mother, as usual, was lost to the TV set.

Slowly another hour passed. Patty called Myles' apartment again, then his garage. "No, Ma'am, he isn't here yet," the same mechanic told her. Yes, something has happened. She was certain of it now. She picked up the receiver again and dialed the police station.

"This is Patty Thompson," she said. "Myles Forbes and my son went to see a doctor earlier this afternoon, and they haven't come back. I know you probably think it's too soon to worry, but I really think they'd be back by now. I can't imagine where they would be."

"What's the name again, Ms. Thompson?" a male voice asked.

Patty repeated the name. "He owns Myles' Auto Repairs."

"Uh . . . yes." There was an unmistakable hesitancy. Patty's heart accelerated.

"Ms. Thompson?" It was a different voice, deeper. The phone had been switched over to someone else—a bad sign, a very bad sign.

Patty gripped the receiver tighter, numbly staring at her hand as it whitened. "Yes?"

"What is your relation to Mr. Forbes?"

"Relation?"

"Sister, friend?" the voice inquired patiently. And gently, Patty noted. "Since your last name is not Forbes, I presume you're not his spouse."

"I'm a friend."

"Do you know if he has a wife, Ms. Thompson?"

"No."

"No, you don't, or no, that he doesn't?"

"He doesn't have a wife."

"Family?"

With her free hand Patty held her stomach. She was going to be sick. Already the room was starting to spin. There was no chair by the phone, so she leaned heavily against the wall.

Weakly, she said, "His parents are dead. I think he has a brother in Ohio somewhere. I'm not sure." There was silence. Patty used it to muster up courage. "Has . . . has something happened to Myles?"

There was an audible, slow intake of breath, then, "I'm afraid I've bad news, Ms. Thompson . . ."

Patty squeezed her eyes shut. *No. Please. No.*

" . . . There's been an accident at Lovers' Point, and Mr. Forbes was found as the occupant of the vehicle, a '77 Ford pickup. I'm afraid your friend is dead, Ms. Thompson."

Patty refused to let the words sink in. Instinctively, her mind slammed shut a door, but the door wasn't strong enough, for the officer's words pushed and pushed until they eventually gained entrance. And when they did, Patty emitted a loud, single sob, then her hand flew to her mouth to quell the next outcry.

"You all right, Ms. Thompson?"

All right? I just lost someone very dear to me. I just lost the only man who was ever good to me, the only man I ever loved. And you ask if I'm all right?

Oh God, this can't be happening!

"What . . . what about Richard?" she suddenly asked, barely audible.

"Who?"

"Richard, my son. He was with Myles."

"I'm sorry, but I don't know anything about your son. At the moment we only know that Mr. Forbes was alone in the accident."

"But . . . but . . ."

"Yes, Ms. Thompson?"

"My son went with Myles. Myles was to take him to see a doctor at the clinic."

"Must have dropped him off somewhere before the accident. How old is your son, Mrs. Thompson?"

Numbly, Patty noted that the officer had switched from "Ms." to "Mrs." after learning that she had a son. "Richard is thirteen," she said.

"Richard Thompson, right?"

Patty nodded, then remembered she was on the phone. "Yes."

"The missing boy who returned a few days ago?" the officer asked, sudden recognition and surprise evident in his voice.

"Yes."

"We'll check on this right away, Mrs. Thompson," he promised. "Don't worry."

"Maybe he walked away from the accident," Patty thought out loud.

She heard the officer clear his throat. "I don't think anybody could've walked away from that accident," he said gently.

Patty said nothing. She needed to sit down, or better yet, lie down. Her legs were too weak, and the phone was suddenly too heavy in her hand. She started to hang up.

"I'm sorry about your friend, Mrs. . . ." The receiver touched the cradle, abruptly terminating the call.

The silence that followed stunned her with its potency. She could hear the droning of the TV set, but that only seemed to magnify the disturbing hush that was closing in on her. She tried to keep her mind blank, to shut that door down again, but the silence made this impossible. It seemed to leave her with no choice but to think solely of Myles. Now she wished she hadn't hung up the phone. It was different talking about Myles than being alone with the silence, thinking about him. She could see his face in her mind's eye, and the realization that she'd never see him any other way, except in a photograph, stabbed at her throat.

"Oh, Myles!" she cried, turning her face to the

wall, pressing against it. "This can't be true. It can't be!"

The silence thickened. She wished there were someone who'd hold her, someone who'd tell her that she had heard the officer incorrectly, that Myles was in the hospital with a broken leg but would be as good as new in no time.

But the silence told her this was not so. Myles was dead.

The silence pressed against her. Dead, it said. Dead, dead, dead.

"Ma," Patty suddenly wailed, desperately needing to be with someone. "Ma!" She pushed herself away from the wall and half-ran, half-stumbled toward the living room, toward the perpetually flickering light of the TV. She was a little girl again, a girl whose cat had just been run over by a big station wagon, and Ma was the only person who could comfort her, Ma who used to be strong and soft and warm.

But something stopped her between the kitchen and the living room.

Richard.

Patty gasped.

"Hello, Mother."

Patty gaped for a long, numb moment. When had he returned? Why hadn't she heard him come in? She glanced into the living room, at the front door for some telltale sign. She saw her mother glance questionably at her from the recliner, and Patty remembered she had cried out for her. Then she looked back at her son. He seemed to have appeared out of nowhere.

"M-Myles," she murmured when she recovered from the shock of her son's presence. "Where is he? He *is* with you." It wasn't a question; it was a statement she desperately wanted to believe was true. She looked around the kitchen, then peered once more past him into the living room. Her mother was still looking expectantly at her. "Myles," Patty said again, as though this would explain it all to Lydia.

Then back at Richard she demanded, her voice harsh, "Where is he, I said."

"Gone."

"What do you mean *gone*?" Hope had flowered like an umbrella-shaped firework, then dissipated into spiraling smoke. "What happened?"

"There was an accident."

Oh God, then it was true. Myles was . . .

"Dead." Richard completed her thought.

Patty shuddered, as though a chip of ice had been dropped down her back. "But you . . . ?"

"I walked away from the wreck," he replied simply.

He was unscathed, Patty noted. His clothes weren't torn, and there weren't any bruises or lacerations that she could see.

"I was out of the truck before it crashed," he said, answering her silent question. His face was an emotionless mask, but his eyes weren't cold or contemptuous as they usually were. Instead, they were surprisingly soft and doleful. "I am sorry I did it, Mother."

Patty felt more ice worming its way down her spine. She said nothing, not wanting to ask what it was he was sorry about, not wanting to hear the reason.

"But he tried to trick me," the boy went on anyway. "I knew the moment he came for me here that he wanted to take me to a psychiatrist. He was a fool, Mother. And you're a fool, too, thinking that a psychiatrist could help me. Only you can help me. All you have to do is—"

"What are you saying?" Patty demanded in a whisper that sounded like a hiss. Like the hope that had mushroomed momentarily inside her, revulsion was doing the same thing now.

"You know what I am saying. I killed Myles."

Patty glared at him. He had admitted what she had suspected. He had killed the love of her life.

"I am truly sorry," he said sincerely.

"Sorry?" she spat, now shivering uncontrollably. Here before her was a murderer, the killer of the man she dearly loved, and all he could say was that he was *sorry*? This was a nightmare. What else could it be? "Why?" she demanded.

"Because almost all that is good in you was given to him. I need all of your goodness, Mother. With Myles I had no chance."

"Goodness? What goodness are you talking about?"

"Love, Mother. Love. You loved Myles so much that you had none left for me."

"And you wonder why we tried to get you to a psychiatrist?" Patty said, exaggerating amazement. "I'm your mother, Richard, not your lover. There's a big, big difference."

Richard shook his head woefully. "You don't understand. Love is goodness. I need as much as I can from you."

"And so because you couldn't get it, you killed Myles?" she said incredulously.

"Yes, and because I was jealous. I lost control. It happens to me all the time. I go into these rages. My feelings take over—"

"How did you—" Patty interrupted, then stopped as abruptly to gather strength for the next word "—kill Myles?"

"It is not necessary for you to know."

"Stop saying that!" Patty screamed. Lydia, startled, looked over at her. Then she quickly looked away, apparently not wanting to become involved, especially with Richard.

"You wouldn't understand, Mother," Richard said, his voice soft, the softest she'd ever heard it.

"How did you kill him?" Patty demanded through clenched teeth.

"Mother, you hate me," Richard suddenly said in alarm. "Please don't do that. It is the worst thing you could do right now. I need your love to help me, not your hate. I have enough of that from Father." He took a step forward and extended his arms, long skeletal fingers splayed and stretched. "I need you, Mother. Please."

She took a step back. "Get away from me."

"But I'm your son. Don't turn me away."

"You killed Myles," she reminded him, her voice strident, on the verge of hysteria.

Again Lydia glanced over, this time unable to ignore the conversation. "What's that, Patricia?"

"You heard right, Ma!" Patty said. "Myles is dead. He just died in—"

"Don't turn me away, Mother," Richard pleaded. "Please."

"—an accident. And Richard killed him but won't say how."

"Accident?" Lydia said dumbly, watching Patty, who was now backing swiftly toward her bedroom.

"That's right, Ma. Myles is dead. He is dead." She reached her room, slammed the door behind her, and threw herself onto her bed.

She was once more a little girl, burying her face in her pillow. She burst into tears, for her world had just ended. When the tears stopped, she wiped her eyes and sat up. She thought she was finished crying, at least for now, but the instant she thought of Myles a fresh flood of tears began.

She cried for the rest of the afternoon and part of the evening, until she finally fell asleep. She never heard Janet nor Frankie come home. And she never felt Richard's hand as he tenderly stroked her hair.

17

The cemetery was cold and sunless. Wind whipped hair and flapped coats as a small group of friends, employees, and a brother gathered around Myles Forbes' flower-strewn grave. Among them was Patty, flanked by Janet and Frankie. There were no more tears. It had taken two days but now Patty had emptied herself of them and was left feeling hollow. She knew she was at a funeral, but somehow it didn't seem real to her. Somehow she had managed to detach herself from her surroundings, from the fact that she had lost the man that was her future.

Richard was at the funeral, too, but stood apart from the others. Patty watched him through dull eyes. The anger and resentment she had felt for the boy had been emptied from her, also. For now, anyway. Only a weary numbness remained. So many emotions and so many troubled thoughts and decisions had plagued her the last two days that she now felt exhausted, drained of everything. It surprised her that she could function at all, standing here before a silver-gray casket that, except for the gloss, matched the color of the sky.

The morning after she had learned of Myles' death and had cried herself to sleep, she called the police and told them that Richard was home, unharmed. She had proceeded to tell them that Richard had admitted killing Myles, but the boy, as though he had sensed her intention from another room, suddenly appeared, glaring at her on the phone and frightening her. Without another word she hung up.

"They would not be able to prove anything, Mother," he had told her. "And it would not solve anything. Myles is already dead."

Patty's hand quickly rose to slap him, but at the last instant she lost courage. She wasn't certain what kind of reaction she would get. She wouldn't have been surprised if he responded violently and attacked her in return.

So her hand hovered in the air for a few seconds, then dropped uselessly to her side. "Get away from me," she had said wearily. She saw hurt in his eyes but didn't care. She just waited for him to leave the room, and when she saw that he wasn't going to do this, she went into the bathroom, locked the door and took a long bath.

He didn't wait by the door for her. She didn't see him again until now.

He was near a large maple that was beginning to sprout miniature clumps of fresh, lime-colored leaves. No one seemed aware of his presence except her. He had not been here when the small crowd had gathered at the grave site; he had appeared quietly in the middle of a prayer. Patty had been staring at the coffin without seeing it, and when she lifted her head and gazed past the priest, she saw her son.

But he didn't see her, or he pretended not to. His face was turned in the direction of the casket, although from this angle and with people circling the grave it didn't seem possible that he could see it. Yet Patty felt certain that he could—probably with his mind rather than his eyes. Patty was surprised to find him there near the tree, but she was not stunned or startled. And she would have dispassionately looked away if it weren't for his expression, which she could see clearly in spite of the distance. He was stricken with guilt and grief. Never had she seen such sadness. But suddenly there was an abrupt change in his countenance. Now he seemed to be laughing silently, his mouth an ugly, complacent smirk, his eyes glinting with delight. For a fleeting moment she thought she could hear a giggle, but it was only the wind, which seemed to have doubled in intensity.

Then the visage changed again and the glint in his eyes was gone. The smirk melted into a frown. Once more she thought she heard a sound from him, this time a wail, but again she realized it was the wind, changing its pitch.

As if sensing her scrutiny, he looked over at her. Then he laughed, tilting his head back as though to mock someone in the heavens above him. He looked back at Patty, then through the people and at the casket. His body shook with sobs, then with laughter again. He reminded Patty of the twin masks of comedy and tragedy that symbolized the theater.

Back and forth he fluctuated, as though literally not knowing whether to laugh or cry.

Finally, unable to tolerate the bizarre changes anymore, she turned her gaze to the coffin. The wind continued to slap at her and change pitch from a deep moan to a piercing shrill. Faintly, she could hear the priest droning on in prayer. When the wind had subsided a little, she looked up again at the spot by the maple tree. Richard was gone.

After Patty left the cemetery she wanted to be alone. She walked aimlessly for miles and welcomed the burning soreness that gradually developed under her feet. At least the pain meant that she wasn't completely without feelings. There was still some life inside her; she hadn't died along with Myles. Only for now most of her feelings were dead. It's only some kind of defense mechanism, she thought dully. Her feelings were dormant, waiting for time to pass—because, as everyone knows, time heals all wounds.

In time everything would be all right, and she would forget about Myles.

Sounds of footsteps suddenly approached her, momentarily jarring her. At first she didn't know where she was, then she recognized the house on her right as Mrs. Mabel's—a grade school teacher. Now Patty knew she was on Crescent Street, about four miles from her own neighborhood.

"Mother?"

Still in a daze, Patty turned around and saw Richard advancing toward her. She calmly looked away, keeping her back to him.

"Don't turn me away like this," she heard him say, his voice a childish whine.

"I need to be alone, Richard."

"I said I was sorry."

"You murdered Myles," she reminded him, her tone dull and lifeless. "Go away."

"Mother, please."

"Go away."

Patty expected another plea, but heard nothing. She looked over her shoulder. The sidewalk behind her was empty except for an elderly woman walking a poodle. Where had Richard disappeared to? Behind a tree? Into somebody's house?

It doesn't matter, she told herself, then walked onward. She didn't want to think about Richard or about Myles. Instead, she concentrated on the increasing agony in her feet. Was this how waitresses and nurses felt? The heels felt flattened and tender, her entire weight pressing down on delicate bones, and her vinyl, almost soleless shoes were suddenly too tight, bunching and rubbing the toes together. Also, there was a tightness in one of her calves. She knew she was going to suffer tomorrow, probably wouldn't even be able to walk, but she didn't care. She kept moving, one street after another.

She saw Richard again. His arms were extended, his countenance pathetically beseeching. She ignored him again.

Madness, she thought, then let only the pain in her feet and legs fill her mind. She continued until she could barely walk anymore. Looking around her, she discovered she had almost made a complete circle around the town. Her own apartment house was only two streets away, but her friend's place was nearby. She could go there, rest for a little while, then return home.

Patty bit down on her lip as she forced her painful legs up the front steps of Kate and Howie's small clapboard home. From outside she could hear loud heavy-metal music, could even feel it vibrating against the front door. She rang the doorbell, wondering if the chime could possibly penetrate the shrill discordancy. She pressed the bell again, then knocked, stinging her knuckles. She was about to give up and continue on homeward when she heard above the music, "Jason, for God's sake, turn that down!" It was Kate's voice yelling at her son.

Then the music markedly dropped and the door opened.

"Why hello, Patty," Kate exclaimed in surprise.

Patty managed a smile. "Hi, Kate. My I come in? My feet are—"

"Of course you can come in." She reached out for Patty's hand and nearly yanked her inside the house, which faintly reeked of cat litter. This smell was quickly confirmed as a Siamese cat leaped off a chair where it'd been sleeping and sprinted out of the room.

"Sit down, make y'self comfy," Kate said, after closing the door.

Patty was more than happy to comply. She sank into a corduroy armchair with a relieved sigh. The living room was cozy, seemingly smaller because of the dark walnut paneling and bright tangerine carpeting. On top of the Mediterranean-style television console was a pseudo-gold and crystal lamp, casting dizzying prisms throughout the room. Kate, she reflected with mild amusement, still had her flamboyant taste.

"Want a drink, kid?" she heard her friend ask.

"No." Patty declined automatically, but then on second thought said, "Yes, something strong."

Kate's right brow lifted in surprise and sympathy. "Like?"

"Vodka and a little tonic."

"You got it." She went to the portable bar, something that Howie, her live-in police officer, obviously had made, for it matched the wall paneling. Above this hung a revolving psychedelic light boasting the cool taste of Busch beer.

"There ya go," Kate said after she had made and given Patty her drink. For herself she had opened a bottle of Miller. "How're you doing?" she asked solicitously.

"Been walking my feet off. God, it feels good to be able to sit down."

Kate, studying her, was not satisfied with the answer. "Want to talk about it? I know it's why you're here."

"I'm here because I couldn't walk another step."

Kate shook her head, refusing to believe her. Gently, she said, "Come on, kid, spit it out."

"I'll be ninety-nine and you'll still be calling me kid," Patty said, but it was with amazement, not petulance. Actually, she liked the nickname; it kept their relationship casual and warm, kept it together and alive in spite of the long absences. She took a long sip of her drink, wincing at the initial pungent taste, then relaxing as the alcohol warmed her. "I walked most of the day, Kate. I must've covered about ten miles."

"Why?" Kate asked, her voice barely audible.

"I don't know, really. I just wanted to do something besides think about . . . about . . ."

"Myles?" Kate supplied gently.

"Yes, Myles." She sighed, then to her surprise and annoyance her chin began to tremble. Quickly she took another sizable sip. From another part of the house tinny rock music still played. "I loved him, Kate," she said. "So much."

"I know."

"We . . . had so many plans. We . . . we . . ." Tears blinded her. "Oh, Kate, why did this have to happen? Why did Richard—" She stopped abruptly, not wanting to talk anymore.

"What about Richard?"

"Nothing."

"Must be something for you to mention it."

Patty sighed, wiping her eyes with Kleenex from a box on a table next to the armchair. She knew her friend would not cease with the questions until she was satisfied with the answers. It was Kate's nature to badger relentlessly, and this was probably why Patty, subconsciously, had come here; she wanted everything that was bothering her pumped out, like poison that she had accidentally swallowed.

She said, "Richard is a stranger, Kate. I'm finding it harder and harder to accept him as my son."

"It's been what, seven, eight years? It's only natural that you two be like strangers. You just gotta be a little more patient, that's all."

"No, Kate. You don't understand."

"Then tell me."

Patty looked up at the ceiling, as though hoping to find the words she was looking for up there. Then she let her eyes roam the room before returning to her friend who was sitting patiently on the couch. "I'm scared of him," she finally admitted. "I think he killed Myles."

Kate stared, nonplussed.

"He was in that truck," Patty went on, "but he didn't even get hurt. Didn't even have a scratch."

It took a few minutes for the words to sink in, then Kate said, "But what makes you believe that he killed Myles?"

Patty told her about the threat on Myles' garage. "He didn't want Myles and me together. I think he was jealous."

"Oh." The single word was a stunned breath.

"Yes. He's not in his right mind, Kate."

"How do you think he killed him?"

"I'm not sure, but I know he did. He even admitted he did, Kate."

"Oh," she whispered again. "Did you tell the police?"

"Yes, and they promised to investigate further, but I don't think they'll ever find any evidence."

"Sure they will, kid. If what you say is true, they'll find out."

"No." Kate shook her head positively. "Richard is too smart for them."

"Don't be silly. My Howie says our police department has some of the best cops and detectives around. They ain't a bunch of hicks like you probably think."

"They never found Richard," Patty reminded her. "He came back on his own."

"Well, yeah, but . . ." Her voice faltered as she failed to think of an explanation.

"Richard's not normal, Kate. He has . . . well, powers, I think."

"What on earth are you talking about?"

Patty saw a flash of skepticism in her friend's face, and she knew her sanity was now being questioned. But, maybe because of the vodka that was starting to relax her, she found herself not caring. She had started this, so she might as well finish. "I think he can read minds," she told her. "He probably can make things move with his mind, too. You know, mind over matter sort of thing. I think that's how he killed Myles. He willed him to drive the truck over that cliff."

"You really believe that?" Kate's skepticism became more evident. Then, to Patty's surprise, it abruptly vanished. Now Kate seemed to be in a pensive trance. There was a long silence, broken only by the muffled, strident music in a distant bedroom.

"What's the matter?" Patty asked.

"I wasn't going to tell you this," she began hesitantly.

"Tell me what?" Patty demanded, at the same time bracing herself, sensing bad news.

"Well, Howie's been hearing talk about your kid at the station. He said that some detective, I think Wheeler's the name, thought he'd found the place where Richard had been staying for the last eight years. Said something about a rundown, deserted building thirty miles from here. Said the place had been in a fire once and was now just a charred shell, rotting away in a dumpy neighborhood. The reason he found the place was 'cuz he'd been asking around if anybody knew a man and a kid who lived together in a boarded-up house. It's what your kid had told him, y'know, and it was the only thing he had to go on.

"Well, he finally found one place that fit the description, and according to a few witnesses the kid had black hair and was slight of build. The man with him, though, seemed to be inconsistent. Some said he was tall and blond, and some said he was dark and squatty. One even said it was a woman who lived with the kid in that house. But most claimed it was a tall, dark man. Very handsome." Kate stopped when she saw that her bottle was empty and that Patty's glass contained only ice cubes. "Want another?"

Patty looked down at the drink in her hand. So absorbed in what Kate was telling her, she was surprised to find she had drunk it all. "Yes, please," she said.

Kate refilled Patty's glass, then opened another Miller for herself. "Anyway," she continued once she was back on the couch, "Wheeler had a picture of Richard."

"It was an old picture I gave him." Patty nodded, remembering. "He was only five."

"Yeah, but everyone from that neighborhood still recognized him. He didn't change all that much, only got taller, that's all. But . . ." Kate's voice trailed away, as though uncertain whether or not to finish the story.

"But what?" Patty prompted.

"But it wasn't him. Couldn't of been."

"Why not?"

"Because they, the police from that town, had found him two months ago in that house . . . dead."

Patty stared at her, not comprehending.

"There had been complaints of a rotten smell, so the cops investigated and found this kid hanging from a rope. It looked like the kid in the picture, but of course it wasn't. That's why Wheeler never bothered to tell you about it."

Patty felt something worm its way inside her. She wasn't quite sure what the something was, but it was cold. Still she could not comprehend what her friend was saying. Or rather, she was refusing to comprehend. "But why are you telling me?" she asked in a small voice.

Kate seemed uncertain herself. "You were talking about your kid not being right, about weird stuff like having powers. So I thought about the weird story

Howie had told me. Gee, I didn't upset you or anything, did I?"

"No, of course not."

"Richard is still alive, so there's no way it
could've been him," Kate said pointedly.

"That's right," Patty agreed. *I've no reason to be
upset. The kid in that house was dead. It couldn't
possibly have been Richard. Only resembled him,
that's all.*

Richard was alive and well, living in . . .

"What—what happened to the man he lived
with?" she asked.

"Disappeared."

The one-word reply was soft, almost a whisper,
yet it had the impact of a bullet. *Disappeared? You
mean, like the way Richard's daddy disappeared that
night years ago, after his mindboggling performance?
Again just before the police came? Did he disappear
like that?*

"Hey, Patty, are you all right?"

"What?" Patty looked up; she had been staring
reflectively into the drink in her hand.

"You're looking pale all of a sudden."

"Oh, I'm fine. Really." She forced a smile, but it
didn't convince Kate. "I think I should be going. Take
a nice hot bath when I get home and then try to get
some sleep." She set the half-emptied glass on the
table and got up. "I'm sorry, but I can't finish my
drink."

"That's okay. Hey, maybe you should sleep here.
Jason can sleep on the couch and you could use his
room."

"Thanks, but there's no need."

"You sure?"

Patty nodded, smiling gratefully. When she left
the house, the smile faded and the cold worm inside
her grew larger and colder.

The kid in that house was dead. It was only a

weird coincidence that he had looked like Richard, and that he had lived alone with a man in a deserted house. But it couldn't possibly have been Richard.

Could it?

Of course not. Nobody can return from the dead.

Can they?

Don't be silly! The dead stay dead.

Don't they?

But when she reached her apartment and glanced into Richard's room and found him staring out the window, she wasn't too sure. Especially when he sensed her presence, slowly turned around and gave her a smile.

For one fleeting moment she could have sworn it was a skull grinning back at her.

PART THREE

PENDULUM

18

Patty locked herself in her bedroom. Repeatedly, she told herself that it couldn't be true that Richard was the dead boy found hanging in an abandoned house. A lot of boys had dark hair and were slender. And besides, the picture she had given Detective Wheeler was an old one, taken when Richard was five years old. No, that boy who had died was definitely someone else.

So why was she still feeling uneasy?

As if of their own volition her hands opened a bureau drawer and rummaged through old letters, empty bottles of perfume, and other items that she had saved as souvenirs. This drawer was her treasure chest, for it held everything that had been precious to her in the past. Her mother used to complain that she was a junk collector, placing value on stuff that most people would burn, but Patty never could part with anything that had been important to her, no matter how cheap the item or brief the time. She still had all her valentine cards from grade school, even a plastic pseudo-pearl necklace that she'd won at a traveling carnival. But now her hands rejected these souvenirs. It was something specific they were seeking, not a stroll down memory lane.

Finally her hand touched a small square box and pulled it out from under the other souvenirs, exposing it to the light perhaps for the first time in over two decades. Patty stared down at the box, which was no bigger than her palm and weighed practically nothing. She asked herself why she had looked for this, but her subconscious remained silent, like a separate being that was ignoring her, at the same time using her body for a secretive purpose.

The small cardboard box in her hand used to be white, but now it was yellowish. She could remember when it was given to her by her mother and father. They had been so proud of her, had hugged her and had thrown a little party that consisted mostly of aunts and uncles. She had been a churchgoer then, a good Catholic. She remembered the white, lacy dress and veil she had worn. And she remembered thinking she was like a bride, except that her legs were showing—legs that were too skinny and knees too big. But the wedding dress, she had told herself, would cover this and she would be much prettier.

Her memory of that day when she had her first communion was all so vivid. The day itself was warm and golden with sunshine. She could almost smell the white carnation that a nun had pinned to her dress. Reverently, Patty ran the fingers of her other hand across the top of the box. When she had made her first communion she had wanted to be a nun, but that had changed along with her body. She finally opened the box and took out its contents—a gold crucifix on a chain.

Moving to the mirror she put it around her neck, surprised that it still fit, although it was tight, looking more like a choker than a necklace. She made no move to take it off. She didn't like the way it looked on her, bringing out the deep ladderlike wrinkles on her throat, but she'd keep it on just the same. Because it was what her subconscious wanted.

Her family's safety became her main concern. Would Richard hurt them, kill them as he had killed Myles? Should she call the police again, plead with them to take the boy away and examine him? She knew she should do something but couldn't decide what.

At length she went to her mother, who had decided to retire early to her room. She was already in bed when Patty knocked on her door.

"Ma, can I talk to you?" she whispered, then glanced around her to be certain Richard wasn't close by.

"Come in," Lydia replied tiredly.

Patty entered, closing the door behind her while her mother, dramatically struggling to a sitting position, reached for her glasses on the nightstand.

"You're wearing a cross," Lydia exclaimed in surprise the moment the spectacles were on.

"Not so loud."

"Why? Who ain't supposed to hear?" Lydia asked, but lowering her voice just the same.

"Richard." Patty sat at the foot of the bed. She could remember when she was a teenager and had sat like this with her mother. They had talked about so many things, about her school crushes, about clothes and hairdos. Her mother had been like a friend of equal age then. It all changed when Dad died. After that her mother aged rapidly, developing one ailment after another.

"What about Richard?" Lydia demanded. "Please don't be too long, Patricia. My neck is killing me. Must've hurt it when that crazy driver made that horrible corner at the cemetery."

"You'll be all right, Ma," Patty automatically assured her.

"Why are you wearing that cross?"

"I'm not sure, but it seems the right thing to do."

"What on earth are you talking about?" Lydia

said impatiently.

"I feel a little more secure with it on."

"You're making no sense, Patricia, and if you don't start soon, I'm going to have to ask you to leave. I need all the sleep I can get, y'know."

"Ma, Myles' death was no accident."

Lydia's face tightened, but she said nothing.

"That's right," Patty said emphatically, "no accident. He was murdered."

Lydia looked away from her, as though not wanting to hear any more.

"Richard did it," Patty ruthlessly went on. Her mother, she knew, was already aware of this but had not accepted it, dismissing it as something she must have heard wrong.

"You don't know for sure," the woman finally said, now looking back at her.

"He admitted it. You were there, you heard him."

There was a long silence. The small clock ticked loudly on the nightstand.

"God, Ma, what am I going to do?"

"You sure he . . . killed Myles?" Lydia still couldn't seem to grasp this.

"Yes, Ma. Yes."

"But how did he do it?"

"I don't know. Richard didn't tell me, only that he did it. But I think he has abilities to do things with his mind."

Lydia stared blankly at her, then said, "Did you tell the police this?"

Patty nodded. "But they have nothing on him. They said they'll keep looking into it."

"And that's why you're wearing the cross?"

"There's more," Patty said, avoiding the question. "I don't know if it's anything, but—"

"Spit it out, Patricia. Don't keep me waiting like this. You and that damn child have been doing a number on my heart as it is."

"Ma, please, keep your voice down." Patty glanced nervously at the closed door and the crack beneath it to assure herself no one was standing on the other side, listening. "I don't want him to hear us."

"Tell me what you were going to say," Lydia demanded, now in a harsh whisper.

"People have recognized Richard in the picture Detective Wheeler has shown them, and they said he had hanged himself."

"A mistake, obviously."

"I guess, but—"

"But what?"

"Well, what if it's true? What if he is dead?"

"Then who's the boy living here?"

"Richard."

"You're not making sense again, Patricia."

"What if he has returned from the dead, Ma?"

Lydia gawked at her, then shook her head, a gesture that was too vigorous to be sincere. "Now you're really not making any sense. Look, I'm tired and—"

"You believe it's too farfetched?"

"Of course it is."

"You saw his father. You were in the room with me," Patty reminded her. "After seeing what happened, would you call it farfetched?"

Lydia fell silent. Her head began to tremble, as though suddenly too heavy for the neck to support. Until now Patty hadn't realized how old her mother actually looked. She appeared weathered, frightened and beaten, like an ancient house gradually weakening through a century of brutal storms and at last beginning to sag and crumble.

A wave of sympathy and guilt surged through Patty. It was all her fault. Her mother hadn't exaggerated when she blamed her and "that damn child" for doing a number on her heart.

"Are you sure?" Lydia asked.

"No, Ma, I'm just assuming. But what if it is true? What do we do?"

"If it's true, then why is he here? What does he want?"

"I don't know."

"Why did he kill Myles anyway? Are you sure of that? Maybe he was lying."

"Maybe, but I don't think so."

"Why not?"

"You wouldn't think he was lying either if you'd seen him. The truth was all over his face, in his eyes. The hate was too real. He had it from the first day he met him."

"The hate for Myles?"

Patty nodded.

"Why did he hate him?"

"Because he wouldn't stay away from me. Richard was jealous, I think."

"Jealous?" Lydia whispered incredulously. "Jealous because a man was with his mother?" She still couldn't seem to believe it.

"It seems that way."

"Oh God." Lydia blessed herself with a quick sign of the cross. "Get him out of here, Patricia. At once!"

"But I've no proof."

"You should've never kept him in the first place. Do you realize that now?"

"Ma, let's not go through that again. Let's just try to be calm and think of what to do."

"Which of course, is obvious. You're not thinking of keeping him here, I should hope."

"It isn't that simple. I can't just throw him out."

"But you can't keep him here either." Lydia's eyes were wild, shiny from the glow of the lamp beside the bed. "God, no, Patricia. If he's some kind of—ghost—get rid of him!"

"I said it's not that easy," Patty retorted, feeling herself on the verge of hysteria. She hugged herself, but still her body trembled. She was frightened and confused, and her mother wasn't helping her any. "I don't know what to do," she sobbed.

Lydia, aware that she was panicking and at the same time disturbing her daughter, began muttering to herself to be calm. Then she reached for a cigarette on the night table. "Maybe we can send him to a foster home," she suggested, after lighting the cigarette.

"He'd never go."

"Maybe the law can force him."

"I don't think anyone can force him to do anything. He refused to see a doctor, so Myles tried to trick him. That's where he was going when . . . the accident happened."

"There's got to be something we can do, but we can't keep him here."

"Why is he back? What does he want?" Patty experienced another cold tremor that a self-embrace couldn't steady. "Maybe he's not dead. Maybe we're overreacting. I mean, there's no such thing as a corpse walking around like a living person, is there? There'd be a smell. He'd be rotting away." Again her body shook, and her teeth began chattering. "Oh God, make it not true."

"Maybe a spirit is preserving the body, making it function," Lydia mused.

"What kind of spirit?"

"I don't know. What do you suppose his father was?"

"I never wanted to think too much about it."

"Cover y'self," Lydia ordered, peeling one of several blankets off her bed. Patty gratefully accepted, wrapping the blanket around her shoulders, although she knew it would not do much to still her. When she was ten she had been caught in a summer storm and had sought shelter from the rain under a big maple. Not too far away lightning struck a pine tree. When she saw the smoking destruction and realized that she could have easily chosen that pine tree instead of the maple, she had begun to shake uncontrollably. It had taken an hour for her to calm down. Fear had gripped and shaken her, exactly as it was doing right now. Nothing would stop her; she knew she'd have to wait it out.

"Maybe you're right. Maybe we are overreacting," she heard Lydia say, apparently endeavoring to soothe her. "First we should be certain about Richard, then we'll go from there."

"How can we prove it?"

There was a laugh, but it came from neither woman. Patty spun around, pulling the blanket tighter around her. She and Lydia gasped simultaneously.

The laughter faded, then Richard's mouth closed in a tight, grim line. Until now Patty had never noticed that her son's lips were chapped and bloodless, almost the same paleness as his skin. She edged backward, until she was close to her mother, who was still in bed but pressing against the headboard.

"Grandmother, Mother . . ." He addressed them slowly, eyeing each woman in turn ". . . do you truly believe that I am—dead?"

No one answered. Patty's hand rose to the gleaming crucifix on her neck. Richard's eyes shot toward it in surprise.

"And what is this, Mother?" His voice cracked slightly. He stared at the golden pendant for a long moment, then looked up at his mother's face, demanding an answer.

"I . . . I got this when I made my first communion."

Richard's gaze fell again on the cross. He seemed

raptly fascinated with it. He took a step forward, then stopped, hesitating. There was something that disturbed him, yet allured him. He reached out, skeletal hand trembling, then drew back, as though recoiling.

"You've been eavesdropping," Lydia accused in false bravado.

Richard slowly turned his head to meet her gaze. "My hearing is acute," he said concisely, then returned to the crucifix, again his hand out in obvious longing to touch it.

Patty moved away from him, until her back was against a wall. She was still shaking, now confused as well as frightened. She couldn't understand what the boy was doing, why he was alternately reaching out and recoiling. What she found more alarming was the abrupt shifting of facial expressions. Whenever his hand was extended an eerie glow would brighten his face and his eyes would gleam bluish, like a sparkling sky. And when he yanked his hand back, as though burnt, the face would darken, the lips lifted to bare teeth, and the eyes would glint reddish, reminding Patty of bicycle reflectors in the dark.

"This is my room, may I remind you," Lydia said, her chin up in defiance.

Patty could tell that her mother was afraid but was determined not to show it. She wanted to warn her not to say anything more, lest Richard's temper flare up, but the changes in her son's face left her mesmerized.

"Why are you wearing it now, Mother?" he asked, stepping closer, pausing, stepping back. It was as if there were a switch inside him that someone was flicking on and off.

"What is it you want, Richard?" Patty hedged.

"Answer my question first."

Patty fingered the cross as her mind searched for an answer. At length she said, "Why should I have a reason? I happened to find it in my bureau drawer and . . . and . . ."

"You are lying to me, and you should know by now that you can't lie to me."

"But I'm not, Richard. No. I really did find it in my bureau."

"You knew it was there all along, and because of me you took it out and are now wearing it." It was a statement and Richard's face filled with contempt as he said it.

Patty took in a long breath, desperately wishing she could stop trembling and garner courage and strength. "Does this bother you?" she asked of the crucifix.

"Yes. No," he said, staring longingly, then resentfully at it. "I don't know. I'm confused. I'm . . . Take it off, Mother!" he suddenly ordered, punctuating the demand with a low, almost inaudible growl from somewhere deep inside him.

Patty flinched, pushing against the wall behind her, gripping the crucifix at her neck. "No!"

Richard glared, the growl rising from the depth of him, rumbling louder.

"No, no!" Patty cried in determination, then squeezed her eyes shut. She tried to think of a prayer to say, but it had been so long. *Our Father who art in Heaven* . . . she began, but couldn't remember the rest. She switched to *Hail Mary, full of grace* but drew a blank.

Then she realized the horrible growling had ceased. She opened her eyes. Richard was now close to her and she could smell the cloying odor of overripe apples on the verge of rot. She tensed, determined not to breathe in.

"May I have it, Mother?" His voice was now gentle and the glow was back in his face. His eyes, she saw, were clear, serene pools. "I need it more than you do. Please, Mother."

Numbly, she shook her head.

"Please." It was almost a sob.

"Go away, Richard. You're frightening me."

"That's right. You heard your mother," Lydia intervened. "And this is my room, so get out—now!"

"Shut your mouth, old lady," Richard snarled, spinning his head toward her on the bed, the pools in his eyes now fiery volcanic craters.

Lydia flinched, but her lips tightened in determination not to quiver. "That is no way to speak—"

Richard suddenly broke into a howl, but it was not in wrath from the woman's words, but from the cross that Patty had unexpectedly broken free from her neck and thrust into his face.

"Get away from me," she commanded in a quavering voice. When she saw that he was indeed retreating she felt a surge of confidence. "Away, I said!"

At the door he hesitated, and she could see his countenance was beginning to change again, to soften. Impulsively, she jabbed his left shoulder with the blunt end of the crucifix. Richard shrieked in excruciating agony, but that was not the only sound that electrified the air and made the hairs on Patty's arms stiffen. There was a loud hiss upon contact, a harsh sizzling that one hears when dropping oil onto a hot skillet.

"Fucking whore!" Richard snarled, grabbing his shoulder. There was no sign of a wound, only a faint tendril of smoke and a sulfuric odor. As he clutched the area where she had touched him, his face completed the transformation. Now there was sadness in his eyes. "Why, Mother?" he cried, like a small child who had just been severely chastised. "Why do you always want to hurt me?"

And before she could answer he retreated from the room, his shoulders hunched forward in dejection.

Minutes after he was gone Patty was still holding onto the cross. She could feel its four tips puncturing the palm in her clenched fist, and still she wouldn't let go, for the pain, although faint, felt good. It made her feel secure.

On the bed Lydia sat in stunned silence, a hand pressing against her mouth, whitening the flesh around it. She stared at the now empty doorway, and her eyes, magnified double-fold by the glasses, mirrored an explosion of terror—terror that until now, she had managed to suppress.

19

In the confines of her room, the door locked with a chair tucked under the knob (just in case), Patty drank vodka, having discarded the tonic water after the first drink, in an attempt to steady her shivering body. After the second glass she finally ceased to tremble, but her mind was still a whirlwind. She doubted if any amount of alcohol would dull it tonight.

Her son was a murderer.

Her son was a walking corpse.

How could she live with that? And how could she expose her family to the dangers? If Richard could kill Myles, he could kill anyone in this apartment. And if it were true that he was not human anymore, then there was no telling what he was capable of.

With one hand Patty lifted the colorless drink to her mouth, and with the other touched the cross that was again around her neck. She fingered it frequently, to reassure herself it was still there.

Was all this happening because she had stopped going to church? And exactly when had she stopped? She remembered being a faithful Catholic. She had gone to confession every month, although there really had been nothing to confess. *Bless me father, for I have sinned.* Was it after high school that she had quit? Yes, it was about that time, she remembered now. She had thought the church was only a crutch for the weak, and since her mother had stopped going (because she couldn't sit on the hard pew or kneel for too long) Patty had done the same. And since then God had ceased to exist in her life.

Was this His way of punishing her?

She wanted to pray and confess to the ceiling as she lay in her bed, but didn't know if He would be offended. Did He ignore those who had ignored Him at times when He was not needed? Or was it true that He was all-forgiving? Patty reached for the gold crucifix, sheathed it with her hand until the metal had grown warm, then let go.

She would have to do something, but first she needed proof—proof that he was no longer alive. Was the hiss and smoke she witnessed when the crucifix had touched Richard's skin proof? No. There could be an explanation for that phenomenon. She needed more.

With the help of alcohol, she mustered courage. She decided she'd confront him, ask him outright what he was. Dead or alive? She'd even demand proof if he should claim the former.

Staggering slightly, she made her way in the dark to her son's small room. She boldly switched on the ceiling light, but to her surprise found the room empty. The bed was still made, smooth without even an indentation of anyone having had sat on it. And come to think of it, when was the last time she'd seen Richard in it? He was usually at the window, in an eerie trance. Was this proof that he was not alive?

Then another realization occurred to her. When was the last time she'd seen her son eat? Since his return he hadn't had a meal, not even a snack that she could recall. Was this more proof?

And where was he now?

A faint smell lingered in the room, and Patty immediately recognized the scent—it was of Richard. It was that overripe smell. Did this mean he was nearby? But where? In the next room, which was the kitchen?

Patty felt her courage slip and wished she had brought her bottle of vodka with her. A thought entered her mind, unnerving her even more. Could Richard be in the walls? Could he be watching her right now?

Patty began to back out of the room, again reaching for the holy emblem around her neck. Then, as she reached the doorway, she spun around. That was when she saw him.

Richard stood in the kitchen, a scant inch away from where the light from his bedroom stopped. He had been watching her. Although he was completely in shadow Patty could see his dark frame clearly and at the unexpected sight of him let out a gasp.

He quietly waited for an explanation.

Patty gulped, refilling her lungs with air that had been snatched away from her. "I . . . I came to talk to you, Richard."

The boy didn't move from the shadows. Was he keeping his distance because of the crucifix? She reached for it. He took a small step back, deeper into the shadows. Or was this only her imagination?

Patty contemplated moving forward and turning the light on in the kitchen, but the switch was on the other side of the room. And she didn't have the nerve to join him in the darkness.

"Richard, please come in here." Where there is light, she thought.

Her son still made no reply, but there was faint, raspy breathing. Again her imagination?

"Richard, *please*."

The harsh breathing subsided, then the boy moved forward into the brightness of his room. Patty half-expected to see a face twisted in a contemptuous sneer and was ready for it, hand still at her neck, but what she witnessed instead was a teenage boy in torment. Richard's head was low, his shoulders high; he was stripped of all spirit and confidence. He glanced at her, then quickly away, as though the sight of her alone was too agonizing to bear. This, she thought, was a picture of defeat.

"Richard, what is happening?" she whispered, feeling her heart reaching out for him. Yet she still could not bring herself to touch or hold him. "Please, tell me. There's so much I don't understand."

His head still bowed, he looked up at her through ebony lashes. "I love you, Mother," he said quietly.

The words did not warm her, as they would if Janet or Frankie had uttered them. Instead, they did the exact opposite—and Richard knew this, for she could see it in his expression. Never had she seen so much hurt in one's face. Briefly, she thought of rectifying this by telling him that she loved him, too, but she knew he wouldn't believe the lie.

"You're not answering my question," she said at length.

"What is happening, Mother, is that you're depriving me of the most important thing I want, what I need."

"That's still not what I am asking."

Richard's head rose an inch from its dropped position. "Just what is it you are asking?"

Patty opened her mouth, deciding to be blunt, but she quickly found it wasn't that easy. A moment passed between them, and Richard's head lifted another inch, now looking evenly at her. Patty licked her lips, then finally blurted out, "Are you alive?"

There was no sudden bellow of laughter, as she had half-expected. No denial or admission, either. Only a quiet question in response. "What do you think, Mother?"

"I don't know."

"You are not being truthful."

"No." She clutched the cross tighter in her fist.

"No what?" he pressed.

"You're not . . . alive." The last word was faint, even to her own ears.

Again there was no eruption of laughter. Richard studied her, and his look of sadness began to fade. The temperature seemed to be dropping in the room, and as it descended, his eyes began to harden, as if they were actually filled with water and were gradually turning to ice.

He lifted his head another inch. Now he was peering down at her.

"You believe you are speaking to a dead person, Mother?" There was amusement in his voice.

"I want proof, Richard," she demanded timidly.

"What kind of proof?"

"Any kind."

"And what will you do if I give you some?"

See that you are back where you belong—in the grave, Patty thought. Out loud, she said, "I'll try to help in any way I can."

This time he laughed, a quick, disdainful bark. "By pushing me into the grave is what you were thinking, Mother."

Patty felt herself spinning, partly from the alcohol she'd drunk and partly from the unrelenting grip of fear. She had momentarily forgotten his ability to read minds.

"Is this why you are here?" he said when Patty didn't respond. "To find proof?"

"I wasn't snooping for it. I was going to ask you."

Suddenly the curtains in the window behind her fluttered, then snapped whiplike in the air. She spun around just in time to see them sigh and settle limply back in place.

"The wind, do you think?" Richard said.

The window, Patty noted, was closed.

"Or do you suppose it was me, Mother?"

Numbly, Patty turned back to her son. Mockery glittered in his eyes.

"Well, what do you think?" he asked. "Your mind is a blank, like Grandmother's most of the time. That can be quite boring. Think of something, Mother. Entertain me."

Evil, Patty thought before realizing what she was doing.

Richard gave another bark of laughter. "Chip off the old block, is that it? Father's block."

"Why did you come back, Richard?"

The cruel grin that had accompanied the laugh began to falter. *The pendulum is swinging the other way again*, Patty thought.

"Yes, the fucking pendulum!" Richard agreed with surprising vehemence. "Back and forth. Black and white. The goddamned, fucking pendulum!"

Alarmed by the sudden shift of emotion, Patty unfastened the chain on her neck and threateningly brandished the crucifix in front of the boy. He recoiled, but only stepped back a few inches. Then, like one who needed time to adjust to blinding light, he moved forward again, no longer repelled by the object in his mother's hand.

The timing was wrong, Patty suddenly realized. His eyes were starting to melt again. She would have to wait until they froze back to ice.

"Do you love me at all, Mother?" he asked abruptly, startling her.

"You're my son. Of course I love you."

"You are lying." He squinted, as though straining to see through her. "I do not sense any love from you, except maybe a fraction. Do you love Frankie better than Janet?"

"Of course not."

"You are lying again. I sense that you foolishly adore Frankie. You are proud that he is the strongest in his class, that he is handsome and can attract so many girls."

"But I'm proud of Janet, too."

"Why?"

The suddenness of the one-word question rendered her speechless for a moment. "Well, because . . . because she studies hard and gets good grades."

"You love them according to their achievements?" He sounded amazed.

"Of course not. Richard, why are you asking these questions?"

"No matter what you say, I still sense it is Frankie you love more."

"Okay, maybe it's true. Maybe I do, just a little bit. But I still love Janet very, very much."

"But not me."

Patty considered denying this, then changed her mind. It was useless, especially since he could sense the truth. But how could she expect her to love him now?

"Do you love Grandmother?" he asked.

"Of course." Actually, she had never given it much thought.

"Grandmother doesn't love me."

Patty, not sure if this was a question or a statement, remained silent.

"She called me a mistake," he went on. "I remember that so very clearly. And I believe that she convinced you of this."

"No, that's not—"

"Do not insult my intelligence. It is so much greater than yours. From the very beginning Grandmother tried to turn you against me. She is one of the reasons that you failed to love me."

"No, Richard, that's not entirely true."

"It is. If she had not repeatedly reminded you that I was someone to fear, you would have overcome it, would have loved me. You did fear me then as you fear me now, didn't you, Mother?"

Patty instinctively shook her head in denial, but stopped abruptly when he said, "But the answer in your mind is yes."

"This is not fair," Patty sobbed.

"Fair? There are so many things that are not fair. You're not fair to me. You love Frankie more than Janet, and Janet so much more than me. That's not fair!"

Patty turned her head away from him, partly with shame, but she could still feel his unwavering scrutiny. It was a full minute before he spoke again.

"I don't like Grandmother, either," he stated. "In fact, I hate Grandmother. I hate her because she stopped you from loving me."

"Richard, please . . ."

"Did you love Myles?" he suddenly asked, startling her with the unexpected change of subject. Even his voice had changed a little, become lighter, although the edge of resentment was still evident. Before Patty could respond, he added, "Or was it his cock you loved?"

"Stop it!"

"You loved everybody, Mother—for all kinds of reasons—but you never loved me. Why?"

"Go away, Richard." She thrust the cross at him, but he ignored it. The eyes were soft and doleful again. This constant change in him was maddening!

She began to shiver, and suddenly she realized she hadn't been trembling for a while. Now it was starting again, and only the vodka and time would quell it.

"Go away," she implored. "Go away!"

The curtains behind her stirred again, then flapped as though the window were a bird and the flanking curtains its wings. She almost expected it to take flight, expected the window to rip itself from the wall and soar across the room. But instead, the curtains tore loose, whisked through the air as if caught in a violent windstorm, and tangled themselves around Patty, who let out a petrified gasp.

"Is it the wind or me?" she heard Richard query in a singsong voice above the angry flapping of curtains, a sound which reminded her of sheets on a clothesline on a windy day. The curtains wrapped themselves around her, cutting off her vision, snaking around her throat. She spun around to uncoil the curtains but succeeded only in tangling herself further. She dropped the crucifix.

"The wind or me?" she heard Richard sing again. This time his voice was high-pitched, almost as sibilant as a wind.

Panic exploded inside her. She frantically tried to peel the thin, translucent material off her face, but it clung to her like spiderwebs. She gasped for breath, already feeling her lungs burn, but instead of sucking in air she pulled in some of the fabric.

Somebody help me! Help me! her mind screamed. She spun around and around, mummifying herself, then collapsed in a heap on the floor as the curtains crushed her knees together.

Help me! Help me! her mind was now sobbing. *God, please, please help me.*

To her relief the cotton serpents began to slacken and became nothing more than innocuous strips of cloth. With ease she found herself able to move her arms and push the curtains away from her face. Had she panicked needlessly? She would have thought so, but as she looked around, still partly wrapped on the floor, she discovered that Richard was gone. And that wasn't all.

The crucifix was gone, too.

20

Through the prompting cheers and applause from the audience as a young black woman spun "The Wheel of Fortune," Lydia faintly heard her daughter calling to her. The voice did not seem real; it sounded distant, from another dimension, from a place called the *Twilight Zone.* Only the sounds from the TV set were real, close to her.

"Ma, did you hear me?"

Lydia stepped away from her particular reality and entered that other world, which she was beginning to dislike more and more. This world was nice when her husband, bless his precious soul, was alive. And it was somewhat tolerable when there were just the four of them. And for a while, when Myles was with them it was okay. But now, ever since . . .

"Ma, are you losing your hearing or what?"

"Yes," Lydia agreed, looking up at her daughter. "I think I am losing my hearing. Might be needing a hearing aid shortly."

"I'm going to see a priest," Patty said.

"Whatever for?"

"I want to talk to him about Richard. Get an opinion. Maybe even some help."

Lydia felt her chest tighten and fought the impulse to clutch it. She heard the TV audience clap and welcomed the uplifting sound, letting it fill her head until she felt closer to the people on the screen and farther away from Patty who was standing mere inches away from her.

"Ma?" Patty's voice was loud now, demanding attention.

"The black woman's winning," she murmured. "But the idiot can't solve the puzzle, and it's so obvious. *A Tale of Two Cities* is the answer. You'd think she'd get it by now."

"Ma, do you want to come with me?"

"I'd love to, but I'm not feeling too good t'day. Something's wrong with my ankle. Must've twisted it the wrong way."

"You sure you don't want to come? Janet and Frankie are in school and you'll be alone with—"

"About time!" Lydia shouted, but it was at the black contestant on the screen. The woman had finally guessed the puzzle, and now the audience was ecstatic. Even Lydia found herself clapping.

"Ma, you're not paying attention," she heard Patty say in a low, harsh whisper, speaking as though she were the mother and Lydia the daughter. Where was her respect? Certainly she didn't raise Patty to talk to her like this.

"What is it, Patricia?"

"I think you should come with me."

"But *All My Children* is coming on next. You know it's my favorite."

Patty hesitated, not knowing what to do. "Ma, you sure you won't mind being alone with him?"

Lydia absently shook her head as she watched the woman on TV select her prizes.

"Well, I won't be gone long," Patty promised, then reluctantly started to leave. It wasn't until she had her spring coat on and was opening the front door that Lydia spoke again.

"All right if I borrow the crucifix?"

Patty stared dumbly at her. "Crucifix?"

"Yes." Lydia pulled her attention away from the game show to look at her daughter. She was surprised to see a face so filled with fear, a hard concrete cage imprisoning eyes that were wild and skittish like two frightened animal seeking escape. "You won't be needing the crucifix to see a priest. So while you're gone why don't you let me have it for a while?"

"I don't have it anymore, Ma. I think Richard took it."

Lydia felt that tightness in her chest again.

"Maybe you should come with me," Patty insisted.

"No, I . . . I'll be all right. My show's coming on in a few minutes." And as if to prove this, she turned her attention to the TV set. "Don't wanna miss it."

"Ma, this is no time to be proud or stubborn. Come with me."

Lydia blocked her out, which was so easy to do, for she had done it many times before, especially to Richard. All you had to do was channel everything into the 19-inch screen and pretend it was the only world that existed. Soon you'd forget the other world, even forget about the chair you were in. Yes, it was easy, almost like magic.

But when Patty finally left, closing the door behind her, Lydia discovered that the magic no longer worked. She couldn't lose herself to the TV program. No matter how hard she concentrated to make the transition from one world to the next, she couldn't forget where she was—alone in the apartment with Richard.

The interior of Richard's narrow porch/bedroom was like the center of a wrathful storm. As the boy stood in the middle of the room he steadily exuded a stream of hate, a force that was as harsh as electricity and as furious as a hurricane. A magnetic attraction began to develop, intensifying as his rage grew. His bed slowly inched toward him, and the curtains that had coiled themselves around his mother the night before slid across the floor, then clung against him, like static-charged socks on a soap commercial. His long hair stiffened, porcupinelike, as the fury mounted. His eyes bulged, filling and swelling with violent emotion, as though ready to pop and explode like summits of volcanic mountains.

His father had been right. His mother did not love him.

The blanket tore free from the mattress, flew toward Richard and adhered itself to him. Another blanket followed, then a pillow, and finally a sheet.

And it was his grandmother's fault. His father had told him about her. Told him that she would never let her daughter love him, although he was the son, a part of her.

The bed touched him. The window bulged, fighting the force that was pulling it inward.

Richard had hoped that there would be a chance that his mother still had some loving feelings toward him, feelings that could help give him what he needed, but he'd seen it all clearly last night. There was only fear in her. Maybe there was a spark of maternal love, but not enough for it to matter. And this realization frustrated and infuriated him.

After his mother had left he stood for several hours in the center of the room, clenching and un-clenching his fists at his sides, letting emotions simmer, then boil inside him. Now they were past the boiling point, vapors gushing out from every pore and filling the room with stormy hatred.

If Grandmother had not interfered, there would have been a chance.

Richard's fists pressed the sides of his head, as though straining to alleviate the pressure within, to keep his skull from bursting. He whined, then howled.

He hated his grandmother. Hated her more than he had ever hated anyone else.

Finally the window could not resist the force any longer. With a loud *pop* it imploded and rained horizontally on Richard, spearing him with countless shards. The triangular splinters were like pins on a voodoo doll, many of them remaining embedded without falling to the floor.

He never cried out in pain, for his hatred toward his grandmother overwhelmed all other feelings.

Lydia heard something.

She tried to ignore it, even telling herself the sound came from the apartment across the hall. It was a dog, she quickly surmised. Although no pets were allowed, maybe someone had snuck one in anyway. Nothing to be concerned about.

The black woman on TV was now trying to win a brand new Chevy wagon and selecting the letters to put into the puzzle.

Another noise. This one didn't sound like a whining puppy. It was more like a howling wolf. The flesh on Lydia's arms roughened to tingly bumps. In her veins cold blood flowed.

She again told herself the sound came from the next apartment. Or from downstairs. Or even from the TV.

A crash! Sharp and violent, as if a light fixture had exploded. No, it would have to be something bigger, she thought. Something like . . . like a window.

It came from next door, she told herself.

The black contestant was now concentrating on the puzzle, and time was running out. But it was so simple. Couldn't she see that the answer was Carol Burnett? How dumb can you be? If you can't guess this, then you don't deserve a new car.

Another noise. Another wolflike howl.

"Carol Burnett, dummy! Burnett!" Lydia shouted at the set, but her voice sounded strange to her ears. It was weak and shaky, filled with fear.

The buzzer went on. The game was over and the woman had lost. She and the audience groaned simultaneously. Then another groan came from—next door? downstairs? TV?—Richard's room.

Lydia reluctantly turned her head in the direction of her grandson's room, which was off the kitchen and out of view from where she was sitting. She could no longer deceive herself or ignore what she had heard. The sounds definitely came from the boy's room, and something was happening in there.

Lydia was tempted to investigate, but was too afraid. She glanced back at the screen. A Hawaiian Punch commercial was on now, and she realized her mouth was dry. After a moment of deliberation, she finally decided to go into the kitchen for a drink. She'd stay away from the boy's room, that's all. But after she poured herself a glass of Diet Coke from the refrigerator, she found herself standing by Richard's door, listening.

At first she could hear nothing, then gradually she made out heavy breathing. It sounded somewhat like a jogger who had just completed his long run, catching his breath. It was loud, labored, and even raspy. No, not a jogger, Lydia thought, more like an animal, like a dog on a hot day, panting, but not panting wearily. No, more like panting . . . peevishly. A rabid dog panting. Yes, just like that Stephen King movie she'd seen not too long ago. *Cujo*. That dog had repeatedly rammed a Ford Pinto, had killed people, had . . .

With a cry Lydia staggered away from the door. She didn't like what her imagination was doing, the way it was scaring her. With her glass of soda in hand, she hurried back to the safety of her recliner. Her soaps were starting now. Good, this would keep her mind off the boy.

But after five minutes had passed, she looked up at the clock on top of the TV and wondered what on earth was keeping Patricia so long. Now she wished she had gone with her. There was an uneasy feeling inside her that she couldn't ignore, no matter how hard she concentrated on the TV program. It was a feeling that something bad was going to happen— very soon.

Richard spun around toward the closed door. He could not see a presence but could sense one. It was his grandmother. The fucking cow was listening, listening as hate poured like black steam out of him, polluting the air with its foul acidity. His breathing was amplified as the emotion strengthened.

Go with it, son, he could almost hear his father say. *Go with the feeling . . . hate your grandmother. Hate her . . . Hate her . . .*

He glared at the door for a long time and picked up the fat woman's stupid thoughts about a jogger and a dog. Then the thoughts faded, and he knew the woman had moved on.

Hate her . . . hate her . . .

Still breathing stertorously, he opened the door and stepped out.

The temperature dropped. Lydia thought it was her imagination running rampant again. Either that or she was coming down with something—as usual. She reached for a woolen afghan and covered her legs. When that wasn't enough, she pulled the afghan up to include her plumpy hips and girth. Then, a moment later, she drew it toward her chin, shrouding her arms and shoulders.

She glanced again at the clock. Only three more

minutes had passed. How long could a visit with a priest take? Maybe she should go to the apartment across the hall. She could lie and say that her apartment was full of smoke from a small pan fire and ask to wait until her daughter came back.

But she was too stubborn to leave the chair. She'd be damned if she'd let anyone push her around. This was a side of her that had made many enemies, had even made her husband walk out on her once. It was a trait that her grandson, Frankie, had inherited. Most people, she knew, didn't call her stubborn or obstinate; they simply called her bullheaded. But whatever they wanted to call it, it was a part of her character, a part that was as real as the shape of her nose and the color of her eyes.

Lighting a cigarette, she stared resolutely at the TV. She would not be afraid. She would not run. Patricia would be home soon, with a solution to get rid of the monster that was in the small room off the kitchen.

The TV screen began to flicker and the sound became sibilant static. Was a storm coming? She switched the channel with the remote control device. An old movie was on with Lon Chaney, Jr., howling as he turned into a wolf. She clicked the transmitter again. This time she saw Gregory Peck and Lee Remick gaping in horror at their young son, the antichrist. Click. Linda Blair spun her head around. Click. Jamie Lee Curtis narrowly escaped the bogeyman and was running. Click. Another horror film. What was this, a special day for monster flicks?

Click. Click. Click. Dracula. Frankenstein. Jason. Damien. Click. Click. Click.

There was laughter behind her.

Lydia found herself unable to move. Without turning she knew whom she had heard. Now there was silence, except for the static coming from the TV. Only the picture seemed to be working. She took a deep drag of her cigarette, then coughed nervously, then took another drag, this time drawing smoke steadily into her lungs. Usually this calmed her, but not now. Richard was behind her, not making a move. Now she could smell him. It was that sickening odor of something on the verge of decay. And the cold temperature in the room—it had happened before, but she hadn't related it to the boy until now.

There was no doubt that he was behind her, probably just right in back of her shoulder, and yet she couldn't move. Fear had literally paralyzed her.

Go away, kid. Go away.

She stared at the screen. A film she'd never seen before was on. There were bodies everywhere, a blurred mass that rippled like an ocean—an orange-red ocean, for a fire off screen seemed to be tinting it and making it glow. The bodies, Lydia noted, were naked and shiny with sweat. There must have been hundreds of them, writhing and squirming like a huge colony of orange maggots. It took her a moment to realize that this was an orgy she was witnessing. Now she could see everything in explicit detail—twosomes, threesomes, foursomes.

But this could not be possible, she suddenly realized. This was not cable TV. Such a film could not be broadcast. With disgust, Lydia then averted her head, and that was when she finally saw Richard.

He was grinning at her, eyes unnaturally wide, pupils tiny pinpoints. Pyramidal shards of glass protruded from his stomach, chest, and shoulders. Lydia cried out, the sight of him startling and chilling her. He chuckled, a sound that was low and menacing.

"Enjoying the show, Grandmother?"

It took a long moment to find her voice. "Get away from me, y'hear?"

"I hear." Richard bowed his head, as though miming a genie. "But I do not listen."

"What do you want?"

Richard ignored the question as he moved closer to her. Lydia cringed, pulling the afghan tighter around her, as though suddenly experiencing an icy draft. Then the boy said, "Look," and pointed at the TV screen.

Reluctantly, Lydia followed his finger. From the ocean of gleaming bodies a man emerged. There was something familiar about him, especially his gait, which was smooth, almost arrogant. Preceding him was an enormous erection.

"Recognize him, Grandmother?" Richard asked, laughter in his voice.

Lydia said nothing, but she didn't recognize the man on the screen, for his head was down, openly admiring his disporportionate penis. Instead of the usual cleft in the head of the male organ there were two slits. And Lydia found herself staring, mesmerized. Soon the slits widened, then snapped open to reveal a set of eyes, yellow with vertical slits, snake's eyes.

Lydia uttered a cry. This was no male organ she was seeing—it was a serpent, for it was now writhing, and the man was reverently stroking it.

Oh my God.

Then the man looked up at her, and her heart froze. It was her husband. He was smiling.

Lydia, stifling a scream, clicked the transmitter. Her husband laughed and stroked the penis-serpent more vigorously. She clicked again, harder, but her husband still wouldn't go away, and the hideous thing between his legs was growing, writhing obscenely in his fist.

"Recognize him now, Grandmother?"

"Make this filth go away," she demanded, her tone nothing more than a croak.

"Offended, Grandmother?"

"Please, make it go away." She clicked

repeatedly, futilely. "Please."

"It's your husband, isn't it? My grandfather, isn't it?"

"No!" she denied vehemently.

"Oh yes, it's him all right."

Lydia, unable to look at the screen anymore, turned her head as far away from it as possible. "Not him, not him, not him," she mumbled.

Passionate moans and groans from the TV filled the room, growing in crescendo until Lydia thought she'd go mad. At length she struggled out of the chair and reached for the plug. She pulled it out of the wall, but still the sound persisted and the orgy continued.

"Do you know where he is, Grandmother?"

"Leave me alone. It's not him. I know it's not."

"Hell, Grandmother. He's in Hell. That's what you're seeing and hearing. Hell."

"No." She shook her head, refusing to believe him, refusing to accept what was happening. "My Leonard was a good man. He's in Heaven now."

Richard threw his head back and guffawed at this. "No place in Heaven for him," he assured her between laughs. "Your Leonard was a bad boy, Grandmother."

"No."

"He fucked anything he could, Grandmother."

"No. No."

"Even fucked his twelve-year-old cousin."

"No!" Now Lydia was screaming, crushing her ears with her palms. Nothing this monster was saying was true. He was making everything up, making her see and hear things on the TV that weren't there, hypnotizing her somehow.

"Angela was her name, wasn't it?" Richard said. His voice, although not more than a whisper, still managed to penetrate Lydia's hands and enter her ears. "Angela Raymond. She was a pretty thing, wasn't she? Delicate and sickly, too. Couldn't have weighed more than eighty pounds."

How did he know about Angela? Lydia wondered. She hadn't seen nor thought about that girl in over 40 years, at least. It was true; Angela was Leonard's cousin and had been an ill child, something to do with her heart. She died at the age of 15, never having had a chance to develop into a woman.

"But that didn't stop him from fucking her," Richard ruthlessly went on. "He didn't care about her heart. He caught her alone in a barn, saw how fragile and helpless she was, so he fucked her. In other words, Grandmother, he raped her."

"No, Leonard was a good man. He wouldn't do that."

"He fucked his way through life, Grandmother. And now, as you can see on that screen, he's fucking his way through eternity."

"No, no, no!" Lydia staggered away from the television and Richard, hands still pressed against her ears. She started toward her bedroom. "Leave me alone, y'hear. Leave me alone."

"He cheated on you." Richard followed her. "He went every Friday night to a whore."

No, he went with his friends. They played cards, she replied in her mind. But she might as well have spoken out loud, for he seemed to have heard her thoughts.

"He never played cards, Grandmother. You were a gullible, stupid bitch. And too old. He liked them young. He paid extra for those whores. You should have seen them, Grandmother. Budding tits, hairless cunts. They were almost babies, Grandmother."

"Stop it!"

Richard threw his head back once more and filled the room with his cruel laughter.

Hand shaking, almost beyond the ability to function, Lydia turned the knob on her bedroom door. It was stuck. She tried again and again, then she pushed her weight against the door, pounding and kicking it.

Why is it stuck? her mind screamed, frantically. It never did this before. So why now?

Of course she knew why, Richard. He was the cause of all this. There seemed to be nothing he couldn't do.

"I am immortal now," Richard said, responding to her thoughts. "I no longer obey the physical laws. I now possess all the mysteries and secrets of existence, of the universe. Hell, Grandmother, is where all the negative energy of the universe is concentrated. There is so much of that in me—thanks, of course, to Father. And now that I am no longer confined to your laws I can use them. There is so much I can do."

And as though to confirm this, viscid substance began to trickle down the door, like thick rivers of purplish-pink gelatin. Lydia stumbled back, repulsed. There was a foul odor like the smell of old garbage on a warm, humid day.

"All an illusion . . . an illusion," she reminded herself, as she headed for the front door. She'd go to a neighbor and wait it out until Patricia returned.

But then this door, too, oozed the same sticky substance, thickly coating the knob. Beneath the door more of the substance was seeping through, entering the room. And the rancid smell was growing stronger, making her gag.

She glanced over at the window, for she noticed the light in the room had dimmed, as though the sun was in the process of an eclipse. But it wasn't the shadow of the earth or moon that was blocking the light; it was the hideous slime covering the window, casting an eerie, dark plum glow. She ran, as fast as her heavy body would allow, toward the kitchen, then stopped abruptly, panting, as though she'd run across a field rather than a small room. Before her was a gelatinous wall where the door to the kitchen should have been.

An illusion, she told herself again. She could probably penetrate this wall easily, but she couldn't bring herself to do this. Instead, she looked around the room in despair, then turned helplessly toward Richard, who was watching with bold glee.

"Stop it!" she pleaded.

Richard reacted with innocence. "Stop what? What you see is not real—that's what you've been telling yourself, isn't it?"

"Please, make it go away."

"Maybe it's like a mirage," Richard smiled. "Maybe it'll go away the moment you touch it." When Lydia said nothing he added, in a lilting singsong voice, "Try and see, and maybe be free."

Lydia stared at the front door, debating. Would it go away like a mirage, or would it consume her like . . .

She heard a scream on the TV, looked over and saw an old black and white horror film.

. . . *The Blob.*

Lydia clutched her chest, her heart thudding painfully against it. She'd never survive this, illusion or no. "Pul-leese," she sobbed.

Then she heard the boy say something in a low, raspy voice that she couldn't catch—something with three words, a long pause between each. The room suddenly seemed still, and the smell of spoiled food was much stronger. Then she heard the three words again. This time they were clear and distinct.

"I . . . hate . . . you."

Never had she heard such intense feeling behind an utterance, so filled with hatred that it didn't even sound human. But then, that was because it wasn't coming from one who was human. "What are you?" she demanded, pressing against a wall to keep as much distance from him as possible. She felt like someone trapped in a cage with a dangerous beast.

"Why, I'm your grandson, Grandmother."

"No, no, I mean . . ." She paused to control her rapid breathing. She was sure she was having a heart attack, but she still had to talk, or she'd go insane with terror. "Your father . . ." She tried again, gulping air like one would gulp water. "What was he? Satan?"

"Satan?" Richard lifted one amused brow. "Why, of course not, Grandmother. Not Satan. But Father is proudly one of his soldiers, though. He is part of one legion. He is the demon Waphax."

"Demon?" Lydia echoed the word with disbelief. Although she had suspected something like this, it wasn't the same as actually hearing it. "How many demons are there?"

Richard shrugged. "Some claim there are six legions. And each have sixty-six divisions. And each division has six hundred and sixty-six companies. And each company has six thousand, six hundred and sixty-six soldiers. Over a billion, I believe. Quite an army, isn't it, Grandmother? The Army of the Night."

"I . . . I don't believe you."

"That's your prerogative."

"Why did your father pick my daughter to . . . to . . ."

"Fuck? Because she was easy. Father told me she didn't even care who he was. She just wanted to be fucked, so he fucked her." There was a cold, hard edge to his voice. Resentment toward his father? Or toward his mother?

Lydia eyed the doors and window again. "Let me go," she implored. "I've never done anything to deserve this."

The boy uttered the three words in the slow, guttural voice again: "*I . . . hate . . . you.*"

"Stop saying that!"

He was glaring fiercely at her now. And for an instant she could swear smoke was coming from his eyes, as though the eyeballs were actually smoldering.

"I've never done anything to you," she cried in defense. "I've minded my own business. Kept out of your way."

"Wrong, Grandmother," he spat. "You were always in the way. You turned my own mother against me. It is because of you she does not love me as she should."

"That's not true."

"You informed her many times that keeping me was a mistake, and now you're telling her to send me away."

"But you're not even human. My God, you can't expect her—us—to live with . . . with a dead person."

"Maybe it is you that should be sent away," he said, ignoring her.

Panic surged through Lydia like an electric current. "No, no. Please, no."

"Would you like to feel your husband's cock inside you again, Grandmother?"

"No."

"Or would you like my father's instead?"

"No."

"Look at the TV screen, Grandmother."

Lydia shook her head, sobbing.

"Obey me, Grandmother."

Lydia finally complied, not because she wanted to but because a force, like a giant hand, was turning her head toward the TV. She squeezed her eyes shut in protest, and again a force manipulated her, reopening the eyes. There was no choice but to watch the horror on the screen.

The mass of sweaty bodies was gone, and now there was an image of her own face, mouth wreathed

in terror. There was no sound, only the annoying
static. Then the face loomed closer, at an incredible
speed. Faster and faster until it crashed into what
looked like a wall of glass, exploding it. After this
there was a moment of confusion as the screen
flickered vertically, then horizontally. Then the
picture was back, this time showing her husband
fondling the serpent again.

Lydia, no longer controlled by a force, looked
over questionably at Richard. What was the meaning
of her image on the screen?

In reply, the force abruptly returned, seemingly
stronger. It wasn't limited to her head as before; it
now seemed to be controlling her entire body,
pushing her downward as well as forward.

"Wha . . . No, please . . ."

She felt as though she were caught in a powerful
current of water. She fell to her knees, and still the
current pushed her forward, sweeping her at a
terrifying speed toward the end of the room, toward
the TV. She tried to anchor herself, wishing she had
claws that could dig into the floor, but it was useless.
The force that was propelling her was too powerful,
and the TV was looming closer. She saw her husband
on the screen; he seemed to be watching her rapid
approach, grinning at her.

"No, stop, stop!" she screamed.

Her head was in perfect alignment with the TV
screen and slammed into it, shattering it, spitting
sparks and billowing smoke. She screamed, felt fire
all around her, then felt the force continue its
ruthless pushing. There was another scream, while
the force pushed and pushed. Bones cracked and
crunched. Blood squirted, then flowed.

TV's too small, I'm too big, she thought hysterically, then her mind screamed once more as pain
filled her. Then the pain and screaming stopped, and
darkness and stillness ensued.

And still the force continued to push her ample

body into the TV, splintering the set, the back of
which was against solid wall. It did not cease until
she was completely inside, blood spilling out over the
broken screen and onto the rug.

And if Lydia were still alive, she would have
heard Richard utter for the last time: "I . . . hate . . .
you."

Driving an old Pinto wagon that Myles had
helped restore, Patty headed home after a short, dis-
appointing visit with a priest. The priest, Father
Ramon, had been neither helpful nor friendly. As
soon as he learned that Patty wasn't a faithful
churchgoer, and that she had never donated anything to the church, he turned distant. And when
she told him that she believed she'd had intercourse
with a demon he accused her of mocking the
religion. He didn't believe her story, but he did agree
to bless the apartment, say sometime next week.

"Couldn't it be sooner, Father?" she pleaded.

"I'm a busy man, Ma'am," he assured her,
quickly glancing at an assignment book that was on
the desk in front of him. "Thursday and Saturday are
bingo nights. Friday I'm scheduled to meet Mon-
signor Sapir. Monday the church is having a frank-
furt and bean supper. And Wednesday . . ."

Obviously he did not take Patty seriously, and
now she had no choice but to wait.

Maybe she should go back to the priest
tomorrow, she mused, and pester him until he
agreed to see Richard sooner. She was certain that
once he saw the boy he'd believe her and commence
whatever needed to be done—an exorcism, perhaps.

But until then a new crucifix would have to
suffice. Maybe she also should wear garlic, she
thought wryly as she reached her neighborhood.

She parked the Pinto in the street and went up to
her apartment.

21

The moment she was inside the apartment house she knew something was wrong. As she mounted the stairs to her floor the uneasy feeling grew progressively stronger. She quickened her pace and was soon skipping steps in much the same way her heart was skipping beats. When she finally reached her apartment she saw that her intuitive apprehension was not groundless. Neighbors were at her door, pounding tentatively.

"Mrs. Thompson? Are you in there, Mrs. Thompson?" The man who lived in the apartment across the hall was calling solicitously through the wooden partition. Behind him was his wife in a housecoat and curlers, and behind her were two young men who shared an apartment downstairs. It was these two men who spotted Patty first.

"Mrs. Thompson!" they exclaimed, almost in unison.

Patty willed herself to remain calm. "What's wrong?"

"We heard a lot of noise, Mrs. Thompson." This was from the woman. She stayed close behind her husband, nervously pulling at the back of his T-shirt. "Screaming and a loud crash."

"Now we hear nothing," finished the husband. "And something's wrong with the door." He stepped back to let Patty through.

"What's wrong with it?" she asked, but found the answer as soon as her hand touched the knob; it was ice cold, refusing to turn.

"I called the police," the husband said. He reeked faintly of cigar smoke.

Patty twisted the knob harder, feeling it gradually warming to her touch. She persevered until it finally turned and the door opened.

Steeling herself, she then stepped inside her apartment. She started to close the door on her curious neighbors, then changed her mind and left the door half-open, so that they could look in from the hallway and rush to her aid if needed.

The cold was the first thing she noticed; it felt like walking into a butcher's freezer. Her breath became puffs of miniature clouds preceding her. The silence was the second thing. Usually there was noise in here, especially in the living room. Usually the TV was on.

That was when she noticed the third thing.

Both of Patty's hands shot to her mouth, and still her scream escaped and filled the room. The neighbors threw the door open the rest of the way and bolted toward her. Then they stopped and gaped in shock at the TV set. Blood trickled from the broken screen, puddling the rug beneath. Inside this screen was a red clump, as if a mass of clay had been pounded into an undersized container. There was a small patch of cloth that somehow was not blood stained beyond recognition. It was a faded floral print. It was part of Lydia's housecoat.

Patty screamed again, then rushed out of the room into the kitchen. There she collapsed at the table, burying her head in her arms, sobbing. She felt a hand on her shoulder, but didn't look up. It was undoubtedly one of the neighbors trying to soothe her.

Grief and rage alternately surged through

Patty—grief for her mother and rage for her son, for there was no doubt in her mind that this was his doing. Also, there was an occasional stab of guilt. She should have insisted that her mother come with her to see the priest. And she should have listened to her from the very beginning, when Richard was a new-born and her mother had pleaded with her to give him up. And now she had lost Myles and her mother. *All because of Richard.*

Patty lifted her tear-streaked face from her arms. Where was he? she suddenly wondered. Behind her was the woman in curlers, patting her back, like one would pat a dog's head. "There, there," the woman was saying. She then went on to say something else, no doubt in an effort to console her, but Patty was now looking around the room, at the walls, at the ceiling, at her son's room, which was open and empty. Where was he?

She got up from the table, walked about the kitchen, as though in a daze. Where? Where? Where? The woman in curlers handed her a tissue. Patty mindlessly took it, wiped her eyes, then her nose. She peered into Richard's room, checked the walls and floor—everything. She was desperately looking for signs that would tell of her son's where-abouts. She went into the bathroom, checked her own bedroom, her mother's, then finally the kids'.

The kids! she remembered in sudden alarm. What was she going to do about them? She couldn't let them see their grandmother like this.

"Patty, you okay?"

It was a man's voice, gentle with concern. She turned and blinked at the face behind her. At first she didn't recognize it, but after a second, she did. It was Howie, the beer-belly cop, her friend Kate's live-in boyfriend.

"I . . . I'm fine," Patty said in a faint voice.

Howie wrapped an arm around her shoulder, and

she fleetingly remembered a time when he had patted her rear behind Kate's back. Patty thought of pushing him away, but simply did not have the strength. She let him help her toward the bed. "Better lie down, I think," he said. "You're awfully pale. Wanna drink of water or something?"

"Yes. Please."

Howie studied her for a brief moment, as though debating whether or not to leave her. Then he was gone.

What's Howie doing here? Patty wondered, then for the first time was aware of voices in the living room. The police were here, and from the sound of it there were quite a few of them. Patty contemplated getting up from the bed to look, but she suddenly felt weak and dazed.

Where is my son? Did he run away? Or was he hiding in here somewhere?

She detected a smell and recognized it almost instantly. It was that sickening overripe stench. No, not overripe anymore, she corrected herself. It was now the smell of rot, no longer sweet but rancid. It was Richard.

He *was* here. In the apartment somewhere. But was he invisible? Watching behind walls? It was possible. He could do anything. He was dead.

Suddenly Patty burst into laughter. She didn't know why but everything seemed funny now, even hilarious, but when Howie returned with a glass of water she was weeping hysterically.

"It's Richard," she told him. "It's Richard, it's Richard, it's Richard!"

He held her tightly against him, repeating over and over, "It's okay. Everything's okay. It's okay."

Through the film of tears she saw faces in the doorway, saw cops, saw a man in a sloppy suit, saw a man with a camera. Then she saw nothing at all.

When she awoke she found herself looking up at Kate's face, which was surprisingly bland without makeup. Her friend smiled, but Patty was too disoriented to remember to smile back. It took a full minute to realize that she was not in her own room, or in her apartment for that matter. Heavy metal music screamed from another part of the house, muted by doors, walls and distance. Hearing this quickly informed her that she was in Kate's house. And this room was her son's, judging from the posters of sports cars, Heineken beer, and rock stars.

Then she remembered that her mother was dead, and she bolted upright. "Ma!" she cried.

"Easy, kid, easy."

Fresh tears burned behind her eyes. "My mother is dead, Kate."

"I know," Kate said softly. "You just relax for a while, and get yourself good and strong."

"How long have I been here? Where are my kids? Do the police know who did it?"

"You've spent the night. Howie brought you here. Your kids are here, too. They're with Jason in the den right now."

"Oh God," Patty groaned, letting the tears brim then spill down her face. The horrible picture of the broken TV and her mother's shapeless body inside it filled her mind. "They didn't see their grandmother, did they?" she asked, hoping the answer was no, for the sight would haunt them for the rest of their lives.

To her relief Kate shook her head. "Howie picked them up at school."

"But do they know what happened?"

"They know she's dead, but Howie spared them the details. Said he didn't know how much you'd want to tell them."

Patty fell silent. Exactly how much did she want her children to know? Of course she'd spare them the horror of how their grandmother had died, but should she tell them of her suspicion? And should she tell them of the possibility that their brother was actually a dead person? She doubted very much that they'd believe her, for she still found it difficult to believe herself.

"Richard," Patty murmured. "Did anyone find him?"

"I'm afraid not, but they're looking. Don't worry, kid. They'll find him," she assured her.

But Patty noticed that her friend had it all wrong. She thought Patty was worried about the boy and wanted him back, but that wasn't it at all. She was worried that he *would* come back—and kill again.

"Howie said the police will question you whenever you're ready."

Patty nodded numbly, but it wasn't until another day had passed that she found herself strong enough to endure what she knew would be an interminable interrogation.

There were two investigators; one was Lieutenant Wheeler, who was beginning to become a fixture in her life, and the other was a tall, slender man on the verge of retirement. His name was Detective Walter Keaton and he was miserable with a cold, his nose inflamed and raw, hidden mostly behind a crumpled handkerchief. He asked most of the questions.

"Have you any idea where your son is now?"

"No."

"Mind explaining why you think he's the suspect?"

She did mind, but told him anyway, as best as she could without sounding deranged. She told the detective that her son was not like other boys, that he was frightening. She told him she believed he was responsible for Myles Forbes' death as well. But when she proceeded to tell them about the boy's powers she caught the skepticism in the men's eyes and quickly fell silent. She could see they were not going to believe her, so there was no sense in continuing further.

When the men left, promising to do everything they could, Janet and Frankie began to bombard her with questions. Until now, Kate and Howie had managed to keep them at bay. They had shed their tears, Janet more than Frankie, and now wanted to know exactly what had happened to their grandmother, whose funeral was less than 24 hours away.

"Someone killed Grandma," she evasively told them.

"How?" Frankie demanded. Janet, unlike her brother, dropped her head, as though suddenly not certain if she wanted to hear this.

Patty told them she wasn't sure how. She only knew that the woman had been slammed into the TV set.

"That must of been horrible, Mom," Janet cried.

"That killed her?" Frankie said doubtfully.

Patty hesitated, then said, "She was forced into the set."

The brother and sister stared blankly at her, not sure if they understood.

"How?" Frankie frowned. "I don't think anybody's strong enough to do that, Mom."

Janet, not wanting to hear any details, abruptly changed the subject. "What happened to Rich? Where is he?"

"I don't know, sweetheart."

"You think he did it?" Frankie's voice hardened as the thought occurred to him. "If he did I'll kill that son of—"

"That's enough, Frankie," Patty warned.

"Well, did he?" Frankie demanded.

"Of course he didn't," Janet declared, then deciding she had had enough, hurried out of the den.

Now Patty was alone with Frankie, who was

studying her, eyes narrowing in suspicion. It was a long time before he spoke. "It is him, isn't it, Mom?" he said confidently. "And he ran away, didn't he?"

"I don't know, Frankie," she said. She thought of telling him the entire truth, and her belief that Richard was the boy who had hanged himself in the abandoned house, but found herself suddenly too weary and tired to do so. Another time, she promised herself, but right now she needed to rest and get her strength back.

At her mother's funeral Patty half-expected to find Richard somewhere near a tree, as she had found him at Myles' funeral, but the boy wasn't anywhere. She told herself she was relieved, but she really wasn't. Although she couldn't see Richard, she knew he was still around, still watching. His presence seemed to grow stronger each day.

After the funeral Janet and Frankie pleaded to go back to the apartment, but Patty was reluctant, thinking Richard was there, waiting.

"Let's stay at Kate's for a few more days," she said.

Janet respected her mother's wish, for she thought Patty was still miserable with grief, but Frankie was impatient to be back in his own room, especially now that he thought his brother was gone.

"Where *is* Richard?" Janet demanded one night, when she was alone with her mother. "You don't really think he killed Grandma, do you?"

Patty could see the hope and dread in her daughter's beautiful blue eyes as the girl waited for the answers. Unable to shatter such hope, Patty said to the first question, "I don't know, sweetheart," and in answer to the second question she pulled her daughter into her arms and held her for a long moment, saying nothing. The girl sobbed quietly, then left to sleep in the den with her brother and

Jason.

Patty reached over from the bed and turned off the lamp on the nightstand. The room fell into darkness, except for the silver patch of light from an almost full moon. The spectral light, slanting through the window, spotlighted a chilling poster of rock star Ozzy Osbourne baring teeth and pink froth. Patty looked away from this poster, and then looked back. The picture, seemingly glowing, demanded attention.

But while she stared at this poster, her mind wandered. She thought of her mother and cried. Then as soon as her eyes were dry she began to think about Myles and cried all over again. Then she thought of Richard, and the tears froze.

Would she see him again? Did he really kill her mother? Why did he kill her? Where was he now? Was he back with his father? And where was his father?

She didn't realize there were so many questions. Until she had the answers to most of them, she knew she wouldn't go back to her apartment. She felt certain Richard would be waiting for her there, waiting to kill her—and perhaps kill Janet and Frankie as well—but she also knew she couldn't stay here forever. So what was she to do?

Patty closed her eyes, hoping sleep would claim her, but the nagging question kept her mind brisk and alert. Now she wished she had thought of sneaking a bottle of vodka into the room, for that would help stagnate her mind.

Then she felt a change in the room. The poster glowed brighter, for a quick instant blurring the picture with glaring platinum light, then it returned to normalcy. While the poster flared, Patty felt something frigid envelope her, tingling her spine. Accompanying this sensation was the familiar odor that Patty had come to associate with Richard.

Patty frantically looked around her in the darkness, but saw nothing. The stench of decay and the cold air lingered.

Richard was in this room.

Patty pulled the blanket closer to her chin, covering her arms and hands, but still the cold penetrated her. She contemplated turning on the lamp, thinking the light might drive her son away. She didn't want to see him now. In fact she was afraid to see him.

Then she heard something, a sound that was faint like the wind—but it wasn't the wind, for the sound was inside the room. And also, there were words blending with the soft wail, words that Patty couldn't catch until they were repeated.

You . . . don't . . . love . . . me . . .

Patty shivered. "Go away, Richard," she pleaded, whispering in the darkness. "Just leave me alone."

You . . . don't . . . love . . . me . . .

At last Patty snapped on the lamp. Light flooded the room, and with it came a sense of security, but not for long. As though in defiance the air grew colder and the stench stronger.

Patty looked around the room, at the stereo, the radio, the set of weights in the corner. She returned her attention to the poster of Ozzy Osbourne. It no longer possessed a spectral glow, but there was still something eerie about it that unnerved her. The eyes had changed. They were now yellow and incandescent.

You . . . don't . . . love . . . me . . .

Patty thought of denying the accusation, then remembered that Richard could sense the truth and read her mind.

"Go away," she demanded, now hissing the words. "Go away!"

The eyes in the poster flared up, as the poster itself had done a moment earlier. Then they faded.

Patty sensed sorrow as the eyes declined in brilliance. It was as though she had seen hope in those eyes, and now hope was dying, slowly and reluctantly. Eventually there was no more light emanating from the eyes or the poster. And the stench and the cold, Patty suddenly realized, were absent also.

Richard was gone.

But Patty wasn't entirely relieved. Grabbing a pillow and a blanket, she went into the den to join the others, who were already asleep. She didn't mind, though, for she just wanted to be near someone rather than alone.

As she lay, wrapped in a blanket on the floor, she stared up at the darkness, knowing she'd never sleep tonight. Richard would return again and again, until . . .

Until what? What would he finally do? Why was he haunting her in the first place? How could she make him leave her alone?

Kill him, a part of her answered. But how could you kill someone already dead?

Patty considered going back to the priest or explaining everything to Detective Wheeler. Then she considered something else—moving far away. Maybe she could lose Richard. Maybe the boy would not know where to find her if she wasn't in her hometown. If she stayed away long enough maybe he'd give up and disappear from her life completely.

It was worth a try, wasn't it?

The next morning, after a sleepless night, she purchased three one-way bus tickets to the farthest place she could afford—a small town in Indiana.

22

On the bus to Indiana Janet and Frankie were silent, each pensive and confused. They had protested against the trip, demanding answers, but Patty insisted this was important. And she assured them they would return—but she could't tell them when.

As Patty packed their belongings, as well as her own, they had complained that they would miss school, miss their friends.

"It's only temporary," Patty had told them.

"It's cuz of Richard, ain't it?" Frankie had said, his tone harsh with resentment.

Patty had ignored him and continued packing, telling herself she'd discuss this later, but first she wanted to get out of town as fast as possible. Later that day she called Detective Wheeler and told him that she needed to get away for a while.

"I'll keep in touch," she had promised.

"Anything new about Richard?" he had asked.

"He hasn't come back. What about you? Find anything?"

"Naw. But don't you worry, we're still working on it. Only a matter of time."

Patty had been tempted to remind him that the last time he'd said that, it had taken eight years for Richard to turn up, and it had nothing to do with intrepid investigations. But she held back.

Now she and her teenaged children were hundreds of miles away from their hometown, away from Richard. When they reached their destination, a small town called Webford, it was dusk, more dark than light. Suitcase in each hand, her kids flanking her, Patty found herself feeling small and alien in the flat, expansive land. The monotonous stretch of fields made the hills back home in Massachusetts look like majestic mountains. Maybe she had made a mistake coming here, picking a place at random, a place she knew nothing at all about.

"Need a ride, Ma'am?" a masculine voice drawled, startling her. She looked around and saw a taxi parked not too far from the bus station. The driver, his head poking out the window, baseball cap partly shielding his eyes, waited expectantly for an answer.

"Could you take us to a motel?" she said, stepping toward the cab. "Something not, er, too expensive."

"Sure thing, Ma'am." He winked, then jerked his head, gesturing for everyone to climb into the back seat.

The motel he drove them to was called, simply, Eat 'N' Sleep. There was a small diner adjoining it, and not too far beyond the weather-beaten structure was a package store. This motel is where all the drunks sleep it off, Patty thought, somewhat repulsed. She was ready to ask the cab driver to take them to another motel, then changed her mind. Maybe this was all she could afford for now.

She paid the driver, ignored the sarcastic show of appreciation as she gave him a meager tip, then headed for the motel office. Janet and Frankie waited outside, suitcases resting at their feet. The smell of stale whiskey and fried food was strong, again tempting Patty to consider another place to stay. But she reminded herself this was only temporary.

Inside, she pounded a silver desk bell several

times before getting anyone's attention. A short, baldheaded man appeared from another room, grunting and fastening his trousers. Apparently she had interrupted him from something. She told him she needed a room, and he bluntly quoted a price, holding his hand out. Then without a word, money and key were exchanged. After this, the proprietor hurried back from where he'd come. He probably had someone waiting for him in bed, but still, the least he could have done was tell Patty the room number, even though it was clearly printed on the key tag.

For the third time the uneasy feeling of being in a strange place haunted her. She forced herself to ignore it, although it was now a heavy rock in her stomach.

With Janet and Frankie following, she searched and found their room—a small, paneled space barely large enough to accommodate a double bed and a flimsy three-drawer bureau, cheaply restored with green enamel paint.

"Somebody's gonna have to sleep on the floor," Frankie muttered in disapproval.

"Temporary," Patty mumbled for the umpteenth time.

Even without touching it, she could see that the bed was too soft and lumpy. There was a distinct smell of Lysol in the air, but there was also another odor that the disinfectant failed to mask—vomit. How many times had people come in here after a night of heavy drinking and thrown up? she wondered as the rock in her stomach grew heavier.

This was no place to bring her children, she shamefully realized. It didn't matter that they were almost young adults. A decent mother would not expose her children to such surroundings.

Something scurried along the wall, then disappeared under the bed. A cockroach? Moaning from the next room was suddenly audible, punctuated by an outburst of passion.

Patty felt her face flame with embarrassment. She glanced quickly at her kids. Janet was equally embarrassed, but Frankie seemed amused.

"Temporary," Patty said, then went into the bathroom to splash cold water on her face, hoping the brisk freshness would lift her spirits. When she returned to the other room she found Janet and Frankie sitting on the bed, waiting for her. There was determination on their faces, and immediately she knew there would be demanding questions, questions that she would not be allowed to ignore.

It was Frankie who had decided to be the spokesperson for the two. "Mom," he began, lifting his chin as though refusing to be deterred, "we think we should know the real reason why we're here. We know you've been hiding something from us, and we don't think it's fair."

With a resigning sigh, Patty joined them on the bed. "I'm afraid Richard may be dangerous," she finally admitted.

"We're running away from Richard?" Janet was stunned with disbelief.

"Then he *did* kill Grandma!" Frankie said.

"We don't know that for sure," Patty clarified.

"Did he kill Myles, too?" When Patty didn't answer, he pressed on. "Well, did he, Mom?"

"He said he did."

"The crummy bastard!"

"Frankie, please."

"But we shouldn't be running away from him," Janet suddenly said. Unlike her brother, there was compassion and concern in her expression, not wrath and contempt. "We should be looking for him, helping him."

"Give me a break!" Frankie snarled.

"But it's true," Janet insisted. "Everybody should

be trying to help him, 'specially since he's had a horrible childhood. That's-why he's not right in his head, but I bet he could be helped." She turned to her mother. "Have you any idea at all where he is, Mom?"

"I'm afraid not." He could be anywhere, Patty thought. He could be back in his grave, or he could be right outside the door.

"You sure, Mom?"

The doubt in her daughter's voice surprised her. "Of course I'm sure."

"You're keeping something from us. I can tell."

"But I'm not," Patty lied. How could she tell them the truth about Richard's father or tell them she believed Richard wasn't really alive anymore? "I'm not," she said again.

The lie seemed to incense the girl. "It's not fair," she declared. "Neither you nor Frankie were ever nice to him. Never! Neither of you ever loved him."

"What are you talking about?"

"It was obvious, Mom. You stayed away from him as if he had . . . had AIDS or something. And you, Frankie, you were so hateful!"

"Wha . . ."

"Don't you what me! You treated him like he had a disease, too."

"There's something I never told you 'bout him," Frankie said defensively, then fell silent as though regretting the statement.

"Well, spit it out," Janet demanded.

Frankie hesitated, looking at his mother, then back at his sister. "He's not . . . I don't know . . . one of us, I guess. He's . . . he's . . ."

"He's what?" Janet was close to shouting, still furious with him and her mother.

"He did weird things," Frankie blurted after a long pause. "He made his shadow change. He . . ." Again he fell silent, unable to continue. He looked at his mother and then at his sister to see if they believed him or thought he was crazy.

"What do you mean 'change'?" Patty asked quietly, barely able to breathe.

Frankie swallowed, then told about the night Richard had scared him with shadows that reached for him, that grew and changed shapes, that had become a devil at one point. That was why had asked to have his own room.

"You probably were dreaming, stupid," Janet said.

"Maybe I was, but . . ."

"But what?"

Frankie started to say something, then shrugged, changing his mind. "Nothing."

"That's why you don't like him, 'cause of a dumb dream?"

He said nothing.

Janet swung toward her mother. "You call that fair?"

"Easy, Janet," Patty urged gently.

"Easy? You broke his heart, Mother. Rich used to come to me and tell me how you didn't love him. Sometimes he'd almost cry. It was awful. He looked so pathetic. I wanted so much to help him, but I couldn't. He . . . He . . ." She suddenly began to sob uncontrollably.

Patty pulled her into her arms and gently rocked her, like she used to do when Janet was a little girl crying about a "boo-boo" or a broken toy. "Easy," she repeated softly, "easy."

"It's not fair." This time the anger was gone from her voice, and Patty held her tighter. The death of her grandmother and the loss of her brother had disturbed her deeply. She needed this outburst.

"The police'll find Richard," Patty said, "and they'll help him."

"And then we'll go home?" It was Frankie, hope

evident in his face and voice.

"Yes, and then we'll go home," she assured him.

After the kids were asleep Patty pulled in a plastic deck chair from outside the room and sat in the dark. She was frightened and unsure of what she was doing. She wept silently, then left the room for the package store and purchased a bottle of vodka, a bag of ice, and the local newspaper. She returned to her room, read the want ads under the bathroom light, and circled promising jobs and apartments. After this, she filled a paper cup with vodka and ice, then went back to the plastic chair in the outer room, where she eventually drank herself to sleep.

To her surprise she found a job the following day; she would be a clerk at a 24-hour convenience store, working the three to eleven shift. Frankie and Janet protested violently, believing this would be something permanent, but Patty eventually managed to appease them, drilling it into their heads that the money was needed for their short stay here.

"Temporary," she emphasized once again.

Then she proceeded to look for a furnished apartment. Luck finally seemed to be with her, for she found a place as quickly as she had found the job. The rent was cheap, the apartment run-down with a broken bedroom window, a piece of cardboard taped to the frame to keep out the rain and wind.

But it was only temporary.

The neighborhood was defiant and indigent, not very dissimilar from the one they'd left behind, Patty reminded her kids.

"It's different when it's our own street," Janet pointed out. "Here we're the outsiders."

"Nobody's going to hurt us," Patty assured her and Frankie.

But when she left her kids behind to work at the

store, four blocks away, she still felt uneasy. From three to six it wasn't too bad, but when darkness fell she found herself constantly worrying about them. She couldn't call them, for there was no phone in the apartment, but now and then she'd call Detective Wheeler back home, each time hoping he'd tell her that Richard had been found and was in their custody and, yes, it was safe to come back home. But a week passed and still there was no sign of Richard.

Except maybe one. There had been a brief smell—that unmistakable stench—but it passed the instant Patty had noticed it. She checked the freezer in the store for spoiled luncheon meat, but found everything still fresh. Maybe it had been something that wafted in from outside from a garbage can in a nearby alley.

Then three days passed without incident. She had gone to a department store and purchased several plastic crucifixes to hang in each room of the apartment. Passing through the book section in this store, one book had caught her attention. It was a thick volume on Demonology, price reduced more than half, for apparently it was a poor seller. Patty actually could not afford to spend her money on something like this, but the book intrigued her. Maybe she would find some answers that would help her understand what she was up against, answers that would solve everything. So, after much deliberation, she purchased the book.

The night began no differently at the convenience store. As the sky darkened and the store lights and street lamps brightened, Patty began to worry more and more about Janet and Frankie alone at the apartment. She called Wheeler about Richard—no progress—then she tried to busy herself with her work.

There were scarcely any customers from 9:00 o'clock on. Usually only the derelicts and creeps came in, purchasing cigarettes or candy bars. There was the perpetual fear that someone would pull out a knife and demand everything from the cash register. She'd been told it had happened several times already, and that was why there was a gun on the shelf beneath the register—for her protection. But Patty prayed that she'd never have to use it. The only consoling fact was that most of the robberies occurred on the third shift, rarely on hers, but still . . .

"Gimme a pack of Marlboro," a boy demanded, shattering her thoughts.

Patty mechanically smiled and reached for the cigarettes on display in back of her. "Anything else?" The kid shook his head. He couldn't have been more than ten. Saying nothing, Patty pushed the pack toward him and collected the money in loose change, mostly nickels. Next, an old man stepped forward, wanting pipe tobacco. That was when she saw Richard.

He was at the other end of the store, watching her. The fluorescent light from the ceiling made him appear paler than usual, made the skin around his eyes darker, almost raccoonlike.

"Hear what I said, lady?" the man said gruffly.

Patty pulled her eyes away from her son. "Oh, I . . . I'm sorry, sir." She forced a smile and reached for the tobacco he wanted. Was it only her imagination, or had she really seen the boy? She would have looked again, but the man before her was asking if she knew what the weather was going to be like tomorrow.

"No, I'm afraid not," she replied politely.

"Ain't been gettin' 'nough rain, ya know."

Patty nodded, pretending that she knew and agreed. Maybe it wasn't Richard, only someone who looked like him, she mused as she maintained her smile.

"Well, the old lady's waiting for me," the man said disgruntedly, then was gone. And Patty was again alone in the store, except for . . .

She looked over at where she'd seen the boy. He was gone now. She would have noticed if he had left via the main door. She studied the convex mirror near the ceiling, where she could see most of the store. No Richard, or anybody else. Maybe he was squatting behind the display of sodas or something, she thought. That way he'd be out of sight from the mirror. Maybe she should go check.

But Patty found herself unable to move away from the cash register and the gun on the shelf.

Someone was still in the store, an inner voice reminded her. That person, Richard or whoever, did not leave. He definitely was still here.

Just the imagination playing tricks, her other voice answered.

Then go check, the first voice challenged. If it's not anything real, then there's nothing to be afraid of. Right?

Still Patty couldn't move.

That smell came back, then faded.

Then a teenage couple, both clad in tight jeans and denim jackets, entered the store. The girl, with long earrings brushing her shoulders, clung to her boyfriend, who seemed sluggish and inebriated. They bought potato chips and cigarettes. Patty made an attempt at conversation with them, not wanting to be alone in the store more than was necessary, but they had other things on their minds. After they left, she saw a reflection of someone in the glass door of the refrigerator, which was filled with milk, juices, and soda. Before she could clearly identify who it was, the image disappeared. She spun around, expecting to see someone round a corner and flee into another aisle of canned goods and products.

But she was alone. The silence seemed to

emphasize this.

Her heart began to race. Her body began the usual trembling.

Richard is here.

She was sure of it now. She had not escaped him. He had followed her.

What was he going to do now?

What was *she* going to do now?

The rest of the night dragged on interminably. When it was finally time to leave she almost cried with relief. Stepping outside in the night air she found herself wondering if maybe she'd only imagined seeing Richard. Perhaps being alone most of the time in the store had made her imagination run wild.

She began to walk toward her apartment.

The air was chilly, silently churning with pending rain. Dark clouds covered the moon. For the moment Patty was alone on the street, yet she did not feel alone.

The relief she had felt a few seconds ago left her. Her damn imagination was back.

A car whizzed past, startling her.

She paused to catch her breath and still her heart, then she proceeded onward. Only four blocks, she told herself, four short blocks and she would be home.

She quickened her pace. The feeling of a presence close by would not go away. She forced herself to ignore it, forced herself not to glance back. And she forced herself not to think.

Three blocks. She'd be home in no time, and she'd be safe.

Why would an apartment be safer? It was that pessimistic voice again.

Three and a half blocks.

Another car sped past, fanning her with cold wind, mussing her hair and causing her to peel strands away from her face.

Then she saw him.

She let out a stunned cry and staggered back, almost falling off the sidewalk. She had forgotten herself for a moment and glanced over her shoulder. When she looked ahead again he was in front of her, as though he had materialized out of nowhere.

"Why did you run away from me, Mother?" he said. The street lamp illuminated only his eyes, which seemed dull with sorrow, while the rest of him was hidden in the night.

Biting her lower lip, as though deliberately filling her mind with pain instead of terror, she ignored him and quickly crossed the street. There were no cars around, and the sidewalks were deserted. All the stores, except for the one she had just left, were closed. Why couldn't she have picked a big city instead of a small town? The inactivity and silence were unnerving.

Richard followed her.

Patty increased her pace.

Another car passed and she absently glanced at it. A mistake, for Richard suddenly appeared in front of her again. This time she let out a scream.

"Don't," Richard urged, a mixture between a plea and a command.

"Get away from me!" She skirted him, going out into the road before returning to the sidewalk, this time on the opposite side of him. "Please, please."

"I am sorry for what I did to Grandmother. You must understand that I had lost control. I didn't mean to do what I—"

"I heard that before. Go away. Go back to where you came from. To your grave—or whatever. Just go away!" Her voice was loud, on the verge of hysteria in the quiet, empty street.

"Don't do this to me." This time it was a plea, almost a sob. "Mother, help me."

Patty walked rapidly away from him.

He moved just as fast, keeping up with her. "I'm your son," he reminded her.

"Not anymore."

"Don't say that. Father never said that."

"Go away!" she screamed for the final time, then broke into a run, this time making sure she didn't look back. She ran blindly, stumbling, ignoring the sharp pain that developed beneath her ribs. She ran on and on, her heels clicking in a steady, frantic rhythm on the sidewalk. Her lungs burned, and still she didn't stop. She ran until she was in her apartment, behind a locked door.

Then she listened, panting painfully, for sounds of footsteps. But there were none.

Clutching her side, Patty collapsed in front of the door. It was a long time before she could move away from it.

23

She nervously looked around the apartment, flicking lights on as she entered each room. Richard could come through walls, couldn't he? The dead can do anything, can't they? She found the bottle of vodka in the kitchen and promply opened it. Hands shaking, she poured herself a drink, splashing some of the liquid onto the floor. She didn't even bother to put ice into the glass.

As she drank, she listened for sounds. The refrigerator, old and beginning to develop a grayish tint, vibrated through the room with its erratic hums and sputters. A TV droned on in another apartment. A car horn beeped outside.

But there were no sounds of Richard.

There were no signs or smell of him either, but intuitively she knew he was near, hovering like a ghost. Patty finished the vodka, having drunk it faster than usual, then she went into Janet's room to check on the girl. To her relief her daughter seemed all right, sleeping peacefully. She kissed her forehead, then quietly retreated from the room. Next, she checked on Frankie. He, too, seemed undisturbed, deep in sleep. She kissed his forehead as well, then returned to the kitchen and refilled her glass. This time she added ice.

She sat at the table and buried her head in her

hands. *Richard is back*, her mind repeated like a stubborn line in a song. *Richard is back . . . Richard is back . . . And there's gonna be trouble.*

She took a sizable gulp of the burning liquid. Slow down, she warned herself, but another part of her refused to listen.

She would have to do something, but what? She knew now that she couldn't escape him, so something else would have to be done, but her mind drew a frustrating blank. She felt as if she were in a corner, stalemated.

Then she remembered the book on demonology that she had purchased a few days ago. She hadn't read it yet, not because there hadn't been any time, but because she had subconsciously hoped that Richard would stay away, making the book superfluous. But now she had to find new hope, and maybe this book would give her some. Maybe it'd give her some answers at least, which was the reason why she'd bought it in the first place.

She pulled the book down from the top of the refrigerator and began thumbing through it. It was a hardcover book from a well-known press, not an ancient tome, and Patty normally would have considered the book trash, existing only to entertain rather than inform, but now she found herself unsure of anything. There was so much she didn't know. Nothing, she realized, was certain. Nothing was absurd. Skeptics could scoff and laugh at things they believed did not exist, but nobody could be thoroughly confident. Life was teeming with mysteries, and maybe all the answers were with death.

Patty scanned the bold-faced subject headings that were on the top of each page. ARRAS WITCHES. CHAMBRE ARDENTE AFFAIR. DEVIL'S MARK. FAMILIARS. INQUISITION. MALEFICIA. POLTERGEIST. SEXUAL RELATIONS WITH DEVILS.

Patty's eyes froze on this last heading. Her heart accelerated a she read beyond.

> Pope Benedict XIV, in De Servorum Dei Beatificatione, made the following comment in reference to devils known as incubi (male) and succubi (female):
> ". . . for while most authorities admit copulation, some writers do not believe there can be offspring. Others, however, assert that children may result, and declare that this in actuality has occurred."

Tell me something that I don't know, Patty thought wryly while her heart continued to race. The following sentence leaped out at her.

> Pope Innocent VIII also believed that it was possible for devils and humans to have intercourse.

Patty had suspected Richard's father was a devil of some sort, but seeing her suspicion in print still disconcerted her. Her alcoholic haze began to thin a bit, so she quickly took a sip of her drink again and read on.

> Three children (Anna Rausch, twelve, Sybille Lutz, eleven, and Murchin, eight and a half) in Wurzburgh, January 1628, claimed to have sexual relations with incubi.

Patty took another sip of her drink, turned a page and read:

> The devil could appear in any form or shape he wished.

Further on down the page:

> Françoise Secretain confessed to
> having carnal relations with the devil,
> sometimes as a black man, and some-
> times as a dog, cat, or fowl. In 1679 the
> Scottish witches at Borrowstones ad-
> mitted to the commissioners that the devil
> had copulated with them in the form of a
> deer.

On the following page:

> Marie de Marigrane, 15, of Biarritz,
> claimed to have seen the devil couple with
> a number of women. The devil would have
> intercourse with the beautiful women
> from the front and with the ugly from the
> rear.

Patty looked up from the book, and noted that
there was a chill in the room. Also there was an eerie
stillness. She thought of closing the book, even
burning it, but her curiosity was not to be deterred.

> Devils can assume the bodies of dead
> men, or recreate out of air and other
> elements a body like that of man.

And after skipping more paragraphs, the text
began to focus on the devils' offspring.

> At Toulouse in 1275 Angela da
> Labarthe delivered a creature with a
> wolf's head and a snake's tail; she was
> believed to have been the first woman
> burned for carnal dealings with the devil.
> In 1531, at Augsburg, a woman gave birth
> to a two-footed serpent.

And:

> *The following famous figures are believed to have devilish orgin: Alexander the Great, Caesar Augustus, Scipio Africanus, Plato, as well as Merlin, and the entire race of Huns.*

The stillness around Patty deepened. Even the refrigerator seemed more quiet than usual. Patty nervously looked around the kitchen, as though searching for the cause of the pervasive silence, but nothing was out of the ordinary. Nothing moved, except the clock on the wall. The long minute hand jerked, then slipped over the short hand, covering it. Midnight.

The bewitching hour.

The borderline time.

The time when night creatures . . .

Patty hastily took a large swallow of vodka to numb her mind some more. Again she contemplated discarding the book and again was magnetically drawn to it.

> *Thievenne Paget claimed that intercourse with Satan was as painful as a woman in labor. Eva of Kenn, from Tyres, in 1572, confessed to intercourse with a devil, claiming it was like an icicle. At sixteen Agatha Soothtell was seduced by the devil.*

On and on the list went, until Patty, unable to read any more on the subject, began flipping through the pages in search of something else. She couldn't believe there were so many accounts of sexual relations with demons. Were they all accurate? How many women—and men—had never reported their experiences, fearing ridicule? Was it more common than she'd thought?

Oh God, she moaned inwardly, there is so much evil in the world. How did you let it happen?

Absently, she continued to turn the pages, then she paused at the heading CIRCLE.

> *To summon a demon, a circle is usually drawn around the conjurer for protection. Usually this is done on the floor with charcoal or on the ground with a sword or an arthame, a ceremonial knife. It is important that the circle be unbroken. It is a powerful symbol of eternity, for it has no beginning or end. The conjurer must remember to stay within the circle. Even if as much as a finger is outside this, he would be doomed.*

At last there was a flicker of hope. It was minuscule, but it was there nonetheless. She didn't have any charcoal to draw a circle, but she couldn't see why something like lipstick wouldn't suffice. The circle, she realized, wouldn't solve anything, but at least it would be protection against Richard.

Closing the book, she downed the rest of the drink, then poured herself another. She was already feeling light-headed and a trifle dizzy, but that was all right. It was best this way. Otherwise she'd probably go mad.

She took a long sip of her drink, then reached for her pocketbook and pulled out a tube of lipstick. She held it securely in her hand, then for good measure took down the plastic crucifix that was on the wall. She held that along with the lipstick. Now she was ready.

Come out, Richard, wherever you are!

She took another generous sip. Then another. And another.

Janet ran all the way home, but her home in Massachusetts was gone. Where the apartment house used to be there was now a big amusement park, and the calliope music from the carousel was annoying and deafening, so much louder than she expected it to be, and the multicolored lights from the spinning rides were too dazzling, dizzying her. And the rides were moving too fast. Someone screamed at her, "Get the hell outta the way!" Janet instinctively jumped back, and just in a nick of time, for a roller coaster car whizzed by. She could actually feel the wind of it as it passed. Then she looked down in alarm and noticed that she had been standing on the tracks. Then another car sped past, and in this one she saw Danny, her boyfriend. Oh, how she missed him! She had pleaded with him to wait for her to come back from Indiana. And now here she was, but he hadn't waited for her. Oh no, he was in the car with Betty, the prettiest and most popular girl in the junior class, and he was doing it to her right out in public for everyone to see. How could he do this to her! How could he!

Janet began to sob, right then and there on the tracks. She didn't care if another car came along. Her life was over as far as she was concerned. She kept sobbing and sobbing, until . . .

She realized it wasn't she who was weeping. It was someone else—something in that other place, that other world. She opened her eyes and found herself back in Indiana, in the lousy, smelly apartment. And the sobs that she had thought were hers were coming from a dark corner in her bedroom.

Janet lay still on her bed, wondering if she hadn't awakened at all from a dream but simply slipped into another one. The weeping sound was now more like that of a dog, a whimpering puppy. Timidly, she reached for the lamp, hesitating a moment before pulling the small chain. Light cruelly blinded her for a few seconds, then she spotted someone in the corner, sitting cross-legged on the floor.

It took several heartbeats to recognize him. "Rich," she gasped.

He looked up at her with the saddest eyes she'd ever seen.

"You're alive," she cried with relief, scrambling across the bed until she was on its edge, closer to her brother. He didn't answer, but then she had asked him the dumbest question. Of course he was alive! "Where on earth have you been?"

Still he didn't answer but only gazed strangely at her. There seemed to be, along with the heart-breaking sadness, a longing. Janet joined him on the floor, tucking her legs in under her, sitting on her heels. "What's the matter, Rich? Why were you crying?"

Again she thought he wasn't going to respond, but at last he said, "If only she were like you." The longing was in his voice, too.

"Who, Rich?"

Once more there was only silence in reply. His doleful eyes were still searching her, reminding her of those hungry kids from Africa who mirrored yearning, agony and hope. She moved to touch him, but he quickly pushed himself away from her.

"No," he said quietly.

Janet dropped her hand. "Why not?"

"You might not like it."

This time it was Janet's turn to stare in silence. She tried to think back to when she had last touched him. She remembered making several attempts, especially when he had first returned, but he had rebuffed her each time. "You said you were sick then," she said out loud. "You were afraid I'd catch something." When he made no attempt to explain, she added, "It was a lie, wasn't it?"

Almost imperceptibly he nodded, but still made no effort to explain.

"Well, I'm glad to see you, even though you're shutting me out," Janet declared.

"I'm not shutting you out. It may seem that way, but I'm not. You are all I have that is good."

Janet nodded, pretending she understood, but she didn't. What on earth could possibly be wrong with a hug between brother and sister? She really was glad to see him and wanted to prove it. She didn't care what her mother and Frankie thought. If it was true that he had killed Grandma and Myles, then it was probably partly their fault. They should have realized that Rich was sick, that he needed love and help. By rejecting him they had only made him worse, made him—

"You are beautiful."

The remark shattered her thoughts, surprising her. She found him staring intently at her face. He was smiling, a faint, adoring smile. Suddenly she felt transparent, as if a door to her mind had carelessly been left open for him to see and read.

"If only she were like you," he said for the second time.

"Who?" she demanded. She wasn't going to let him evade the question again.

He seemed surprised she didn't already know. "Mother," he finally said.

The answer momentarily stunned her. "Why do you wish she were like me?"

"You are not afraid to love me."

"Why would I be afraid?"

The silence again. How could he say he wasn't shutting her out if he kept ignoring her questions?

"I'm not shutting you out," he reassured her.

Janet blinked stupidly at him. "How did you

know what I was thinking?"

"Perhaps I went about it all wrong," he said pensively, automatically avoiding her question. "I frightened her. I was too desperate. Or maybe I didn't try hard enough. Every time I tried, the other half seemed to get in the way."

"What are you talking about? Frightened who?"

"Mother."

Janet shook her head in confusion and frustration. "I don't understand. Why is she frightened of you?" As soon as she asked the question she wanted to retract it. She didn't want to know the answer. Maybe this was what he'd meant when he said he wasn't shutting her out; actually he was protecting her from something that would damage their relationship. She told herself to remember the old adage—"What you don't know won't hurt you."

But this time he didn't ignore the question. "I killed Myles and Grandma."

There, she thought, he said it, and now there was no turning back. Her brother was a two-time murderer. She should be filled with loathing and recoiling from him with shock and revulsion, but all she felt, along with disappointment, was sympathy. Only God knew what her brother had gone through when he lived alone with his father. His mind had been twisted, for certainly a sane mind would not have eaten rats and bugs. He needed help, and no one would give it to him. Maybe that was why she felt such strong compassion for him—because he was alone and she was the only one willing to help him.

"I couldn't help it," Richard went on, and Janet could see that he was sincere about it. No actor, no matter how gifted, could express remorse like this.

"I lose control. Father's half in me is so strong, Janet. You wouldn't believe how strong it is. If I feel even just a spark of jealousy it grows into a rage. It

grows and grows until . . ." His voice faltered, indecisive as whether or not to continue.

"Tell me everything, Rich," Janet encouraged.
"It's not good to keep things bottled up inside. That's
what Mr. Carringer always says." Mr. Carringer was
her psychology teacher.

Richard nodded faintly, as though deciding that
she was right, that he should express his feelings and
let them flow. "There's a constant pulling in me,
Janet. It's as if Father is pulling one way, and Mother
the other. But Mother is weak, and that's why I'm
back."

"I don't understand."

"I don't want her to be weak."

"Rich, I still don't—"

"Of course you don't understand." Richard
sighed in weary frustration.

"Explain it to me."

Richard searched her face, and she could see that
he was afraid to tell her something, afraid that she
might think differently of him if he did.

"Nothing would ever change my feelings toward
you," she promised. "You're my baby brother and I
will always love you."

Something in his eyes softened. At length he said,
"I'm not human like you, Janet. I . . ."

Janet nodded, encouraging him to go on.

"I am a part of my father, and he . . . he was not
human."

Janet frowned, puzzled, but said nothing.

"I hate my father," Richard continued, "but then,
he would want it no other way. He taught me to feed
on negative feelings, to make them grow, but I'm not
completely like my father. I am also like Mother.
She's part of me, although she seems to want no part
of me. She . . . she . . ." He tilted his head back, his
face twisted in torment, and for a moment it seemed
he would howl like a stricken wolf caught in a trap.

But instead, he squeezed his eyes shut, silently endured the hurt until it subsided, then reopened his eyes and said, "I need her help."

"I'm still confused, Rich, but maybe I can help you."

Richard shook his head, emphasizing that this was not possible. "She is my mother. She is half of me. If only she weren't so weak."

"How could Mom help you?"

"By fighting with my father's half in me."

"Your father is in you?"

"No, Janet," Richard said patiently. "Father is gone from this world and back in his. It is what he passed on to me that I'm talking about."

"Oh." Janet found herself more confused than ever. She also began to suspect that Richard was confused himself. His father, no doubt insane, had influenced him and twisted his mind to be like his. Now Janet hoped it wasn't too late for psychiatric help.

"No."

"What?"

"No psychiatrist."

Janet stared imcomprehensibly at him, then felt a chill rush through her. "How did you know I was thinking about a psychiatrist?"

"I told you, I'm not human."

"Then what are you?"

"You would not understand. I recreated the body I had from its flesh, and from the air, the moon, the sun. The power of life is everywhere; it abounds us. And I absorb heat from the air, the sun, and whoever is around me; I absorb it to give my own body temporary life. Sometimes, I fear, I take too much and leave the air and those around me cold. I do this to be with Mother. I need her help."

"Are you saying you're some kind of . . . ghost?"

"I'm not alive," Richard said. "At least not in

your sense of the word."

"You really believe this?"

"It is obvious that you don't."

"Well, it is—" she swallowed, then continued in a calmer voice "—kind of farfetched."

Richard fell silent, and because of this silence Janet found herself believing what he had said. Shouldn't he have tried harder to convince her? And also, the truth was evident in his face, in the way his expression suggested that he wished otherwise—to be alive and human.

"My God, it is true, isn't it?" she whispered incredulously. He said nothing, and she experienced a ripple of horror but fought it. There was nothing to be terrified of, she adamantly told herself. Her brother—whatever he was—was pleading for help, and this was no time to flee, screaming, like one who had just caught a glimpse of the bogeyman.

"You're afraid," he said.

"No," she denied, a little too hastily.

"I suppose it doesn't matter."

Never had she seen him so downcast. It brought back a memory, of when Frankie and his friends had made fun of him. Richard had cried then, and she had comforted him since Mom was too busy and Grandma was watching something "important" on TV. He was only three years younger than she, but she held him in her lap and rocked him as though she were his mother. He used to fall asleep in her arms, and she used to feel so much love pour out of him and seep into her.

She wished she could do that now.

He looked at her, apparently aware of her thoughts. "It's different now," he reminded her.

"What would happen if I touched you?"

"Mother didn't like it, even when she was sleeping. I would have never touched her if I didn't want so desperately to be close to her." Facing Janet, he said, "You might not like it. You might be—"

"Scared?"

"Yes."

Janet thought about this for a moment, then declared, "Maybe not. Come on, Rich, let me hold you."

Richard shook his head, but the gesture wasn't firm. "I don't think it'd be—"

"But I hate seeing you so unhappy," Janet protested. When he made no further objection, she knew she had won. She could hold him, like she used to. And then for a moment she found herself suddenly reluctant. Would she actually be touching a ghost, or whatever he was? Swiftly, she swept the question away as though it were a speck of dirt, then she moved closer and gingerly wrapped an arm around her brother's frail shoulder.

The contact took her breath away. It was like the first splash of cold water in the morning. Janet shivered involuntarily, then willed herself to endure the cold. She had never thought a body could be this frigid—but then, this was not a living body. Resolutely, she forced the gruesome realization from her mind.

"You don't have to prove anything," she heard Richard say as she drew him closer. "You can let go."

"No." And to prove this, she wrapped her other arm around him, hugging him tighter. Now it didn't seem so bad, so cold. Repeatedly, she told herself that this was her brother in her arms, and that she loved him. Nobody, it seems, loved him, but she did. She loved him so very, very much.

"Don't you hate me for killing Myles and Grandmother?" His voice betrayed amazement.

"Don't talk about that now," she said. "Just relax. Everything's going to be all right."

But Richard was still tense, yet not as cold.

"Relax," she ordered softly. "Rest your head

against me, like you used to."

Richard hesitated.

"Go ahead."

He sat in front of her and leaned back until he was resting against her, her arms around him, cozily comforting him. Then he tucked his head beneath her chin.

"Everything's going to be all right," she whispered. He seemed so harmless now, as harmless as a baby. He was a baby—her baby brother—and she probably loved him so much because nobody else did.

And he was no longer cold, but warm just like her. She smiled and found herself relaxing.

"You are helping me," he said gratefully. "But it is not enough."

"Shhh. Everything's going to be all right," she repeated.

And foolishly, she believed it.

24

Richard reveled in the warmth that shrouded him like a palpable blanket. So often he'd be cold and have to absorb heat from the air and from those who were around him, but Janet was liberally supplying him with warmth by her embraces. It had been a long, long time since he had felt this wonderful, and now he almost felt strong enough to combat the other feelings inside him, the one that was implacably pulling toward that fiery end—almost, but not enough. Only his mother could make him strong enough, for she was half of him, his father the other. One must dominate the other, for the two could not coexist harmoniously.

And Richard longed for his mother's half to dominate, but longing was not enough. The jealousy, contempt and bitterness were usually uncontrollable. He sometimes felt like those wife- and child-beaters he'd heard about. The violence could not be restrained, although remorse and pleas for forgiveness invariably ensued. It was a constant pulling, but one was weaker than the other.

A pendulum. Back and forth.

And right now Richard was experiencing a warm glow. His sister loved him, and he loved her. Such an extreme, he found himself thinking. He loved his sister more than anything else, whereas he hated Myles, Grandmother, and, oh yes, Frankie, more than anything else. Love and hate. Back and forth.

He wished the pendulum would stop, exactly where it was now, but he knew it wouldn't. It would begin to swing the other way, toward his father.

Behind him, arms still protectively around him, Janet fell asleep. His body, deathly cold at first, gradually warmed and lulled her. Now she was leaning a side of her face against the top of his head and was breathing softly. Richard wanted to stay this way, to freeze this wonderful moment for an eternity, but he also wanted to see his mother. When the pendulum was in this position there was hope, hope that his mother would suddenly break through the doubts and fears and cherish him the way she cherished Janet and Frankie. Hope—a thin positive force in a sea of negativism, but existing just the same, glimmering faintly.

Gently, he extricated himself from his sister, then carried her back to her bed. He covered her, gazed adoringly for a long moment, then leaned forward and kissed her cheek.

"I love you," he whispered.

She stirred in response but did not awaken. He studied her for a moment more, then quietly left the room, closing the door behind him.

He found his mother in the kitchen. At first he thought she was asleep, her arms on the table, cradling her head, but a pungent scent permeated his body, and like a computer he methodically analyzed it and came to a deduction. Vodka. The woman at the table had overindulged and was now unconscious.

As he'd done with his sister, he stared lengthily at his mother. A blend of compassion and pity swept through him as he slowly moved closer to her. He was certain she had been drinking because of him, and it was because she was afraid of him, because she knew the truth of what he was, but she didn't understand. He wished there was a way he could remove the fear that was clouding the light, but there seemed to be no way. In his desperation he had worsened things. He had got Myles and Grandmother out of the way, but this had not smoothed the path as he had hoped; it had only made his mother run farther down it.

He reached out to touch her, to stroke her pretty hair, then something he saw stopped him. One of her hands was closed in a tight fist and two objects protruded from it. Richard stared curiously at the hand, gradually recognizing the objects. One was a cheap crucifix, and the other a tube of lipstick. Lipstick? He frowned, then gently began to unfurl his mother's fist.

Upon cold contact Patty grunted, but she was too inundated with alcohol to move, let alone protest. Richard then proceeded to open her hand wider and completely disclose the cross and lipstick. The latter still puzzled him. Had she started to apply it to her lips before passing out? He tried to concentrate on her mind to learn something about this, but it was too hazy with sleep and drink. But the crucifix, he knew, was to protect herself from him. She had already tried this before. What she didn't seem to realize was that the cross was useless when he wasn't controlled by his father's half. This was how he had taken his mother's other crucifix, the golden one she'd worn around her neck. He had kicked it with his foot in his dark rage until it was hidden under a bed, then, when he was calm again, had retrieved it, keeping it until his mood began to change. In fear and contempt he hastily had flushed the golden pendant down a toilet.

Now he reached for the plastic crucifix, coveting its warmth and serenity, but as his hand reached for it a voice stopped him.

"Keep your fucking hands off her!"

Without moving his body, Richard slowly turned his head toward his brother in the doorway. Frankie, clad only in fleece pants, was stabbing a finger in warning at him. His face was twisted in a snarl, a face that Richard knew was merely the mask of a bully.

"Get away from her!"

Richard eyed him silently. Yes, just a mask, he decided. Beneath it Frankie was still as scared as that night when he had pissed in his pants.

"This does not concern you," he quietly told him, "so take a walk."

Frankie's stabbing finger curled and his hand became a fist, which he waved in the air at Richard's face. "Y'deaf or something? I said get away from my mother."

"Don't make me angry," Richard warned, already feeling a change occurring inside him. He was going the other way now, toward darkness. "Go," he commanded his brother.

But Frankie defiantly came closer, now both hands clenched in readiness. "I ain't afraid of ya, murderer! This time I'm prepared for ya."

"Shall I send my shadow after you?" Richard grinned maliciously as everything around him seemed to darken. He could feel the familiar heat grow and spread inside him, the burning heat of hate and resentment toward the muscular teenager in front of him.

"Those shadows were only a dream," the boy said, his voice steady but a trifle too high. "I was half-asleep that night."

"Are you asleep now?" Richard widened his grin, taunting his brother.

Frankie ignored the question. Instead, he repeated, "Get away from my mother."

"You speak as though she is your mother only and not mine," Richard said, then looked over at the woman at the table. She was still unconscious, face hidden in the crook of her arms. Turning back to Frankie, who was now almost thoroughly concealed in darkness, he added, "She loves you very much, but alas, not me."

"Cut the goofy crap and get the fuck—"

"I don't accept orders, big brother. You should know that by now."

The snarling mask slipped, but Frankie quickly shifted it back in place. "Look, if ya don't—"

"What's the matter, you don't trust me with *our* mother?"

Frankie said nothing, clenching his fists tighter.

"Are you afraid I'd do what I've done with Myles and Grandmother?"

"You killed them, didn't you, you bastard?"

"Tsk, tsk, let's not get nasty."

"You're not gonna get away with it."

"I'm not?" Richard mocked surprise.

"No, I'll make fucking sure y'don't."

"My, my, such language. You think you are quite the big boy. I imagine you even believe you are already a man. Are you already a man, Frankie?"

The brother refused to answer. When Richard took a menacing step toward him he stepped back, then quickly caught himself and moved forward, attempting to erase his retreat. He squared his naked shoulders in defiance. Ain't afraid of you, ain't afraid of nothing, his stance declared.

Richard laughed, then his grin vanished and his countenance became grim. "Well, are you a man, Frankie? How many pretty cheerleaders have you fucked?"

"None of your business. Look, I don't know where you've been lately, but why don'tcha go back, huh? Just get away from Mom."

"Why are you so worried? She doesn't even know I'm here. It is for yourself that you should be concerned."

"I said I ain't 'fraid—"

"You see, big brother—or is it big man?—I don't like bullies. They remind me of pesty houseflies. They're too stupid to leave you alone, and the only way to get rid of them is to swat them."

Frankie's face paled, but his fists and shoulders remained firm and challenging. "What're ya talking 'bout?"

"How much clearer do I have to be? I abhor bullies, and you are a bully and always were. I had to bite you once. Remember that? And so since I hate bullies, I hate you."

"I don't giva shit if you hate me or not. Never liked ya much anyways."

"Of that, I was always full aware."

Frankie glared at him, then with obvious force moved past him toward his mother. "Are you all right, Mom?"

The woman grunted but did not move. He shook her shoulder. "Mom?" When she failed to respond again, he snapped at his brother, "What did you do to her?"

"Do? She's drunk, idiot. The bitch doesn't like to think about me, so she drinks." He lightly shrugged his shoulders, but his voice betrayed a hard bitterness.

"I'm calling the police," Frankie suddenly decided, "and don't you try anything funny."

"You mean, like disappearing?"

"Yeah."

"I don't see any phone in this sty."

The nearest phone was in the apartment across the hall, and Frankie wordlessly made a start for it. But when he reached the front door to his own apartment he found it jammed. He struggled with the knob, pulled at it, twisted it, and even kicked the door itself. He kept at it until he heard Richard laughing. He spun around and was startled to find his brother only inches away from him.

Frankie opened his mouth to say something, an obscenity no doubt, but changed his mind. Uncertainty and fear flickered in his eyes, then determination took hold. He returned to his struggle at the door. "Open up, y'fucker!"

Richard continued to laugh, a sound that was faint and low in his throat, like a rumble that was more felt than heard.

Frankie ignored him as he doggedly worked at the door. Repeatedly he swore at it, yanking, wiggling and pulling at the knob. He was so blind with determination that, at first, he did not feel the change in his palm, did not notice that the knob had become cold and wet like borderline ice, like frigid slime. He did not notice until he felt something move and ripple in his hand. Even then he was too frantic to pull away. It wasn't until he experienced a sharp pain, something like a razor blade slicing the center of his palm, that he jerked away. He was in time to catch a glimpse of a yawning slit on the knob and a row of ragged, diminutive teeth before it closed and blended with the smooth surface of the dull, brass knob. He gawked at it and wouldn't have believed what he'd seen if it weren't for his hand; it was bleeding at the palm, like a holy stigma.

"It . . . it *bit* me," he whispered incredulously.

Richard's laugh was no longer confined to his throat. It rose, whistling through his teeth.

"Stop it!" Frankie pressed his wounded palm with his other to stem the bleeding.

"As you would usually say—'make me, big man.' "

Frankie ignored him and glanced quickly around the room in search of something to stop the bleeding. When he couldn't find anything, he went back into the kitchen and found a dish towel to wrap around his hand. Patty, still at the table, lifted her head as he and Richard entered the room, but her eyes were glassy with alcohol, not fully comprehending what was happening. She opened her mouth but only uttered a grunt. Then, too weary to keep her head up any longer, she went back to sleep on her arms.

"It is my turn to be a bully, big man." Richard grinned.

"Get the fuck outta here."

"Make me."

Frankie stared, and his fists almost seemed to be pulsing with tension, but he didn't make a move, didn't dare, no matter how much his ego demanded of it. And Richard's eyes glittered complacently at this. "Afraid, big man?" he mocked, tilting his head to one side. "Cluck. Cluck."

"No, I'm . . . I'm not afraid."

"Well, you're not seeing me—as you suggested—getting the fuck out of here."

Sweat broke out in bubbles on Frankie's pallid face. "Look, I don't want no trouble, okay? Leave Mom alone, okay?" Suddenly something invisible shoved his shoulder, pushing him back a step. "Wha . . ."

"How do you like being pushed around?"

Before Frankie could answer, he was pushed back another step. The shove was quick, yet violent, nearly knocking him off his feet. Now alarm and uncertainty were more than a mere flicker in his eyes. "What's going on?"

Another shove.

"Bully, bully," Richard taunted, eyes fixed on him, arms calmly folded across his chest. "I'm the bully now, bully."

"How did you—" He couldn't finish. He was as scared as that other time, and Richard expected him to piss in his pants again. But he didn't. Instead, he began to mumble, "Dream . . . dream . . ."

"No dream," Richard assured him, and as though to prove this he let another force slam into his brother. This time Frankie hit a wall with his back.

"Dream!" he screamed, refusing to believe otherwise.

The outcry was loud, and Richard was certain someone would awaken in the building and pound on the door. But nothing happened; even his mother was still out of it. She had briefly lifted her head to see what she had heard, but that was all. To ensure himself that nothing like this would happen again, for he wanted this to be prolonged and without interference, he willed the towel around his brother's hand to unwrap itself, rise and force its way into the boy's mouth, plugging it.

Frankie tried to let out a scream, but it was muffled. He then made a frantic attempt to reach for the gag but found his arms paralyzed.

"I'm the bully now," Richard sang in a sepulchral voice.

Frankie grunted, straining to move his arms, trying to push and spit out the towel. Blood rushed to his face, reddening it, yet he still struggled. Stubborn bastard, Richard thought as he watched the face darken to a purplish shade. It amused him that his brother was fighting strenuously while he was imprisoning him with such ease. Negative forces, like loathing, resentment and revenge, were quite powerful, indeed. They could move mountains, lift boulders and, of course, lift . . .

Pressed against the wall, Frankie began to slide upward. Realizing he was leaving the floor, his grunts became louder and more frantic. He kicked his feet and thrashed his body, but his arms were still limp and lifeless. Disbelief and terror were wild in his eyes.

He rose until his head touched the ceiling, then stopped, pinned like a butterfly to the wall. He was looking down at Richard, his face probably pleading for mercy, but Richard wasn't sure, so potent were the negative feelings that he couldn't see his brother clearly anymore. He had plunged completely into darkness as his insides burned with rage and hatred. All he could see now was the dark outline of a squirming teenager against a background that was a shade lighter.

Frankie thumped and kicked at the wall with his body and feet. The panic and desperation amused Richard, even delighted him, but he again worried that others in the building would hear and intervene. There was so much more he wanted to do. So he willed his brother's legs together, tied them with mental rope, then forcefully pressed against the midsection until there was a strangled cry of pain and all movements ceased.

Then he pushed Frankie, inch at a time, across the ceiling. He still could not see the face because of his darkened vision, but he knew the other was looking down at him, at the floor. The acrid smell of fear was strong in the room, and Richard grinned victoriously, feeling the black force inside him intensify. It filled him, then shot out at his brother on the ceiling, as violently as water from a fire hose.

"Bully . . . bully," Richard chanted, then abruptly severed the flow.

Frankie crashed to the floor, face slamming into the surface, nose cracking on impact. The boy bit the towel in agony as blood gushed from his nostrils. Then Richard willed him to roll over until he was on his back, swallowing the blood. Frankie gasped and coughed, managing only to suck in more of the towel. Then Richard sat him up, manipulating him like a marionette.

Eyes now glazed with pain, Frankie began shaking his head, mutely beseeching him to stop.

"Did you ever stop when you were the bully?"

Richard questioned.

But Frankie seemed too filled with agony to hear him; he kept shaking his head, tacitly pleading for pity.

"You never stopped, did you? You kept pushing those boys around until they couldn't move anymore. Isn't that right, big man? Janet told me you mostly bullied those who were younger and smaller than you. Isn't that right?"

Back and forth his brother's head went. No more no more no more . . .

Richard then concentrated on Frankie's left leg. He stared at it until it began to curl upward at the knee, the thigh fastened to the floor. Frankie's eyes widened in pain and liquid sounds bubbled in his throat. Then there was a sharp, bone-splintering crack, and Frankie's eyes squeezed shut in a silent scream.

Frankie began to whimper, his head back to rocking, pleading no more no more no more.

"Enough, big man?"

No more no more no more . . .

"You're a piece of shit. Do you know that?"

No more no more . . .

Richard focused on the other leg, willing it to rise and curve.

No more! Please!

Crrr-aaack!

Now the rocking became frantic and wild. Please, please, please!

"I don't know why Mother loves you so much," Richard said, "but she does. She loves you best. Did you know that?"

His brother, crazed with pain, was beyond hearing.

"Yes, she loves you best, and yet you are nothing but a lump of turd. And because she loves you so much, she forgets about me. Why should she bother with me if she has you, right? But—" He paused to let this last word linger "—if you didn't exist, big brother, then she couldn't love you best anymore. Now could she?"

The implication managed to penetrate Frankie's pain-filled brain. He stopped rocking his head and was gawking at Richard in horror.

"Now could she?" Richard repeated, quietly demanding a response.

But Frankie's eyes only grew wider as he stared.

"Shake your head. Yes or no?"

Faintly he began to move his head left to right. No more no more.

"I can't see you. You're not shaking your head enough."

Frankie rocked his head more visibly.

"That's not enough, bully. I still don't know if it's a yes or a no."

No! Frankie seemed to be screaming now. No, no, no!

"Maybe I should help you," Richard suggested, then commanded Frankie's head to move to the right, then slowly to the left, stretching the skin on the neck. "Was this what you wanted to answer? You wanted to say no, didn't you? Like this?"

He willed his brother's head to turn to the far right again, pushing and pushing, until he could almost hear it creak in resistance, until Frankie's eyes were bulging with pain.

"Too much?" Richard asked, mocking concern.

Frankie could only goggle, horrified.

Richard smiled, then forced his brother's head toward the left, pushing, pushing, pushing.

Another creak and now Frankie's eyes looked as if they would actually pop out, like newly exploded popcorn leaping from a vat of hot oil.

Then Richard heard frantic moans and grunts

behind him. Without losing his hold on his brother, he turned slightly to glance at his mother. She was staring at him and Frankie and was struggling to push herself up, but she was clumsy with drink.

"Nooooo, noooo," she was pleading, blinking furiously to clear her vision and head. "Stop, Richard. Stoooooo . . ."

But Richard didn't want to stop. He had gone with the flow, something that his father had so often urged him to do. And once you were caught in the flow, there was nothing you could do except let the rapid current sweep you along.

He turned his brother's head the opposite way and pushed and pushed.

"Stop!" his mother cried, quickly coming out of her daze now. "Stop it, Richard!"

Frankie screamed, a sound, although guttural, that managed to escape through the towel.

Richard laughed, then pushed harder.

"Please!" His mother started toward him, but fell to the floor the moment she left the chair. She scrambled frantically the rest of the way and grabbed his legs. She was momentarily stunned by the icy touch, but did not pull away. "Please," she repeated.

Ignoring her, he pushed again, forcing the head beyond its limit. There was a crack and a jolt of horror on Frankie's face, a look that betrayed disbelief as well, then froze into a permanent mask.

Frankie was dead, and still Richard did not find himself sated. He kept pushing and pushing.

"Oh God," his mother moaned at his feet. "Oh . . . my . . . God."

Richard twisted and twisted, as though Frankie's head were a bizarre light bulb. He twisted and twisted and twisted—until it came off. Then he heard his mother break into a deafening scream. And after that came another scream—Janet.

That was when the turbulence of the current ceased and the darkness began to break, like the coming of dawn.

25

Patty was certain she was hallucinating, no doubt from all that vodka she had drunk. She had been dreaming about drowning in a dark, almost black body of water when she heard grunting noises. She had thought it was herself screaming for help underwater, but when she opened her eyes she found her two sons in the kitchen—the older on the floor, his lower legs hideously contorted, bent forward, almost on his lap. Then she saw his head turning and turning.

She screamed. Janet abruptly appeared in the doorway, stopped short, and also screamed. When the head twisted loose with a final, violent rip, Patty knew the sickening wet sound would stay in her head for the rest of her life. She had wrapped her arms around Richard's legs in desperation to stop him, but it was like clutching a granite statue—cold and unyielding.

Finally she let go and scrambled toward her other son's headless body, then froze halfway, unable to go any closer. Blood was gushing from the opening between his shoulders, and she recoiled, then vomited on the floor.

Then she saw Richard move toward her. "Get away from me!" Never in her life had she shouted so loudly. The alcoholic fuzz suddenly evaporated and the picture was shockingly clear. Wiping her mouth with the back of her hand, Patty quickly rose to her feet and recoiled toward her daughter, who was still rooted to the doorway. This was when she spotted the crucifix and the tube of lipstick on the floor, near the table where she must have dropped them. She hesitated, debating whether or not to retrieve them, then made a dash for the items. She ran swiftly, as though expecting Richard to seize her as she passed, but he only watched without moving, his shoulders bent, his arms limp at his sides.

"'Don't be afraid, Mother," she heard him say.

Afraid? Now why would I be afraid? So what if my other son is dead on the floor in two pieces! That's still no reason to be afraid, now is it?

Patty felt a crazy impulse to laugh, but the laughter died quickly, smothered by terror. She snatched up the tube of lipstick and the crucifix, then rushed back to her daughter.

"Let's get out of here!" Taking Janet's hand she forced her to run with her to the front door. Behind them Richard continued to watch, his arms now extended as though silently imploring them to come back to him.

The door was jammed, Richard's doing undoubtedly. She spun around and found him walking toward them, moving in slow, almost fluid steps. His arms were still outstretched. The ugly rage she had seen on his face earlier was now completely gone. It was almost as though he had slipped on another mask.

"You must forgive me, Mother," he said. "And you must help me."

"Don't . . . don't come anywhere near us," she warned.

But he didn't listen and kept moving forward—until pounding was heard on the other side of the door. "Hey, what's going on in there?" a masculine voice demanded.

Hope surged through Patty. She started to yell for help, to ask for the police, but found her voice was gone. It was as if something had gripped her voice box and squeezed and paralyzed it. She frantically glanced at her daughter beside her, hoping she'd shout something through the door, but she too was rendered speechless. Then Patty saw that Richard was staring intently at them, at their throats.

As he kept her and Janet silent, he said to the man on the other side of the door, "We're just having a family quarrel, sir. We're sorry we disturbed you."

There was a pause, then a gruff reply. "Well, keep it down, will ya. It's after midnight, for Christ's sake."

"We will. And again we're sorry."

There was another pause, then footsteps retreated from the door. When they could no longer be heard Patty felt the grip inside her throat slacken. Absently, her hand reached for her neck. Was there anything Richard couldn't do?

He moved closer.

"No! Stay away!" Her voice was not as strong as before. "If you take another step, I'll . . . I'll . . ."

"Please, Mother, try to understand."

Patty thrust the crucifix at him. He stopped, not because of the holy object but because he suddenly seemed to see the futility of it all. Too much damage was done. It was all beyond repair now.

His outstretched arms dropped in defeat to his sides.

But although he seemed harmless, Patty wasn't taking any chances. Grabbing Janet, fiercely and painfully by the wrist, she pulled her closer, then opened the tube of lipstick.

"Mom, what are you doing?" Janet demanded, frowning.

Patty said nothing. Keeping a watchful eye on

Richard, she knelt down on the worn, cracked linoleum and drew a circle around herself and her daughter. When she was done, she instructed, "Don't step out of the circle, Janet. Don't even let a finger be outside of it."

Janet's frown deepened. "Why? What is this?"

"A circle will protect you from demons." Feeling somewhat safer, she then sneered at Richard. "That's what you are—a demon, isn't it?"

Richard looked at her sadly. "It won't work," he said after a long silence. "I am not a demon, and the circle is useless. It would not stop me."

A trick, a voice warned Patty. His father was a demon. What else would you call a creature who had grown before your eyes and then disappeared into thin air? And since he was a demon, and since his son was dead and talking to her right this very instant, then that made him a demon, also. Right?

Of course she was right, and the circle would protect her. How do I know? her mind crazily sang. The book told me so. Again she felt that fleeting impulse to laugh. Did this mean she was finally going crazy?

She hugged Janet, for the girl was all she had left. She held her tightly, desperately, nearly suffocating her, at the same time keeping a wary eye on Richard. "Go away," she hissed. "Leave us alone."

Richard lifted a foot, then deliberately planted it inside the circle, to prove his point.

Patty gaped in disbelief, then panic swept through her. The book was wrong!

"I'm not a demon," Richard reiterated. "I have half of you in me, and you're not a demon."

"What do you want from me?" Patty wailed in frustration, backing away from him, taking Janet with her.

"I've told you many times what I wanted. But you won't listen."

"What?" she screamed, her voice now fully recovered, now strong.

Janet's hands around her tightened. "I think I understand, Mom," she told her. "He wants you to love him. Don't you see—"

"Didn't *you* see?" Patty interrupted hysterically. "Didn't you see what he did to your brother?"

Now it was Janet's turn to embrace tightly, to protect what was precious to her. "Oh Mom, Mom. Yes, I did see, but I'm trying to keep it out of my head right now. I'm trying to think clearly. I'm trying to—"

"I love you, Mother," said Richard.

"Shut up!" Patty shrieked.

Richard's face crumpled, as though she had slapped him.

"Mom, Mom," Janet's voice shook her, demanding attention. "He wants your love."

"Love? How can you expect me to love him after what he did to—"

"Mom, listen," Janet demanded sharply. "Try to understand. There are two opposing forces inside Rich. He needs your love. He wants you to help him fight that other force. You understand what I'm telling you, Mom?"

But Patty was thinking about poor Frankie. What had he done to come to such a horrible end? He had been a strong, healthy boy—good-looking and popular with the girls. He had everything going for him. It wasn't fair. Richard had no right to kill him like that.

"Goddamn you!" She spat in Richard's face. "I hate you! You hear me? I hate you!"

"Mom, no!" Janet pleaded.

"Yes, yes!" Patty extricated herself from her daughter and bolted for the kitchen. At the sight of Frankie's severed corpse in a crimson puddle she let out a heart-wrenching sob, staggered backwards, then fought for composure and plunged toward her destination—the cutlery drawer.

Hastily rummaging through the instruments she finally found what she wanted—a chef's knife.

Can't kill something that's already dead, idiot! an inner voice reminded her.

But what else could she do? The crucifix and circle were useless. There was no phone in the apartment, and the door was jammed. And she had already tried shouting for help.

Clutching the knife, feeling a little secure, she returned to the other room. "If you don't get out of here by the count of three," she said, struggling to keep her voice steady, "I'm going to do what you did to Frankie. Got that?" When there was no response, she began: "One . . . two . . ."

Richard made no move. The knife in Patty's hand shook, nearly blurring.

"Three!"

"Mom." Janet tried to placate her. "We all know the knife won't do anything."

"But I've got to do something." And with that she raised the knife, then plunged it into Richard's neck. He didn't flinch or cry out in pain. She lifted the knife again, this time burying the blade in his chest. Again he stood firmly, enduring the attack, as though she were merely slapping him with her hand. She pulled the knife out once more and made another attempt, aiming for his heart—if there was one.

No blood flowed. The knife made deep gashes, and a foul stench, a damp smell of swamp and sewer, escaped each time she made a wound, but that was all.

"You are making me angry, Mother." It was a quiet warning.

She looked into his face, saw that doleful mask changing. She felt the air chill around her. Yet she clung to the knife, pulled it out and slammed it back into him.

"Mother."

Janet's hands were suddenly on her shoulders, tugging her away from Richard. "Mom, stop it. This isn't going to work. Stop it!"

Panting heavily, Patty held the handle of the knife with both hands. She stopped plunging but would not let go of the weapon. The blade, instead of stained red, was partly smeared with a grayish mudlike substance. This too stank of rot and death, but she still refused to part with it. She wasn't certain why, but this felt more secure in her hand than the cross had.

"Please, Rich, you've got to try to understand, too," she heard Janet say. "Please."

Richard's countenance, which had started to darken with anger, began to soften again.

"We have to be calm, discuss this," Janet went on. "It's the only way."

Patty gripped the handle tighter, whitening her knuckles. "He killed my son," she reminded her in a broken voice. "And he killed—"

"You never told me anything about his father." Janet deliberately cut her off.

"What?"

"Where did you meet him? What did he do? What was he?"

"I met him at the Red Lantern. I wasn't myself then, upset and down because your father had left me, and so I brought this stranger—monster—home."

"What was he?" Janet asked again.

"I don't know. Ask him!" Patty jerked her head toward Richard. "All I know was that he was a shape changer and evil."

"Why didn't you tell me this before, Mom?"

"Because I was ashamed. I didn't want you to

think your mother was a . . . whore."

"Oh, Mom."

Patty's chin shook as a violent wave of grief and fury flooded through her. To Richard she shouted, "Why did you kill Frankie? What did he do to you?"

"I lost control," he said.

"You always lose control. That's because you're evil. Like your father. Evil! So why is my love so important?"

"It is because of you I could see that other side at all. It was only a glimpse, very faint, but I saw it. Now I want to see more of it, but I'm not strong enough. I need you to nourish me, to help me make that climb."

"You never talk clearly, never make any sense. Do you know that?"

"I will try then. That is, if you will listen clearly."

"I just want you to go away, leave me and Janet alone."

"Listen, Mother!" Richard demanded, so vehemently that Patty found herself silent and obedient. When he saw that he had her rapt attention he lowered his voice, and began, "Father was full of hate and anger, and he encouraged me to be like him. He would always goad me, pick on me until I lost my temper, then he would continue to needle me and feed the anger. Sometimes he would charm a bird into his hand, then give it to me when I was in the middle of a rage, and he would urge me to crush the bird. And I would give in. And he'd laugh—proud of me—and I'd be proud of myself. But then I'd feel this guilt, and I would think of you and miss you. I told Father about this, but he convinced me that you didn't love me.

"He tried to make me hate you, but that was something I couldn't do. I wanted to be like Father in every way, but because of you I couldn't be completely like him. There was a war inside me, Mother, a war that wouldn't end. I told Father of this and he said that there was only one way to stop the constant pulling within me—death—and he said in death everything would be complete. Not only would the battle inside me be finished, but I'd be exactly as he was. I would join him in his eternal place and never be disturbed by guilt anymore.

"Believing him, I hanged myself while he watched. But the war inside me did not cease; it only became worse. Father had lied. I found myself in the middle of darkness. Above me to the right I saw a bluish-white light and I could sense its peace and sweetness. Something from that light reached me, caressed and calmed me. It left a part of itself in me before retreating to its source, and below to the left I saw a different kind of light; it was orange-red. It flickered with wild excitement. It tempted me, even aroused me in a sexual way. Both lights, each in a different way, attracted me."

Richard paused, lookin at Patty, then at Janet, as though wondering if they were grasping what he was saying, if he was wasting his time. But he could see that he still had their full attention, even if his mother was avoiding eye contact with him and was hugging herself, trembling.

He continued. "I tried to move toward the bluish light, but found myself too weak to make the climb. It would be easier to descend toward the red light. Not much strength would be needed. It would be like running downhill. I could sense my father's presence down there, urging me to join him. I could even feel his wrath as I hesitated, as I kept looking up at the other light."

Patty stared at him, wonder momentarily replacing horror. Were the lights he were referring to actually entrances to Heaven and Hell? Had he entered one or both of them? Seen what they were like?

Reading her thoughts, Richard said, "I was close
enough to catch a glimpse of the red side, but I did
not enter it. It was rich with the smell of meat and
fire. Actually, a tempting scent for me. There were
cries of agony, also beckoning and arousing. There
was a mass of bodies fusing and separating to fuse
again on something else—all kinds of imaginable
bodies, ranging from humans to common houseflies.
It was a mass orgy where all life-forms participated
together. Tempting," he said again. "This was at the
entrance. Beyond, I could see flat land. At first I
thought it was a grassy meadow rippling, tinted
reddish from the light, but then I saw that the 'grass'
was actually maggots or something similar. This
field seemed to stretch infinitely. At one spot there
was an opening in the ground, like the mouth of a
volcano, and this was from where the orange-red
light projected. I wanted to peer into this opening
and imagined it being an immense well leading to the
core of this strange world. Yes, I was very curious to
peek into the well, to participate in the ultimate orgy.
I could feel, hear and smell Father all around me,
urging me to enter. Yet I couldn't.

"I kept glancing upward, at that other light. It
nagged at me. I knew that if I passed through one of
these entrances it would be something permanent,
no turning back, but I wanted at least a glimpse of
the bluish world before making the decision. So
against Father's protestations, I commenced the
climb, but the climb proved to be too difficult. I
simply did not have the strength. It was like trying
to scale a steep mountain without the correct equip-
ment. It seemed I had no choice but to enter the red
side. Either that or remain in between.

"But the blue side would not free me of its
temptation. There was a balming something—air, I
guess—that kept filtering through me, teasing me. I
wanted more of it, but as I've said before, I

simply wasn't strong enough to reach it.

"So, while Father continued coaxing me, occasionally bursting into rages, I contemplated making myself stronger. It wasn't long before I came to realize that Father dominated me and the red side was where he belonged. As for you, Mother, there was only a small trace left inside me, and you, I knew, would belong to the blue side. But the small trace that was inside me was enough to tempt me to want more, and so I knew only you could help me—at least to make a decision. Maybe a glimpse into the blue side would be all I needed. Maybe it was only curiosity. So I came back—to you."

"To me . . . from . . ." Patty couldn't finish, for it all seemed so incredible. She hugged herself tighter, but this didn't do much to ease the trembling. She wished her mind were still coated with alcohol, but she couldn't bring herself to move toward the nearly empty bottle of vodka in the kitchen. "To me . . ." She tried again to understand what he wanted from her.

Richard said, "I have so much hatred and negative feelings inside me, but I wish to know more love and positive feelings to offset it. And where best to find this but from my own mother?"

Patty, unable to answer, stared at him. She looked away, then stared at him again.

"I want you to love me, Mother. That's all. Show me that good is stronger than evil."

Patty glanced over at her daughter. How could she show her son this? she silently asked. How?

But it was Richard who was aware of the question. "Hold me, Mother," he answered. "I will feel it. It felt so good when Janet held me." He held out his arms, bony fingers splayed in desperation.

Like a zombie groping for a victim, she thought. She involuntarily took a step back, again looking frantically at her daughter, tacitly pleading for aid.

Her daughter seemed at a loss, blankly staring back at her. Then slowly, Janet nodded. "Show him you love him." Her voice was soft, scarcely audible.

Patty looked back at Richard. How could she show it? He repulsed her. He smelled not only like a stagnant swamp but also a damp grave. His hands were streaked with blood—with Frankie's blood.

"I . . . I . . ." She shook her head. She couldn't. She just couldn't.

"Please, Mother, please." There was desperation in his voice.

She retreated another step, but he took one forward. He was closing in on her, but she couldn't.

"Please."

Patty felt herself pressured and succumbing to the importunate pleas. Looking down at her arms that were embracing her body, she was somewhat surprised to find the knife still in her hand. Should she use it again? Maybe if she kept plunging he'd go away.

Or should she drop it and give him what he wanted and hug him?

"Yes," Richard urged. "Hug me. Drop the knife."

For a long moment Patty searched her daughter's face, which was pale, filled with horror and grief, then she released her grip on the knife. It clattered onto the floor, a sound that almost escaped her ears.

Richard took another step forward, and this time Patty didn't move back. Instead, she braced herself, waited for her son's arms to furl around her. *Death*, she suddenly thought, suppressing a violent shudder, *is going to embrace me.*

The arms wrapped themselves around her. Patty sucked in a stunned breath. The contact was ice cold, cold as death.

Oh, God in Heaven, please help me.

"No, help *me*," Richard said. The embrace was not tight, but still Patty felt horribly trapped.

"Cold," was all she could think of saying.

"You can make me warm."

"How?"

"Hold me in return."

Patty's mind ordered her arms to move from her sides and embrace her son, but they wouldn't comply.

"Hold me," Richard reiterated. The desperation in his voice reached her heart and she experienced a rush of emotion. But it was pity, not love, she felt for him—and guilt. It was her fault that Richard was tormented like this, torn between two places.

He pleaded again for her to return his affection, and this time her arms listened. She raised them and circled his skeletal body, her hands meeting on his back. She forced herself to endure the cold.

"You're tense," he said.

She forced herself to relax, commanding each limb and shoulder to loosen. She even tried to force her heart to reduce its frantic beating.

And she forced herself to think good thoughts about her son, knowing he would read them. *He's my son and I love him. I love him just as much as I love Janet or Frankie. I love him just as much as I'd loved Myles. I love my son. I love him very, very much.*

Richard leaned his head against her cheek. Patty instinctively stiffened, then caught herself and relaxed. He didn't seem as cold as before. Was she warming him?

He held her tighter. "More, Mother," he pleaded softly.

She hesitated, then stroked his licorice-black hair, as she used to do with Janet and Frankie when they were little.

I love you, Richard, her mind started again. *You should never doubt this.*

"Yes," Richard urged. He was as warm as any living human she had ever touched. "Now say it,

Mother. Say the words out loud."

"Words?"

"Tell me you love me."

"I . . . I love you."

"No, that was not sincere."

She swallowed, then tried again. "I . . . love . . . you."

"Yes. That feels wonderful. Yes. You mean it, don't you, Mother?"

Patty forced her mind to say yes, then said the word out loud to confirm it.

"I'm not sure, but I think you mean it," he said.

"Don't doubt it," she reminded him, and soon began to feel herself enjoying the embrace. She had never held her son this long and was now experiencing a sweet glow she had never felt with him before. He *was* just like Janet and Frankie. She never should have neglected him the way she had. She did love him. Yes, she truly did.

She brushed back a long strand of hair and kissed his pale forehead. "I'm so sorry," she whispered.

"Yes, yes!" He was ecstatic. "Oh Mother, yes! This is what I want."

"Shush." She held him closer, then closed her eyes and let the glow swell inside her. For a long moment there was serene silence, mother and son together in a frozen waltz.

Then Patty made the mistake of opening her eyes and looking into the kitchen.

Frankie's head, sitting on the floor, was staring back at her.

The horror returned, full force. Patty pushed away from Richard, only to find herself locked in his arms.

"No," he said, panic and desperation in his voice and grip. "Don't stop now. Please, don't!"

But Patty couldn't recapture the glow she had felt. Frankie's face was still a mask of horror and shock, and he seemed to be gawking at her also with the shock of seeing her embrace his killer. She pushed against Richard again. "Let me go!"

"No," Richard wailed, tightening his hold on her. "I'm feeling revulsion, loathing. Stop those feelings, Mother. Give me more of the positive feelings I was getting."

"I can't." She swung her head away from Frankie, but the image of his head remained vivid in her mind. "Can't," she sobbed. She continued pushing, then pounded her fists against his chest. Although he was thin, he was incredibly strong.

"Don't push me away," he warned. His body, she noted, was losing its heat. At an alarming rate it became icy.

"Let me go," she screamed.

"Come on, Mother, come on." He was crushing her now, suffocating her. Panic exploded in her brain. He was going to kill her. She was sure of it.

"Come on, come on!" He was bellowing with rage and frustration.

Patty knew she should try to calm herself, to do everything she could to retrieve the glow, but she couldn't. Her mind was out of control, wild with the thought *I am going to die!*

She kicked at him, squirmed and thrashed, but he held on, imprisoning her in an iron cage.

"Come on! Come on!" he roared.

"No, Richard. No!" Janet screamed.

The implication of her daughter's cry penetrated Patty's horrified brain. It wasn't until now that she fully realized what was happening. Richard was crushing her in his powerful grip. Suddenly she was aware of the hot pain in her chest as she heard her ribs crunch. Hysterically, she was reminded of a bag of chips being squashed. Crunch . . . crunch . . . crunch . . .

She opened her mouth to let out a scream, but

none came.

Oh God, please help . . .

Blood streamed from her mouth, nose and ears. She gagged, then coughed, spraying red froth. The pain was excruciating, and still it grew. And grew.

"Damn you, Mother!" she dimly heard, then the pain exploded like a balloon that had stretched beyond its limit, and then there was nothing.

Richard tossed the limp body aside, as though disgusted that it could not move anymore. Then he dropped to his knees with a heavy thud, threw his head back and wailed at the ceiling.

Janet stood at the doorway, too frozen with shock to move. Her hand was over her mouth, suppressing both a scream and a need to vomit. She stared at her brother as he continued to wail, her mind too numb to even carry a thought. It wasn't until the wailing stopped that she broke out of her catatonic state, and even then her mind refused to grasp everything. It seemed to have developed a protective haze.

Still kneeling, Richard looked over at her. "She wouldn't love me. Why?" he demanded in a voice that betrayed resentment.

Janet opened her mouth to speak, but had difficulty finding her voice. Everything seemed detached from her. After a moment, she said, "I think she was too afraid of you."

"But I never did any harm . . . at first."

"It was because of your father." It was easy to talk now. She just had to numb herself a little, keep her attention on her brother, keep it away from . . . from the rest of the room. "She was afraid of you because of him."

"But that wasn't right."

"I know."

"If she'd given me a chance, maybe things would have been different." Resentment was quickly turning to something stronger—contempt and hate.

"I've always loved you," Janet said to appease him, not wanting the horrible rage to return.

"I know. I never doubted it." He studied her face for a lingering moment. There was almost a smile, but the storm in his eyes quickly killed it. Then he began to lose substance and fade. Through him Janet could see the kitchen beyond.

"Where are you going?"

"Father wants me. I know now it's with him I belong."

"Oh, Rich . . ."

"Good-bye, Janet," he said, and she knew it was final.

She watched the kitchen behind him grow clearer as he faded further.

"Good-bye, Richard."

Her legs no longer able to support her, she moved toward a chair and collapsed into it. She heard pounding at the door, a gruff voice demanding entrance, but she paid no heed, for she had started to cry—not for Rich, but for everyone she had lost.

She was still spilling tears with no sign of stopping when the police came.

26

Darkness was all around him, except for two beams of light at opposite ends. Above to his right shined the white-bluish light, rays splayed, dazzling like a sunburst. And below to his left was the orange-red light, a solid beam penetrating the dark like a powerful spotlight. In a diagonal line these lights would have met if the distance between them wasn't so great. And in the middle was Richard, ready to decide.

He sensed his father's presence, felt the victorious glee that he had returned. He also felt a strong attraction toward the red entrance and scarcely any for the other, yet he looked up, as though to be certain. As he stared at the bluish light he thought of his mother, of how she had rejected him, but instead of feeling sadness and regret, he felt only burning contempt. He no longer wanted a glimpse of the side above him, and the sense of peace and sweetness that he had experienced before was absent this time. The light itself, he noted, did not seem as bright; it seemed to be waning.

No, he did not want any part of this side anymore. And as he made his decision he abruptly turned away from the fading light.

At last he knew where he belonged.

Father, here I come! he cried voicelessly. He hesitated only for a fleeting instant, then hurled himself downward.

EPILOGUE

TO THE RED LANTERN

It was midnight, the winter solstice. The temperature was below freezing, but the cold did not deter her. She moved effortlessly through the woods, relishing the frigid wind as it whipped at her thick, ebony hair. She wore a red dress and a black woolen shawl, and these, too, flapped violently in the wind. She wore high heels yet moved gracefully in ankle-deep snow.

She was beautiful and knew she'd have no problem finding a man. Reaching the edge of the woods, she stopped, and for a moment gazed at the street that abruptly began ahead of her, at the lounge faintly illuminated by a Miller sign above its entrance. Then she headed for it, confidence apparent in her feminine, catlike stride. When she reached the bar, two men immediately approached her, offering her a drink. It was so easy.

But she declined, wanting to appraise the entire lounge first and select her own man. At length she found him. He was a blond with rugged features—a construction worker, perhaps. She stared at him until he felt her gaze and glanced over at her, then she licked her lips and smiled. He blinked in surprise, then quickly composed himself and re-

turned the smile. She lowered her eyes, as though
bashful, letting him see her long, black lashes, then
looked up through them at him. He visibly puffed
out his muscular chest in a burst of confidence and
determination, reached for his glass of beer, and
made his way across the crowded bar toward her.

Yes, it was so easy.

He sat at her table. "Can I buy ya a drink?"

"Sure. A Bloody Mary."

Nodding, as though in approval, he signaled a
barmaid and ordered the drink and another beer.
When the drinks were served, he asked her name.

"Samantha," she told him.

When the drinks were finished, she said, "I find
it terribly stuffy in here. Do you think maybe we
could go somewhere else . . . somewhere alone?"

The construction worker's eyes gleamed in
anticipation. "Sure, hon. My place or yours?"

She licked her lips again, glistening her red
mouth. She let a minute pass, pretending to weigh
the question extensively, then said in a throaty voice,
"Your place, loverboy. Mine is much, much too far
away."

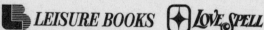